THE LAST DARKNESS

Glasgow, December: In this city of biting sleet, icy pavements and Christmas street decorations battered by arctic winds, the body of a well-dressed man is found hanging from a railway bridge. Investigating the case is Lou Perlman, a detective whose idea of a good suit is anything that fits him. Perlman feels that this is no suicide, and that something about the corpse reminds him of his boyhood in the Gorbals. For Perlman is a man with secrets of his own and, as one death follows another, the hunt for the killer takes him into a territory of deceit and greed — a world of old allegiances that are lethal to reawaken.

Books by Campbell Armstrong
Published by The House of Ulverscroft:

CONCERT OF GHOSTS
DEADLINE

Campbell Armstrong was born in Glasgow and educated at Sussex University. After living in the USA for twenty years, he and his family now live in Ireland. He has been in the front rank of modern thriller writers for many years.

CAMPBELL ARMSTRONG

THE LAST DARKNESS

Complete and Unabridged

CHARNWOOD
Leicester

First published in Great Britain in 2002 by
HarperCollins Publishers, London

First Charnwood Edition
published 2003
by arrangement with
HarperCollins Publishers, London

The moral right of the author has been asserted

This novel is entirely a work of fiction.
The names, characters and incidents portrayed in it
are the work of the author's imagination.
Any resemblance to actual persons, living or dead,
events or localities is entirely coincidental.

British Library CIP Data

Armstrong, Campbell, 1944 –
   The last darkness.—Large print ed.—
   Charnwood library series
   1. Jews—Scotland—Glasgow—Fiction
   2. Police—Scotland—Glasgow—Fiction
   3. Detective and mystery stories
   4. Large type books
   I. Title
   823.9'14 [F]

   ISBN 0–7089–4942–8

Published by
F. A. Thorpe (Publishing)
Anstey, Leicestershire

Set by Words & Graphics Ltd.
Anstey, Leicestershire
Printed and bound in Great Britain by
T. J. International Ltd., Padstow, Cornwall

This book is printed on acid-free paper

For different kinds of assistance,
my gratitude goes to Erl and Anne Wilkie,
Brenda Harris, Stephen McGinty,
Hazel Frew, Jeannine Khan, Kirsten Wilkie,
Sydney Altman, Robert Burns, Joy Frew,
Tomasso, Ed Breslin, Diana Tyler,
and my wife Rebecca

This book is dedicated
to the memory of my mother,
May Black, 1919-2001.

1

Lou Perlman stood on the dark riverbank and gazed up at the body dangling from a girder under Central Station Bridge.

This was the second hanging he'd seen in his life.

The first — long ago, almost fifty years — had been a milk delivery-man called Kerr who'd hung himself from an oak in a scrubby little park at the edge of the old Gorbals. Perlman hadn't thought about Kerr in ages, but now he remembered the dead man had worn a white work uniform with the logo Southern Cooperative Dairy.

Dresses for work, hangs himself instead. Little Lou, about six and chubby, had watched cops cut Kerr down and place him on the grass. *Obviously a suicide*, one of the cops had said.

Lou had never heard that word. He'd looked it up in his father's big dictionary. '*The act of killing oneself intentionally.*' It had seemed strange to him that anyone would take his own life. Years later, as the recipient of several hard-won diplomas from the academy of rough streets, it no longer astonished him. Depression, melancholy, debt, terminal weariness — there were a thousand reasons or more for slashing your wrists in a bathtub or swallowing fifty Temazepam or tying a noose round your neck.

The air beneath the bridge smelled dank. A

goods train rumbled overhead. Perlman watched the wagons as they passed out of view. He stamped his feet for warmth. The tip of his nose was an ice-cube. He could sense snow in the air, an early December downfall. He searched the pockets of his coat for his gloves, but could find only one. Christ knows where the other was. He was always losing gloves. Socks too. Anything that comes in pairs I lose one, he thought. Why couldn't they sell gloves and socks in threes?

He glanced at his watch: 1:15 a.m. He lit a cigarette and watched two cops climb an extension ladder. Another uniform was already up in the girders fiddling with the knotted rope. An ambulance appeared. A couple of medics came out carrying a stretcher, which they set at the foot of the ladder. Perlman scanned the casual observers who stood here and there, the night people, the homeless, the curious who just happened to stumble upon this unexpected cameo of the city.

Suicide. That's from the Latin, of course, Colin had said. Perlman remembered how his brother had remarked, in a smartarse offhand manner, that the word was derived from *sui*, oneself, and *cidium*, a killing. Clever Colin, four years older than Lou and even in those days the proud owner of a Very Big Brain, top of his class in everything.

Poor Colin, all things considered. Two days ago he'd been a Polaroid of good health. Strong, fit, lean. A weight-lifter, cyclist, non-smoker, a man who abstained from all toxic ingestion

2

except the occasional glass of good wine. Very good wine.

Things change, zoom, zap, God never gives warnings.

The cops were lowering the body now. Carefully, in slow stages, they brought the dead man down. Perlman looked at the corpse's herringbone overcoat; expensive wool, no *shmatte*. The fellow's scarf was grey silk and his slip-on shoes gleamed in the headlights of the ambulance. One trouser leg had ridden up, showing a short black sock and a stretch of white skin. He wore a plain gold wedding ring. He'd come here, rope presumably in coat pocket and, stalked by God knows what horrors, he'd either climbed up into the girders from the stone support plinth on the riverbank, or he'd descended from the railway line above.

Then he'd made the necessary killing attachments and jumped.

Perlman stepped towards the stretcher, looked down at the dead man. What had driven him to finish his life hanging from the underside of a railway bridge that straddled the River Clyde in the middle of Glasgow? Eyes open, lips parted, head tilted limply to one side, the guy had black and silver Brylcreemed hair parted in a razor-sharp line to one side. He might have been dressed for a night out, a serious date. He was sixty, Perlman guessed. Maybe more.

Perlman bent over, and his bones creaked, and he thought how, especially on these biting wintry nights, you could hear the Reaper's advance signals in the realignment of joints. He studied

3

the rope, one end of which lay across the dead man's chest; the other was bound hard round the throat and gathered at the back of the neck in a big thick slipknot that looked like a cancerous growth, a lethal melanoma. The end that had been fixed to the girder was stained dark and oily from the city's emissions, from railway residues and lubricants and leakages.

'I had to cut that top knot, Sergeant. With my knife.'

Perlman looked up at the young policeman who'd spoken. How like kids they seemed to him these days, callow boys, some of them barely at the age of shaving. This one was called Murdoch. He had an open pink face that shone from the cold and earnest eyes.

'I couldn't work it loose with my hands,' Murdoch said. 'I tried.'

Perlman shrugged. 'No big deal, son. We couldn't leave the poor sod hanging up there until we'd located somebody with nimble wee fingers, could we? Might've taken all night.' He wondered why the young cop sounded so apologetic: eager to please, he assumed. Young and keen, didn't want to *wreck* what might have been a vital item of evidence, in this case a knot in a length of rope recently tethered to a girder.

Perlman sometimes had an unsettling effect on young cops. God knows, he always tried to be friendly and understanding, even compassionate, but maybe they were intimidated by the longevity of his career, or his legend as a cop who knew just about every ned in the city. Or they were perturbed, as ambitious young men

4

and women might be, by his refusal to accept promotion beyond the rank of Detective-Sergeant. *This* was so tough for these kids to understand? It was simple: he didn't want to get caught up in the internal politics of the Force, which grew more complex the higher you rose. He'd seen too many useful cops taken off the streets and shackled to their desks, clamped in the chains of administration. He thought: if I don't want to get my arse kicked upstairs, it's because this is my job and this is my city, and I don't want to change a bloody thing, not even a situation like this, kneeling on the bank of a black river in the freezing night air in the cold cold heart of Glasgow.

He rummaged in the pockets of the coat. Empty. He fingered the wedding ring, checked it for an inscription, found none. He felt the softness of the dead man's palm. He undid the buttons of the coat, slid his fingers inside. He had an uneasy sensation, a stark sense of trespass. Going through a dead man's clothing in front of twenty or so night-crawlers — he knew he ought to have waited until the poor bastard was inside the ambulance before starting this rudimentary exploration, but he'd always been impetuous. A weakness in his psychological structure, too late to fix.

He called to Murdoch. 'Son, get these bloody gawkers out of here. Scatter the whole crew of them. And don't be polite either. Use the authority of the uniform, and *lean* if you need to.' He gestured to the small crowd. Murdoch and his fellow uniforms began to make the appropriate loud noises, *Come on, move along, nothing for you to see here, shove off the lotta you.* The pedestrians began to shuffle away. They'd regroup further down the street, of course: death was magnetic.

Perlman took off his glasses, wiped them on the cuff of his coat, then returned to his examination of the suicide's jacket. The label read: *Tailored in Italy for Mandelson's of Glasgow.* Mandelson's was an expensive menswear shop in Buchanan Street: it wasn't where Lou Perlman bought his clothes. He slipped a hand into the inside pocket. Two spare buttons wrapped in clear plastic, nothing else. No wallet, no keys, nothing. It was the same with the side and breast pockets. All empty. Perlman frisked the trouser pockets: nothing — no loose change, hankie, crumpled slip of paper, matchbook. A dead man, a well-dressed, well-nourished Caucasian, with no identification and only one personal possession, an anonymous gold ring.

Chilled, Perlman cupped his hands and blew into them. He stood upright. His joints felt like fused metal. He gazed at the man's face and for a moment had a fleeting sense of familiarity. From where? He turned and squinted across the narrow river where the old Renfrew ferryboat lay at anchor: a relic of a dead Glasgow, it had once carried passengers downriver. Now it had been adapted as a floating venue for theatrical and musical events. Perlman had attended a concert there some time ago, a swing revival band from Rotterdam.

6

He looked down at the suicide again. No ID. No farewell letter.

Maybe that was the way he'd planned it. Just a nobody at the end of a rope with nothing to say. Sad. Perlman nodded at the two orderlies from the ambulance.

'You can take him,' he said.

They lifted the dead man into the ambulance. Perlman caught himself staring at the corpse's shoes, and he thought of the man's soft hand again, and he had one of those moments when you realize, with a quickened skip of pulse, that appearances are only surface. Stir the pond and the silt shifts and sometimes something unexpected emerges from the murk.

2

The young man walked through the park with his hands in the pockets of his big heavy coat. He listened to a breeze rattle the skeletal branches of trees. He saw a half moon in the sky. Glass from broken lamps and hypodermic syringes littered the ground. He passed a bench, glanced at a man who lay there in a tattered sleeping bag that oozed pieces of insulation. The man's head was covered in a hood, and he snored. A drunk, a beggar.

Beyond the sleeper, the young man saw the statue and a pale light hanging above it. *You'll find a figure carved in stone. That's the place where you wait.* He tried to read the inscription on the base, but couldn't make out the letters because too many vandals had come this way with spraypaint. Who was this fellow who'd been honoured by a statue? A political hero? a great poet? He couldn't have been so very important if he'd been placed in this tiny swathe of park so far from the city centre.

The young man wondered how long he'd have to wait. He walked round the statue and tried to keep warm — a problem in this refrigerated city so far from home. Now and then he touched his short black beard, which was cold. The breeze came up again, arctic, and he lifted the collar of his coat against his neck.

In the darkness to his right the headlights of a

car flicked on then off, and again. The sign. He walked forty or fifty yards until he reached the street. He was aware of tenement windows on the edge of his vision, so many families living one on top of the other, creatures in hives. He smelled food frying, and realized he'd eaten nothing save some tangerines and a banana and handfuls of *garinim* in the last twenty-four hours. He remembered the long shuddering train journey from one end of Europe to the other, and before that the voyage on the rusted fishing boat that ferried him from Port Said to Athens, and the stench of rotten sardine in the airless hold where he'd been obliged to travel, a foul odour he could still feel at the back of his throat.

He reached the car. The passenger door swung open.

'Get in.' The face of the man behind the wheel was in shadow.

The young man climbed in, closed the door.

The man behind the wheel said, 'Call me Ramsay.' *Cawmeramzay.*

'Please . . . You will have to speak more slowly.'

'Going too fast for you, Abdullah?'

'Abdullah? That is not my name — '

'Look, if I choose to call you Abdullah, that's your name, okay? Stick your backpack on the floor and show me your passport.'

'Why?'

'You could be anybody. That's why.' This Ramsay, concealed in shadow, spoke English with an impenetrable accent. Words ran together, letters fell from the end of words, it wasn't the well-schooled English of the teachers in the schools the young man had attended. Cautiously, he handed his passport to Ramsay, who opened it and checked it with a glance.

'You look like your photograph, Abdullah,' Ramsay said, passing the document back.

'Of course. But my name — '

'Fuck the name. Who gives a shite? Me Ramsay you Abdullah. Let's keep it nice and simple.'

The manner in which he said 'Abdullah' was offensive. It was a joke name; as if all Middle Easterners were called Abdullah. The young man thought of the passport he'd been given in Athens, which identified him as Shimon Marak, a naturalized Greek of Israeli birth, and he realized that assumed names were simply tools of deception, and unimportant so long as you never lost sight of your real identity.

Ramsay said, 'Here's how it is. One, I'll drive you to a place where you'll live. It's not fancy, but I don't expect you're accustomed to the Ritz. The address is 45 Braeside Street. Commit it to memory. Two, don't ask me any questions because the chances are I don't know the answers anyway. You follow me?'

'Yes, yes. I follow.' The young man had expected a warmer reception. He'd anticipated an ally in this alien city, somebody at least kind. But Ramsay's attitude was the opposite.

I constructed an ideal in my head, Marak thought. Now I must absorb the reality. I am not here as a tourist with a camera. Ramsay's hostility was unexpected, but what did it matter in the long run?

10

Ramsay turned his face, and Marak saw his profile for the first time. The nose that terminated in a sharp point, the backward slope of forehead, the strange way the chin ran almost without impediment into the neck. Ramsay's hair was thick and brushed high from his scalp. One wedge, perhaps gelled, jutted from the front of his head, a promontory.

'I'll drive you to your new home, Abdullah.'

'I'm tired. It's been a long journey.'

'I don't want to know anything about it,' Ramsay said.

The young man fell silent and stared from the window. He was aware of crossing a narrow river, the same one he'd travelled over earlier on his way to meet Ramsay. He'd ridden in a black taxicab driven by a pockmarked man who spoke as incomprehensibly as Ramsay. Laughing, the cabbie had said, *You another fucking illegal then?* He'd agreed with the driver: Yes yes. Illegal yes. Another foreigner. *Och, there's always a shortage of dishwashers at the kebab joints.* He'd smiled at that too and nodded eagerly. I understand nothing, Mr Driver. I am moron. You do not know if I am Palestinian, Israeli, Lebanese, whatever. I am just idiot from a distant country.

He saw the glare of the city, the night sky ablaze with electricity. Ramsay switched on the radio and listened to some kind of popular American music.

'You like the golden oldies, Abdullah?' Ramsay asked.

'Pardon me?'

11

'Ah, the tunes of yesteryear,' Ramsay said. 'The memory lanes of our lives and times. The way we were.'

Splish splash I was taking a bath, the singer sang.

'Bobby Darin,' Ramsay said.

The young man glanced at Ramsay as the car passed under a streetlamp and saw that the protruding bolt of hair was a peculiar yellow emerging from the blackness of scalp. He wondered about this decoration, this dye, and whether it signified anything.

'Bobby Darin,' Ramsay said again. 'You're listening to a dead man's voice. Amazing when you think about it, Abdullah, intit?'

Abdullah. *Enough.* The young man looked at a red traffic light. The colour of his feelings. He pressed his palms together hard. 'Call me Shimon. I prefer that.'

'Whatever bangs your bongo, pal,' Ramsay said, and beat a hand on the dash in time to the song. '*I was splishing and a-splashing. Splashing and a-splishing.* Got it? Altogether now, Abdullah.'

3

Sidney Linklater, forensics expert, was a Force Support Officer, a civilian attached to the Strathclyde Police. He was in his early thirties and spent all his spare time in wellies and raincoat trudging through the mud of ancient graveyards in pursuit of his hobby, charcoal rubbings of headstones.

Perlman thought this ghoulish, given the nature of Linklater's work, which took place in a world of decaying corpses and maggots channelling through rancid flesh. Why didn't Sid have a hobby that took him well away from death? There was nothing sickly or weirdo in young Linklater's appearance; he had the healthy open face of an eager boy-scout making his first successful sheepshank. Maybe he just felt at ease with the dead: they couldn't hurt your feelings, couldn't let you down. Had some flighty young number broken Linklater's tender heart?

He needs another life, Perlman thought.

Presently, Linklater hovered over the body that had been removed from the Central Station Bridge. Undressed, stretched on an examination table, the corpse had the look of a man just a little annoyed by his departure from the world. Things left undone, that cruise of the Nile never sailed, *Crime and Punishment* only half-read.

His flesh was pallid under the glow of two arc-lights. Linklater carefully examined the blue-purple marks left by the rope. Lou Perlman, who couldn't quite shake off the tiny feeling of familiarity the dead man had aroused, turned and gazed into the shadows beyond the lamps. He didn't like forensics labs, organic matter floating in bottles, amputated hands or feet suspended in formaldehyde. He didn't like the smell of chemicals and medicinal soap.

He said, 'Don't know about you, Sid, but I'm seriously convinced he's dead.'

'He's crossed the great divide all right,' Linklater remarked, and looked at Perlman over his glasses.

'So is there a chance we can wrap the poor bastard up and get the hell out of here?'

'Indeed we can,' Linklater said. He drew a sheet over the dead man's body, then scrubbed his hands at the sink.

Perlman stepped into an adjoining room, a storage area for chemicals and equipment; there was a shaky table and an electric kettle, mugs and tea-bags. He plugged the kettle into the wall and set two mugs beside it. One of them contained a dead fly, which he dumped on the floor. He dropped a tea-bag in each cup.

'Bloody cold in here,' Linklater said. He found a stool and sat on it, stretching his long legs.

'Is there milk?' Perlman asked.

'*Milk?* Lucky there's tea, Lou.'

'I like mine milky.' Perlman couldn't wait for the kettle to boil. When the water was hot, he poured it into the cups, and shoved one towards Linklater.

'We don't have a spoon either,' Linklater said. 'Cheers.'

Perlman poked a fingertip at the tea-bag, then sipped his tea. Utter pish. He made a face. 'Right. One dead man. Apparent suicide.'

'Apparent,' Linklater said.

'Except. No evidence he climbed the concrete column to the girders. No wee crumbs of concrete under the fingernails or on the soles of the shoes. No rough or broken skin, no chipped fingernails. Just oil stains.'

'Agreed.'

Perlman swirled the awful tea around in his mouth before swallowing it, and thought how quickly you could get used to rubbish if you had no alternative. We are obliged to choke down a load of shite and we don't even taste it after a while, especially the utterances of politicians. Bad mood, Lou. Fatigue, three in the morning and a corpse you don't need, *ballocks*.

'All right, Sid, so no evidence the poor sod did any climbing. And if he came down from the rail tracks above, how come he's not totally *covered* in crap? We're probably talking about a half century of oil leaks and who knows what substances on the track.'

'I don't think there's any deep mystery here, Lou. There's grease on his coat.'

'My main concern is whether it's enough. You come clambering down from that bridge to the underside, Sid, and it's not going to be here a smudge, there a smudge, is it? You'd be *bathed* in black lubricants. I also bet there's layers of soot trapped up there from away before the Clean Air

15

Act. You might not remember our fair city in its foggy heyday. Darkness at noon. The air was pure *schmutz*. You know what the people looked like? The Living Dead, Sid. You could leave the house nice and clean at eight a.m. and your pores would be clogged with coal smoke in a matter of twenty minutes . . . The good old days, Sid, when you sucked down a ton of pollutants on a daily basis.'

'Excuse me for pointing this out: the city's still polluted, Lou.'

'Polluted?' He lit a cigarette, a Silk Cut. 'You should've been here when they didn't have pollution in the dictionary.'

'I see you're smoking,' Linklater said.

'My choice,' Perlman said. He could smell that old Glasgow suddenly, the stench of soot and smoke and how, when you blew your nose, your mucus was black and had a metallic whiff; even the wax in your ears turned black. 'So do I get the speech about killing myself, Sid? I smoke because I like it. Also because my nerves cry out for it.'

'Studies show that nicotine isn't a tran — '

'Fuck the studies. They're all anti-tobacco propaganda. Back to our man at the end of the rope, Sid.'

'My theory.'

'Let's hear it.'

'Give me a minute.'

Linklater left the room. Perlman took another sip of tea, then poured the rest down the sink. He didn't want to hear Linklater's theory: he guessed it would match his own thoughts,

16

basically. He wanted this to be a suicide. He didn't want it to be something else, even if he already suspected it was heading into perplexity and turbulence, questions without obvious answers, sleepless nights. *I need my bloody sleep*, he thought. He envisaged the dead man's face: who was he? This Brylcreemed man with a hair-parting that might have been made by a precision instrument, and the expensive coat from Mandelson of Buchanan Street, and the unengraved wedding ring?

Linklater came back. He carried the dead man's clothes in a neat pile, shoes on top. He set everything down on the small table, then picked up the shoes. He turned them over, pointed to the soles. 'A couple of grease-marks, but not a lot. And nothing to indicate he'd climbed a concrete pillar, certainly. No scrapes. Nice shoes, by the way. Soft and Italian, new. Expensive.'

'So's the coat,' Perlman said.

'Anyway,' and here Linklater held the shoes, one in each hand, beneath Perlman's face. 'Regard the heels, Lou. See. They're seriously scuffed.'

'I saw that when they were lifting him into the ambulance.'

'Deep scuffs. Which suggests?'

Lou Perlman adjusted his glasses. They kept slipping. He needed those little nonslip pads you could buy at an optician's. Check that for another day. Check so many things for another day. A loose filling at the back of his mouth, the occasional shot of pain when cold liquid was going down. Library books months overdue. A

17

Thelonious Monk CD — *Solo* — he still hadn't disinterred from its cellophane, and an old vinyl album of Gram Parsons's *Grievous Angel* he'd found in a second-hand shop and longed to hear. 'In My Hour of Darkness': yes indeed. Life marched all over you in tackety boots and somehow you couldn't find the time to arrest its progress. His mood was blackening. He might have had rooks nesting inside his head.

'It suggests he was *dragged*, Sid,' Perlman said.

'Exactly. Consistent with these stains on the back of his trousers. See?' Linklater touched the garment, then studied the oil stain between his thumb and the tip of his index finger. 'A man crawling along the girders would have stained the front of his trousers. Unless he slithered along on his back — '

'He wouldn't have to slide flat on his back. There's room under that bridge.'

'Now the coat.' Linklater set the trousers to one side. 'Oily marks on the back of the coat, again consistent with dragging. You'll notice the 'smudges' you referred to earlier are confined more or less to one central area of the back of the garment, corresponding to the spine. The front of the coat is *relatively* unsullied.'

Perlman tossed his cigarette into the sink. 'Don't tell me what I don't want to hear. Feed me pleasant fictions, Sid. Lie to me.'

'I'm saying there's a possibility somebody killed him.'

'And hung him from the bridge and wants it to be written off as a suicide.'

'Just so. The killer — or killers — hauled him along the track, lowered him to the underside, knotted one end of a rope round his neck, the other round a girder, then pushed. Away he goes. A pedestrian sees the body and phones the Force. And here we are, you and me, alone in this godforsaken place at this bloody awful hour sifting a dead man's clothes.'

'Because it's what we do,' Perlman said. 'We keep awful hours.'

He looked at the back of the coat. There was more oil on the herringbone garment than he'd first noticed. He could smell the lubricants. He was reminded of foundries and forges and pits where mechanics examined the underbodies of cars. He was reminded of trains racketing into bad-smelling tunnels that plunged beneath rivers. Dragged, he thought. Had the poor fucker been killed elsewhere and taken to the bridge and hung? It wasn't likely that he'd gone willingly along the bridge and down into the girders. *Walk this way, chum. Let's have a palaver beneath the Central Station Rail Bridge.* So where had he been slain, and how?

Perlman coughed. There. That little twinge in the chest. You don't want to know what it might *really* mean. Twenty cigarettes a day for thirty years, give or take: that was a massive intake of smoke and wear on the tread of the lungs. Calculate. No, don't. More than 200,000 cigarettes. *A quarter of a million?* Oy, fuck. That *many?* He felt giddy. How many times had he inhaled? Say a dozen times for every cigarette. Multiply a dozen by a quarter of a million and —

Change subject.

'The suicide ploy isn't very clever,' he said. 'Whoever did it wasn't blessed with smarts. The assumption we'd overlook the evidence is . . . ' He groped for a word. 'Amateur.'

'Or arrogant,' Linklater said.

'Somehow I prefer to think I'm dealing with an amateur.'

'You could be dealing with an arrogant amateur, Lou.'

Perlman stared into the sink where his discarded tea-bag lay like something washed up on the bank of an industrial river. 'I'll need to run his fingerprints. See if I can give him a name at least.'

'I'll arrange a post-mortem,' Linklater said, and glanced at Perlman as if he wanted to expand on the subject of autopsy, but he knew Perlman didn't have a scientific turn of mind, and grew bored with technicalities. 'If he wasn't a suicide, Lou, then maybe he was killed by some means other than strangulation. Leave no stone unturned.'

'Is that your motto too?' Perlman asked.

'Look at my dirty fingernails, if you will.'

Perlman said, 'Aye, manicures are pointless in this line of work, Sid. You're not alone.' He held up a hand for Linklater to look at.

'You bite your nails, I see.'

20

'I'm devouring myself quietly, old son. Piece by piece.'

'Better no nails than no lungs.'

Perlman walked to the door. 'Nag nag. I'm away. I've a report to write.'

4

Artie Wexler peered from the bedroom window into the street at the parked cars shining under lamps. He knew all the cars in this prosperous cul-de-sac, Sinclair's red Land Rover, Tutterman's antique Jaguar, fifty years old and still as showroom-glossy as a wax apple, Mackinlay's silver Lexus, all of them. I'm looking for something else, he thought. But what? A car I've never seen before? Too much imagination. Something goes wrong in your schedule, an old friend fails to keep an appointment, and you feel little breakdowns inside. He closed the slit in the curtain. The palms of his hands were damp.

Ruthie was out cold in bed. Artie glanced at her. Artie and Ruthie, man and wife, thirty years of matrimony. She was ten years younger than him, and a handsome woman. He loved her as much as the day he'd married her. A different kind of love, admittedly, a matter of comfort and mutual support, it had long ago ceased to be the hot seething passion of youth. You couldn't keep that up, the sexual energy, always grabbing each other any chance you got. Love changed. A settlement took place in the foundations of marriage. You didn't have the old appetites.

Ruthie's sleep was Dalmane-induced. She raised her face suddenly and peered at him, eyes slits.

'How was dinner?'

'He didn't show up,' Wexler said.

'Strange. Did he call?'

'No.'

'Maybe . . . ' Ruthie didn't finish her sentence. She turned on her side, slipped immediately back into sleep. Artie Wexler walked out of the room and went downstairs. He turned on the lights in the kitchen. He heard the dog, Reuben, a quiveringly fat Dalmatian, growl in the back yard. The kitchen was overbright. Artie blinked, lit a cigar.

He thought about the broken engagement again. There had to be some good reason. Something came up, last-minute business, whatever. He'd waited in the restaurant for a while, sipped a G&T slowly, fidgeted with cutlery, then he'd left. He'd stopped for a drink in the Horseshoe, thinking perhaps somebody had seen Joe there. Nobody had. It was odd, and hard to dismiss. A monthly dinner, same night every month, same place and time, La Lanterna at nine, Artie and Joe. What am I, obsessive? Let it go.

He turned his thoughts to another matter troubling him.

Miriam.

Too late to telephone. Maybe. He blew smoke and it hung in the eyes of the spotlights overhead. Ruthie loved the spotlight effect. She'd installed twenty spots on a series of tracks in the ceiling. She also liked stainless-steel appliances, the fridge, the oven, the big extractor hood over the stove.

He picked up the telephone and punched in

Miriam's number. It rang for a long time. He thought, hang up, leave it until morning. He tightened the cord of his robe and listened to the central-heating system come to life, the whisper of hot air flowing through vents. Ruthie liked the house hot.

He heard Miriam. 'Yes . . . '

'It's Artie,' he said.

'Artie, do you know the *time?*'

'Just tell me how he is.'

Miriam was quiet. Artie pictured her exquisite face, the dark Mediterranean eyes. She'd been a beautiful young woman and you could still see the ghost of that loveliness about her; time had refined the overt sexuality of her youth. She was graceful now, and elegant. Women admired and envied Miriam. *She's so thin, how does she keep her figure, and that smooth skin, what's her secret?*

And if that isn't enough she's talented as well.

'He's just the way he was when you called before, Artie. Were you expecting divine intervention?'

'I don't know what I was expecting,' Artie said. 'You'll keep me informed?'

'Yes yes.'

'This was all so bloody sudden.'

'One minute I have a healthy husband. The next.'

'When can I see him?'

'A few years go past and you don't see him, and suddenly you can't stop asking after him?'

Artie Wexler knew this was true. But so was the reverse. 'He didn't contact me either,

24

Miriam. It's not my fault completely.'

'The trouble is, Artie, time slips away. Then one day it's too late for renewing old friendships.'

He said, 'Maybe,' and knew it sounded feeble. Time. Once, you had it in abundance. You thought you had a surplus. 'What hospital is he in?'

She told him.

'That's Rifkind's hospital. I know him quite well. He's a good doctor. Maybe we can pay a visit together tomorrow.'

'Fine. I'll be in touch.'

Artie Wexler hung up. He saw his cigar had died but he didn't light it again. He wandered up and down the kitchen, restless. Outside the dog barked and the sensor lights tripped in the yard and Artie stared out and saw wind shake the trees and ripple the grass, which had long ago shed its rich summer lustre. The swimming pool glimmered like a sea of spilled oil.

He watched the dog prowl back and forth, sniffing air, disturbed no doubt by the way Ruthie's wind chimes — souvenirs of a trip to the Grand Canyon: or had it been that time in Jerusalem? — bonged ever so quietly on the patio. The sensor lights went out and the wind receded and Artie Wexler, pausing to check on the security system, climbed the stairs to the bedroom. Ruthie said something in her sleep, a sound dredged up from the unfathomable sludge of the mind.

Wexler lay down beside his wife and stared at the ceiling and listened to acid rumbling in his gut. He thought of circles interlinking, old acquaintances renewed, a history, and he felt sweat form on his skin. He fell asleep and dreamed of the empty chair at his table in the Lanterna, and when he woke at 4 a.m. he was soaked.

5

There were no pyramids in Egypt, Glasgow, where Lou Perlman lived. He'd wondered many times about the name of this neighbourhood, which lay pocketed in the East End of Glasgow between Shettleston Road to the north and Tollcross Road to the south. Small area, a cluster of a few streets, some two-storey blocks of 1930s vintage, none of the classic Victorian sandstone tenements you found in other parts of the city. On some maps Egypt wasn't even noted, as if cartographers were so baffled by the origins of the name that they ignored it. It was, Perlman often thought, a place lacking character. It was certainly not scenic. You wouldn't drag tourists out here from such picturesque places as the Botanic Gardens or the Glasgow Art Gallery. But there was an anonymity about it he enjoyed, a sense of privacy, tucked away from the roar of traffic rolling east and west along the main roads.

He guessed he was the only Jew living in Egypt. The Jewish community in Glasgow — some 4,000 out of a total population of around 610,000 (about 1.2 million if you included the whole Metropolitan area) — had usually lived in the Southside, particularly in the slums of the old Gorbals, where they'd first come at the turn of the twentieth century as immigrants from Eastern Europe. Later they'd graduated to the suburbs of Shawlands, then

Giffnock, and later still into the prosperous beyond of Newton Mearns. Perlman's family considered it an act of defiance on Lou's part to live this far into the East End, and typical of his contrary nature, but he didn't give a damn what that cake-making, tea-drinking rabble of aunts and uncles and cousins thought.

I'm a Jew in Egypt, and I like it.

Five-twenty a.m. and freezing when he parked his dented Mondeo and hurried, head bent, towards his house, which was one of two old blackened sandstones in the street. He stuck the key into the lock, shut and bolted the door behind him. He switched on the light in the hallway. Superstitiously, he touched the mezuzah on the door jamb. It had been painted over many times in the years Perlman had lived here. Now it was covered in the same dull blue gloss as the door itself.

This faded house seemed to gather itself around him as he walked, turning on more sixty-watt lights, into the living room. He struck a match and held it to the gas fire and heard the familiar swish of blue flame rushing through the old-fashioned mantles. He spread his hands for warmth. What the house needed was modern central heating with thermostats. The bloody house needs more than heat, he thought. It needs new paint, new roof, new carpets, furniture, all kinds of *stuff*. He sat down in a chair close to the fire and kicked off his shoes and pushed his toes towards the gas flames.

Living like this, he thought. Tut tut. Upstairs rooms you never use. Cupboards crammed with old newspapers and magazines you don't get round to throwing away, and books in haphazard stacks, and a bird cage for the canary you once considered buying, but didn't. Nice to have something yellow and chirpy and fluffy, you'd thought in a lonesome moment. But the bird would have died from neglect.

Perlman, canary killer.

He gazed at the framed photographs above the fireplace. He'd hung these years ago in an attempt to make the house feel like a place where a person actually *lived*, but now as he looked at them he remembered his own desperation at the time. That instinct to connect yourself and your history to the soul of this house, as if you wanted to belong in the same way as the mortar, the bricks, the floorboards. The photographs were of immigrant families taken in the early years of the twentieth century in the Gorbals, unsmiling bearded men and their plain sturdy women and their shoeless kids. Some of the men had a rabbinical intensity about them. The women looked careworn.

The black-grey tenements, a little fuzzy in the background, seemed already to be vanishing into a future that would demolish them. Lou had found these pictures in a cardboard box at the Barras market, and when he'd first hung them he'd pretended they were family members, but they were just unknown Jews from this *shtetl* or that, Poles, Russians, Latvians: they'd journeyed to a new life from the anti-Semitism and pogroms of Eastern Europe only to find a different form of purgatory in the Gorbals.

The one personal photograph in this gallery of strangers was of his parents, Etta and Ephraim, who'd fled the menace of Bavaria in 1935. Etta, small and fair-haired, almost Teutonic; Ephraim dark-eyed and secretive, Semitic. They'd chosen Glasgow because Ephraim had a cousin who operated a small car-repair business in the Gorbals, and there were promises of work and accommodation. Ephraim laboured grudgingly in the shop for three years — *pishtons, carberryators, what do I know of zuch zings?* — before he found work in his old trade as a printer. Overjoyed, he and Etta had moved out of Cousin Lev's cramped quarters in Nicholson Street just before the outbreak of war, and settled in a two-room flat in Kingston Street. How proud Etta had been of this spacious paradise, how tidy and particular, forever sweeping, polishing, attacking cobwebs with a broomstick, setting and emptying mouse-traps. Lou could close his eyes and see her, all whirl and purpose.

He gazed at his parents for a moment longer. When Lou was ten Etta died suddenly. One day she'd been bright and industrious, the next dead on the kitchen floor, surrounded by the broken pieces of a porcelain bowl and the browning crab-apples it had contained. Ephraim overnight became old and distant, wedded to a grief. Lou remembered how his father would sit in front of the fire, hunched over a copy of the *Evening Citizen*, scanning the front page endlessly as coals sparked and kindling spat and split in the chimney. If Ephraim heard these sounds or absorbed anything of the newspaper, he gave no sign. He went through the motions of a life for another ten years before he followed his wife. His death was recorded as cardiac failure.

Heartbreak, Lou thought, was nearer to the truth.

At the funeral, Colin had whispered in his ear: *This is only a shell we're burying, little brother. The real man died the same day as his wife.* Lou had felt an unbearable sadness at the waste of his father's life, and his eyes had filled with tears during the service. By contrast, Colin had seemed detached, as if death was something that happened only to other people. The expression on his face said: *This isn't going to happen to me, oh no.*

Perlman looked away from the picture of his parents.

Once, many years before, he'd hung another picture alongside that of Etta and Ephraim, but he'd taken it down. He thought of it now, that lovely oval face and the mouth so intelligent you knew it belonged to a woman who'd never utter anything shallow or dull. *I desire her,* he thought. It's wrong, and I know it, and I can't help myself any more than poor Ephraim could help being married to the dead.

He found the CD he hadn't opened, and he ripped the cellophane from it and slid the disc into the slot of the player: his sound-system, a Bose, was the only expensive thing he owned. He sat back and listened to Monk play 'Dinah'. The sound was mischievous, pert, Monk having some fun. Lou listened, tapped a foot. 'I Surrender

31

Dear' came up next, slow and touching and then briefly upbeat. By the time 'Ruby, My Dear' played, and the room filled with the melancholy of the tune, Lou Perlman was asleep.

Troubled sleep.

He dreamed of black iron girders, which were strangely aligned, joined in defiance of logic. He dreamed he was walking beneath them and they cast weird shadows across his face. He dreamed of a man hanging, not from a rope, but from a nylon stocking.

He woke cold even though the gas fire hissed and the mantles glowed red. Wrapping himself tightly in his coat, he stumbled towards the stairs and staggered up to his bedroom, which felt like the inside of an ice cube. There was a narrow unmade bed and a heap of clothes and shoes and newspapers and a poster on the wall of the Celtic team that had won the European Cup in 1967. The Lisbon Lions.

Old heroes.

He lay face down and slumped back into sleep, this time dreamless.

6

The telephone ringing in the kitchen woke him shortly before eight a.m. and he rose, dry-mouthed and befuddled, and made his way downstairs. He grabbed the receiver, dropped it, went down on his knees.

'Lou?'

Detective-Inspector Sandy Scullion had one of those voices that was always sunny. Scullion, ginger hair and pleasant looks, could deliver bad news and make it seem like you'd just won the bloody lottery. Perlman supposed it was a gift, the knack of cheerfulness.

'Lou, did I wake you?'

'Aye, it was a long night.'

'I read your report. I fear it's going to be a long day.'

Perlman listened to the old Aga humming comfortingly. The hot core of the room. He edged closer to it. Somewhere in the night he'd removed his coat, but not his suit. Brown and crumpled, a double-breasted number that had come into fashion and then gone out at least twice in the time he'd had it. He owned only two suits and the other had been in the dry-cleaners for months. He couldn't remember where he'd left the claim ticket. He gazed round the kitchen, not really seeing it. Without his glasses the world was an acceptable sort of blur.

'No record of your dead man's prints, I'm

afraid,' Scullion said.

'So he was a law-abiding citizen.'

'Why does a law-abiding citizen get killed, Lou?'

'Good question. If it *was* a murder.' Perlman opened the refrigerator and looked inside. He grabbed a carton of apple juice and slugged some back.

'He shouldn't be too hard to identify,' Scullion said. 'Sooner or later somebody's going to report a missing person.'

'Unless he lived alone.'

'Not everybody lives like a monk, Lou. Anyway, he had a wedding ring.'

'It doesn't follow he had a wife,' Perlman said.

Scullion was quiet a moment. 'The coat's distinctive. Somebody might remember him at Mandelson's.'

Perlman saw his day stretch ahead in a series of little investigative jabs. The coat. Probing the memory of a salesman. Who bought this damned garment? Trudging through the cold. Making out reports. He wanted to sit here and hug the Aga. He looked at the window. A few soft snowflakes drifted against the pane. Dark as night out there. The city in winter had a feel of having been abandoned. The sun was rare, and even when it shone it had all the warmth of a tangerine stored in a freezer.

He plugged the electric kettle into the wall. Coffee, hot coffee, kick the day in the arse. And music, that was what he needed for the full blast. He took the phone inside the sitting room and found his glasses lying beside the Bose. He slipped them on and stuck Gram Parsons's 'Grievous Angel' on his old turntable, and lowered the stylus carefully to 'Cash on the Barrelhead'. Volume up, fast fiddling, whooping voices of merriment. Just the thing for clearing out the tangled webs of morning. *Lord they put me in the jailhouse* . . . He thought of Scullion in his office at Force HQ, an architectural conundrum of buildings jammed together in Pitt Street, close to the city centre. Scullion's little room was decorated with bright drawings his kids had made. Stick figures with big grins and smiley-face suns in the sky.

'What's that racket, Lou?' Scullion asked.

'Gram Parsons.'

'Who?'

'Your idea of music is Barbra Streisand warbling.'

'It's more than that — '

'Okay. I'll throw in Shirley Bassey.' Perlman attempted to sing, managed a croak. 'What now my love . . . '

Scullion said, 'There's a word for you.'

'Slovenly? Cantankerous?'

'They go without saying. I was thinking eclectic.'

'That's the sweetest thing you ever said to me, Sandy.'

'Jazz concerts, classical, that country stuff, there's no limit to your taste,' Scullion said.

Perlman said, 'I draw a line at reggae.'

'McLaren's doing the post-mortem later this morning.'

Perlman lowered the volume of the music.

35

'McLaren? His hand's about as steady as a live toad in aspic.'

'Then we should be thankful he works only on the dead.'

'A small mercy.' He went back inside the kitchen, poured hot water into a cup, stirred in a big spoonful of instant coffee.

'Are you coming in?' Scullion asked.

'Give me about an hour, Sandy. I'm popping in to see my brother first.'

'I heard about that. I hope he'll be okay.'

'We all do.'

When Perlman hung up, he drained his coffee and went back upstairs and stripped. He stepped inside the shower, a narrow fibreglass cubicle with a plastic curtain, and turned on the taps. He let the force of water needle his skull and run down his body, then he dried himself and hurried inside his bedroom where he found an old dark-blue blazer with silver buttons, and a pair of baggy flannels that needed pressing. He discovered a clean but crumpled white shirt. What the hell. You were investigating a death, not posing in a fancy cardigan for a knitwear pattern. He couldn't find a tie. All right. So he was going into the office looking like a downmarket yachtsman, blazer and bags and silver buttons. All he needed was a captain's cap and a collapsible telescope. Ahoy.

He put on his glasses, brushed his teeth, looked at himself in the bathroom mirror. What could you say about that face? A battered duffel-bag pummelled by the demands of too many long nights working the streets, climbing

36

staircases in rundown tenements, ringing the doorbells of sleazy flats whose occupants were psychotic, homicidal, and often armed, too many years wading through the guff the city barfed up from its lower intestinal levels, the pervs, scumbags, dossers, alkies, druggies, molesters, wifebeaters, the whole sad lawless crew that lay concealed in Glasgow's gut.

My eyes have life at least, he thought. Of a kind. Unflinching, albeit bloodshot from lack of sleep. Years of interrogation had gone into those eyes, years of asking questions and watching for the tics and funny little mannerisms that indicated somebody was lying. He scanned the map of his entire clock. The underchin was fleshy. The cheeks, you could say, had a slight hollow quality. The hair, aye, well, he'd tried for years to do something about it, and nothing had worked, and he wasn't going to grease it down at his age. So he'd yielded to a spiky look, tufts of silver rising like sharp shoots from a thin lawn of dark grey. Politely, it was a failed crewcut.

He stepped out of the house. The morning was blurry with snow that fell through streetlamps. A figure appeared under a lamp and moved towards him, a woman dressed in a long brown coat and a headscarf. She reminded Perlman of a bowlegged table.

'Maggie,' he said. 'I forgot it was your day.'

'You'd forget your bum if it wasn't welded to you,' the woman said. She had dentures that slipped and clicked as she talked. She was a widow who'd been cleaning Perlman's house for years.

'How's that pigsty of yours?'

'The kitchen is spotless. It's like a model home — '

'Aye, right, you were on your knees all night long scrubbing the floor in the endless war against e-coli. I'll do your bedroom and bathroom, then I'll get stuck into the kitchen. If there's time. Which I doubt. What you need, Lou — '

'Maggie, don't say it — '

'A wife, Lou. You need a wife.'

'I had one once,' he said. 'It didn't take.'

'Find another.' She took a key from her pocket. 'Watch how you drive. The road's slippery.' She entered the house, closed the door. Where would he be without Maggie McGibbon? In more chaos. He unlocked the Mondeo and got inside, turned the key in the ignition. Battery dead, very very dead. Fuck it *all*. December in Glasgow, snow as thin as consommé, the rag and bone end of the year.

7

The man whose passport identified him as Shimon Marak had slept for ten hours after Ramsay delivered him to a top-floor flat in a Maryhill tenement, on the north side of the city. *You'll like it here, Abdullah*, Ramsay had said. *It's a lovely flat, and very quiet, and none of the neighbours will trouble you.* What Marak discovered, shortly after waking, was that Ramsay had been lying. Construction work took place in a tenement across the street, hammers and drills and the clatter of discarded rubble rushing down disposal chutes, and labourers playing their radios. As for the neighbours leaving him be, more lies: a thin-faced woman with bright-green hair had come to his door to sell him raffle tickets for the renovation of a church, she claimed, but Marak noticed how she sweated, and the circles under her eyes, and he guessed she was on drugs. She grabbed his sleeve and said, *Please mister buy some tickets, eh.*

Shaking his head, he closed the door. He heard her curse on the landing. *Bloody Arab bastart.* Then she kicked his door a couple of times before she went away, still swearing.

Arab, he thought. What an easy racial assumption.

Half an hour later a man claiming to be the blonde's husband turned up on the doorstep. He was dressed in black leather motorcycle gear. He had an ugly face, thick-lipped and malicious. An old scar trawled the length of his cheek. His hands were tattooed with blue snakes. He pushed Marak hard in the chest. *You chancing your arm with my wife, eh? You taking certain liberties while I'm working, are ye?*

Marak backed off, tried to shut his door. The man leaned into it with his shoulder. *Ya fucken piece of shite. You think you can come here and help yerself to our women, ya wanker.* Marak met the brutality of the man's eyes and held them. He wasn't afraid. He knew he could maim this intruder, but the last thing he needed was trouble. The idea of the police coming here — no, he couldn't have that.

Smiling like an idiot and nodding, he told the man he meant no harm, and finally forced the door shut. The man had made a strange baying noise, like a wolf maddened by moonlight, and then he'd gone downstairs, and within minutes loud bass-driven music had begun to play from below, sending reverberations up through the floors and walls to the rooms Marak occupied. He hadn't been able to escape the music.

He spent a few minutes taking clothes from his backpack — two pairs of black Levi's, a couple of black flannel shirts, socks, underwear — and folding them neatly inside a chest of drawers in the bedroom. The drawers were lined with yellowed newspapers, pages of the *News of the World* dating from the mid-1970s. He took his toilet items into the bathroom. Somebody's turds, in an advanced state of deterioration, floated in the bowl. He flushed the cistern and the water roared.

Before stacking his toiletries inside a rusted medicine cabinet, he cleaned the shelf with water and tissues. He aligned his things carefully: razor, shaving soap, comb, toothbrush, toothpaste, and the small gold-handled scissors he used on his beard. The scissors were special. A gift from his father. His initials had been carved in tiny letters on the blades.

He walked through the rooms, expecting the phone to ring, thinking about Ramsay and his 'lovely' flat. When a man tells one lie, usually he tells many. He felt a distinct uneasiness: how could Ramsay be trusted? Marak had come a long way. He'd received promises, and made promises in return. He'd sworn an oath.

Patience, have patience.

He paced the three dull rooms with their dirty curtains and shabby furniture. The kitchen was filled with mouldy food left behind by a previous occupant. He came across some edible bits and pieces in the refrigerator, bread and cheese and two imploded pears, not enough for sustenance.

Hungry, he left the place and walked through the poor morning light to a small grocery, where the staff was Pakistani. He bought milk, tea, cheese, pitta bread, oranges, houmus, a packet of dates. He paid, counted his change. He examined the coins and notes, trying to familiarize himself with them.

Back in the flat, the telephone rang. He dropped his groceries on the floor as he rushed to answer.

41

Ramsay asked, 'What the fuck do you think you're doing, Abdullah, eh? Leaving the premises?'

'You're having me watched. Why?'

'I'm protecting our interests,' Ramsay said.

'I don't like being observed.'

'Get used to it.'

'I had to go out for food.' He walked to the window, peered down into the street. A very light snow was falling. The morning sky was heavy, bruised. He saw no sign of observers. Unless there were spies among the workers, somebody on the scaffolding, or up on the roof. How could he tell? 'Do you have information for me?'

'Memorize this name, Abdullah. Joseph Lindsay. You got that?'

'I'll remember.'

'Now the address. No pen, no paper. Understand?'

'My memory is good.'

Ramsay uttered the address slowly. 'Got it?'

'Yes, yes, of course. But where is this place?'

'Take a taxi, you'll find it,' Ramsay said. 'Oh, and one last wee thing. Look inside your fridge. Bottom shelf. Okay? Hey. Know this oldie, Abdullah? *It's gotta be rock 'n' roll music, if you wanna dance with me.* Chuck Berry.'

'I have not heard of this Chuck Berry.'

'You know absolute shite about Western culture. Get with the programme, man.'

Ramsay laughed. *Hardyhar.* Then hung up.

Marak walked into the kitchen, found a brown envelope on the bottom shelf of the fridge. A photograph slid into his hand. He stepped to the window, examined the picture, a man's face snapped in grainy shadow, a little fleshy, late fifties, difficult to tell, heavy-lidded eyes like small hoods, a weak mouth, black-grey hair.

He turned the picture over. A name was pencilled on the back: Joseph Lindsay.

A name, a face. What you did with that information was up to you. How you performed the deed, that was left to your own discretion. No help from Ramsay. No weapon. Nothing. He wondered what Ramsay had contracted to do, if there were to be other kinds of assistance, something more than this depressing flat and the provision of names.

All right, if he had to go through this on his own, that was his destiny. Joseph Lindsay: he said the name to himself several times until it had begun to sound like a mantra. He stuck the picture back in the envelope, then it struck him that Ramsay or someone in his employ had a key to the flat and could come and go at any time.

An intruder. I have no privacy, Marak thought.

He left the flat. Outside, the air was unstintingly cold, shark's tooth sharp. He couldn't conceive of summer and sunshine in this place. He longed for home and the people he loved. His brothers, sisters. His mother —

Inevitably, he made the leap to the memory of his father. Inevitably, he saw him lying in that hot street and heard the echo of gunfire and he remembered shadowed faces in dark-blue doorways the sun couldn't reach, and a hawk sweeping the cloudless purity of the sky, and how he'd rushed to be with his father, how he'd held his father to him, and the man's eyelids had flickered and the pupils became whites and his lightweight summer suit was wet with blood, blood flowed and everything was red, the sun, the hawk in flight, everything deepest red, and an ambulance wailed in the distance and his father said *I do not want to leave you, but this hurts, how it hurts, hold me, do not let go . . .*

These memories filled him with an unbearable sorrow.

Calm. An uncluttered mind was what he needed. Clarity. The address, think about the address. And Joseph Lindsay. How to meet Lindsay? How to know if he lived alone, or was married, where he worked, the hours he kept — so many elements.

Ramsay had been parsimonious with information.

Marak reached a main thoroughfare and scanned the passing traffic, double-decker buses and lorries and cars, looking for a taxi. It occurred to him that if anything happened to Ramsay, if Ramsay decided to disappear, say, or some accident befell him, what would he do then? Ramsay was the one who provided the names. Presumably for security reasons, they were going to be drip-fed to him one at a time, like this Joseph Lindsay. Fine. But without Ramsay there would be no names at all.

The whole undertaking seemed suddenly precarious to him, and he backtracked to the fat bearded Moroccan, Zerouali, the proprietor of a felafel restaurant called Tahini in the Arab

Quarter of Haifa, who'd furtively given him a wad of money and blessed him for his courage, *you are doing a wonderful thing, young man, and may God be with you, and if you need a word of moral support at any time, telephone me here*; and the kibbutz boy in aviator glasses and a UCLA T-shirt who'd driven him by jeep to Port Said, then the funereal vodka-charged Greek skipper who'd ferried him to Athens, and the white-haired man in the glasses with bright-green plastic frames who'd handed him an envelope with the passport in the foyer of the Hotel Kirkeri in Athens — the connections, the links, how had they been forged? That wasn't any of his business. All he needed was the belief that the enterprise was sound from beginning to end.

Snow still fell. It felt strange against his lips and melted in his beard. When he saw a black taxi come towards him, he held out his hand and the cab stopped. He climbed into the back seat.

'Where to?' the driver asked.

'Bath Street.'

'What number, john?'

John? 'Anywhere will do.'

The driver shrugged. 'Jump in. Glasgow's your oyster.'

The cab carried Marak across a short stretch of droning motorway into the heart of the city, where the streets were narrow and traffic was dense. Fumes hung in the serrated air.

'Right you are,' the cabbie said. He braked.

Marak stepped out. 'This is Bath Street?'

'Unless they changed the signs since this morning,' the driver said. He was a plump man with a good-natured smile.

Marak thrust some money into his hand and said, 'Keep the change.'

'Actually, um, you've underpaid me, john.'

'Underpaid? Sorry. I am not used to the money.' Marak held his open palm towards the driver, who picked out two chunky little coins.

'Lucky for you I'm an honest man,' he said. 'Mind how you go, squire.'

Marak watched the taxi pull away before he turned and walked. He looked at numbers. Ninety. Eighty-two. Restaurants, insurance offices, art galleries, banks, shops, a world of commerce. Some had Christmas decorations in their windows. Trees, bright lights, silver strands.

Snow, picked up by a gust of fresh wind, blew into his face like cold white lace. He walked until he came to the number he was looking for, and he checked the collection of brass plates screwed into the doorway, then moved on. He crossed the street, passed below the strange blue lighting of Bewley's Hotel. It had an hallucinatory effect. He thought he was strolling through a dream.

He stopped, looked directly across: the narrow building consisted of four floors. In an upstairs window which bore gilt letters he saw a good-looking blonde woman inclined over something, a computer perhaps, a typewriter. When he thought she was about to move the angle of her face and look out, he hurried away, huddled deep inside his coat.

On the next corner he went back across the street again and he walked past the front door of the premises, for a second time checking

46

the brass plates. *Addendum Research World-wide. Calico Interiors Ltd. Scottish Domestics Agency.*

At the bottom: *Joseph Lindsay, Solicitor.*

He glanced back up at the window where he'd seen the woman moments before. She was gone. The scroll on the pane read: *Joseph Lindsay, Solicitor.*

Marak reached the corner of Bath Street and West Campbell Street and he stopped, and just for a moment yielded to a certain dismay: how was he supposed to engineer a discreet meeting with Joseph Lindsay, one so private nobody must ever know it had taken place?

He walked until he came to Queen Street Station, a large clamorous structure echoing with the sound of timetable announcements and train cancellations. He found a public telephone. He called the operator, and was connected to Directory Inquiries, where he obtained Joseph Lindsay's office number, and punched it in.

A female voice answered, 'Good afternoon, Joseph Lindsay and Company,' and Marak wondered if this might be the woman he'd seen in the window.

'I wish to speak to Mr Lindsay,' he said.

'I'm sorry. He isn't in today.'

'Can you tell me when he is expected?'

'Probably tomorrow. May I say who called?'

'Can I phone him at home?'

'I wouldn't be able to give you his private number, sir. If you tell me your name I'll have him contact you.'

Can this call be traced? he wondered. It didn't

matter. A public phone. So many people used it. He hung up. In the station bar he found a directory and flicked the pages. Plenty of J Lindsays. He took the photograph of Lindsay from his pocket and he tore it into small pieces and dropped them into a rubbish bin. He had the face memorized.

Probably tomorrow, he thought. He went out of the station and even as he yearned for sun and resurrection, the unobtainable necessities of his life, he wondered what he'd do next. Whatever it was, he understood that death had to figure somewhere in the equation of his future.

8

Lou Perlman had his kaput Mondeo jump-started by the driver of a passing bread delivery-van who spoke at length about the need for regular battery maintenance in cold weather. Chastened, Perlman drove away scattering promises of future good behaviour. It was after ten a.m. when he reached the Cedars, a small private hospital in Mount Florida on the south side of the city. In summer, the building would have been invisible from the street because of the density of trees but now, in this stunted season, Perlman could see the structure beyond the branches. Once, the Cedars had been a motel, and you could still detect its origins in the low-slung utilitarian look of the place, although it had been tarted up with balconies and slatted blinds at the windows and a couple of antique statues placed here and there on the lawn.

He drove into the car park, got out, hurried towards the entranceway; a wind-devil of dead leaves chased him, swirling around his head. Breathless, he shut the door behind him and looked at the receptionist. 'Bitter out there,' he said.

The receptionist wore a fashionable black suit. A glossy fringe of hair hid half her brow. She raised her face, gazed at Perlman as if he'd come here to collect for a charity of which she disapproved. 'Do you have an appointment?'

'With Dr Rifkind.'

'Name?'

'Perlman. Lou.'

'Take a seat.' The woman picked up a phone and spoke into it quietly. Perlman sat in a sofa so soft and deep it engulfed him. He scanned the waiting room. It was all muted shades in the Cedars, rusts, tans, browns. The prints on the walls were spartan, bleached of bright colour. This sedate place was several universes removed from the hospitals of the National Health Service, which in Perlman's experience were desperate abattoirs filled with the smells of stale body fluids, and out-moded equipment, and waiting rooms stuffed with all the sad bastards who'd been maltreated or carelessly overlooked by an arse-backwards system. The Cedars, private and expensive, was where you came to be pampered in your infirmity, and to hell with cost.

The receptionist said, 'Fine, Mr Perlman. Take the door to your left and go down the corridor.' She pointed with a yellow pencil. 'The doctor will meet you.'

Perlman walked down a long corridor. He saw only one nurse, and she moved soundlessly on rubber-soled shoes; no shrill intercom announcements here, no emergency calls, just the kind of quiet you'd expect in a library. The air was slyly perfumed with a scent redolent of baby powder. Nobody left sweat in the atmosphere of the Cedars. Nobody's emissions remained for long in bedpans.

Martin Rifkind appeared at the end of the corridor. He was a lean muscular man in a white coat. He had a large skull, a dome. It was the first feature of the man anyone noticed. Across this *duomo* lay a frail latticework of white hair. Years of bedside visits had given him a friendly manner. *I'm more than your doctor, I'm your chum.* Nothing happened in this small hospital without his imprimatur: he was cardinal, chief physician, God. Lou Perlman had met him a couple of times in the past. He was one of Colin's people. Lou had always felt distanced from the coterie in which Colin moved — they were all too bright, too classy, or just too obviously *ambitious*. They favoured sleek places and smart cocktails and holidays at expensive bijou hotels on the lesser-known islands of the Caribbean.

Rifkind held out a hand and Perlman shook it.

Rifkind said, 'It must be, what, a dozen years?'

'Who counts time any more? It's too depressing.'

'I remember, it was the anniversary . . . ' Rifkind paused in mid-faux pas. 'Ooops.'

Perlman listened to the word 'anniversary' reverberate in his skull and he remembered that night, oh Christ did he remember that night. The twentieth wedding anniversary of Colin and his wife, a hundred guests, tuxedos and glittering dresses and fancy jewels. The room was gleaming, brilliant, *wonderful*. But the humiliation . . . He'd begun drinking before his arrival because he was nervous, he didn't want to attend, and when it came to alcohol he was an utter lightweight who rarely drank. It roared immediately to his brain and distorted all his

51

notions of time and propriety.

He remembered sitting at the head table, one of the anointed. He remembered rising at some point, unbidden, to make a toast to the happy couple. Spilling things. Coffee pot, milk jug, ashtray. Getting his feet tangled together and listing forward and clutching table linen and thinking he was on the *Titanic* and here's the iceberg coming. He remembered the anniversary couple turning to look at him. *Aghast*: that was the word for their expressions.

Pished out of his skull, Lou raised his glass in the air and tried to make a joke, while the room swivelled and the punch-line deteriorated in mid-structure, and when he jerked his arm upwards to emphasize the sincerity of his toast the glass shot out of his hand and zoomed like a missile across the table and struck Colin in the forehead and rebounded, spilling globes of liquid into Rifkind's lap, and then Lou had staggered out into the garden, bending double, boking vigorously into a bed of violets and pansies for all the guests to hear. And then Colin was bending over him and saying, *You're humiliating, a fucking total embarrassment to me, this was an important night for us, arse-hole, I'm sticking you in a taxi and you're out of here and no goodbyes* . . .

Perlman looked at Rifkind. 'That was quite an evening, Martin, eh?' And he tried to laugh it off, a drunken misadventure, a silly wee thing, tut-tut pooh-pooh.

'Ah, we all act daft sometimes,' Rifkind said. 'Even doctors like me have been known to

52

consume a cocktail too many. Hard to believe, right?'

Too too kind, Perlman thought. I behaved disgracefully. 'Never drink on an empty stomach. So they say.'

'Plays havoc with the system all right,' Rifkind remarked.

Perlman looked at his watch. He wanted to see his brother and get out of here. Things to do. 'Can I visit him, Martin?'

'For a minute.'

'How is he?'

'He'll get over it in time, Lou. But his heart won't take another hammering. Go in room nine. Two doors down. Just keep it short.'

Lou Perlman entered the room. He realized he rarely saw his brother. Once a year, maybe twice, if that. A shame. Colin Perlman, handsome but pale and weary-eyed, head held up by a bank of pillows, offered a tiny smile.

'Well well, wee brother, *le gendarme*,' he said.

Lou Perlman approached the bed. Colin was attached to an IV drip. A machine monitored his heartbeat. 'So, Colin. How do you explain this state of affairs?' Lou gestured with his hand.

'Explain it?' Colin Perlman had Etta's blue eyes. He had a few fair strands in his thick grey hair. His face was square-jawed the way Etta's had been, his nose straight exactly like hers. 'I was jogging along minding my business, when out of an orange-coloured sky — '

'I know the song,' Lou said. 'Flash. Bam. Alakazam.' Etta had played it constantly on her old record-player, he remembered. But who the

53

devil had been singing it?

Nat King Cole: got it.

'It was like a bloody stake going deep into my heart, Lou. The pain was . . . utterly fucking *appalling*. I was suffocating. Blacked out. Rifkind says if I hadn't been treated so quickly you'd all be putting me in a box. Me, the fit one. Addicted to gymnasiums. I don't smoke, I get a serious heart attack. You smoke like an old blacksmith's forge, you get off scot-free.'

'So far,' Lou said.

'I had chest pains a couple of weeks ago. I thought heartburn. Wrong? I hate feeling this weak. That quack Rifky tells me I'll still have a quality life. Mind my diet. No fats, no butters, no cream. Alcohol? One tiny glass of vino on special occasions, thank you very much, doc. Oh, and don't overdo things. I'm supposed to walk with a bloody stick and pat the heads of all the nice geraniums I've grown and thank my lucky stars for the *quality* of my life? Well, fuck, I doff my hat to the constellations.'

Lou said, 'Bad shite happens to everybody.'

'Not to me it doesn't. This is a bitch.'

Lou gazed at his brother. Everything Colin touched, abracadabra, pure gold. He could take donkey droppings and turn them into doubloons. He invested money, it multiplied tenfold, twenty. He was a respected member of the Jewish community, not just in Glasgow, but in London, New York, Los Angeles. He went to the finest tailors. He flew first-class. He probably didn't even *realize* there was a rear cabin where all the *shlukhs* sat. He'd been kissed by a benign God.

One heart attack later, he knew he was mortal after all, and he didn't enjoy the discovery that, despite his good fortune and intelligence, he was exactly like everyone else: doomed. Those well-honed muscles in arms and legs, what good were they to him if his heart was a joker?

Lou touched the back of his brother's hand, and he felt a certain sadness that had its source in the understanding that they'd come from the same womb and seed, they'd grown up together, they'd seen their parents die; they were past middle age, and when it came to the blood of family they were the end of a specific line. There were no young Perlmans to carry on what Etta and Ephraim, fugitives, had begun. There were aunts and uncles, and a clamour of cousins, but that wasn't the same thing.

He turned his face to the window: the light outside was gloomy. More frail snowflakes fell. He thought: I've never told my brother I love him. Not in those words. Do I love him the way I should? He admired him, sure, and — God forgive him — envied him too. Not for his material wealth, flash cars, good suits; he wasn't lured by material items. *Stuff* was always replaceable. But love was just a damn tough card to play. The heart was reticent, the tongue lead.

He skipped around these thoughts. 'Do you remember that guy who hung himself when we were kids?'

Colin Perlman shook his head slowly. 'What guy?'

'He was a local milkman. Kerr . . . I think that was his name.'

'I have absolutely *no* recollection of any Kerr. Is there a point to this, Lou?'

'No, not really, just . . . ' But yes, yes, there is, I'm searching for common ground. Fraternal glue. The shared history of brothers remembering childhood. You told me about the word *suicide*, Colin, how could you forget that?

'You're waxing all nostalgic, Lou. Is this some age thing?'

'Must be, right enough.'

Lou Perlman was uncomfortable. Trying to bond, and failing. Why did it always have to be this way with Colin? 'I'll come back and see you tomorrow,' he said.

'Of course you will. But in the meantime make sure you keep the streets safe for respectable folk.'

'I try.'

'You do your best. You always did.'

'So did you, Colin. Except your best always seemed that wee bit better than mine.' No, Lou thought. Oh shit, why take this flight path? It was the wrong way to go, it invariably led to memories of childhood, to the old feeling that Colin had been Etta and Ephraim's favourite, and Lou some kind of afterthought, a footnote to the Perlman family. But was there a hard truth in that? He couldn't remember either his mother or father favouring Colin with specific gifts or treats. Maybe the feeling had its origin in the fact that greater things were always expected of Colin, because he was the sharper one, the gifted one — and Lou was the plodder, more persistent than brilliant. One time, Etta had said: *Colin, I think you'll do something with words, a journalist maybe, write for a newspaper. And you, Lou, you'll be a schoolteacher, I can see it.*

Prediction obviously hadn't been Etta's metier.

Colin said, 'You didn't have to be a cop, Lou. Who forced you? Who said sign on the dotted line and you'll be a policeman?'

'True. I might've been a businessman like you.'

'Don't knock it. I offered you the chance. Come in with me, I said. Make some real cash. But no, you always gave me the feeling that you looked down on what I did for a living, you didn't approve of what you once called get-rich-quick schemes. You had other . . . let's say, honourable motives.'

Honourable, Perlman thought. Was that the word? 'I never disapproved of what you did for a living. I never really understood it enough to approve or disapprove. And I don't remember ever describing anything you did as a get-rich-quick scheme, you're twisting my words — '

Colin shook his head. 'I don't think so. You didn't want to get involved. No filthy old capitalism for you. You didn't have the spirit of acquisition about you, Lou. You were never a swashbuckler. You lacked that buccaneer element — ' He contorted his face, didn't finish his sentence.

Lou asked, 'You in pain?'

'A twinge. Do me a favour. Send Rifkind in.'

57

Lou moved quickly to the door. He opened it, called out for Rifkind, who came down the hallway.

'He's in some discomfort, Martin.'

'I'll deal with it.' Rifkind entered the room and shut the door behind him. Lou Perlman walked back into the reception area. I've got an unidentified dead man on my hands, he thought. And I've got a brother who's just had a heart attack and I don't know too much about him either. The mysteries of people. What secrets they stash.

The outside door swung open just as he moved towards it. He saw her in the frame, dark against the morning sky and the pale snow, and his heart reared.

He wasn't conscious at once of the man who stood directly behind her, holding her elbow, he was transfixed by the sight of her, and anything on the edges of his vision faded to black. And then he was flustered, wishing he'd brushed his hair properly, that he was better-dressed, manicured and groomed, instead of looking like a bloody *nebbish*.

'Lou,' she said, and his temperature rose.

Was he blushing?

When she approached him, in long plum-coloured coat and scarf, and stepped into his embrace, he thought: *I showered, shampooed, I'm fine.* But does my clothing smell of mothballs? He remembered the photograph of her he'd hung in his house, right next to the picture of Ephraim and Etta, and how, guilty and ashamed, he'd taken it down, and removed it from the frame, then rolled the picture into a tube and stuck it in a drawer. I should've kept it on the wall where it was. I wasn't brave enough to face my own delusions.

She felt light in his arms. Delicate. He longed to kiss her, not some polite little dab on the cheek or forehead, but open-mouthed and passionate. He was in the grip of an absurd fever: how long was he destined to carry this yearning? There was no future in loving your brother's wife — and if this wasn't love then it was one hell of a counterfeit, and built to last. He trembled as he let her slip out of the embrace. Did she know? Had she suspected over the years? He imagined his face gave everything away, even to passing strangers. Apparently not. Somewhere along the way he'd become adept in the craft of camouflage.

'I'm so glad to see you, Lou,' she said. She had her long hair pinned up under a beret that matched her coat. He imagined undoing the pins one by one, slowly.

'I didn't expect,' and he let the sentence wither. You twittering *dunderheid*. She robs you of speech, for Christ's sake. She infiltrates you and steals your power.

'Did you see Colin?' she asked.

When he looked into her dark eyes he thought of reincarnation. Could they meet under different circumstances in an afterlife of sorts? It would have to be corporeal — none of that airy-fairy disembodiment kack — because his feelings were instilled with a serious carnal longing. God have mercy on me, he thought;

59

sometimes he'd imagined her in his bed with thighs spread and that long brown hair falling over breasts he wanted to kiss. Honourable Lou Perlman: aye, right, maybe in some respects — but was it honourable to lust after your sister-in-law and envy your brother because he was married to this woman?

'I saw him,' he said.

'What do you think?'

He noticed a wifely concern in her eyes, and understood — as he always did — that his longing was useless. She loved Colin. Nothing had changed. Nothing ever would. 'He'll be all right.'

'Rifkind says he'll have to take things easy. Can you imagine him pottering round the house?'

'No, I can't.'

'Neither can I.' She smiled sadly, and Lou Perlman was lost once more in her face, drawn into her smile and sent spinning through the tunnels of his emotions. Even at fifty her face seemed unworn. She had the lush mouth of a torch-singer in an after-hours club. She looked as if she knew deep secrets. There might have been blemishes, faint lines at the corners of the lips, even some slight slackening of flesh at the throat — but he was blind to her faults. She was still the girl he'd first met years ago, the astonishing girl hanging on Colin's arm, smart and exotic and vibrant, her presence suggestive of blue ocean voyages and tropical jaunts and rum drinks. And sophistication. Paris. Florence. Milan. She'd studied art in these glam places.

He was possessed by a daft urge to proclaim his feelings. In another world, yeh. In a comic strip reality. *True Love Rescues Trapped Maiden from High Tower Hell*.

Miriam, *neshuma*.

'I read somewhere you got a lectureship,' he said. 'I meant to phone and congratulate you.'

'You never phone, Lou. You never come to the house. But thanks for the thought.'

'Art School . . . right?' He knew the answer. He'd read the two small paragraphs in the *Herald* half a dozen times. He'd hunched over them like a Talmudic student scrutinizing some sixth-century proverb for its concealed meaning. He was proud that Miriam's oil paintings, big bold ambitious explosions of colour, hung in collections and galleries and banks. The ones he'd seen suggested nebulae detonating in space.

Miriam said, 'I'm teaching figure-drawing. Just for a year.'

'Well, if you're ever short of a model,' he said, and wondered if it was a joke too far. Sitting naked in a class of students, Miriam watching and assessing him, thinking he was pale and a little overweight, muscles in dire need of toning. She'd compare him to Colin, and she'd find him lacking. In the red corner, Colin, sick and handsome. In the blue, Lou, lumpen cop. No contest. KO.

'I'll keep that generous offer in mind,' she said, and she turned to the man who'd escorted her inside the hospital. 'Artie Wexler. You two *must* know each other?'

61

Artie Wexler said, 'We go back a long long way.'

Lou remembered Artie Wexler well, one of Colin's inner circle. Sixtyish, square-faced, brown hair thick and unreal, a weave maybe. Lou accepted Wexler's outstretched hand, which was hot and firm. Something at the back of Lou's mind prevented him from wanting to hold the hand for long. Something buried. He wasn't sure what.

'How are you?' Lou asked. He wondered if there was anything between Miriam and Wexler, but he set this aside as the fevered fear of the anxious lover, even though he didn't have a lover's proprietary rights.

'Considering the mileage, I'm fine,' Wexler said, and laughed in the easy way of a man who has prospered in life.

'Tell me about mileage,' Lou Perlman said.

'Still with the Strathclyde Police?'

'Can't find my way out.'

'Must be interesting work.'

People always said that. 'It has its moments.'

Miriam said, 'I'm going to look in on Colin now. Lou, phone me soon?'

'I will.'

'Is that a promise?'

He put a hand over his heart. 'On my word.'

Wexler said, 'Good seeing you.'

He walked behind Miriam and they passed through the door to the corridor. Wexler looked back once across the reception area and smiled at Lou, who wondered if he saw something a little possessive in the expression. Miriam and

Wexler. *Aw, ballocks, your head's stuffed with keech, Lou.*

He stepped outside and lit a Silk Cut. Miriam's scent hung in the fibres of his coat. He had work to do, a dead man to identify; funny how the silent mysteries of the dead had kept him busier all these years than the noisy cravings of his heart. He walked to his Mondeo and, annoyed with himself, annoyed with the world, *his* world, booted the right front tyre hard a couple of times and said *she's not for you, she's not for you.*

Dear Christ, she's been married to your brother for thirty-two years. Thirty-two long years. That's a whole world, and you're not a part of it. So it's time, Lou, to grow up and move on, it's time.

9

Club Memphis, bankrupt, stripped of assets, was located in a loft not far from the Gallowgate. The club had been the property of a man called Bobby J Smith, more commonly known in Glasgow entertainment circles as BJ Quick. He wore tight blue jeans and a white T-shirt and a brown leather jacket. He was forty-five years old and lean as a whippet. He had an ear-stud attached to his left lobe, and a thin gold chain around his neck.

Quick fingered the chain and said to the man in the chair, 'You're telling me you're fucking penniless. Don't have a brass fucking *farthing* to your name?'

The man roped to the chair wore only Y-fronts with a cross of St Andrew design. He had bald legs. 'If I had the dosh, BJ, you'd get it. If I knew how to lay my hands on it, you'd have it. So let's get these ropes off and act like rational men.'

'Rational? I've lost my club. I've lost my fucking livelihood. I've lost my *dream*!' BJ Quick gestured round the long drab room. A few old rock posters, cracked and creased, remained on the walls. The Killer thumping his piano. The King in black leather jump suit, lank of well-oiled hair hanging over forehead. Chuck Berry doing the duck walk, guitar held in bazooka position. 'This is all I got left after the vultures came in. Life's work. Life's fucking

64

work, arsehole. People like you put me outta business. Cretins. *Wankers!* People who wouldn't come up with the readies when they said they would.'

'These are competitive times in the club business, BJ,' the man said. He had a big round face the colour of an unlit fluorescent tube. He was known as Vindaloo Bill on account of his addiction to fiendishly hot curries. 'If you don't keep up, BJ, you go under.'

'I didn't keep up, eh? That what you're saying?'

'Rock Revival, big yawn. Okay for a couple weeks, man. But kids want acid dance or just a general fucking rave. You're a dinosaur, pal. Elvis is dead, by all reliable accounts. Jerry Lee's an old-age pensioner. These kids want Backyard Babies and Micronesia one week, and God knows what else next. You can't keep up with their tastes. You were beating off a dead horse, BJ. Even the name. Club Memphis? Past tense, pal. I mean, *you* might be obsessed with dead music — '

'Fuck you, Vindy. Stick to the subject. You owe me *fucking money*, you hairy-arsed tub of shite.' BJ kicked Vindy Jim's kneecaps hard. 'I dug in my wallet for you when times were tough. Here's a grand, Vindy. Here's another. Let me help you.' He bent an arm, tensed it, and drove the ramrod of his elbow into Vindy's face and blood poured out of a suddenly split lip.

'Ah fuck,' Vindy said, spitting out a dollop of tooth.

BJ Quick looked at the blood dripping on

65

Vindaloo's Y-fronts. He was furious, he missed his club, he ached for the nights when the place was packed and the music was loud and money was rolling in like tumbleweed in a gale. Okay, moronic oversight to forget setting loot aside for the tax people, and the VAT man, and the assorted legalized proctologists who probed his bum with rough instruments for the government's cut. Okay okay, mistakes were made. But he was damned if he'd suffer for his generosity to wallies like Vindaloo Bill. And he was damned if he'd hear his beloved Club Memphis criticized as *old-fashioned*. He walked to the window. He looked out. Snow blew in powdery swirls over chimney tops. He turned and stared the length of the loft.

Willie Furfee stood in shadow at the far end. He was a big man dressed in the neo-Edwardian mode that had been popular in the late 1950s, long jacket with velvet collar, drainpipe trousers, suede shoes with thick soles: brothel-creepers. He was a fully paid-up Teddy Boy, an anachronism. Sometimes at revivalist rock concerts he encountered fellow travellers and they smoked skunk together in the toilets and talked about funky little shops where you could still lay your paws on some authentic threads from the old days. They remembered legendary concerts they'd attended. No fucking Beatles she-loves-you-yeah-yeah shite, or poncy Rolling Stones stuff. Furfee and his like were pioneers along the rock frontiers, sworn to Little Richard, or Jerry Lee, sometimes even

Gene Vincent or Eddie 'Three Steps to Heaven' Cochran.

'Got your blade, Furf?' BJ Quick asked.

'Always, BJ.'

Vindy turned his head. 'Blade?'

Quick chucked Vindy under the chin. 'Time for some serious biz.'

'A fucking blade, man? No way. That's not on.'

'Oh but it is. The Furf doesn't like to use his razor, because basically he's soft-hearted. But he's awfully good with it, *pal*, and a man shouldn't be denied the chance of practising his skills now and again, right?'

Vindaloo shook his head vigorously. 'I'll get you your money. I will.'

'Aye, when pigs crap gold. Fuck *you*. I'm tired waiting.'

Furfee walked across the wooden floor, which had been burned and gouged by millions of cigarette ends and stiletto heels. He took an old-fashioned bone-handle razor from his jacket. He opened the blade, and it gleamed like a terrible mirror.

Vindaloo said, 'Youse are kidding me, right?'

Quick asked, 'Are we kidding, Furf?'

Furfee said, 'Do I look like I'm kidding?'

Quick said, 'The Furf never kids. What's your sign, Bill?'

'Sign?'

'Star sign, arsehole.'

'Fuck. Pisces. So what?'

BJ Quick said, 'Do us a fish, Furf,' and he grabbed the left arm and held it, and Furfee brought the blade down and carved a curving

67

line in the skin of the backarm, and blood surfaced quickly where he'd cut. Vindaloo roared and wriggled around in his chair and tried to break free of the ropes.

'Oh, for fuck's sake, don't cut me again,' he shouted. 'Come on, BJ, we go back years, tell this guy not to cut me, eh? *Please*.'

'Sit still and shut your face. Here, this'll help,' and BJ Quick stuffed a filthy rag he found on the floor into Vindaloo's mouth, just as Furfee drew another curving line with the edge of the blade, joining it to the first incision he'd made. Now he had two five-inch lines, each bleeding. Vindaloo tried to scream, but the thick rag muffled his sound.

BJ Quick said, 'Nice work, Furf.'

Furfee took the razor away. 'Want me to finish this, BJ?'

Vindaloo Bill shook his head with vigour. 'Blllblllwoobbb,' he said.

'Is that a no?' Quick asked.

Furfee said, 'Hard to tell.'

'Do the eyes of the fish now, Furf.'

Furf bent over the arm and made two deep punctures between the curved lines with a slight stabbing motion of his hand. The blade was wondrously sharp. Blood spewed down Vindy's arm and over his belly.

'Star sign,' Quick said. 'Scar sign more like.'

'Ha ha,' Furf laughed.

'The tail, Furf. Don't forget the tail.'

'I wish this fucker would stop wriggling.'

'You hear that, Vindy? Be still. Be very still.' BJ patted Vindaloo's cheek gently. 'A fella cuts you, it's going to hurt like hell. Just think, this could be much worse. Eee gee, I could ask the Furf to *skin* you. He's got a diabolical skill for that. Skinning's worse than anything. You see somebody slice off the top layer of your skin and you start to think, what the hell will it be like if he skins my whole fucking *body*? Try and imagine yourself without your outer covering. Got the picture? Not a very pretty sight . . . '

'*Abbbekkkkkmmml.*'

Quick ripped the rag from Vindy's mouth. 'You trying to say something?'

'No more, please, BJ, I can't take it. The bloody pain — '

'I'd like to finish the tail,' Furfee said. His eyes had the beatific light of a man in the extremes of pleasure. 'You want me to go on, BJ?'

'That's up to Vindy.'

'I'll find you money. Swear to God.'

'You hear that, Furf?'

'Man swears to God. An old story.'

'Ach, finish the tail, Furf.'

Vindaloo said, 'Wait, no, listen, I can get you five K. That's all.'

'Five K, eh? Zatso? I'd want it tonight.'

'Aye. Tonight. No problem. Absolutely.'

BJ Quick said, 'Eight sharp.'

'Eight sharp, worda honour.'

'Just remember this, Vindaloo. We know where you live.'

Furfee said, 'Right. Ranfurly Road, Penilee.'

'And does he live alone, Furf?'

'Wife Mary, age thirty-four. Two kids. Tom,

69

ten, and Cindy, seven.'

Quick said, 'Wee doll that Cindy. A Gold-ilocks.' He untied the ropes, let them drop to the floor.

'Don't come to my house, for Christ's sake,' Vindy said, picking up his clothes and groaning. 'Please. I'll meet you anywhere.'

'Govan subway station.'

'Right. Fine. Fuck's sake, I'm bleeding all over the fucking shop here,' Vindy said.

'Get dressed, Billyboy. Go home. Get the money.'

'Dressed? I'm leaking *pints*, BJ. You got any bandages, anything like that, stop all this?'

Furfee laughed, a sound like a poker raked through cinders. 'We look like a chemist to you?'

'He'll be wanting rubbers next,' BJ said.

Furfee laughed again and wiped his blade dry against Vindy's shirt, which the injured man was trying to button with fingers shaking.

Vindaloo Bill, human colander, dripped blood all over the floor.

'You can find your way out, I take it,' BJ Quick said.

'I'm going, I'm going.' In slow measured steps, Vindy moved towards the door. He went out, stumbling, weeping.

'What do you think?' Furfee asked.

'I think it's bloody magical he can find money when he swears left and right he doesn't have any.'

'Carving affects people,' Furfee said.

BJ Quick stepped around puddles of blood and walked to the window. He looked out at

70

snow drifting lazily across the city. He observed a ghost of his own image in the glass and touched the promontory of hair that rose from the centre of his head and powered out over his brow. It was yellow, like a bird poised for flight from the bush of surrounding black hair. This style, a jutting pompadour with attitude, was rock 'n' roll, flash, up yours.

'Five grand's not going to get me the ante for a new club. Kilroy wants another ten before I can get this place back.' He breathed on the pane and drew the letters KILROY WAS HERE in the condensation with a fingertip, then rubbed them out. Leo Kilroy was the owner of the premises and he'd promised, in thon sleakit way of landlords, that BJ could have first option on the place if he could lay his hands on twenty-five K. *I can't hold that offer open too long, BJ.*

'I want my fucking *club* back.'

'Five grand plus the ten you already gave him,' Furfee said. 'That only leaves another ten to get.'

'I can do the bloody arithmetic, Furf.' Ten grand up the chimney and into Kilroy's coffers.

'What's this Arab guy like?' Furfee asked.

'Tense as a nun's twat.'

'What's he here for?'

'He's here, that's all I fucking know and all I want to know. Which reminds me. Has Wee Terry called?'

'Not in a few hours.'

'Get him on the horn, Furf. Let's see what our wandering Arab has been up to.'

'Wilco.'

BJ Quick shook his head and thought how his

71

present predicament could be traced back to a single moment in time: an autumn night in 1969, his thirteenth birthday, when his father, Frank Xavier Smith, chauffeur to the director of a real-estate company with a dodgy reputation, had given him Jerry Lee's *Greatest Hits Volume One* as a present.

'Whole Lotta Shakin' changed BJ's life. It steamrolled his heart. He became a True Believer. His conversion on the road to rock 'n' roll Damascus took only a few seconds and the first phrase of a song — 'Come on over baby we got chicken in the barn' — and after that he'd given years to the cause. It was more than love of the music, more than an obsessive pastime — it was a calling, and he an apostle determined to spread the gospel.

Right, he thought. Look where it led me.

Bankruptcy, much dope smoked and much dope sold, three broken marriages, eight kids here and there, acts of violence; and a bloody mysterious alliance, for mercenary purposes, with some intense bearded character from the Middle East.

He thought: Messages from somebody I don't know and I pass them along despite the fact I don't like working in the fucking dark, but I need the green infusion, and I was paid 10K down — which went straight into Kilroy's plucked pigeon of a fist — with a promise of another 10K on completion. And I have a feeling the people I'm working for are *right bad bastards* who wouldn't look kindly on me shirking my duties.

He gazed round the empty room. The rubble

72

of Club Memphis. He felt a sense of withdrawal as desperate and as bleak as that of any junkie abruptly cut off from his source. I bankrolled this fucking place. It was my dope, and I smoked it, snorted it, mainlined it. It was mine and mine alone . . . and now, and now. He booted aside the chair where Vindaloo Bill had been bleeding, and he thought: I should've listened to Father Georgeann, parish priest, when he said rock 'n' roll was Satan's music. Man had a point there.

10

At Force HQ in Pitt Street, Lou Perlman went to Sandy Scullion's office. The kiddie drawings on DI Scullion's bulletin-board had a cheering effect, all those innocent yellow suns and square houses and matchstick figures waving from windows and funny doglike things running on lime-green lawns. Sometimes he wished he had a life like Scullion's. Would he know what to do with it? *I'm home, love. What's for dinner? My day was a nightmare, darling ... I'd die for a G&T*. He scanned the drawings while Scullion finished a conversation on the telephone.

When he hung up, Scullion asked, 'How is Colin?'

'Impatient. Champing at the bit. Thinks his life is over. Colin loves control over events, and one thing you can't control is a serious cardiac arrest. Or its consequences. So he's flattened and a wee bit angry. You haven't met him, have you?'

'No. What's the prognosis?' Sandy Scullion frowned, ran a hand across his thin ginger hair. He was a genuine man, and when he was concerned about something he couldn't hide it.

'Doctors don't say a lot.'

Scullion said, 'I'm sorry, Lou. Really. Still. Might have been worse. A total eclipse.'

'Might have been, right enough,' Perlman said. He thought of Colin and how, before he'd married Miriam, he'd been through a stream of

74

girlfriends, dumping them ruthlessly. He had charm, which he used as a weapon. Master of heartbreak. Miriam seemed to have tamed that cruel streak long ago. She had strength, and Lou admired her for it.

'Are you close?' Scullion asked.

'Not as much as I might have wished. He went his way, I went mine. He liked banking, sitting in his big London office and wheeler-dealing obscene sums of money from one numbered account to another. He thrived on that stuff. When he quit the bank business and returned to Glasgow, he set himself up as a financial consultant. Hordes of clients. They came in greedy droves. Make me rich, Colin, they cried.'

'And did he?'

'I imagine he did.'

'Will he retire?'

'Might not have a choice,' Lou said. Fatigue dimmed his mind. How many hours had he slept? He thought of the bridge, and the dead man's identity; he also thought about other cases demanding his attention — a charred skeleton that had been found in a sewage-pipe under a building in Stobcross Street last week, and a young wino clubbed to death in Sighthill Park three nights ago — all things he ought to get focused on. But Miriam's appearance had knocked him off-balance.

'I got some pics of our hanging man, Lou.' Sandy Scullion opened a folder on his desk. Lou found himself looking at photographs of the corpse's face. He sifted the assorted black and whites, and listened to office noises seep into his consciousness: phones, clackety-clack of conversation, banter between cops, a kettle boiling, somebody humming 'Those were the Days, My Friend'. This face. This guy. I *know* him, I've *seen* him. Where oh where? His memory was too often a wayward instrument. He had to coax it to work, and sometimes it took too long. He removed his coat and tossed it across a chair.

Scullion, in dark suit, neat white shirt and dark tie, went back behind his desk and said, 'By the way, Lou. I love the threads. Planning an ocean voyage? Got your sextant packed, and your hardtack bickies ready?'

'You're a right chucklefest. It's a fucking *blazer*, Sandy. An old fucking *blazer*. I got dressed in the dark. Okay, so it's got brass buttons. So what. I make no excuse for the flannels either.'

'I'm not the fashion police, Lou. I'm only slagging you — '

'I don't have somebody to iron my shirts and see I'm turned out all neat and tidy, do I?'

'Oh Lord. Remind me to hang a sign on my door. No Curmudgeons Need Apply.'

'Bloody winter depresses me, Sandy. Dead trees, nothing *growing*. It gets longer every year. Roll on spring.' Perlman swatted a hand through the air in a gesture of irritation, sat down, longed to smoke. One reason he hated the confines of Pitt Street. Tobacco-Free Zone.

'Anyone reported missing lately?' he asked.

'Usual runaway kids, sad stories, anxious parents. A woman who said she was going to the corner shop for cigarettes, never came back.

76

Nobody matching the face in the photographs, Lou. Not yet.'

Perlman stood up. He had to get out. This place was overheated, he was sweating, and the sirens of nicotine were ululating. 'I'll pop over to Mandelson's,' he said. 'Take one of those glossies with me.'

'We can send a uniform, Lou. We've got the Stobcross Skeleton on the desk. And that kid who was beaten. It's not like we're looking for something to do — '

'I know, I know. I need a walk, Sandy. Clear my head.'

'Is your mobile powered on?'

Perlman patted his pockets, searched his coat, couldn't find his mobile. Then he remembered seeing it last on the kitchen table.

Scullion said, 'Take mine. And remember not to switch it off. I want to be able to call you in case McLaren's finished the P-M before you come back.' He slid a slimline royal-blue gizmo across the desk. Perlman shoved it in his pocket, then struggled back into his coat.

'See you shortly, Sandy.'

Scullion, who'd worked his way up through the ranks under Perlman's guidance, watched him step out of the room. He was very fond of Lou; he couldn't imagine a time when Perlman would retire, any more than he could conceive of him ever leaving Glasgow. The sometimes abrasive nature of the city, the often melancholy countenance of the place, found correspondences in Perlman's character. And just as the city could be good-natured and gregarious, so could Lou Perlman — a scratched gem of a man, and too often alone for his own well-being.

Scullion's wife Madeleine adored Perlman, although she'd once famously remarked that, like Lagavulin, he was an acquired taste. Sandy made a little note on a slip of paper. *Invite LP to dinner soon.*

11

Artie Wexler entered the driveway and drove towards the house, which was big and imposing, a redbrick Edwardian monstrosity far too large for one man. He'd told Joe Lindsay this a hundred times. You're alone, go live somewhere smaller, and Joe had rambled on about all the happy memories of raising his kids here, and how his long-dead wife had loved this house, and what a wrench it would be to find some bloody little box in which to live.

There was no sign of life. Even Joe's Mercedes, usually parked at the front door, was missing. Wexler braked, got out of his Lexus, rang the doorbell. No answer. Bloody weird. Joe's gone, and so's the Merc. Business trip? Last-minute thing? He peered through windows. Saw nothing. He walked round the house. Back door locked. He rapped on it anyway, even if he knew he wouldn't get a response. It was something to do, an action. He was at a loss.

He stared across the garden; Joe's vegetables were all dead and gone, limp stalks, brown relics of broccoli leaning to ground. He had an uneasy feeling as he looked at the garden, somebody walking on his grave.

Joe, Joe, where did you go?

Wexler returned to his car. This house was giving him the creeps. His life was a series of watertight compartments. Marriage. Business.

79

Old friendships. History. Secrets he kept from Ruthie. When something didn't *feel* right, when an irregularity occurred, it threatened the entire structure. He couldn't have that. Insomniac hours. Night sweats. *You worry too much,* Ruthie had told him. *You hear a car backfire in the distance and imagine a nuclear reactor explosion. Every little upset is like your own personal Hiroshima.*

He adjusted his scarf, shivered. He took his mobile phone from the glove compartment and punched in the number of Joe's office. He got Joe's secretary, a divorcee called Wilhelmina, or Billie as she liked to be called.

'Is he in?' he asked.

'No, and he didn't call. I'm a very unhappy woman. People have been phoning all morning, looking for him.'

'He didn't keep our dinner engagement last night, and that worries me. Any idea where he is?'

'There's nothing in his appointment book. He didn't tell me he was going anywhere. Usually he tells me everything.'

'Maybe he left town, Billie. Something urgent.'

'Excuse me for saying so, Mr Wexler, but nothing urgent *ever* happens here. This isn't some hotshot criminal practice, as you well know. Sometimes he changes a will for a client — which might involve a mad dash to get to the deathbed in time, I grant you — but he deals mainly in land transactions, which is hardly the stuff of legal thrillers. I'll get him to call you when he shows up.'

'Fine, fine, Billie.' Wexler killed his phone and stared at the house and thought how big empty houses filled him with dread; all those quiet rooms, darkness in an attic.

What if Joe lay dead inside?

But the Merc was gone.

Somebody might have stolen it. Killed Joe, stolen the car. These things happened.

Your own Hiroshima, Artie Wexler.

He backed up the car quickly and drove through the streets of Langside in the distracted manner of somebody lost. He had the feeling that the fabric of his world was about as strong as an old canvas sail in a tempest.

He turned left on Mansionhouse Road and wondered: who do I talk to about my apprehensions?

One name occurred to him.

12

Perlman walked out of Force HQ, head bent at an angle against wind blowing out of the north; he could taste the frigid deeps of winter. Beyond the city, in the Campsie Hills and on Ben Lomond, snow would be falling heavily and quietly. Inside Glasgow, it had quit for the time being, but the wind was a bastard.

Eyes smarting under his glasses, lips chilled, Perlman lit a cigarette behind cupped hands, then crossed West George Street, two blocks south of Bath Street. Walking east, he had some cover from the cold except when he came to cross-streets, Blythswood Street, West Campbell, Wellington, where he was exposed. Folly, maybe, to have left his car behind in Pitt Street, but on a normal day he enjoyed this walk. From Force HQ to Buchanan Street took only — what? five minutes at most?

He stopped for a traffic signal at Hope Street, cursing the fact he didn't have gloves. His hands felt as if they were ice-bound in his coat pockets. One thing about this air: it kept you awake.

'Mister Perlman, that you?'

He turned when he heard the girl's voice. He looked at her. She had the beauty of an angel totalled in a car crash. Black mascara ran down her cheeks. Her lipstick was askew and her hair, tinted maroon, hung uncombed around her unhealthy white cheeks.

'Sadie?'

'You remember me, that's nice, Mr Perlman.'

'Jesus Christ, girl, you'll catch your bloody death.'

'Aye, it's cold.' She wore a thin velvet blouse and a short tight black skirt. No coat. No scarf.

'You're using again,' he said.

'Gets me through the hard times.' She leaned close to him and he wondered how a girl so heavenly, so blessed by looks — and brains when she wasn't drug-addled — had squandered her possibilities. She'd been busted three years ago for possession of heroin, and sent for counselling and Methadone treatment.

'Drugs don't get you through a damn thing, Sadie,' he said.

'You're not hooked.'

Thanks, but I've got my own addiction, he thought. The kind you can't buy in some alley behind a pub. He noticed a bruise staining her flesh from the corner of her left eye to the edge of her ear. 'What did he hit you with this time?'

'He drinks, he gets carried away, Mr Perlman.'

'I know where I'd like to carry *that* bastard,' Lou Perlman said, angry. 'You've got a tattoo on your forehead, love, and it says V for Victim. Which is how come you attract scum like that sadist Riley, who has all the charisma of a bloody stormtrooper. You pick up these arseholes who batter you the first time they've had enough booze. Big men. Tough guys. You're drawn to these wasters. What is it with you?'

'We've been this road before, you and me,' she said.

'Am I talking to a brick wall, Sadie?'

She shivered violently and stamped her feet in a flamenco manner for warmth. She was turning blue. Perlman took off his coat and draped it over her shoulders. She'd been in rehab, seen shrinks, but she always ended up in the same trap, wasted on smack, and always with the moronic Eric 'Moon' Riley as her lover and violator and part-time pimp. He wanted to find Riley, an altogether ugly fucker, and bust his head open as you might take a sledgehammer to a watermelon, but what was the point?

The last time he'd leaned on Riley the dumb little fuck had got himself a low-rent lawyer who'd threatened to bring a police brutality lawsuit — even though Lou hadn't laid a hand on the guy. Fuckers like Riley, so quick to violate the rights of others, screamed navy-blue murder when they imagined their own rights under attack. Now, standing in front of this shivering girl, Perlman had the urge to seek Riley out again. He repressed it. You can't be the avenger, Lou. You can't go strutting around protecting people like Sadie. It was a thankless task. There were just too many Sadies on the streets of Glasgow.

'I can't take your *coat*, Mr Perlman,' she said. She looked small in the folds of the garment.

'And I can't see you die of hypothermia, love. Just take the bloody thing.' He took two fivers out of his blazer and stuffed them into her hand. 'Your mother still living in Partick?'

'Aye.'

'Then jump in a taxi and go home. Go on.'

'Riley'll find me there.'

He patted the side of her face softly, and felt sad for her. Face like that belonged in a fashion magazine. But she'd end up dead before she was thirty unless she made a big-time life change. 'Go home. Get warm. Do me a favour, eh?'

She closed her hand round the money. 'Thanks a lot. One day I'll maybe do something for you.'

'Return the coat to HQ?'

'You've got dimples. You know that?'

'No, love, my jaws are collapsing where the dentist yanked out the back teeth, that's all.' Perlman called a passing cab, then helped her get inside. 'Go home, Sadie.'

He slammed the door and watched the taxi pull away and he realized his little act of charity had deprived him of his coat and the wind blowing down Hope Street cut through his blazer and bagged up the legs of his flannels. Act of charity — she'd probably take the cab round the corner and get out at the nearest bar and have a drink, then she'd phone Riley and he'd come for her and the sorry cycle of her life would continue.

Ah, fuck it, you did what you could. You hoped. You sent out lifeboats, and some of them never came back.

He hurried now into Buchanan Street where there was no shelter. The Christmas lights overhead failed to project warmth: just a sort of chill sterility. He entered Mandelson's. Hot inside, deliciously so. The air had that comforting smell of new clothes, of expensive Harris tweed jackets and wool trousers and hand-finished linen shirts. Rubbing his palms together, he approached the counter where a skinny-faced assistant with an effete manner assessed him in a sniffy way.

'I know, I know,' Perlman said. 'It looks like the charge of the hoi polloi, and I'm the advance scout.'

'Mmmm,' the assistant said. 'Perhaps I can interest you in something?'

Lou fished his wallet out and showed his ID. 'This is the only thing I'm interested in, son.' He produced the glossy, and laid it on the counter in front of the assistant. 'Tell me who that is.'

The man looked at the photograph just as the phone in Lou's left pocket rang. Sandy Scullion had set the ringer to play the first bars of 'The Yellow Rose of Texas'.

Lou answered. 'That's embarrassing.'

'I knew you'd like it. My kids set it,' Sandy Scullion said. 'Okay. The news of the hanging man isn't pleasant.'

'And I was longing for cheap and easy closure.'

'Sorry to let you down, Lou.'

'I'll be right back, Sandy.' Perlman killed the connection.

The assistant said, 'I *think* I know him. It's hard to be sure. He looks awfully like one of Mr Mandelson's personal customers.'

'So what's his name?'

'Let me talk to Mr Mandelson. A minute, please.' The assistant went into a back room.

Perlman wandered around the racks. He

scanned a heavy coat in navy-blue wool, and he checked the price-tag, which was hefty enough to dry the saliva in his mouth. He tried it on anyway, looked at himself in the mirror. He was smart all of a sudden. He'd buy this damn coat and sod the price. It was time to treat himself.

The assistant came back, followed by an arthritic old fellow with a pear-shaped pink face. This was Mandelson, a gent of the old school, a time when suits were bespoke and young men of means paid their accounts quarterly.

'May I take a wee peek at this photograph, please?' he asked.

13

When Perlman returned to Force HQ in Pitt Street he found Charlie McLaren, pathologist, in Sandy Scullion's office.

McLaren asked, 'How come you're not out chewing the cud yet, Lou?'

'They can't retire me, Charlie. I know where all the skeletons are stored.'

'I bet you do.' Charlie McLaren, who had a roaring laugh and a big red face, wore a three-piece pin-striped suit and an old school tie. He had a public-school manner; you could imagine him, legs parted, roasting his arse against the blazing fire of a gentleman's club on a cold afternoon. Old port in hand, maybe the occasional sly fart aimed towards the chimney. He had a very refined Scots accent. 'Personally, Lou, I'm seeing the finishing line. I did a reckoning the other day, and I calculate I've cut open five thousand corpses in my time. That's an awful lot of dead flesh and dipping your hands inside wet carcasses. Hard to stay enthusiastic about the job.'

'Enthusiasm's as slippery as a bar of soap in a bathtub,' Lou said. 'Now you have it, now you don't.' He couldn't imagine losing his own zeal altogether. Weary at times, sure, jaded, but he always bounced back. Something always cropped up to crank his motor. The unforeseen. An unexpected turn of events.

Sandy Scullion picked up a plastic Ziploc bag from his desk. 'Have a gander at this,' he said.

Lou Perlman looked at the bag. He saw what appeared to be small pieces of shredded latex, but it was hard to be sure. 'I give up, Sandy. What is it?'

Scullion said, 'The remains of a condom.'

Charlie McLaren said, 'Right. Damnedest thing.'

'Explain it to me,' Lou said.

Scullion said, 'There was a french letter in the dead man's stomach.'

'His stomach?'

'Burst in his gut,' McLaren said.

'He'd *swallowed* a condom?'

'Right. And it killed him.' Sandy Scullion poked the plastic bag with a fingertip.

'More specifically, the *contents* of the contraceptive killed him,' McLaren said.

'And what were these contents?' Lou asked.

'Cocaine. Fatally high concentrations of the substance in the subject's blood. I'd say very pure cocaine, pharmaceutical quality. The condom splits, cocaine melts into the blood-stream, whack, heart isn't equipped to handle the chemical blast. Positively *atomic*. A few seconds of clammy terror. If that. Then death.'

'Cocaine in condoms, everyday smuggling tactic,' Scullion said.

Perlman perched himself on the edge of Scullion's desk. 'If you're a smuggler, right. But tell me why Joseph Lindsay, respectable solicitor — if that's not an oxymoron — would swallow a condom filled with prime cocaine?'

'You're sure he's Lindsay?' Scullion asked.

'No two ways. According to Frank Mandelson, Lindsay had been his customer since Moses came down from the mountain. Had an account there. Never in arrears. I had a feeling from the minute I saw Lindsay's body I knew him from him somewhere. Then when I heard his name the mist rolled back. Nine or ten years ago, he was involved with some group advocating peace and coexistence in Palestine. The name of the group was Connect. No, wait, wrong, it was Nexus. Or *The* Nexus. I was hijacked by one of my liberal relatives into attending a bloody *awful* chicken dinner in honour of a visiting Israeli luminary. The man who introduced this Israeli to the assembly was Joseph Lindsay. Offices in Bath Street, Mandelson says, and a house in Langside. Butter wouldn't melt. So how do we go from being a quiet-mannered lawyer to somebody with a coke-filled rubber in his gut? That's a leap, Sandy.' He looked at McLaren and asked, 'Who uses pharmaceutical cocaine these days in conventional medicine?'

'Ear nose and throat fellows,' McLaren answered. 'It's not in great demand.'

'Except by drug dealers,' Perlman said.

'Who steal from pharmaceutical warehouses.' McLaren's stomach rumbled. 'Before I leave you chaps to get on with your investigative matters, let me just say you'll have my full report in the morning, cc to Detective-Superintendent Mary Gibson, although I understand she's away at some law-enforcement seminar until tomorrow. For your immediate purposes, the drug definitely

90

killed him, and he was hung post-mortem. Also, that he died last night between eleven and midnight. Lord God, I'm famished. I need some grub.' He picked up his overcoat and said, 'Happy hunting,' then stepped out of the room.

'Lucky sod,' Scullion said. 'He just drops the ball and walks away.'

'He had the brains to attend medical school, Sandy. He doesn't have to sit round with grunts like us, does he?'

'Grunts? Speak for yourself.' Scullion switched on his desk lamp. Although it was only early afternoon, the sky was darkening and the office grew dim. 'How do you force somebody to swallow something he knows will probably kill him? Hold a gun to his head, I suppose.'

'It's a good way of getting what you want. Lindsay takes the condom into his mouth and gags it down. Better than a bullet in the skull, he thinks. At least he's alive for a wee while longer. And where there's life etcetera. I'd swallow a barrowload of coke myself if somebody was pointing a gun at my noggin.'

'What had Lindsay done, I wonder.'

'He was a lawyer, Sandy. You show me a lawyer and I'll show you a man with a few enemies.'

Scullion tilted his head back, studied the ceiling. 'Whoever did the deed took his wallet, money, anything that might have identified him.'

'Except the ring. Which I'm assuming was maybe too tight to yank off.' Perlman walked round in slow pensive circles. He was back on the riverbank, hearing the goods train roll across the railway bridge. He imagined somebody dragging Joseph Lindsay along the edge of track. Somebody strong — unless the task was split between two. Why go to the trouble of trying to make it look like suicide?

'Lindsay was a widower, Mandelson says. There are a couple of kids. One in Australia, he thinks. The other in Canada. He's not sure. I'll ask around. Since Lindsay was connected in certain Jewish circles, I'll probably get any personal information I want without too much trouble — unless I'm persona non grata with my relatives for what they think of as my anti-social behaviour. Frankly, Sandy, I'm weary of my aunts trying to fix me up with allegedly eligible women. If I lived back inside the circle, I swear I'd never go short of food. There'd be beef casserole or gefilte fish every day. I'd be a sitting target for the widows' brigade. Do I look like marital material?'

'Not quite. But the coat's very nice. You clean up pretty well, Lou.'

'I thought you'd never notice,' Lou Perlman said.

'Let's get this show on the road.' Scullion stood up, stretched his arms. 'Lindsay's office first, I think.'

'What about the Stobcross bones?' Perlman asked.

'Still no ID. The skeleton's been buried in that pipe for more than twenty years, Sid Linklater estimates, so you're looking at a very cold trail.'

'And the dead kid in Sighthill Park?'

'Uniforms are still taking statements. The

usual painstaking stuff. Time-consuming. It'll keep, Lou.'

Perlman walked to the door. *It'll keep*. He hated leaving investigations in mid-air, things unfinished, questions unasked. The criminal puzzles of the city could drive you mad if you let them. Don't spread yourself too thin, Lou.

Scullion said, 'I already called Lindsay's secretary. She's waiting. And before I forget, where's my mobile phone?'

Perlman took the phone from his pocket and handed it back.

'I thought you'd lose it somewhere,' Scullion said.

'I never lose anything that isn't mine, Sandy.' Perlman followed Scullion downstairs and into the street, away from the hubbub of Force HQ and out into the miserly afternoon light.

14

Terry Dogue, whose cracked Docs leaked, mumbled into his cellphone. 'He went down Buchanan Street to the river. Stared into the water. Turned round. Gawked in the window of that shop selling knives, know the one I mean under the bridge? Victor Morris? Now he's going back up Buchanan Street. He's turning about a block ahead of me. I bet he's going back to Bath Street.'

BJ Quick said, 'Anything else he's done?'

Terry said, 'Aye. He went into Queen Street Station earlier and made a phone call.'

BJ Quick said, 'You get close enough to hear him?'

'Naw, no chance. It was over and done in a flash. Listen, BJ, my arse is as cold as a witch's tit. My feet are ice — '

'You're getting paid,' Quick said.

Terry Dogue said, 'I haven't seen a penny yet.'

'You'll get some scratch tonight, wee man.'

'That'd be welcome.'

'Phone me, eight-thirty, nineish.'

Terry Dogue heard the line click dead. He had a mind to phone Quick back and tell him to piss off. Terry Dogue didn't do dogsbody jobs like this, Terry Dogue may be five feet tall but he had dignity, and Terry Dogue didn't didn't *didn't ever* work without pay. But he held back. The last thing you did was get on the wrong side of BJ.

Let's not overlook the Furf.

What a pair: Mr Quick and Mr Razor. Fucking terrorists. Terry Dogue had spent time in Barlinnie and he knew some hard cases. But Furfee and Quick were something else: total fucking nutters, headcases of the first order.

Terry Dogue screwed his Northern Arizona University Lumberjack's dark-blue baseball cap on to his frozen skull. He'd always had a mysterious *thing* about Flagstaff, although he'd never visited it in his life. When he'd first heard the name of the town as a kid he'd imagined a stark white flagpole in the middle of nowhere. *Magic*. Then he'd seen pictures in *Arizona Highways*, and begun a lifelong yearning for a sight of the San Francisco Peaks or a quiet stroll through the old town on a soft summery night when the air was said to be scented with pine.

Flagstaff, Az, dream destination.

He needed to win the Lottery, buy a plane ticket, piss off into the skies.

But. Here he was. Glasgow. His lot. The only place he knew. He was trapped like a doomed fly in a jar of Dundee marmalade.

The crowds streamed past him down Buchanan Street, walking under Christmas tinsel and bright lights strung between buildings. 'Good King Wenceslas' issued from a loudspeaker somewhere. Who the hell was Wenceslas and what was so good about him anyway? Terry Dogue wondered.

Up ahead he saw the Arab moving, and he hurried after him.

Lose the Arab, you lose your credibility. Maybe also something else.

One slice of the Furf's blade and, whoops, gelded.

★ ★ ★

Marak entered a cafeteria for soup and a sandwich. But the soup, in which the letters of the alphabet floated, was lukewarm and didn't heat him. The weather was depressing. He felt blunted by the way the clouds hung low in a dismal sky.

He walked back to Bath Street and stood directly across from the premises of Joseph Lindsay. Light burned in the window. Soon people would be leaving work. He'd already decided on a course of action. It was a risk, certainly, because it meant he'd have to come out into the open — but in the absence of any practical guidance he saw no other way. His father used to say: if you have faith in your heart, the world will one day make sense.

Yes, I have faith in my heart and my father's blood in my veins and memories that go on and off inside my head like electric signals that have short-circuited. He thought of his mother and the white-walled room where she lay in Haifa, just below HaZiyonut Boulevard, and the nurses who'd been bringing her medication in little plastic cups for years. He saw the ceiling fan going round and round, stirring dust and dead air and desiccated insects snared in webs. He saw his mother's dry lips and the distance in her eyes and remembered how he'd sit on the edge of the bed and swab her mouth with a damp cloth.

She still screamed now and then in her dreams. Awake, she spoke incoherently of scorpions and ghosts. She recognized nobody. Dr Solomon had said, *Lifamen anashim kol kach mitrachakim she aynaynou yecholim yoter limsto· et ha derech elayhem le olam* . . .

Sometimes people go away where we can't reach them . . .

And if we can't reach them, we can't recover them.

Marak thought: They killed my father. They drove my mother to an inaccessible hell. The whole intricate mosaic of family destroyed.

Traffic along Bath Street was ponderous now. The work-day was winding down. Streetlamps were lit. He walked to the corner, stopped, looked this way and that. He saw no sign of the little man in the baseball cap he'd observed hours before, but he was sure he was somewhere nearby.

Ramsay's spy. He wasn't very good at spying.

Marak turned, walked back, looked up at Lindsay's window. The woman would come out, he knew that.

He'd worked out his approach. He'd rehearsed it in his mind.

Yes yes. It would be fine.

15

Lou Perlman thought: This Billie is a real peroxide chickadee. She reminded him of a latter-day version of Betty Grable, or maybe Lana Turner, except when she opened her mouth what came out was more Castlemilk, with affectations, than California. She wore a brown suede skirt and a silk blouse and calf-length boots that matched the skirt. She had a pert face, pointy little nose, blue eyes, red lips just a little too full. Loads of navy eye-shadow, and a bunch of silvery bracelets that clanked when she moved. She might have been thirty, probably more.

'It's bloody tough one to take in,' she said. 'He was such a . . . well, a sweetheart. A nice man.'

Sandy Scullion, solicitous, said, 'I'm sorry. I wish I had an easier way of telling you.'

'A man's been murdered. How can you rephrase that so it's digestible? You can't.'

They were in Joseph Lindsay's office, high-ceilinged, corniced, over-elaborate plaster plums and cherries and apples. The window looked directly down into Bath Street. Perlman glanced down at the streetlamps; fresh snow began to drift into the lights.

He surveyed the room as Billie Houston pulled Kleenexes from a pop-up box on the desk and pressed them to her eyes. He absorbed the surroundings — peach walls, cutesy little prints

98

of mushrooms and toadstools he attributed, rightly or wrongly, to Billie's influence, certificates attesting to various legal qualifications and memberships of this or that society, or good citizenship awards. Joe Lindsay had been civic-minded, a trophy-gatherer.

Perlman wondered if Billie had been one of his trophies. Nubile secretary, sixtyish solicitor, throw them together into the cauldron of an office — had Lindsay been set alight by Billie? Ageing men could be such idiots, he thought. All the remembered appetites of youth they tried to recapture. Hunt the Erection. No more Mister Softee.

'Was anyone bothering him? Was anyone *threatening* him?' Scullion was asking. He was just so bloody *good* at putting questions in a mild way that you half-expected him to whip out a prescription pad and write you a script for Librium.

She said, 'No, I don't think so . . . '

'Would you have known?' Perlman asked.

'I knew a lot about his business, Sergeant. I can safely say he wasn't being . . . *menaced* by anyone. To the best of my knowledge.'

'Did he seem, um, oh, troubled?' Scullion asked.

'No . . . '

'Any strange phone calls, or unusual visitors you might remember?'

She shook her head, blew her nose. The bracelets chinked. 'I don't believe so.'

'You can't think of a reason why anyone would want him dead?'

99

'No. Really. He was a decent man.'

'Tell us about his life,' Perlman said. 'Hobbies. Friends. Anything you can think of.'

'He grew vegetables,' she said. 'He occasionally played bowls.'

Vegetables and bowls, Perlman thought. This wasn't what you'd call a keg of dynamite.

'He specialized in growing different types of broccoli.'

Perlman wondered if his heart could take these revelations. 'The problem is, Miss Houston, broccoli and bowls aren't the kind of things that get men killed. Drug deals, theft, revenge, aye, definitely. But growing broccoli isn't a dangerous pursuit.'

'You're looking for something underneath, right? Solicitor's sleazy secrets, stuff like that. I can't think of any, Detective.'

'Forgive me for this, but I have a personal question — '

'You're going to ask if we were an item, right?'

'You're a mind-reader.'

'We were friends. Nothing more. We sometimes had dinner. He behaved very well towards me. He didn't try to grope me under the table. Are you satisfied?' She looked at him with some hostility, as if he'd wrongly attacked her virtue.

Lou said. 'I'm sorry. I had to ask. Look at it from my point of view. What if you had a boyfriend who was jealous of your relationship with Joseph Lindsay, say, and what if this boyfriend, in a fit of insane jealousy, decided to kill the lawyer?'

'But I don't have a boyfriend — '

100

'Fine. So we eliminate that possibility. One less road to explore. Saves time.'

'You always suspect the worst of people?' she asked.

'Not always,' Perlman said.

Sandy Scullion interrupted. 'What about his clients, Miss Houston?'

'Generally old people with too much money and property. Mr Lindsay handled a lot of wills.'

'I'll need a list of them,' Scullion said.

'I can do that for you.'

'I'm also going to need access to his house.'

She hesitated. Scullion said, 'It's necessary.'

'There's a spare key in his desk.'

'His family. What do you know about them?'

'His wife died sixteen or seventeen years ago. A stroke, I think. His daughter Michaela lives in Australia. His son David is in Canada. Both married. They don't come back to Scotland often.'

'Do you have phone numbers for them?'

'They're in Mr Lindsay's address book. I don't envy you the job of calling them with news like this.'

Scullion said, 'You haven't mentioned friends.'

'He wasn't an outgoing man. I'd say he had acquaintances more than close friends. He used to do work for a committee that had something to do with Palestine, but I don't know a whole lot about that part of his life. He'd drifted away from it, though.' She fell silent, buried her face in a clump of Kleenex, and sobbed quietly.

Lou Perlman's instinct was to comfort her, because he was a sucker for a weeping woman;

101

show him a woman crying and he'd rush to the nearest flower shop and buy out the whole lily supply and have it wrapped and ribboned, toot sweet.

Scullion was already uttering sympathy. 'Take your time, there's no hurry.'

Billie Houston dropped the tissues into the trash and looked up at the ceiling and sniffed. 'I'm sorry,' she said. 'When you've worked for a person for eight years you . . . '

'It's all right,' Scullion said.

'I can't *believe* somebody *killed* him. And the *way* he died . . . Where were we? Friends. Right. He had dinner once a month with a man he'd known for years. An old friend from university.'

Scullion asked, 'Do you have a name?'

'Yes. Artie Wexler.'

Perlman was instantly intrigued. 'Artie Wexler? Fellow of about sixty, sort of square jaw, hair like a wig?'

'I only saw him once,' she said. 'I don't remember what he looked like. Once a month he and Mr Lindsay had dinner at La Lanterna.'

'You know this guy, Lou?' Scullion asked.

Perlman said, 'Unless there's another Artie Wexler I never heard of.'

Scullion was quiet a moment, then he looked at Billie Houston and said, 'I'd like you to keep our conversation completely confidential, Miss Houston. For the time being at least.'

'I will. Don't worry.'

Artie Wexler, Perlman thought, and remembered the man's smile as he'd escorted Miriam out of the reception area at the Cedars and into the corridor beyond. That smirk. No, Lou, you only imagined it that way. It was a straightforward smile, maybe even sympathetic: *Sorry about your brother, Lou.* You could read all you liked into an expression. And quite often you read the wrong things — especially, it seemed, when it came to Miriam.

Forget her. Think of something else.

This new coat, say. Bloody brilliant. It suits me. I feel well-dressed. Raised in class and status. Spend a great wad of money and it uplifts you.

Scullion's mobile rang and he fished it out of his pocket, answered it. 'For you, Lou.'

Perlman took the phone and heard Miriam's voice. 'I don't mean to disturb you, Lou. Can we meet later?'

'Of course.'

'Is seven suitable? Outside the Art School?'

'I'll be there.' He was about to ask the purpose of the invitation, but she'd hung up. He gave the phone back to Sandy Scullion and thought: What does she want with me?

What did that question matter?

She could have asked for a meeting in an igloo in Greenland or an assignation on a dying space station and he'd have gone anyway, with or without explanation.

16

Marak saw the blonde woman step out of the building, but as he prepared to cross the street and squeeze through traffic he realized she had company. Two men, one tall and straight-backed with hair the colour of sand, the other bespectacled and a little round-shouldered, escorted her along the pavement. They stood on either side of her like guardians. Marak had a feeling about these two, that they represented some branch of officialdom — lawyers, perhaps, tax or immigration inspectors, policemen, he wasn't sure. They had a certain air, almost a watchfulness, such as he'd seen on the faces of bodyguards.

They all stopped on a corner and exchanged a few words, and then the woman walked away. She was alone now. He watched the men continue to move along Bath Street.

The woman went south into West Campbell Street and Marak hurried between slow traffic lest he lose sight of her. She walked about ten yards in front of him. There were no Christmas decorations along this street. She turned a corner, and Marak went after her and saw her step into a building with the letter P outside. P, Parking, yes, of course, she was going to fetch her car. He moved behind her, closing the distance, aware on the edges of his perception that there were no pedestrians, only a few cars coming down the exit ramp, and there was nobody waiting outside the lift where the woman had paused.

She pressed the call button and Marak noticed she wore pink fingernail varnish. The lift hissed in the shaft and the door opened and the woman stepped inside. Marak entered behind her. The door slid shut. The lift began to climb.

Marak said, 'I don't intend to hurt you.'

The woman looked at him. 'Hurt me? What the hell are you talking about?'

'Tell me what I want to know, and I will leave you alone. You'll never see me again.'

'And what could I *possibly* know that you'd like to hear, you creep?'

'Where to find Joseph Lindsay.'

'Wait a minute. You phoned today, didn't you? I remember your accent.'

'Just tell me where he is.'

'Why don't you piss off,' she said. 'You don't scare me. I don't have to tell you a bloody thing.' She stretched out a hand and held the tip of her index finger over a red button marked ALARM.

He said, 'No, don't do that.'

'Then back off. And if you want to know anything about Joseph Lindsay, I suggest you call the police. Talk to a detective called Perlman. Or Inspector Scullion. I'm sure they'd be delighted to answer your questions. I hate this — a woman can't go anywhere in this bloody city without some fucking perve annoying her. Bugger off.'

'Please,' he said.

'This is where I get out.'

The lift slowed, halted. The door opened. The

woman moved to exit, Marak stepped in front of her. He pressed a button and the door closed again.

'I don't want to talk to the police,' he said. 'Tell me where I can find Joseph Lindsay. This is all I am asking.'

'Open that fucking door,' she said.

He struck her. He hit her once with the flat of his hand and her nose bled. The blood ran down her overcoat. Marak was devoured by shame. He'd never hit a woman before. He'd always respected women, always. He took off his scarf and reached towards her face to stem the blood and she misinterpreted his movement — perhaps she saw herself strangled — and she backhanded him, a sharp ring on her right hand piercing the skin of his upper lip. The pain stung him. His range of vision was filled a moment with all kinds of disturbances. The lift door opened, the woman shoved him and moved past, and he stepped after her, catching her as she hurried towards a rank of parked cars. He swung her round to face him. He was furious with himself. Shame and anger and pain. In his mind he'd seen this all differently. He'd ask the question. The woman would answer. A civilized exchange. He'd go away. That was it. Distilled and simple. Not like this.

'I am sorry, the blow, I didn't intend . . . ' he said. 'Just tell me what I want to know, please.'

'I wouldn't tell you the time of day if you were on your hands and knees and begging. Go on, hit me again, I dare you,' and she turned her face up to him, offering him the target, taunting him.

106

She knows how to fight, he thought. She'd fought before. This was nothing new to her.

'Go on, smack me again, big man, what's stopping you?'

He took a step back. It had all gone wrong. He tasted blood in his mouth.

'Well, you bastard? Can't work up the balls, eh? Well, *fuck you*,' and she turned and walked in the direction of the cars and Marak was about to chase after her again when he was aware of a man in a navy-blue uniform emerging from a doorway to his right. Security.

He turned and ran towards a stairway that led to the street, and he clattered down the steps, slipping where pedestrians had left slicks of melted snow, and clutching the handrail to break his tumble. He heard the guard shout *Hey you* and the voice echoed in the stairwell. Marak made it outside, but it wasn't the place where he'd first entered the building. He found himself in a narrow alley, and he ran until he reached the main street again where the illuminated letter P hung in the dark sky. He used his scarf to wipe blood from his mouth: the wrong approach, but how could you know she'd act like that? You have no powers of prediction. You thought she'd be scared enough to tell you what you wanted to know. And that would be the end of the matter. You'd be polite, firm, but not violent. He thought about the Moroccan in the Haifa restaurant, and remembered what he'd said: *you have courage, and you have been patient, and now you are doing a wonderful thing —*

A wonderful thing, yes. Hitting a woman. And

107

running away like a jackrabbit. He raged against himself. His dead father rose in his head, furious as a thunderstorm. *This is not the way. Violence is never the way forward.* He tossed the scarf over his mouth and walked, thinking, no, I can't yield to panic, cannot, people are depending on me.

He spotted the little man in the baseball cap slip deftly into the doorway of a darkened shopfront a few yards along the pavement. He thought, this is who I want, exactly, this man who watches me hour after hour, this damned dwarf in black leather jacket, does he think I don't know he's been trailing behind me all day?

Marak walked until he came to the doorway and he reached quickly into the dark space and his hands came in contact with the man's neck and — *forgive me, God forgive me, this is madness* — he squeezed hard, thumbs digging into windpipe while the little man stammered N-n-n, but Marak, trapped in the impetus of violence, kept pressing hard, then harder, his fingertips throttling the throat, squeezing shut the passage of air, *N-n-n-n*, the little man's breath smelled of spoiled things, cheese left in the sun, old meat hanging in a marketplace too many days. Appalled by himself, he let the man go, and his hands slithered down the smooth front of the leather jacket. The man slid slowly against Marak's coat to the ground and lay there like a bundle of refuse dropped by somebody who didn't give a damn about litter, or a package nobody wanted to sign for — a limp heap in a black doorway in a bitter-cold city where Marak felt displaced and abandoned.

17

Outside Force HQ Scullion asked, 'Who's Wexler?'

'Somebody I knew once,' Perlman said. 'I saw him this morning at the hospital. First time in years.'

'Small world.'

'If you're a Jew in Glasgow it's even smaller than that.'

'What does Wexler do?'

'Last I heard he had a finance company. Borrow ten grand and pay off all your debts in one swoop, you know the kind of racket — but the small print says you repay Artie Wexler's company twenty grand over three years, or whatever the going rate is. Fucking Shylock. He's probably retired, living off the fat he accumulated in a lifetime of moneylending.'

'I gather from your tone of voice you're not a big fan of the man.'

Perlman stood still, as if reluctant to enter the building. The lights from windows illuminated slow-falling snowflakes. Three uniformed cops went past in their long coats. One of them said, 'Okay here's what *really* happened,' and the other pair laughed in anticipation. When you only hear the start of a story it makes no sense, Lou thought. When you're at the beginning of an investigation, likewise, nothing is clear. He was trying to draw a line on an imaginary graph, joining Colin's heart attack and Joseph Lindsay's murder, and extending this series of dots in the direction of Artie Wexler. But it didn't take him anywhere, nor did he expect it to. It was head doodling, a brain game, playing with names and associations.

He looked at Sandy and said, 'I was remembering when I didn't belong. I had my nose pressed to the window; looking in. Always looking in.'

'Are you confiding something in me?'

'Ach, just thinking aloud, Sandy. I was the wee brother who was sent to fetch bottles of lemonade and sweeties for Col. Now I remember having to run to the shop and pick up a bag of soor plooms or sherbet for Artie Wexler as well. It wasn't just Colin who bossed me around, I was Artie's runner too.'

'What are you telling me?'

'Just old stuff I'd totally forgotten. I resented being the errand boy. I kept hoping somebody would pass a Wee Brothers' Emancipation Act and set me free. Then one day Colin and Artie grew up, Colin went to London, Artie to St Andrews University . . . and my little world was empty for a while. Then I joined the Force when I was twenty-two and suddenly I had a whole new purpose.'

Scullion smacked his gloved hands together and frowned. Sometimes Lou could go off into a thicket of apparent digressions, and there was no point following him. 'You coming inside, Lou? It's freezing.'

'I'd like to get a hold of Artie Wexler. Talk to

110

him about Lindsay.'

Scullion had resigned himself long ago to the fact that Perlman kept to a schedule of his own. If you let him run loose, he sometimes got results, sometimes not. You took a chance on him because he'd never knowingly let you down. 'Okay. But remember to keep me posted. Here, take my phone again. I'll pick up Bernigan and Bailey and we'll run out to Lindsay's house.'

Bernigan and Bailey, two young Detective-Sergeants detailed to Scullion, were known around Force HQ as Rodgers and Hart because each had some musical ability: Bernigan sang bass in an *a cappella* vocal group, and Bailey played cello in a string quartet. Or was that the other way round? Perlman couldn't keep the pair apart. There was even some physical resemblance. Both men were slender, both had a kind of dark Pictish intensity. They were devoted to the serious ministry of law and order. They also thought the sun shone out of Sandy's arse.

'I'll be in touch, Sandy.'

'Tonight.'

'Absolutely. I promise.'

Perlman walked to the end of the street, thinking what a weird contraption memory was, how it released images like a flawed steampipe issuing vapours. He'd somehow obliterated Artie Wexler's part in the formative years of his life. *Fetch me this, bring me that, chop chop wee Louie, shake a leg.* And then memory kicks in and three boys from the demolished slums of the Gorbals assume new forms. One an investments adviser with a serious heart condition, the other

111

a retired loan shark — don't even *look* for a euphemism, Lou — and the third a cop.

And then he remembered something else, how Colin and Artie had secret words they used, coded words, like the private language of a club Lou could never enter. He'd accepted this fact without rancour. They were Big Boys, after all. They smoked cigarettes behind tenements. When they couldn't buy cigs, they tried to smoke cinnamon sticks. They flirted with girls. They talked about condoms. Sleeping bags for mice, they called them. They talked about 'getting their hole'.

A melancholy buzzed Perlman. Patterns of the past resonate in the present. A man acquainted with the dead Joseph Lindsay, perhaps even his closest friend, was a ghost from Lou's boyhood. Did that mean anything? If so, what? He tried to imagine Lindsay's dying. He tried to imagine that feeling, the condom leaking in the acids of the stomach, the cocaine rocketing into the bloodstream, the heart exploding. A ride on an express train to Infinity.

Lost in his thoughts, he collided with a young policeman who was hurrying along the pavement. It was Murdoch, the cop who'd cut Joseph Lindsay down from the bridge.

They did a little shuffle together, one trying to make room for the other. 'Sorry, son,' Lou said. 'Get to my age and your head wanders all over the shop.'

'No, it was my fault, Sergeant, I wasn't looking where I was going.'

'Where's the fire?'

'A woman was attacked in a parking garage just south of Bath Street.'

'Badly hurt?

'From what I hear she's fine.'

'You take a statement yet?'

'I'm on my way, Sarge. Just got a call from security at the garage.'

'Don't let me keep you.' Perlman stepped aside and young Murdoch kept moving. The energy of youth, the elasticity of muscle and sinew. How quickly all that betrayed you. Perlman considered the dread of retirement and wondered what he'd do with his life when he didn't have this job any more. The lack of a daily function, an identity. The city would seem strange to him then, like a place he'd seen once on a postcard.

Retirement, ballocks. He didn't want it. Not ever. Die on the job. He was still working all the shifts that came his way. He crossed Sauchiehall Street. Christmas decorations strung between buildings were garish. Sleighs and electronic reindeer, no sign of a Jesus anywhere. Christmas was all Hollywood these days.

He reached the junction of Dalhousie Street, then walked until he came to Renfrew Street. Here, on the edge of Garnethill, the neighbour-hood that rose above the shopping centres and pubs of Sauchiehall Street like a fortress of tenements, he paused and took the phone out of his pocket. He punched in Directory Inquiries and asked for Artie Wexler's number. He got it, tapped it in, a woman answered.

'Is Artie at home?'

'No, he's not. Can I take a message?'

'You can tell him Lou Perlman called. I'd like him to get back to me — '

'*Lou Perlman*? Don't you remember me?'

'I'm sorry.'

'Ruth. Ruthie Cowan. Well, Ruthie Wexler nowadays. We met at your brother's wedding.'

Perlman brought the memory up like a struggling fish reeled in from the deep: Ruthie Cowan, a slender young woman with lips that were a little sluttish, the kind of mouth that held out guarantees of a damn good time, dirty talk included gratis. He wondered how much of that appeal remained. He couldn't remember Artie Wexler getting married. He was out of touch. He didn't read the *Jewish Telegraph* to find out who'd wedded whom, who'd been born and who'd died. Hatches, matches, dispatches. He wasn't keeping up with tribal information.

'That was more than — oh, I hate talking about the years,' Ruth Wexler said. 'You in good health, Lou?'

'The clockwork runs. Just about. You?'

'I keep fit,' she said.

'If I said that, I'd be a barefaced liar.'

Ruth Wexler said how sorry she was to hear the bad news about Colin. She hoped he'd return to good health. He'd always been so 'robust'. Robust, Perlman thought. It was a word he'd heard to describe his brother a few times, usually by women who recognized that he had a wild energetic streak in him.

Perlman looked up Renfrew Street: he saw the

Art School ahead and wondered if Miriam was waiting.

Ruth Wexler said, 'I'll tell Artie you called.'

'He can reach me through Pitt Street HQ. If not, I'll call back.'

He switched off the phone, stuffed it in his pocket. He walked uphill. The huge windows on the upper floor of the Art School threw out a soft light. Fancy wrought-iron work characterized the building. He needed a cigarette, but he wanted clean breath when he met Miriam. He wondered if he had a mint somewhere, rummaged in his pockets, found the crinkled remains of a packet of Polos, but no sweetie.

He approached the lights, saw her standing at the top of the stairs beyond the curvature of iron that spanned the gateway, and she raised a hand in recognition and he thought: This must be how wives greet their husbands when they arrange to meet them outside cinemas or restaurants or wherever. A little fluttery signal, *I'm over here, my love, thrilled to see you.* The thought appealed to him. He'd bound up the steps and clasp and kiss her under the lights. Her hair would glow. The kiss would burn and their bodies tremble.

She came down towards him. She had such grace in her movements she looked as if she could walk a highwire without pausing to consider the possibility of falling. You have this woman on a pedestal, he thought.

She slipped her arm through his and said, 'New coat?'

'Sewn and stitched this very day,' he said.

115

She smiled. 'Fancy escorting me a little way?'
'You lead,' he said. 'I'll follow.'

As in a dance, he thought, a waltz across an empty ballroom. They moved together along Renfrew Street and Lou Perlman dreamed he was on the threshold of a thrilling new life, even as he understood he was travelling steerage on the same old battered boat of wishful thinking.

18

Artie Wexler looked from the window of Shiv Bannerjee's library across the expanse of the Clyde where it flowed, the colour of black ink, past Helensburgh, a few miles beyond the boundaries of Glasgow. Bannerjee's mansion, built by a tobacco merchant in the mid-nineteenth century, and embellished by subsequent owners, had a conservatory and a billiards room. Shiv had added a climate-controlled aviary where he kept tropical birds, flashy parrots and bug-eyed cockatoos imported from the rainforests.

Wexler turned when the door opened and Bannerjee entered the room, walking lightly as he always did; you always half-expected to see him in ballet slippers. His grey double-breasted jacket was fastened, and a black silk handkerchief flopped an inch or so from the breast pocket. A dandy, Shiv Bannerjee, everything about him just so, white hair immaculate, fingernails perfect: you could never imagine Bannerjee spilling a drop of food on himself, or tolerating a speck of dandruff on his collar.

'I'm sorry to keep you waiting, Artie,' he said. He had a distinct but refined Glasgow accent. 'You come on a sad night, old friend.'

'How's that?' Artie Wexler asked.

'Colin's heart attack for one. And now this. Look.' Bannerjee carried a brown paper bag in his hand. He walked to his desk, opened the bag, and allowed its contents to slide carefully out. A small red bird, stiff. 'Poor little chap croaked an hour ago. We had him on an IV drip and penicillin. But sometimes, so far from their habitat, they don't make it.'

A bird on an IV drip, Artie Wexler thought. What world did Bannerjee occupy? Artie feigned an interest in the dead creature. Under lamplight, the feathers were the rich red of blood.

'Shame,' he said.

Bannerjee stuck the dead bird back inside the paper bag. 'Wine? Scotch?'

'I'm fine,' Artie Wexler said.

'Not so.' Bannerjee wagged a finger. 'From the look of you, you're a long way from fine.'

Artie Wexler sat down and glanced glumly round the tall bookshelves, antique volumes in shadow. This room intimidated him — perhaps the weight of knowledge contained in the books overwhelmed him: so much he didn't know, so much he'd never know. About the world, about himself. Especially himself.

Bannerjee poured two glasses of sherry from a decanter and gave one to Artie, then he stood with an arm stretched along the mantel of the marble fireplace. He was a second-generation Indian immigrant who'd worked in his father's wholesale outlet in Rutherglen, trading in those items called 'sundries' — cheap footballs, aspirins, flashlights, batteries, corner-shop staples. Determined to improve himself, he'd studied

118

hard, gone to Glasgow University, graduated with a first-class degree in Sociology, then entered politics and risen through the ranks of various Labour Party advisory committees. In a parliamentary by-election in 1993 he'd won a narrow victory over a Tory opponent in a vicious contest for the seat of a working-class area of Glasgow; and so, off to Westminster in a glow of glory, MP, possible Cabinet material — Minister for Scotland, perhaps, as some local newspapers predicted. He was Going Places. Magazines profiled him on glossy pages, drum-banging about what Asians could achieve in British political life.

His fall was as swift as his rise. The scandal was intricate, and difficult even now to unravel, involving the deposits of large sums of money to accounts held by Bannerjee's aides. Those who'd 'donated' funds received in return preferential treatment — UK passports processed quickly for wealthy immigrants, payments for questions asked in the House on behalf of vested interests. It was tawdry, High Sleaze, unworthy of the honest Bannerjee the media had created. When he was exposed and tried for tax fraud and jailed for three months, his only excuse was that the pressures of power had affected his judgement. He'd been blind to his principles.

Greed induces amnesia, Wexler thought. Amen.

Shiv Bannerjee had worked hard at redemption. Fallen politicians often good-deeded their way out of their misdemeanours and felonies, and that was the route Shiv took. He toured

119

blighted African countries, got himself photographed in famine zones wearing khaki safari suits and holding shrivelled babies over whose eyelids flies crawled. Shiv *schmoozed* on a global level and had set up a charity. And so he'd risen a little way, he had some measure of respectability again.

Wexler sniffed his sherry, turned the glass round in his hands. He couldn't shake his mood, his sense of doom.

'What's on your mind?' Bannerjee asked.

Wexler rose, walked around the room, glancing at book titles. *A History of Jainism. The Jain Cosmology.* 'I shouldn't have come here,' he said.

'But you did,' Bannerjee said. He had a lovely smile: women were charmed by it. His diminutive hands were the colour of milk chocolate. 'Unload, Artie. Tell me why you're here.'

'Lindsay's disappeared.'

'Disappeared? Explain.'

'He missed dinner with me last night. He didn't turn up in his office today. His secretary doesn't know where he is. There's no sign of life at his house. His car's gone.' This litany seemed thin to Wexler as he recited it; there were scores of reasons for missing a dinner, or failing to turn up at your office. *Scores of them.* Not if you were Joe Lindsay, there weren't. You could set your fucking clock by Joe. 'It's upsetting. It's uncharacteristic.'

'You're letting Lindsay's apparent disappearance get to you, Artie.'

120

'Do you ever wonder — '

Bannerjee held up a hand like a traffic cop. 'Don't finish that question. The past is dead. The moving finger and all that. I'm sure there's some simple reason for Lindsay's absence. Perhaps he has a mistress you don't know about. Perhaps on an impulse he flew her off to Rome or Biarritz — '

'He's the least impulsive man I ever met,' Wexler said.

'Finish your drink,' Bannerjee said. 'Unwind. Stay for something to eat.'

'I better get home. Ruthie will be wondering.' He walked to the window, peered out. A boat sailed on the river, lights on water, snow flurries. 'I feel this heavyweight guilt sometimes, Shiv. I know it's pointless, but it's a fact. I saw Colin today, and he looked like shite, and I thought — is this how the ending begins? Then I figured Lindsay's vanishing act into some kind of equation.'

'Colin has a heart attack, and Lindsay behaves unpredictably, and you lump these things together and what do you come up with — fear of karmic retribution?'

'Are you laughing at me, Shiv?'

'I'm a little amused by the way you shackle yourself to your own imagination. How could there be any connection between Colin's cardiac arrest and Lindsay's quote unquote disappearance?'

Artie shrugged. 'If I had an answer for that, you think I would have driven out here to see you?'

Bannerjee said, 'Sleep. You'll feel better when you wake.'

'Do you sleep?'

'I sleep like a suckled baby, Artie. I wake with zest. I left my conscience in Westminster.'

'I lug mine around like a bloody rucksack filled with broken bricks.' Wexler drained his glass. 'Everything haunts me, Shiv. I can't sleep. I sometimes take one of Ruthie's pills. So I sleep a couple of hours. Big deal. The dreams are always upsetting. Waking is a reprieve.'

'Have you considered counselling?'

'And tell a shrink what? The truth?'

Bannerjee shrugged. 'Maybe some version of the truth, Artie.'

'There's no such thing as *some* version of the truth.'

Bannerjee picked up the bag that contained the dead bird. A red feather floated to the floor. 'I don't know what more I can say, Artie. Except that Lindsay will turn up.' He patted Artie Wexler on the shoulder. 'Don't fall apart, old chap.'

'Easier said than done,' Wexler remarked.

19

At the end of Renfrew Street Miriam said, 'I like this street.'

Perlman shivered, tried to hide his discomfort. 'Me too.'

'In summer especially.'

They'd walked as far as the Garnethill synagogue. Lou had forgotten the last time he'd been at *shul*. Years. He'd drifted. What was it — lack of faith or laziness? Or just too little time? Feeling guilty, he glanced at the gate, which was padlocked.

Miriam said, 'Up here on a summer day you can see for miles. So many spires. The university. Churches. The old Trinity College.' And for a moment she was lost in contemplation of the lights of the western reaches of the city. He wished he was inside her head, caressing her thoughts: the ultimate intimacy.

The wind whipped at her coat. 'It's cold. You want to get a drink somewhere?'

'Why not?'

They went down the hill to Sauchiehall Street to a bar which had a kind of Latino ambience. It was exactly the sort of place — trendy, patrons who talked about themselves in very loud voices — Lou Perlman would never have entered in his life. But here he was, arm in arm with Miriam: I'll go anywhere.

'Let's have margaritas,' Miriam suggested. Her

face was bright from the cold air, and there was something childlike about her, a little girl who'd come indoors after building a snowman.

'Fine by me.' He'd never had a margarita.

'Are you on duty, Lou?'

'In a way,' he said.

'You're always on duty, aren't you?'

'I have free time. Sometimes.'

She touched his arm. 'You hate this place, don't you?'

'Does it show,' he said.

'You're gritting your teeth. It's too ritzy-phony. It's trying to be enchanting, only it isn't working. It's just not your style.'

Lou smiled. 'Do I have a style?'

'You like grubby little dives. You like bars where all you can get is bad blended whisky and beer, and the conversation is more football than Kafka.'

'Is he that midfielder Celtic tried to sign last year from Sparta Prague, only he couldn't get a work permit?'

'Come on, Lou. I think you're a wee bit ashamed of admitting you know something about books and paintings and classical music. It doesn't go with your gritty image.'

'Me? I have an image?'

'You're this long-serving city cop who lives his life in the streets. You're crumpled and dented. Glasgow bruises you and the work devours you and you mix with some bad people. But you still see a little light of goodness at the end of the tunnel. Justice will always prevail in Lou's world.'

'You wouldn't be suggesting I have a wee streak of optimism, would you?'

'You're a decent man, and you know it.'

Would you think me so decent, Miriam, if you knew the feelings in my heart for you? He watched the barman make the margaritas in a blender. He suddenly thought of cocaine fusing with Lindsay's blood. Neural meltdown. Pharmaceutical cocaine, McLaren had remarked. Pure.

'Hello?' Miriam said.

He turned his face away from the liquid churning in the blender. He'd drifted. Always on duty, right. It didn't stop. The brain kept processing. You didn't have to be at the scene of the crime. In fact, it was sometimes better if you were elsewhere, free of place, of specific things. Your mind could roam then.

'Sorry,' he said.

'It's okay. Work and sleep, sleep and work. Lou Perlman's life.' She removed her beret and tossed her head, freeing hair to tumble, and it did, it tumbled in great strands on her shoulders. Oy: he ached to wind them round his fingers.

Their drinks came. Lou looked at the frothing yellow-green liquid. He sipped. He thought he was swallowing neon. Miriam was watching him over the rim of her glass, waiting for a reaction.

'It's fine,' he said. 'Sharpish. Tangy.'

'Hot when it gets down,' she said.

'Aye, I'm feeling it now.'

'Cheers,' she said. 'You know the last time you came to our place for dinner?'

'Last year, I think.'

'More like three years ago, Lou. You avoid us.'

Yes, true, he avoided the whole domestic situation, Colin and Miriam, Miriam and Colin, the little touches between them, the common references they were so used to sharing they failed to realize they excluded other people from their world. The perfect couple in the perfect reality. Nothing could be *that* perfect, he thought. Why didn't he ever catch some hint of stress in their marriage? Some sense that they ever disagreed about things? Their world was like smooth glass.

'I'm busy more than I want to be,' he said. 'Don't forget bachelors get the short straw when it comes to working the worst shifts, Miriam.'

'I suspect you just don't like seeing married people because it reminds you that you live all alone in a damp old house.'

'I'm *that* transparent?'

'Is there never going to be a woman, Lou?'

'I got out of the swami business. The future's impenetrable.'

'You have a lot to offer,' she said.

'So my aunts keep telling me,' he said, thinking of those Southside crones, Aunties Hilda and Marlene and Susan and all the others who got together and concocted marital schemes. 'They sit over a cauldron in Giffnock and brew up love-potions.'

'Because they care about you,' she said. 'You ever hear anything from Nina?'

'Nina? A blast from the past. Not a word in . . . must be ten years. Probably more.'

'Ever think you'd *like* to hear from her?'

'We don't have anything to say to one another. So no, I don't want to hear from her. Everybody should have at least one failed marriage just for the experience. Mine was mercifully short.'

'Somebody told me she was in New Zealand.'

'That's pleasantly far away,' he said. He picked up his drink, tasted it. Funny how you could be married to somebody, how you could achieve a certain depth of intimacy, and then it disappeared as if it had never taken place. He could hardly remember Nina's face, her body. Their lovemaking was a blank. She left no scent. He had no photographs of her, no reminders. He was thirty when he'd fancied he could find love with her, and so they'd married, and the union had lasted one year before she bolted in pursuit of her own distant star. *I have it in me to be a great writer, Lou. But you cramp me. Glasgow cramps me, I'm suffocating here.*

A writer, he thought. All of a sudden I'm married to Virginia fucking Woolf. She took to sitting up nights composing stories in a big yellow-paged ledger. She never asked him to read what she'd written. And then one day — bye-bye, baby — she was gone. London, he heard. Then Paris. After that nothing. Down the Chute of Creativity, he guessed. He hadn't pursued her. What was the point? He'd known he hadn't loved her, the marriage was a hollow undertaking, an act of self-delusion. It was history now, and withered, a shrub in winter.

Miriam had fallen silent. She set down her glass and played with her beret on the bar. Her expression darkened. She shut her eyes and inclined her face forward. He risked touching her, laying the palm of his hand over the back of her wrist. Her skin was cold. In this one connection of flesh, Lou Perlman felt more of a charge than he'd felt in a whole year's marriage to Nina.

'What can I do to help?' he asked.

'I don't think you can, Lou.'

'You wanted to see me. You have something to say.'

'Right. It's . . . Rifkind tells me . . . ' She turned, faced him. 'Rifkind says Colin has to have this bloody bypass surgery as soon as possible,' and she made her lovely hands into tight white fists. 'And I wish that wasn't the case, because I keep thinking of them cutting Colin open, and people doing things to his heart. And I'm afraid. What if he dies on the table? What if he dies?'

'He's not going to die, Miriam.'

'Heart surgery is risky, Lou.'

'Rifkind's good. Anyway, people have these operations every day, they're commonplace.'

'But still risky, Lou.'

'They've got sophisticated new techniques. I understand they don't work by gaslight any more.'

'Seriously. I read these stories about people who don't come round from the anaesthetic. What if that happens . . . '

'Colin will come through it. He's strong.' He thought of his brother, chest cut, skin clamped back, beating heart exposed, merciless lights shining down into the cavity of his body.

'He's not as strong as we all thought,' she said.

'Strong up here,' and he tapped his head. 'Where it counts.'

'The op's scheduled for tomorrow at noon.'

She finished her drink. She studied the dregs in her glass a little wistfully — the expression, Perlman thought, of a young girl clutching a bittersweet farewell letter from her lover — then glanced at her watch. 'I have an evening class to teach,' she said. 'It helps take my mind off things.'

'Call me any time,' he said.

'You're a sweetheart, Lou.'

Yeah, I'm a saint, he thought. A St Bernard more like. You need me, Miriam, I'll come running, small barrel of brandy attached to my neck. 'You want me to walk back with you?'

She reached for her beret. 'I'll be fine. Thanks for coming to meet me.'

He kissed her quickly on the cheek, a sparrow's peck, and she began to move away.

'Oh, Miriam, wait — one last thing. Do you know if Colin's acquainted with somebody called Joseph Lindsay?'

'Lindsay? A lawyer?'

'That's the one.'

'He came to the house a couple of times for dinner a while ago.'

'What did you make of him?'

'Oh, a quiet wee man. Pleasant in his own way. Why do you ask?'

'Curious.'

'You're working on something, aren't you?'

'I can't tell where work stops and life begins,

lassie,' he said, and watched her go outside. His eyes followed her as she passed the window, her face sad and her hair tugged by the wind and flopping against her shoulders. When she'd gone he felt lonely. He wished he could do something, perform an act of magic, that would make her worries vanish.

He lit the cigarette he'd been gasping for, dragged smoke into his lungs with a satisfying feeling. He studied the comforting red glowing tip.

Connections then. Wexler knew Lindsay. Colin knew Wexler. And Joseph Lindsay had come to dinner. There was really no great surprise in this, was there? Glasgow social circles were small; and Jewish ones incestuously so.

Had Miriam served lamb chops with caramelized onions? Or her beef and paprika ensemble? She did both those dishes well. The wine, he knew, would be good; it was always good at Colin and Miriam's table. They favoured a certain Nuits St George Colin imported by the case. The conversation: how had that gone? What had they discussed? Miriam would be up and down between dining table and kitchen, playing hostess, leaving the small-time solicitor and the hotshot financial adviser to carry the talk on their own much of the time. It was probably business, Perlman thought. Simple dull business.

Money and the law, those twisted partners. *Yack yack yack.* He left the bar and shivered on Sauchiehall Street. He flicked his cigarette away and looked in the direction Miriam had taken, but there was no sign of her now. He imagined her climbing up into Garnethill, and he thought of her slim form passing under streetlamps.

Beautiful Miriam, a flash of loveliness in a city where the charred bones of an unknown man had been found stuffed inside an old sewage-pipe, and an alcoholic kid had been battered to death in Sighthill, and Joseph Lindsay, solicitor, had perished in a cocaine explosion.

20

BJ Quick and Willie Furfee arrived at Govan underground station on the south side of the city at five minutes to eight. Leo Kilroy met them there. He was short and enormously fat and wobbled like a flesh-coloured blancmange when he moved. He wore a long camel coat and a red silk cravat. He also wore a homburg hat as outmoded as the cravat, and a brocade waistcoat. He had clusters of rings on his plump fingers. He carried a walnut cane with a brass handle. He was a man of wild ostentation and as out of place in the dreich surroundings of Govan as a peacock at a ploughing contest.

'You think this varlet will show up?' he asked. He had a strange honk in his voice. His vowels might have been porcine in origin. Some people referred to him as Fat Pig, but not to his face: he allegedly controlled a number of local rackets and could count on some heavy muscle, and so it was imprudent, perhaps downright lethal, to offend him.

'Aye he'll show,' BJ said.

'And if he doesn't?'

'We go to his house,' BJ answered.

He gazed into the sleet. Govan depressed him. Black tenements. Dead shipyards. Social security. Shuttered shops. No glamour here. Just a daily grind. This was the Third World. He wanted big lights and neon in his life. 'I'm thinking next time I'll call the club some other name.'

'Smart lad,' Kilroy said. 'Dissociate yourself from your failures.'

'I'm thinking Club Farraday.'

'Club who?'

'Where Jerry Lee was born. Farraday, Louisiana.'

'Oh, laddie, no. It lacks a certain *oomph* factor. Pizzazz, BJ. Electricity. Something that will blaze in the sky at night. Think of Glasgow clubs that have any kind of longevity. What names come to mind?'

BJ Quick said, 'King Tut's Wah-Wah Hut, but — '

'My very point,' Kilroy said, and prodded Quick in the chest with his cane. 'King Tut's been in business for *years*. Great name. But Club Memphis? I ask you. And Club Farraday? I don't care if Farraday was the birthplace of Elvis, Jerry Lee, Chuck Berry and Jesus *Christ Almighty* all on the same damn *day*, it's not going to go down with the average punter, laddie. Think again.'

'Right,' BJ Quick said. 'I will.' He thought: It's my club and I'll call it anything I like, you fat wank.

Kilroy looked at his gold wristwatch. 'It's five past the hour. Where is this scruff we await?'

'Late,' Furfee said.

'Punctuality is everything in business,' Kilroy said.

Quick said, 'He'll be here, Leo, I swear it.'

'With my five thou?'

133

'Absolutely,' BJ said.

'How are you acquiring this capital? And how did you raise the first ten?'

'Old debts,' BJ said.

'But not drug-related, I hope?'

'No fucking way.'

'You know how I feel about narcotics, BJ. They're evil. If you're connected in any way with drugs, you won't find me so easy to deal with, rest assured. So is this five grandees another old debt or what?'

'Cash I loaned in a moment of weakness,' Quick said. Why was Pig putting him through a third-degree here? What difference did it make where the cash came from? A measly 5K and Pig wants its history. Sometimes Quick had a vague feeling that Piggy Kilroy was playing a game with him.

Kilroy asked, 'Name of debtor?'

'You wouldn't know him, Leo.'

'Tell me anyway.'

Quick sighed. 'A fellow called Vindaloo Bill.'

'Small-time?'

'Very,' Quick said.

'Just need to know what you're up to, BJ.' Kilroy looked across the street and shuddered. 'By God, Govan's like a portal to hell. I usually love a wee bit of slumming, but this . . . '

'Another few minutes,' BJ said.

He tried to keep any note of desperation out of his voice. Be cool. He didn't want Kilroy to slip away. He needed to press a wad of dough into Pig's hand, so Kilroy could hoof off cheerful in the knowledge that he already had 10K of BJ's money, and in a few minutes he'd drive away in his 1956 Bentley with another five: total fifteen. And still BJ had to find the final instalment, another ten. 25K total, it was a miserable pittance, the kind of money he'd piss and party away in a couple of days, young hookers and drugs and champagne. By God, he wanted those good times to roll again.

He heard an underground train *shooosh* to a halt way below.

If that fuck Vindaloo lets me down, he thought.

A woman of about forty approached. She wore a plastic rainhat and a red raincoat and red galoshes, and she had the expression of one whose life has been a sequence of bruises and disappointments: now, she regarded the world with neither expectation nor fear.

She asked BJ, 'You're Quick? He told me to look for a guy with a right stupid hairdo. I've brought you this,' and dug into her purse and drew out a package wrapped in a copy of the *Daily Record*. Quick ignored the insult to his hairstyle, and ripped the newspaper. He counted the banknotes quickly and removed two hundred for himself.

Kilroy said, 'Tchhh-tut-tut.'

'I need running expenses, Leo,' BJ said. 'Petty cash.'

'I'm keeping records. Deductions will be made.'

The woman regarded this transaction with a hostile frown. Her forehead resembled a furious map of intersecting motorways.

BJ asked the woman, 'You the missus?'

'He can't come himself,' she said. 'He's so badly cut. He had to go to the bloody hospital. You bastard. You paira bastards.'

'Whoa,' Furfee said.

'I'd like to kick you in the balls,' she said.

'Be the last thing you did,' Furfee said. He stepped between Quick and the woman and forced her away.

'I find this unsightly,' Kilroy said, and he reached out and picked the package from BJ's hand. 'Call me when you know the ETA of the last payment. Which, I might point out, should be soon.'

'Like when?'

'I'll leave that open, laddie. I'm being wildly generous to you. But I have a weak spot for dreamers, hence I'm giving you a chance to get back in the biz. You have the inside track on the lease.' He raised his cane — *ciao* with a flourish — and vanished into the sleet.

Quick watched him go. All that money disappearing in Kilroy's fat hand. Made him sick to his heart.

The woman was still harassing Willie Furfee. *You should see the state you left him in, you evil bastard, you know how much blood my man lost? I hope you choke on the money. I hope it kills you.*

Furfee shoved her back against the wall. Quick said, 'Let's get out of here, Furf.'

'Bastards! Fucking *bastards*!' the woman screamed.

Quick and Furfee walked outside. They

hurried to where Furfee had parked his car. The woman came after them and, oblivious to both weather and spectators huddled in shop doorways, screamed and rushed at the black Peugeot, hammering on the side windows and kicking the hubcaps as Furfee slipped the vehicle into gear and drove away.

'What a bloody carry-on,' BJ Quick said. He yanked the rear-view mirror and checked his hair: flattened by sleet, ruined. A stupid hairdo, my arse. That bitch.

'You got the dosh,' Furfee said.

'Aye. For a few lovely seconds before Fat Pig took the bulk of it. Jesus, I'm freezing. Crank up the heater, Furf.'

'Wilco. Is Kilroy a poof?'

'I don't know what he does for sex, Furf. I'm not about to ask him either. You better get me Wee Terry on the phone. Find out about that Arab.'

'Right away,' Furfee said, and punched a number into his mobile with one hand, while he steered with the other.

He passed the unit to BJ, who asked, 'Terry?'

The voice that answered was authoritarian. 'This is Dr Nimmo. Who's this?'

'Nimmo? I don't know any Nimmo. This must be a wrong number.'

'Are you by any chance trying to reach Terence Dogue?'

'Right.'

'Then you'll find him here at the Royal Infirmary,' Dr Nimmo said.

21

Perlman rushed through a rage of sleet on his way back to Force HQ. By the time he stepped inside the building his new coat was sodden. Probably ruined already. Bloody winter. I want the tropics. I want al fresco dining, mangoes dangling on trees. He climbed the stairs slowly, taking off the coat as he moved. He pondered Colin's bypass operation, Colin going under the knife tomorrow afternoon. Rifkind wasted no time. Maybe there was no time to waste.

He entered his cluttered cubicle and sat at his desk and was about to try Artie Wexler's number again, when PC Murdoch's benign young face appeared in the doorway.

'That woman who was attacked,' Murdoch said.

'Refresh an old duffer's memory, son.'

'The one in the multi-storey parking garage?'

'Oh, aye, right,' Perlman said, but he felt scattered, preoccupied with Wexler, Colin, Lindsay, old associations, confluences of a shapeless past. He yearned for a younger man's agile brain, recall like a razor, a thousand details brought to mind in a flash of time. Sometimes his brain felt like a turnip in his skull, fibrous roots clotted with soil.

'She wants to see you,' Murdoch said.

'Can you deal with her for me?'

138

'Says you talked to her earlier. Name's Billie Houston.'

'She was the one *attacked*?' Perlman stood up.

Murdoch said, 'Some guy hit her.'

'Send her in, send her in.'

Murdoch went away a moment, then ushered Billie Houston inside the cubicle. The young cop vanished. Billie Houston sat down. Her nose was slightly puffy, eye makeup pale.

'Great service around here. I got a cup of tea and a ginger snap.'

'That's a damn sight more than *I* get,' Perlman said. He blew into his cold red hands. 'I'd murder for a cup of hot tea. So what happened to you? Who attacked you?'

'He didn't pause to introduce himself, Sergeant.'

'They seldom do,' Perlman said. 'What was he after? Purse? Those bracelets?'

'Robbery wasn't the motive,' she said. 'He wanted information.'

'Funny way of asking for it.'

'Dead funny,' she said. She crossed her legs, and her coat fell open to expose the short suede skirt and the matching knee-length boots. He imagined Joe Lindsay eyeballing the legs while he dictated letters. Why did a quiet wee man get murdered?

'What information was he so keen to get?'

'Wanted to know where he could find Mr Lindsay. Desperate to know.'

'Desperate enough to thump you.'

'I got him back,' she said.

'I bet you did.'

139

'I'm not a punching bag for some arsehole. No way.'

'Strange he didn't come to the office in Bath Street if he was looking for Lindsay. Why follow you into a parking garage?'

'I think he phoned hours before you turned up. I remember his accent. I told him Mr Lindsay hadn't come in and he asked for his home number, which I didn't give, of course.'

'What kind of accent?'

'I don't know. I don't have an ear for things like that. I can't place it.'

'What did he look like?'

'Dark beard. Dark hair. Quite good-looking. He wouldn't be my type. I can't imagine him ever relaxing, enjoying a night on the town. If I was forced to pin it down, I'd say he looked Middle Eastern. Iranian, I dunno. An Arab. That kind of complexion.'

That kind of 'complexion' covered all sorts of nationalities in the Middle East, Perlman thought. Arab was an easy label, a generic. 'Anything else you remember about him?'

'Sure. He was sorry he hit me. Even apologized. Oh — one other thing. I didn't tell him Mr Lindsay was dead. I told him if he wanted to know anything about Joe, he ought to ask you or Inspector Scullion.'

'So I can expect to be assaulted on my way home?'

'I doubt it. He might phone you, though.'

'People who've committed an assault don't usually telephone the police for the information they've failed to get by violent means,' Lou Perlman said.

'No, I suppose they don't,' she said.

He considered Lindsay's life: what had he been hiding? An act of fraud, fiddling the ledgers of somebody's estate? Perlman wasn't inclined to buy. The cocaine bothered him. The staged suicide also. A desperate man who might be from the Middle East — that niggled him as well. Lindsay had been part of that group, Nexus, which advocated peace in Palestine, Jew and Arab, good neighbours together. Could a connection lie there? Some disaffected person who had a serious grudge against Lindsay? But the solicitor had seemingly drifted away from the movement, if that's what it was. So Billie Houston had said, and Perlman had no reason to doubt her.

'Unless you have any more questions, I'll be running along,' Billie Houston said.

'You want somebody to escort you to the garage?'

'I think I'll be fine.'

'I'd feel negligent if I didn't get PC Murdoch to make sure you were safe.'

'If you insist.'

'I do.' He picked up his phone, pressed a button, asked for Murdoch. The young policeman appeared within moments. How eager, Perlman thought. A young dog panting to please. Did I ever have such enthusiasm? 'See that Ms Houston gets back to her car safely, would you?'

'No problem, Sarge.'

From his doorway, Perlman watched Murdoch lead Billie Houston across the outer office towards the stairs. He listened a moment to the ringing of phones and the upraised voices of policemen and women indulging in the joking banter that made the job of law enforcement tolerable. A dedicated crew, he thought. Most of them fresh, most of them keen as young Murdoch. Many of them would become jaded and stale in time. In the tumult of the city's criminal world, a few would even lose their way entirely and break down in exhaustion and nerves, and occasional delusions of grandeur, *I'm above the law, I can swagger and throw my weight around and do whatever the hell I like.*

He started to punch in Artie Wexler's number when a tall stout man loomed in the doorway. Bloody hell. Was he *never* going to get the chance to call Artie? He put the handset down and, slipping his fingers under his glasses, massaged his eyelids. 'And who the devil are you?'

'Tony Curdy. Clyde Valley Security.'

Perlman regarded the man's dark-blue uniform. Nice little red shoulder chevrons, he noticed. 'And what brings you to my lair?'

Tony Curdy had a sorrowful face. You could see him doing a tearful clown *shtick* in a circus. 'I have a videotape. Your Constable said you might like to see it. It's the incident in the garage?'

'You have *that* on tape?'

'We maintain extensive CC surveillance of the garage twenty-four hours a day, Sergeant.' He talked like a sales brochure. He tugged a video cassette from the pocket of his coat. 'You got a VCR somewhere?'

Perlman remembered there was one in Scullion's office. 'Follow me,' he said. He walked through the outer office, and Curdy came after him. They climbed the stairway to the next floor and went along a corridor to Scullion's office, which was empty and dark. Perlman switched on an overhead light and indicated the VCR and TV in the corner of the room. Curdy slid the cassette into the slot and turned on the TV.

Perlman watched grey static on the screen, and then the picture cleared, and he saw the inside of a lift and the face of Billie Houston, and her image made him uneasy because he knew what was going to happen to her. The camera swivelled and another face appeared in the frame and this was the bearded man she'd described, the attacker. The *Arab*. Perlman braced himself for the inevitable moment of the assault. Words were exchanged: mouths opened and closed in silence. The lift door opened. Billie Houston started to make an exit, but then her face was rendered invisible by the man's body as he stepped in front of her.

The camera angle changed. Perlman saw a quick downward gesture of the man's hand. Billie Houston's face jerked back and then blood came from her nose, and again the angle of vision changed and Perlman saw the assailant's face in close-up. An expression that might have been one of self-disgust, regret. The attacker dragged the scarf from his neck and held it out to Billie like a peace offering, and that was when she belted him.

Clearly you didn't mess with Billie.

Then both characters vanished off camera and Perlman found himself looking at an empty lift.

Curdy said, 'Wait, we pick it up again. Right here.'

A row of parked cars. The bearded man was moving after Billie and caught up with her, an image wrapped in shadow. He turned her around so that she faced him. Oy, she looked tough, her expression one of determined self-preservation. She shoved the guy away, and then she hurried out of the shot and was lost entirely. The attacker moved in the opposite direction and then he too was gone.

Perlman's eye was drawn to another figure who appeared briefly between parked cars. Wait, he thought. Who's the wee lurker? 'Can you roll it back and freeze it?'

Curdy rewound, then stopped. 'This the spot you want?'

Perlman moved closer to the screen, peering at the dim shape loitering among motionless cars. 'Him,' he said.

'I noticed him too,' Curdy said. 'He must've seen the confrontation between the man and the woman, and buggered off.'

'Can you make it clearer? Can you zoom in or something?'

'We don't have that capacity, but I could leave you the tape and your tech guys could enhance that image for you.'

Perlman didn't have the patience to wait for technicians. He got in as close to the screen as he could. The face that looked out, from beneath a baseball cap, was familiar. Perlman wasn't sure.

The image was grainy. He stepped away, took off his glasses, replaced them, looked again. Yes. No. Maybe.

Curdy said, 'If this guy interests you, there's one more bit you might want to see. A street sequence. We've got cameras outside the building as well as in.' He fast-forwarded the tape, then played it. The picture depicted a pavement, a few lights reflected from surrounding offices. The image was gritty, as if the picture had been shot through sand. A man rushed into the frame, stopped, looked back. It was the guy from the lift. He turned, then moved away from the camera. A few yards ahead a second figure appeared — and this time Perlman, down on all fours, gazed at the picture like an assessor evaluating a painting of uncertain provenance. The 'Arab' moved a few paces towards the second figure, a small man who slipped quickly into the doorway of a shop and out of sight. The bearded man stopped and abruptly disappeared into the same doorway, and the frame was empty for perhaps twenty or thirty seconds, before Billie's attacker emerged and ran along the pavement and finally out of the camera's range.

The second figure, the small man in the baseball cap, didn't reappear.

Curdy said, 'One guy goes into the doorway and doesn't come out again.'

'Maybe he *couldn't* come out,' Perlman said.

'Probably the bearded joker kicked his arse.'

'Why not? The little guy's a witness to the fact the other guy committed an assault.' Perlman stared at the pavement, the reflection of lights in

145

wet stone. It resembled an artsy monochromatic photograph: 'Glasgow Sidewalk in Winter'. He stood upright, massaged the sides of his aching legs. Shouldn't go down on all fours, he thought. Harder than ever to get up again.

'Run it back a little for me,' he said. 'To where the guy in the cap slips into the shop doorway. Then hold it.'

Curdy obliged. Perlman stared at the face under the peak of the cap until his eyesight began to vibrate. You're sure. But not one hundred per cent.

Sandy Scullion came into the room. 'Home movie night, eh? What's showing?'

Perlman said, 'Have a close look.'

Scullion walked to the frozen image on the screen. 'When did Terry Dogue become a film star and what the devil has he been up to?'

Confirmation. Terry Dogue, felon, drug-dealer, credit-card thief. Lou Perlman smiled and said, 'Keep watching, Sandy. Wee Terry's about to vanish right in front of your eyes. So much for the fragile nature of stardom, eh? Let me tell you the story so far.'

22

PC Dennis Murdoch was fond of WPC Meg Gayle. He liked her tall flat-chested body and the touchingly self-conscious way she slouched to diminish her height. Some people considered her awkward in her movements, but not Murdoch. He loved her laugh — a bell's sound, he thought — and the way she cut her black hair in a bob.

He shone his flashlight into the doorway of the shop. Sleet pierced the narrow beam of light. Bending, Meg Gayle examined the space illuminated by the torch. There was no evidence anything out of the ordinary had occurred here, no body, no bloodstains, just a plain old doorway, a few scraps of uninteresting litter — Crunchie Bar wrapper, dented Tizer can, spent matches — and a darkened insurance office beyond.

'What are we supposed to be looking for, anyway?' she asked.

'Evidence of violence. This is where the encounter took place.' Murdoch directed the beam around the space again. He'd been taught to be thorough. Look, and if you see nothing, look again. Then a third time.

'Perlman showed me the videotape.'

She said, 'I bet he doesn't want to be out in this weather, does he?'

Murdoch smiled. 'I don't think he gives a monkey's about the weather. He's too busy thinking. He's got, how would you describe it . . . an elsewhere look? I like him.'

'They say his bark's worse than his bite.'

Murdoch said, 'Ah, he doesn't bark that much.'

'All the worse when he *does* bite,' she said.

'I sort of admire how he goes about his business.'

'And you want to be just like him when you grow up, Den?'

'It'll be years before I grow up.' Murdoch smiled and killed the beam.

He stood with Meg Gayle in the doorway. He enjoyed the intimacy of this, him and Meg and the empty street. In other circumstances, off-duty say, he might have reached for her hand and warmed it between his own. He imagined undressing her in a half-dark room. Red scarf draped round a lampshade. That flat body. The hard stomach. Flimsy knickers, peel them off gently, slide them down over her legs. You've a mind like a cesspool, he thought.

'We might as well drive back,' he said. 'I'll call in, tell Perlman there's nothing at the scene.'

'Spose.'

They rushed to the patrol car parked nearby. Inside, melting sleet dripped from Murdoch's black and white chequered cap. Meg Gayle blew her nose quietly into a Kleenex. Sniffle weather, Murdoch thought. Weather for coming down with bugs and calling in sick.

The carphone rang and he answered. He heard the throaty voice of PC 'Diamond Jim' Brady. 'Come in, Dick Tracy, speak your mind. Diamond Jim's here most of the night to answer your calls, ease your worries, soothe your concerns, give you good advice on loving and living, on vitamins and nutrition, alternative medication as against traditional, anything you need, you just ask the Diamond — '

'Christ,' Murdoch said. 'The Mouth Machine. We're just on our way back. Anything happening?'

'Possible victim of violence Terence Dogue was taken by a passer-by to Emergency at the Royal Infirmary.'

'Have you told Perlman?'

'Yepski. He was out of here like a whippet in heat.'

'Any instructions for us?'

'Aye. You're to meet him for tea and cream buns tomorrow afternoon at the Willow Tearooms. Two-thirty, don't be late. His treat. And wear your best suit. As for you, WPC Gayle, Perlman wants to see you there in a really skimpy mini-kilt and transparent blouse and absolutely no bra. Something utterly suggestive, he said. Something you can see your nipples through. I'd suggest PVC.'

'Piss off,' Meg Gayle said.

'You don't *believe* me?'

'You're up to here in crap, Brady,' Murdoch said.

'And damnably proud of it,' Brady said.

'Bampot.' Murdoch cut the connection. Back to Pitt Street through the sleet. He looked at the wipers and thought of Meg Gayle in mini-kilt and see-through blouse. Aye aye. Hot thoughts on a nippy night.

He needed a steaming cup of Bovril.

149

23

At nine p.m. Lou Perlman parked the Mondeo at the Royal Infirmary. Sandy Scullion was with him. As they rushed across the car park, Scullion said, 'Lindsay's house is neat and tidy, at least until I send the technical boys in tomorrow. Newspapers folded. The kitchen shipshape. Bed made. Absolutely immaculate. Just like your place in Egypt, Lou.'

'Aye, right enough, sounds like home,' Perlman said. 'Did you find anything interesting?'

'Would you call the *Jewish Telegraph* interesting?'

'My aunts all love it, if that means anything.' Perlman said.

Driving sleet skelped his face. He heard the wind blow out of the Necropolis, where it roared between headstones and crosses and mausoleums, and battered the gothic structure of Glasgow Cathedral before it thudded the big dark edifice of the Infirmary. This was the cervix of old Glasgow, where the city had been birthed in the sixth century by a wandering monk later canonized as St Mungo. His bones lay interred in the Cathedral.

Perlman and Scullion entered the hospital, and found their way to Emergency, where they asked a bustling nurse the whereabouts of Terry Dogue. She was Irish and pretty, and held a bedpan over which lay a soiled towel. 'It's Dr Nimmo you'll be wanting to see.'

'And where might we find him?' Scullion asked.

The woman jabbed a finger in the air. 'Down there, office on the right,' and then she was gone, bedpan held aloft.

Perlman and Scullion moved along a corridor thronged with sorry people awaiting medical attention. They passed curtained partitions where they glimpsed bleeders, accident victims, the casualties of everyday violence. One screaming child had a long nail hammered through her right nostril. This is where they come, Perlman thought, Glasgow's wounded, the accident victims, the wrecks of domestic or criminal violence. They come for drugs, stitches, bandages, tourniquets, hasty surgery. And some come to die.

A big man in heavy black-framed spectacles came out of an office. He wore a plastic tag that identified him as Dr George Nimmo.

Perlman said, 'Just the man we want,' and flashed his badge.

'Bloody hell,' Nimmo said. He had a harassed expression. He lived along the borderline between life and death, a location that made him impatient and nervy. He was also very English, and in his most stressful nightmares had probably never imagined he'd end up working in an Emergency unit in a huge Glasgow hospital. Some Englishmen, Perlman knew, didn't travel well. Especially to barbaric Scotland.

151

'I've got better things to do than chat to you police chaps — '

'I'm sure, doc,' Perlman said. 'We want to ask about Terry Dogue.'

'Dogue?' Nimmo blinked, puzzled. 'Oh, Dogue, of course.'

'He was brought in here, correct?' Perlman asked.

'Some kindly Samaritan found him in a sorry state. Half-dead from asphyxiation. Seems somebody tried to throttle him. I'll make out the necessary police report for you fellows whenever I have a minute to sit down. God, I've been going non-stop for fifteen hours and it doesn't look as if I'll ever get a chance to put my feet up — '

Perlman interrupted. 'You have my sympathy. You're doing a terrific job. Can Dogue talk?'

'There's damage to the larynx and if he tries too hard to speak the damage may well be permanent.'

'We'll need a minute of his time,' Perlman said.

Nimmo sighed. 'Spare room. Last door on the left. We're awfully short of space. One minute.' He dashed off, white coat rising behind like a sail in an updraft.

Scullion and Perlman entered a room that was in disarray, a half-dozen empty beds stripped of sheets, bed-screens, cardboard boxes filled with bottles of disinfectant, a rubber bucket that caught leaks from a dripping overhead pipe. A single low-wattage lightbulb was screwed into the wall and cast a sad light. The back rooms of the NHS. The underbelly. Forty watts and leaking pipes. What did that scream about the system? Perlman surveyed the place. There was no evidence of Terry Dogue in the clutter.

'Check behind the screens,' Scullion said.

Both men did. No Dogue. Just more empty beds. One had been used recently. The pillow was indented, and damp where the last sliver of an ice-cube melted. Probably Dogue had been given an ice-pack to hold to his throat, and a single cube had slipped loose when he'd decided to get out of bed and scarper.

Perlman stepped into the corridor. Scullion followed him. Nurses hurried this way and that, the child with the nail in her nose still screamed, a young man with half of his left leg missing lay unconscious on a gurney pushed by orderlies who formed a blood-soaked caravan. Perlman thought it was like rushing through a nightmare that just kept coming at you. He took off his glasses. The lenses were streaked. The world was sometimes better viewed without them. Edges softened, nobody was wrinkled, nobody grew old in this world.

He stuck them back on and saw the Irish nurse again. She was bent over the face of a very old man, and she had a cotton swab in her hand she was trying to apply to the man's eye.

'It was a fly,' the man said. 'Flew right in. Cheeky bastard. Gonny hurry, nurse.'

'Hold your head still, Mr Mckay.'

'I can feel the fucker crawl in there. Probably laying bloody eggs.'

'I doubt it.' She rolled his eyelid back and

153

peered into the white.

Perlman interrupted her. 'Dogue's gone.'

'I know. Daft old gobshite. I saw him leave five minutes ago. Couldn't stop him. This isn't a jail.'

'Did he leave on his own?'

'He had company. *Jaysus*, will you hold your head still, Mr Mckay?'

'Come on, nurse. Get that damn fly out before my head's filled with maggots,' the old man said.

'Can you describe the company?' Perlman asked.

'One man. Tall. Very very wet. He had a coat, looked sort of old-fashioned. Long, sort of a jacket more than a coat. Black velvet collar. What do you call these people who think it's still the early 1960s?'

'Beatniks?'

'No. Oh, what's the term? Teddy Boys?'

Teds. Teddy Boys. Perlman remembered them. Their world was lost and sunken, mainly found nowadays in souvenir or nostalgia shops. Shoes with fat crepe soles. Stovepipe trousers. Long sideburns. The Teds were anathema to parents who had wild-spirited teenage daughters. You rarely saw them any more. Now and then some ageing geezer could be spotted wandering along in full Edwardian gear. A curiosity.

'They left in a rush,' the nurse said.

Perlman thanked her. He and Scullion hurried along the corridor in the direction of the exit. They stood behind the glass doors and scanned the car park for a sign of a car zooming off, or two figures running through the vile weather.

Nothing, nobody out there.

154

Perlman sighed and said, 'So what have we got, Sandy? Dogue's in the parking garage at the same time as the bearded guy. The Arab, as Billie Houston described him. Then this 'Arab' attacks Dogue. Do we know why? No, we don't. Was Dogue just loitering with intent? Did he fancy breaking into a car? Was he following the Arab, for some fiendish purpose of his own? A mugging? Fucked if I know. Then Terry skips hospital, accompanied by this . . . Teddy Boy. I'm not all that worried about Dogue. I just wonder who his companion is. Anyway, Terry's not going far. I don't think he's ever left Glasgow in his life. He'd have withdrawal symptoms and nosebleeds a few miles beyond the city limits. I'll give young Murdoch a bell, and get him to check on Dogue's last known address. Meantime, I'm going home, get an early start in the morning. I'll drop you off at Pitt Street if that's all right with you.'

'Fine. I'll make sure we get prints of the attacker and float them into circulation tonight.'

Perlman thought of pictures going out to the various Sub-Divisions throughout the Strathclyde Region. He pondered the assailant's young face, the intensity of expression, and how upset he'd looked when he struck Billie Houston. Did he feel just as bad about throttling Terry Dogue, or did his regret extend only to women? Maybe he'd broken a rule of his own code of ethics: you don't hit women. He didn't look brutal. It wasn't a thug's face.

Scullion said, 'There's also been the usual babble of media inquiries about the case of the

155

hanging man, and I'll have to deal with that. The telly people grind you down. I hate making public statements anyway.'

'What's the party line?'

'Apparent suicide,' Scullion said. 'For the moment.'

'The hacks and hackettes will love you to death for that one. They always want a murder. Suspicious circumstances at the very least.'

'They'll have to be disappointed for a day or so. I pilfered a photograph of Lindsay from his house. I'll give them that much.'

'You still happen to have that key to Lindsay's? I thought I'd drop in there on my way home.'

'Since when was Langside on your way home?'

'Have you never taken a detour in your life, Sandy?'

'I always regretted it when I did,' Scullion said.

They went outside. The night chucked sleet at them with the abandon of an enraged wife throwing cutlery at an errant husband. The car park was slushy, *goor* roaring in gutters.

'Ready to make a run?' Perlman asked.

'Any time you like.'

Perlman pushed the door open, and the night pounded him like the hoofs of an icy black cavalry. He ran as fast as he could across the car park and by the time he reached the Mondeo he was chilled deep into the bone, he couldn't catch his breath, and slicks of icy water slid down the surface of his glasses, blinding him.

24

The Kelvin, a tributary of the Clyde, flowed in spate between Glasgow University and Kelvingrove Park. In summer, the banks were leafy and pleasant to walk; on a vicious winter night, when the Kelvin churned, the place was wild and hostile. Empty plastic bags, casually discarded by pedestrians, were snared on bushes and trees, and crackled under the force of wind and hard rain.

BJ Quick said, 'He fucking saw you, he fucking *saw* you, wee man. That was the first mistake.'

Terry Dogue's voice was an emphysematous whisper. '*He tried to kill me, BJ.*'

Quick said, 'You were supposed to be a shadow. But no, he sees you. He *spots* you.'

'*No big deal,*' Dogue whispered.

'No big *deal?*' He slung an arm round Dogue's shoulder and walked the wee man to the edge of the muddy bank where water, whipped well and frothed, roared past. 'Let me explain it, Dogue. The fellow sees you and then gives you a bit of a hammering.'

'*He choked me,*' Dogue croaked.

'And the consequences of this choking? The kindness of strangers allows wee Terry to be whisked off to the Royal for treatment. The doctor examines you, you babble too many details of the attack — '

'*Had to tell him something — *'

157

'But why the truth, for *fuck's* sake? You could've said you got your head stuck in a revolving door, Terry. You could've said you were choked by an athletic hooker while you were head down in her muff. You didn't have to say you were attacked by a madman. You have no fucking *imagination*. Does he, Furf? No imagination.'

'None.' Furfee stood straight-backed and indifferent to the sleet. Once a Private in the Scots Guards — discharged after he'd drunkenly razored an eyeball out of a hoor in a Libyan brothel — he was accustomed to an assortment of climates.

Quick rubbed water from his eyes and said, 'The thing is, Terry, these doctors make reports to the police. See where I'm going with this?'

'*I wasn't thinking.*' Terry Dogue didn't like the weight of Quick's arm round his neck. That whole area was sensitive. Cold water soaked through his baseball hat. He felt like a dookit Halloween apple.

'You should always be thinking, Terry. *Always.*' Open-handed, Quick smacked the back of Dogue's head with a wet hand. Once, twice, a third time for emphasis.

'*Hurtsssss,*' Dogue whimpered.

'Consider this, Terry. The doc's report lands on some cop's desk. He sees your name — a name you were fucking *idiot* enough to give the fucking doctor in the *first* place. And that was mistake number two. The cop says, aye aye, somebody did a serious number on wee Terry. What's this all about? So this cop thinks, smells

158

juicy, I'll check into it, might be drug-connected. Mibbe I'll squeeze some information out of the wee man. Mibbe I'll get news of a drug deal and I'll look good and I'll get promoted. Cops think that way.'

Dogue shook his head vehemently. *'Naw, naw — '*

'Terry. Your breaking point is so close to the surface you can practically see it under your skin. A few questions, a wee bit of pressure, and you'd tell the polis anything.'

'Naw, BJ. Swear to God.'

'I can fucking hear it now. *I was doing a job for BJ, following this Arab tit about —* and then before you know it, Terry, the shite lands on my fucking doorstep, and I'm left there to take the heat, I'm standing there trying to answer questions, who's this Arab, why are you having him followed, and okay, I can fucking *lie* to these cop cunts and get them out my hair for a wee while, but at the same time I've probably *ruined* the work I'm being paid to do, which means no more fucking *income*, and quite likely some violence coming down on my head from people I don't want to know, Terry. And I value my scalp, wee man. I seriously do. Are you seeing where I'm going?'

'Naw,' Dogue said. Flagstaff, I wanna be in Flagstaff. Fly me there. Take me home, country roads. Take me to the tall pines. I dream of the valleys and the San Francisco Peaks.

'You'd land me in the *shite*,' BJ Quick roared, and squeezed harder on Terry Dogue's neck. 'Five minutes, mibbe ten, and you'd be singing

159

to the fucking cops like Madonna. And that's a risk. Intit, Furf?'

'High risk,' Furfee said.

'I blame myself,' Quick said. 'I selected the wrong man for the job. Simple as that.'

'*I wouldn't speak,*' Dogue said.

'Too big a chance for me to take, Terry.'

Dogue suddenly felt weird, as if he was somehow floating over the sleet level. Maybe a consequence of the painkillers he got at the Royal. Or else connected to the dread that devoured him. His baseball cap felt like a band of cold wet steel on his skull and his heart was going like a bell calling the faithful to Mass. He opened his mouth to speak and it filled up with ice-cold water and his larynx felt like raw hamburger. The river churned past, threatening to rise and engulf the whole world. Somewhere high above were a few points of light from the University, specks in the sleety mist.

'I'm sorry, I am,' Quick said.

'*Sorry* — '

'Furf,' Quick said.

Furf said, 'Wilco.'

'*Naw naw naw,*' Dogue whispered. '*Please, BJ. Oh please, I'll do anything, I'll lie, I'll tell the polis nothing* — '

Furfee gripped Dogue by the neck and dragged him moaning and kicking and clawing to the edge of the Kelvin and forced him to his knees in the wet grass and sodden broken-necked nettles, and just as he opened the blade of his razor and drew a single line across Dogue's throat, like a man slaughtering a sacrificial creature, Terry clamped his teeth into Furfee's knuckles and whispered *The Monte Vista Hotel, ya bastart*, as if it was the first phrase in a prayer of deep longing, and Furfee said, 'Fucker,' and finished the cut with one last angry stroke.

Dogue fell face forward and Furfee rolled him into the river with the toe of his sodden blue suede shoe. The little man floated in a flamingo-tinted rinse down through the black waters of the Kelvin.

'Let's fuck off out of here,' BJ Quick said.

'Cool,' Furfee said.

Quick said, 'I need a bloody good drink.'

'Just the job.'

★ ★ ★

They walked to a pub called The Brewery Taps at the extreme western end of Sauchiehall Street. They were drenched by the time they reached it. The place was empty.

'Two pints of heavy,' BJ Quick said to the barman. 'Graveyard in here, intit?'

The barman, whose name was Bear, had the chest and arms of a weight-lifter. He pulled two pints. 'Aye, the weather keeps people at home, BJ.'

'No kidding,' Quick said.

'I think money's short as well,' the barman said. 'Mibbe a recession coming.'

'When is there never a bloody fucking recession coming, Bear?' Quick didn't want to hear about such shite. All he wanted was to reopen his club, and great wealth would follow. Media profile: *BJ Quick, Owner of club farraday* — lower case made it feel more hip, gave it more cred — *speaks freely of his success.*

Recession. Shag that.

The barman said, 'By the by, got something for you.' He reached under the counter and produced a manila envelope. He slid it across the bar and Quick picked it up.

'Who left this?' Quick asked.

'A delivery-boy on a bike. Same boy as before.'

Quick took the envelope, opened it carefully when he was at a table, glanced at the photograph, saw a man's face stare back at him. He flicked the pic over and registered the name, but at some level he really didn't want to know. Normally he valued information as a commodity. But the vibes right then were not copacetic. He stuck the thing in the pocket of his coat. He'd deliver it to the Arab.

Quick thought: Fuck me, this is crazy. Somebody on the end of a phoneline tells you you'll get twenty K in two halves, and all you have to do is carry messages to this third party, this Arab. Clean hands, in and out. Easy-ozey. No questions asked.

He swallowed half his beer.

club farraday here we come in neon. The Rajah of Quick is coming HOME, Glasgow. I'll kick King Tut's Wah-Wah Hut and any other competition into the Clyde.

Somebody on the end of the bloody phoneline.

Somebody you never met. Somebody who says

162

he sympathizes with your 'fiscal' problems.

Ten K gets delivered by messenger to the Brewery Taps. Crinkly old notes. Instructions attached. Pick up a certain guy in a certain place at a certain time. Drive him to an address in Maryhill. Key enclosed. Provide him with occasional information. Keep an eye on him, watch his moves.

That's all you have to do. No unlawful act involved. No nasty strings.

Who the hell are you? BJ Quick had asked.

You don't need to know that. Think of me as your Santa Claus, Mr Quick.

Quick didn't recognize the voice. He thought at first the accent was Edinburgh, maybe some posh part like Morningside. But the accent during the second call was different, raw Glaswegian. Maybe the second call had been made by a another person altogether. Maybe maybe maybe. He wondered often who was behind the deal. He knew a lot of dodgy people, so there was a cartload of candidates. His business problems were well documented, and his private life had been exposed in a Glasgow tabloid pursuing a vendetta against him: a tangle of alimony demands, an affair with a teenage lap-dancer, nooners with a convent schoolgirl. One headline had read: *Club Czar's Convent Conquest.* There was also an alleged connection with a paedophile ring. (Okay, so he sometimes scanned certain *borderline* websites. So what? So did a lot of people.) Anyone with a need for utter discretion may have surveyed the wreckage of Quick's life and said to himself: *This is the git*

I'd hire for a dubious job.

Furfee drank half his pint and belched. He sat down and gazed at the TV. BJ Quick sat beside him.

'I hope Dogue didn't have rabies,' Furfee said, and looked at his hand.

Both men stared at the telly for a time.

Quick finished his pint and when he reached the end of his drink he saw, through the base of the glass, a distorted image of the screen: as a fish might see things, he thought. The photograph of a black-haired man floated in the bevelled disc of sudsy glass.

I know that face, Quick thought, and the thought speared him.

A TV voice said: *Joseph Lindsay, sixty-two, was a Glasgow solicitor . . .*

There was a stock shot of a bridge.

He was found shortly after midnight hanging from Central Station railway bridge, an apparent suicide . . .

A police spokesman, whose name came up on the screen as Detective-Inspector Scullion, said, '*He left no note, the investigation is ongoing . . .*'

The glass slipped from Quick's hand and shattered on the floor.

'You awright?' the barman called out.

'Wee accident,' BJ Quick said.

'No problem, squire,' the barman said. 'I'll clean it up.'

BJ Quick looked at Furfee, who was staring at the TV as if hypnotized, and said, 'What the *fuck*.'

164

25

Perlman parked outside Lindsay's redbrick house in Langside. He got out of the Ford, surveyed the area at the front of the house. No car, no garage attached to the house. He slipped the house-key into the front-door lock, stepped inside. The air smelled of expiry, flowers rotting in stagnant water in a distant room.

He turned on lights as he walked. Comfortable home, the kind of furniture that was expensive and solid and built to last until the apocalypse. Dark patterns, dark carpets, brown velvet curtains: all too *heavy*, Perlman thought. Too funeral parlour.

In the kitchen he opened the refrigerator. He found a slab of cold lamb, sniffed it, plucked a big pink chunk from the bone and chewed on it. When had he eaten last? He couldn't remember lunch. He poured a glass of flat seltzer water from a bottle, washed down the lamb, then wiped his greasy fingertips in a paper towel.

He roamed the house. In the upstairs master bedroom photographs of Lindsay and his late wife hung on the wall. One depicted Lindsay in tux, wife in long ballgown. Happy days. There were also silver-framed pictures of children and grandchildren, the kind of blue-sky shots expatriates sent home to their parents in Glasgow. Here are the grandchildren sitting by the azure-tiled swimming pool. Here they are dressed in cowboy hats. Here's little Jessie on her piebald pony.

Perlman imagined Lindsay gazing fondly and sadly at these photos. Maybe on cold wet nights, when he was more lonely than he could abide, he filled a tumbler with Scotch and looked at the pics and thought about death and distance, and how life was altogether too fleeting.

He leaned towards a picture of Lindsay. Who forced an ignominious death on you, Joe? Who did it?

He headed back downstairs and stood in the middle of the living room. A hefty TV in a mahogany cabinet dominated one wall. Television disguised as furniture. He finished his seltzer and listened to the hush of the house, which hung around him like the folds of a curtain. The place spooked him. His aloneness troubled him. *I have to go home to a house as empty as this*, he thought.

A menorah stood on an upright piano. Lou took out his cigarette lighter and lit all seven candles — maybe for a sense of inner warmth, maybe because it was just something to do. Eyes shut, he listened to the small plosives the flames made. *Blessed art thou, O Lord, who has chosen thy people Israel in love*. A fragment from the *Siddur*, something he remembered old Rabbi Friedlander reading aloud. Friedlander's tiny mouth was invisible behind his enormous white beard. His voice seemed to emerge from some place even older than his face. All the little kids thought he was God, or at least God's best pal.

He'd enjoyed Rabbi Friedlander, whose

solemn words suggested that some truths were immutable, that there were constants in the world, if only you took the time to look, the time to worship. What happened, Lou? Why did you fall off God's wagon?

He opened his eyes and admonished himself for idling in memory. You should be going through Lindsay's papers, poking in the drawers of his desk, rummaging for a clue that would lead you to the killer or killers, evidence say of a terrible crime on Lindsay's part, something that got him whacked. Open a drawer, eek, there's the very thing you need. It never happened that way in life, only in the fictions perpetrated by TV and movies. In life an investigation stuttered along, a process that sometimes resembled quiltmaking, you added this thread to that, this stitch to that, and maybe at the end of all your labours you had something resembling a design from which you could glean an insight into the whys of a crime, and the identity of the criminal.

He heard the doorbell ring. He looked at his watch. 10:20.

He walked to the front door, opened it.

Artie Wexler said, 'Why did you want to meet me here, Lou?'

'You look drowned, Artie. Come inside the living room, take your coat off.'

Artie Wexler threw his coat over a chair. 'That's not answering my question.'

'You, ah, haven't heard?'

'What's to hear?'

Shite. Perlman had hoped Artie Wexler would have learned from radio or TV about the death

167

of Joseph Lindsay. Maybe Sandy Scullion hadn't made any announcement to the media gang yet. Or Wexler had missed it. Whatever, the dirty work falls to me, he thought.

'A drink, Artie?'

Wexler shook his head. 'I'll smoke. You don't mind?'

'Mind? You go ahead.'

Wexler lit a cigar. Lou fished Silk Cuts from his pocket and smoked, and couldn't keep his attention from straying to Wexler's hair. It's a thatch, he thought. He used to have thinning hair, Lou was sure of that. So this is a thatch, a weave. It's not his own.

'Here we are, puffing like old men,' Wexler said.

'Speak for yourself, Artie. You're older than me. You're about the same age as Colin.'

'Poor Colin.'

'You've heard about the surgery tomorrow?'

Wexler looked surprised. His small eyes widened. 'What kind of surgery?'

'Bypass.'

Wexler sucked on his chunky cigar. 'I'll call Miriam in the morning. See if I can do anything to help.'

Like what? Assist at surgery? Lou Perlman let this mention of Miriam slide past him. 'Funny, I was remembering just today the times when you and Colin used to boss me around.'

'When was that, Lou?'

'The old days. Remember, Artie, when I used to run and fetch you Irn-Bru or a poke of sherbet at that wee shop at the corner of Bridge

168

Street and Norfolk Street?'

'Your memory's clearly better than mine, Lou. I get a distinct sense you're stalling about something.'

'I'm stalling, aye, you're right,' Perlman said.

'It's Joe, it's about Joe.'

Perlman nodded. 'Yes.'

'I knew it. I've had this feeling all day long.' Artie Wexler held his cigar as tightly as a man clutching the safety-barrier on a rollercoaster ride. 'What's happened, Lou?'

Perlman told him. Wexler listened, then placed his cigar in an ashtray and watched it burn. He said nothing for a long time. He tugged at his lower lip with the tip of an index finger. He looked, Perlman thought, like a lost boy.

'Let me get this straight,' he said finally. 'It was supposed to look like suicide.'

'That was the idea.'

'But he was definitely killed.'

'Cocaine overdose. The interim official line is apparent suicide.'

'Why?'

Interim official line: Perlman was ashamed of this jargon. When had he learned to spout such guff so easily? 'It's a strategy thing. It gives us some breathing space to make quiet inquiries without the fucking press hammering us. Think of it like a pressure valve we turn off. Frankly, I think it's a load of shite, and the truth should be set loose, but I don't make these decisions.'

Wexler didn't seem to be listening. He got up, walked to the piano, looked at the burning candles. He lowered his head, turned his face away from Lou. 'He was a good guy. I know he was very private, kept himself to himself, and some people found him standoffish, but when he befriended you — you couldn't find a more loyal person.'

'So who had it in for such a paragon, Artie?'

Wexler let his hands hang loose at his side. His eyes were wet. The menorah candles glowed in the polished wood surface of the piano. He said, 'I can't imagine.'

'Somebody wanted him dead, Artie. Somebody went to a lot of trouble and expense. Cocaine isn't cheap. Any ideas?'

'Absolutely none.'

'You probably knew him better than anyone. Think. Tell me about this organization he belonged to.'

'What organization?'

'The Middle East thing, I went to one of their dinners years ago. Joe was the MC on that occasion. Nexus.'

'You got roped into one of those dinners too? Ruthie dragged me along to one, I don't remember when exactly. I don't remember much about the entire evening, to be honest. I know Joe got disenchanted with that stuff long ago. He told me they just squabbled all night, achieved sweet Fanny Adams, waste of time. I don't think they exist any more.'

'You dined with him every month, right?'

'Regular table in La Lanterna. He liked their *fegato*.'

'Did he ever strike you as being worried about anything?'

'Nothing he couldn't deal with.'

'Obviously there was *something* he couldn't fucking deal with, Artie, or he wouldn't have ended up the way he did, would he?'

'Obviously. But I don't know what. He didn't tell me.'

Perlman stared at Wexler for a few seconds. He thought Artie's flesh by candlelight looked like waxpaper. He realized he'd never liked Wexler. Not as a kid, not as man. And he remembered why, and it had nothing to do with any misconceived suspicion that there might be some form of union between Artie and Miriam, because that was beyond the limits of credibility: Miriam wouldn't be attracted by this bewigged *ganef*. No, it was back a long way before that, back in childhood, and it had to do with concealment of truth, with stolen money, and the memory, abrupt as it was, jangled inside Perlman's head like an old Salvation Army tambourine. Colin had a secret stash of coins, perhaps a pound or two in change, old florins, half-crowns, some big flat heavy pennies, cash he kept wrapped in a handkerchief stuffed into the space between the back of the wardrobe and the wall in the bedroom the brothers shared, and one day this money was gone, and Colin accused Lou of taking it. No, it was beyond accusation, Colin was absolutely *certain* Lou had swiped the hankie with the cash. The only other person who knew about the stash was Wexler, plump Artie, Colin's bosom buddy, his best friend in the history of the world, and therefore totally beyond blame. Colin had thumped Lou a few times, and

171

forced his hands behind his back and threatened to break his arms if he didn't confess, but Lou couldn't confess to something he hadn't done, and yet — and yet at the same time he'd never accused sly Wexler of the crime, he'd never pointed at Artie and said, *he's the bloody thief, Col, not me.*

And Artie had never confessed.

A pound or two in coins, a boyhood theft, Christ, he could even remember the metallic smell of the big old pennies and the way the coins had rubbed off on the cotton handkerchief and how the hankie had become discoloured. Money smelled different back then, and it was heavier, it rattled more cheerfully in the pocket.

You were a sorry sack of shite in those days, Artie. And you're still a sack of shite, even more pathetic than you used to be, a retired moneylender, a legalized thief.

Perlman picked up his overcoat. 'I'm going home, Artie. You staying here for a while?'

'Here? I don't think so. I'll walk out with you, Lou.'

They turned out the lights and left the house. The wind blew hard, but the sleet had died. The sky was black, no stars, no moon. Perlman said, 'I assume Lindsay had a car.'

'A Mercedes. There's no sign of it. I thought probably it had been stolen.'

'You know the year, the model?'

'It was silvery grey. About two years old. Model, I don't know.' Wexler kicked at some damp dead leaves.

Perlman took a few steps towards his car, then

stopped. 'Tell me this, Artie. You remember taking that money?'

'Money? What money?'

Perlman laughed. 'If you don't remember, I'm not telling you.' He got into his car and turned on the headlights. Wexler, staring open-mouthed at the Mondeo, was white-faced in the beams. He had an arm upraised, as if to signal Lou to brake. But Perlman drove past and out into the street that would take him to Langside Road and along the eastern edge of Queen's Park, then north on Victoria Road and through the new Gorbals, where *nice* little houses had replaced the richly populated tumbling-down tenements of his childhood, and to Bridgeton and up to Duke Street where the tenements formed the walls of canyons, and then east, finally east to Egypt and sleep.

26

When Marak answered the door of the flat it was almost midnight. Ramsay and another man, dark-eyed and muscular with long black sideburns, stepped inside. They walked without invitation straight into the living room, leaving a beery scent in the air. Marak followed them. They were here to berate him for attacking their little spy, what else? He'd been expecting a reaction.

Ramsay's hair was flattened against his skull. The blond shock had collapsed. The other man stood with his back to the red bars of the electric fire, hands clasped in front of his coat.

Ramsay said, 'What's the game, Abdullah?'

'Game?' Marak asked. Although he addressed his question to Ramsay, he was acutely conscious of the taller man, who emitted an air of violence held very loosely in check. This was the dangerous one, he thought. This was the brute and Ramsay pulled his strings. Be careful.

'Where in your job description does it say you're allowed to strangle my people?'

'I lost control,' Marak said.

'Hear that? Abdullah lost *control*. Mr Cool here just dropped the ball. You don't *fuck* with my people, Abdullah. You fuck with my people, and I take that personally.'

'I don't like being followed,' Marak said.

'You think you're all grown-up and don't

need somebody to watch over you in this strange city, eh?'

'I don't like being followed,' Marak said again.

Ramsay fidgeted with the ruined clump of blond hair as if he were trying to adjust his personality. 'If I say there's to be a bloodhound, you think I'm saying it because I *fucking* like the sound of the word? I say there's to be a bloodhound, Abdullah, because I *mean* it. Got that?'

He shouts too much, Marak thought. It was a sign of somebody close to an edge. Marak stood very still in the centre of the room. He felt tense. He was anticipating an aggressive move from the big man and he wanted to be prepared for the contingency. But it was best, he knew, to be conciliatory. Too much was at stake for him to provoke these men needlessly. He understood that. He couldn't go home without accomplishing what he'd come for.

Failure was no option.

Why had he yielded to the urge to hurt that little nuisance in the doorway? He was a nothing in the scheme of things, less than nothing, an insect. And yet he'd wanted to trample him. He'd descended to a level of rage that had no connection with his purpose. Why? The desire that brought you all this way blinded you, that was why. It fogged your judgement.

Ramsay walked up very close to Marak, face to face. The smell of ale on Ramsay's breath was strong.

'Tell your spy I'm sorry,' Marak said. 'Such a

thing will never happen again. I give you my word.'

'You're bloody right it'll never happen again,' Ramsay said.

'Aye, ha ha,' the big man said. 'Never again.'

Ramsay looked at Marak. 'And as for Lindsay — you've come a long way for fuck all, Abdullah. Whatever you wanted from Lindsay, you can scratch it.'

'What do you mean?'

'No TV, I see. No radio. So you don't know he's dead.'

'Dead?'

'Offed himself, it seems.'

'Offed? I am sorry, this word — '

'He hung himself, squire.'

'No,' Marak said.

'He committed suicide.'

'You're making this up,' Marak said.

'Oh aye? Why would I do that?'

'I don't know why . . . '

'Get it through your head, pal. Lindsay's dead. Okay?'

Marak looked hard into Ramsay's hard blue eyes, then he turned and walked to the window. The truth, yes, Ramsay was telling the truth. Down in the dark street rain fell. He felt a strange little chug of loneliness. He needed somebody to confide in, a trustworthy person he could ask: How does Lindsay's death affect my task? He thought of putting this question to Ramsay, but Ramsay's role in this undertaking was simply a mercenary one, and you couldn't ask advice from a man whose only interest was

176

money. A call to the Moroccan in Haifa then? But no, not now. Lindsay had killed himself. Maybe there was justice enough in the act of self-destruction.

Marak pressed his face to the cold glass and said, 'Because of Lindsay, and people like him, my father is dead. Lindsay deserves to be dead,' and the words escaped him before he knew he was blurting them out.

Ramsay said, 'Hey hey hey. Your problems have got *fuck all* to do with me. I don't want to hear about them. I don't want to know what you're here for, any of that shite. Understand?'

'Do you have a father, Ramsay? Do you have a family you are close to?'

'A father? Get to fuck. What I've got are ex-wives and too many weans and too many fucking demands for child support.'

'Weans?'

'Crumbsnatchers. Kids.'

'You are not close to them?'

'*Close* to them? Ha bloody ha. Their mothers wouldn't let me within a hundred fucking *miles* of them. Close to them! What a fucking joke.'

'The bad husband,' Marak said. 'The bad father.'

'Hold on there. I never gave you permission to get personal, friend. Let's just keep this on a business level. I don't want you turning our relationship, whatever it is, into some family counselling session. I don't talk to you about my family, and you don't tell me about yours. Don't tell me about your dead father or Joseph Lindsay, and I won't tell you about my assorted

177

wives and all the fucking problems I haul around like bags of coal. I see that as a fair basis for a working relationship, right? In the immortal words of the late Hank Williams, Abdullah, if you mind your own business, hey, you won't be minding mine. Makes great sense, eh?'

Marak studied Ramsay. Ramsay didn't care; he'd said as much. He didn't know why Marak had come all this way, and he didn't want to know.

'You like to keep a distance,' Marak said.

'Too bloody right, I want to keep as far away from you as possible. I do my job. I get my cash. Anything else, I don't give a monkey's fuck.'

'No curiosity?'

'I stifle it, sonny boy. Curiosity's a killer.' Ramsay dug an envelope from his pocket. 'Here. This is for you.'

Marak snatched the envelope, opened it. It contained a photograph and a sheet of unlined paper on which was written a name and an address.

'Delivery complete. We'll piss off.' Ramsay and the other man moved towards the door.

'This address,' Marak said, holding the paper forward. 'Where is it?'

Ramsay raised a hand in the air like a traffic cop working a busy junction. 'Do yourself a favour, Abdullah, and splash out on a Glasgow A — Z. Dirt cheap at any bookstore.'

'What is this A — Z?'

'A book of maps, my friend. Street maps. Awright?'

Ramsay and the big man went out into the hall.

Marak listened to the front door open and close. There was the sound of footsteps descending on stone. He sat down, gazed at the photograph. A man. You couldn't look at this face and see any suggestion of evil. It was only a picture of an unfamiliar man looking back at you. A man you'd pass on the street without noticing him. But evil was rooted in the ordinary.

He drifted, thought of wind blowing through dry scrubland. He saw a Land Rover approach in a storm of dust. The vehicle stopped and the man who stepped out was his father. He wore a handkerchief, bandit-fashion, over his face. His father said, *They don't believe me.*

Marak said, *You haven't done anything.*

They say I am guilty, and I cannot prove otherwise.

There has to be some way, Marak said.

The sand blew, swirling around the Land Rover and into Marak's eyes, and the handkerchief his father wore flapped up and down. Sunlight came ruined through stirred grit.

There is no way. They say I'm a thief.

Marak looked down at the photograph in his lap. The face, so bland and self-assured and well-fed, gazed back at him. Don't ask me for pity, Marak thought. Because I have none.

The well of mercy is dry.

27

Lou Perlman hurried quickly through freezing rain towards the entrance of his house. He stumbled over the girl huddled in the doorway, coat drawn up over her head, her knees clamped together.

'Sadie?'

She looked up at him. Rain fell into her eyes. 'Riley said he'd kill me, Mr Perlman.'

'Let's get inside.' Perlman unlocked the door. He helped her to her feet and led her into the house, and kick-slammed the door behind him. For years he'd considered going ex-directory, but the argument against that was simple for him: a public servant should be listed in a phone book. Accessible, accountable. He had nothing to hide. So clearly Sadie had looked up his name and found him.

She was sodden. Hair, coat, blouse, jeans. What was he supposed to do with her? Step one. Show charity. He propelled her towards the kitchen, which was warm, and he stuck a kettle on the stove. He rubbed his hands together for heat.

'You'll need to get out of those clothes,' he said. He recognized the old coat he'd given her.

'I didn't know where else to come,' she said.

'It's all right, love, it's all right,' he said, and he had the momentary panic of a lifelong bachelor presented with a baby whose nappy needs changing. What to do first?

'Just get out of those clothes. I'll make some tea.'

'What will I wear?' she asked.

Step two. Find warm dry clothes. He ran upstairs, puffing, rummaged in his bedroom, found a thick flannel robe, stopped in the bathroom to grab a towel, and then rushed back downstairs. Sadie had already removed her coat, blouse and jeans. See nothing, he thought. She had fine small breasts. He held the robe out towards her, and the towel.

'Dry your hair,' he said. 'But put the robe on first, eh?'

She stood up. With his back to her, Perlman fussed with the kettle. He whistled, hummed. Boil, kettle, boil. He heard the sound of her wrapping herself in the robe.

'Come nearer to the stove,' he said. 'Get warm.' He touched her hand as he moved a chair from table to stove. 'You're ice, girl. How long have you been sitting out there?'

She shrugged. 'I don't have a watch.'

Step three. Make tea. He dropped a tea-bag, his last, into a cup, filled it with boiled water, rescued the bag and lowered it into a second cup, which he also filled with water. 'Here, pet,' and he passed her one of the cups.

She blew on the surface and smiled at him.

Oh, this is cosy, he thought, the policeman and the junkie, the warm Aga, the cups of tea, the beauty in the flannel robe. This was a picture, right enough. If you were paranoid you might imagine blackmail, a hidden snapper somewhere, click-click. He was weary enough to entertain such fantasies: fatigue was a crucifix, and he was nailed to it. He sipped his tea, hoping for a brief revival. But his eyelids were weighted with lead like the bases of those little Subbuteo football figures kids played with. Relax, relax, Lou. This is just an everyday occurrence at Chez Perlman, the flash of a lovely girl's breasts, her nakedness swaddled in an old robe.

He opened a packet of cigarettes, offered her one, and she took it. He lit hers first, then his own. Ever the gentleman. 'You said Riley threatened you.'

'With one of them knives people use to cut lino,' she said.

'A Stanley knife.'

She nodded, sipped tea. Her dark hair was flat against her scalp. She looked childlike, lost, skittish. He gazed at the bruise on her face and felt a profound loathing for Riley.

'You want to press charges?'

'You know what'll happen, Mr Perlman.'

'Bail, then he'll come looking for you.'

'Great system, intit,' she said.

'Flawed to fuck,' he said.

She looked into her tea. 'I'm scared.'

Perlman set his cup on the edge of the stove and slipped off his glasses. He massaged his eyes. 'I'd love to send a couple of big fat uniforms round to see him.'

'What? *Lean* on him?'

'Right.'

Where the *hell* was he drifting with this kind of cockeyed notion? Two fat-necked red-faced uniforms looming up in Riley's doorway with violent intent? Illicit use of force. Against the law. But the idea tempted him because this girl needed his protection. He gazed at her. Some kinds of beauty couldn't be erased by narcotics. You could always see the remains of it. A flower battered and wilted by acid rain: it still held a little of its wonder. This Sadie was a bundle of possibilities. Was it too late to rescue her?

Send me your junkies, your addicts yearning to be free.

'Riley's not *your* problem,' she said.

He finished his tea. *Riley's my problem all right*, he thought. *I'd be remiss if I ignored him.* But the violent road wasn't the way. Two huge cops in a doorway. It wasn't an option.

'Is it all right if I stay here tonight?' she asked.

'There's a couch,' he said. 'It's not great. I'll show you.'

They walked into the living room. He indicated the couch. Brown corduroy, old. How depressing it seemed. How drab this room. This whole bloody house. I should move. Pack up, head to the Southside, let my aunts find me a nice Jewish wife, matzo balls and chopped herring, tzimmes, blintzes, weddings and funerals and a slew of functions to attend. *Shul* even. A new life.

But he was attached to the old one, that was the problem.

Sadie looked at the photographs on the wall. 'Family pictures?'

'Some of them.'

'I like old photos.'

He picked up a newspaper from the couch and tossed it to the floor. 'This okay for you?'

'It's fine, it's great.'

'I'll find a blanket.'

'Listen, are you sure you're not bothered I'm here?'

'Not at all,' he said. A lie. *I'm just a wee bit uneasy.* He left the room. He discovered an old grey blanket in a closet. When he went back he found her looking at his record collection.

'You like the old-fashioned LPs,' she said.

'It's an age thing.'

'CDs are more convenient. Take up less space. Or DVDs.'

He spread the blanket. 'This should keep you warm enough.'

'Great,' she said. She sat down. She rolled her head from side to side, relaxing.

He said, 'I need to get some sleep, Sadie. If you want anything, you know where the kitchen is. Slim pickings, though. A mouse working three shifts a day couldn't make a living in the emporium that's my kitchen. He'd strike. He'd call the other mice out for industrial action. All rodents down tools.'

She smiled. She had perfect white teeth. A lot of users had teeth missing, or rotten and discoloured. But not Sadie. Not yet. He was taken by an urge to press a paternal goodnight kiss on her brow. He resisted it.

'You want me to leave the light on?' he asked.

'Please, I don't like the dark,' she said.

'See you in the morning then.' He stopped on the way out of the room, and his head filled up with a sense of the city stretching off into the rain, and the infinite permutations of relationships between inhabitants, the buzz of commerce, legal and illegal. He turned to look back at Sadie. 'One question for you, love. Do you ever have dealings with a man called Terry Dogue?'

'Now that would be clyping,' she said.

'Honour among dopers, eh? Come on, dear.'

She ran both hands through her hair. 'Okay. I've scored off him a few times.'

'Where does he hang out these days?'

'The last time I went to a flat in Ruchazie. I took a bus. I remember that. I went past Barlinnie Prison, and a golf course. I think.'

'You remember the address?'

She stretched the corners of her eyes with her fingertips and looked oriental. Perlman imagined her in a kimono. Sadie Geisha. She let her hands drift down to her lap. 'Dunottar Street.'

'Any number?'

'Come on, lucky I remember the *street*, Mr Perlman.'

'Thanks.' He went into the kitchen and took the portable phone upstairs. The air in his bedroom was cold. He lit the gas fire. Yellow-blue flame burned. He undressed. He put on an old pair of pyjamas with a check pattern that had faded over the years. He shivered, sat on the edge of the bed, and telephoned Force HQ. He gave his name and asked to be connected to PC Murdoch. The operator had a hard nasal Glasgow accent. She brutalized her words. 'Please hang on,

185

Sergeant.' It came out as *Pleaz hing oan Sarjint*.

Perlman waited. He heard the couch creak downstairs. Sadie lying down, turning over, getting comfy. It was weird, somebody else in the house. A funny thing. A girl sleeps on your sofa and your solitude's dynamited, and suddenly winter's over and it's nearly spring, hey nonny no.

'Murdoch here, Sergeant Perlman.'

'Do a wee job for me. See if you can locate a man called Terry Dogue. He might be at an address in Ruchazie. Dunnotar Street. I don't have a number. You could ask for some assistance from Easterhouse Office, see if anybody there has a specific address.'

'I'll get on to it, Sergeant,' Murdoch said.

Easterhouse was where the ED Sub-Division operated along the extreme eastern edges of Glasgow. This area encompassed a number of housing schemes, Ruchazie, Garthamlock, Cranhill, Easterhouse itself, pebbledash gulags where Glasgow City Council had shipped many thousands of inner-city inhabitants in the late 1950s and early 1960s, an exodus from old tenement communities to a Promised Land that turned out to be a sorry deception in which people exchanged a familiar but decrepit world for barren estates, and a lack of social facilities, and every face belonged to a stranger. Instead of compassion and the friendship of your long-time neighbours, you got a brand-new two- or three-bedroom flat with hot and cold running water and, if you were lucky, a balcony.

A balcony, Perlman thought.

They took your known world away and they gave you a fucking *verandah*.

You drank tea and looked out at people on other verandahs drinking tea. What was that all about? So you could imagine you were the sahibs of the schemes, lords of some new order?

He turned off the lamp and lay down, pulling blankets up around his body. He shut his eyes and tried to let the day seep out of his mind. He thought of Billie Houston, and remembered the face of her attacker. Angular, dark-bearded: it wasn't a face that smiled a lot. Who was he? And why had he throttled Terry Dogue? Simply because Terry had witnessed the attack on Billie — or was there another explanation Perlman couldn't think of? He wondered about the identity of the man who'd taken Terry Dogue out of the hospital.

The night was popping with questions. And he had no answers.

He listened to the metallic tick of the cheap alarm-clock. Typical this, sleepy — and his damned head wouldn't stop churning. He thought of Colin, his damaged heart, the operation. And Miriam, dear Miriam's concerns. He felt privileged that she'd chosen him as the repository for her fears. She'd *needed* him. He remembered the feel of her hand on his. That intimacy. You're far too old to be infatuated, Perlman. Infatuation is what you grow out of, you *alter bokher*.

And he slid to sleep, down into the black canyons, and he woke only when he heard the girl climb into bed beside him.

'I'm cold downstairs,' she said. 'D'you mind me coming up to your room?'

He felt her body against him. How long since he'd shared his bed with a woman? Oh, Christ, years: he lived a monastic life. He occupied a cell of his own making. Was Sadie really cold, or was this some skimpy pretext, and she wanted to screw? Vulnerable and attractive — what in Christ's name could she possibly see in him?

Easy. You're kind and generous to her. Hers is a brute world. Scraping along, scoring dope. Living in fear of an arsehole like Riley. And you, Lou, you're fatherly. She doesn't have a father. That's it. She's a frightened wee girl a long way from home.

She caught one of his hands and rubbed it between her palms. 'Nobody ever gave me the coat off his back before,' she said. 'I want to give you something in return.'

'There's nothing I want, Sadie.'

'You don't find me attractive, eh?'

'No, you're beautiful.'

'You say the nicest things. Here I am. All yours.'

He turned on the lamp. He looked into her face. He hoped he appeared stern, resolute. Her eyes were dark, appealing. *Please take me, Perlman*.

'You want me to go back downstairs?' she asked.

'Oh *Christ*,' he said.

'If you're worried about Aids, don't be. Honest, I'm HIV-neg.'

How foreplay had changed since his heyday. Here's the result of my clinical test, love. Now can we get down to it? He said, 'I'm sure you're clean, love. Look, I'm almost fifty-six years old, and I appreciate your offer, it's generous beyond anything I deserve. It's just — I'm not a one-night-stand sort of person,' and he knew this was a lie, he desired her, in the muted light of the bedside lamp she looked alluring. But also innocent and easy to hurt, and he wanted to enclose her in his arms and just hold her and tell her the world was going to be fresh and clean again, if she gave it a chance, if she worked at it. His head was filled with conflict.

He felt a faint tingle in his scrotum, electrodes of sexual longing.

'Sadie, love. This isn't the way.'

'Okay, you tell me the way, you tell me what you want.'

'You sleep here. I'll take the couch.'

'It's not how I want it, Lou.'

'It's the way it has to be, love.'

He shoved the blanket aside and stepped out of bed. I'm crazy, he thought. Leaving this girl and a warm bed for solitude on an uncomfortable couch. A bed of stones. What was he — some Jewish mystic, dressed only in a loincloth, freezing his willie off in the desert?

She said, 'I want to thank you.'

'No need,' he said.

'I can't remember the last time anyone's been so kind.'

'I'm not looking for repayment, Sadie.'

'I'll fuck you, Lou. Whatever you fancy.'

'No, love, no.' He moved out of the room before she could say anything else, because sooner or later he'd falter, and he'd be unable to convince himself that he *should* leave, and he'd get back in bed and they'd make love, or some semblance of it, and for a few minutes he'd be gratified, then when morning came he'd feel bad because he was just another bandit who'd used this girl, he was only one short rung up the moral ladder from that fuckwit Riley. And he wanted to believe he was better than that.

I don't want to fuck you, he thought.

Only to help. A helping hand. Accept that, lassie. You owe me damn all. But in Sadie's world when somebody did you a good turn, you owed that person. You paid back with the only thing you had. The debt was cleared.

Downstairs he lit a cigarette and lay on the couch with his eyes open. He felt tense and cramped, and his groin ached, and for a moment he thought — what the fuck difference will it make if I go back upstairs? would a spoke get twisted out of shape in the great cosmic wheel if an ageing Glasgow cop got it on with a junkie girl he'd busted a few years before? Man, woman, cop, junkie, these liaisons happened, desire, mad lust, what did it matter? You could always avert your eyes at dawn.

He crushed his cigarette out in an empty tea-cup and thought of an old truism: *a fuck missed is a fuck missed*. Stay upstairs, Sadie. Don't come down here. He summoned pictures of Miriam. He thought of her splattering a big canvas with paint, bold strokes of a brush. He

190

imagined her standing outside the synagogue in Garnethill, the light-show of Glasgow spread beneath. Miriam Miriam. He adored the name, the way it began and ended with the same letter. The perfection of that closure. Eventually he floated into sleep listening to rain. It was a sleep so deep he didn't hear Sadie descend nor did he feel her kiss him lightly on the side of his face before she let herself out of the house and into the wet morning-dark streets of Egypt.

28

Artie Wexler woke afraid and confused. The red digital numbers of the bedside clock shimmered like the scales of tropical fish in shallow water. He had a sense of his throat closing, but he knew no physical agent was responsible for it, it belonged in the dream he'd just aroused himself from — dream? no, more a nightmare of a cold lime-green room and ornate iron grating overhead and the shadow of a man walking back and forth above him. The click of steel-tipped shoes on metal.

He was dry as a dead fire, needed water, reached for the glass he usually left beside the clock, couldn't find it. He sat up. He remembered he'd taken one of Ruthie's sleepers, maybe that was what had dehydrated him —

The dream had been about money. Right.

Tell me Artie, you remember taking that money?

Perlman's voice in the dream, and yet not; the way of dreams was to buff the edge of the known and replace anything familiar with a skewed facsimile.

He sat up on the edge of the bed. Ruthie was dead to the world. The digital clock read 4:25. The window of the bedroom was black. The sleet and rain had quit, no wind blew. Thirst scorched him. He'd have to go downstairs for water. He walked out to the landing, flicked a switch that

192

turned on lights downstairs.

Halfway down he paused. He thought of Joe Lindsay dead. He thought of Nexus and the way Perlman had asked about it, and all that seemed such a long time ago. He reached the foot of the stairs, headed towards the kitchen. He pressed the button that turned on the spotlights. He wondered if Perlman really knew anything, or if he was firing from the hip — why had he mentioned money?

And then he remembered, as if the recollection were a small incendiary device from the past, the day he'd stolen Colin's hidden stash, and young Lou had taken the blame for it. I'd forgotten that, he thought. Maybe that's what Lou Perlman had been referring to: Colin's coins. That's all. Nothing more serious than that.

The little theft made him feel ashamed now.

He thought of places in the past where events had come together. You want to go back and change things round. Shift the furniture of your history. Revise the way you'd lived, the stuff you'd done. *I am falling to bits*, he thought.

Somebody killed Joe. Had that been in the dream too? He couldn't remember. He heard the wind-chimes shiver, a soft timpani in the night.

Wind-chimes. But no wind.

He felt a wave of vulnerability. He imagined his skull in a sniper's scope. He walked slowly to the sliding glass doors in the living room. The sensor lights shone in the yard. He pushed his face to the glass and, holding his breath, squinted out, looking for a sign of Reuben. The dog's movements often triggered the lights. But that didn't explain the chimes in the motionless dark.

The dog wasn't around. Probably curled up somewhere and sleeping. Poor Reuben, growing old and infirm, diminished vision and hearing. Artie Wexler felt a huge affinity with the dog. Going downhill, man and dog together.

He was about to open the door to call for Reuben when something at his back cast a shadowy reflection in the panes. He thought: ah, Ruthie, Ruthie's come down to look for me, and from outside came the bong of the wind-chimes again, a sweet rippling effect as one chime collided with the next, and the next. He said, 'I couldn't sleep,' and he turned, expecting to see his wife, but it wasn't her, and before he could register this fact he heard glass shatter violently behind him, a scattering of pieces as jagged as stalactites of ice, and he felt himself pitched back into pain, into the fury of wreckage, and back further, and as he fell through shards he reached for the hanging chimes and caught them, and brought all the hollowed bamboo sticks suspended by thin wires down around him, and he kept on falling like an axed tree, teetering back until he stood on the lip of the swimming pool, where he dropped with a splash, and sank through icy water.

In the depths of the freezing black pool his eyes registered nothing.

194

29

8:20 a.m.: Perlman ventured out into the rush-hour city, a cold morning, sky heavy, squalls of wintry rain. As a kid he'd always thought of winter as witches' weather, imagining pointy-hatted women scowling as they floated on broomsticks across chilly silver moons. The season diminished the city, and the tenements seemed withdrawn in a kind of anguish, disillusioned old men seeking comfort.

He drove in the direction of Mount Florida and listened to a tape of Brad Mehldau's Trio playing 'Monk's Dream', and he thought of Sadie, who'd left some time in the dark hours. She'd scribbled a thank-you note on an empty Silk Cut Blue packet on the kitchen table. *Ta, see you, S.* She was out there in the city somewhere, dodging the monstrous Riley, and he wondered what kind of practical help he could give her. The idea of dispatching two big uniforms to eclipse Riley's doorway — that was laughable, something his tired head had tossed up. There had to be another avenue he could explore — but first there was Colin to see, and Lindsay's bizarre death to explore, and Dogue to track down, and the identity of the bearded guy, and Christ knows what else.

How could he make time for Sadie?

She came to my bed, he thought. And I didn't touch her. Bully for you. Now what did he feel?

Hypermoral? Self-satisfied? None of the above? Face it, Lou. Not many young women throw themselves at you these days. And when one does, big shot, you toss her out of bed? Okay, so she wasn't exactly the Immaculate Virgin of Lourdes, but she was *sexy*. Some would call you a total *shmendrick*. Take the chances that come your way, Detective. The nights are long and lonely. Fuck it, fuck this debate, what it comes down to is this: I didn't screw her. Couldn't. End of. Who needs turmoil?

He turned on the wipers. Tenements and street-signs and traffic were thrown briefly into blur mode. The Trio had begun to play an idiosyncratic version of 'Moon River'. It wasn't one of Perlman's favourites. He killed the tape. He was in Aikenhead Road now, southbound, passing close to Hampden Park, the refurbished National Stadium, downsized from the big funky crumbling bowl it had once been. Now it was neat and tidy, lacking any character.

He took a right turn into a grid of narrow streets, and when he found the Cedars he parked and walked inside. The lobby was empty. The woman at the reception desk was the one he'd encountered the day before. He hadn't noticed her ID badge before. Now he did. Fiona Marshall.

'Mr Perlman?'

'You remember me.'

'I have a good memory,' she said. She had one of those posh accents as clipped as a well-kept hedge.

'I'd like to have a minute with my brother,' he said.

The receptionist glanced at her watch. 'Take a seat.'

Perlman wandered around the reception area while the woman made a phone call. She hung up. 'You know where to go,' she said.

Perlman thanked her and went down the corridor to Colin's room. In the doorway he hesitated. Bad timing, the worst kind of timing for bringing unfortunate news, and asking a few questions that might be a little delicate. Colin's mind, reasonably, would be concentrated elsewhere.

Perlman stepped into the room, a bright hospital-visitor smile in place. Colin was sitting upright, gazing at a TV propped high on the wall. It played soundlessly.

'Hey, my wee brother,' he said. 'Twice in two days. Some kind of record, eh?'

Lou Perlman approached the bed, glanced at the drip hooked into his brother's arm. 'Probably.'

Colin nodded at the TV. '*The Man in the Iron Mask*. I know it by heart . . . which may not be the right expression for somebody in my condition.'

Lou looked at the screen briefly. 'When's the op?'

'Noonish. Rifkind says it's essential. Life-saving. I asked for a second opinion. He declined. I feel my rights have been infringed here. Whose heart is it anyway?'

'Rifkind's not going to mislead you,' Lou Perlman said.

'Fucking quack. Loses more bloody patients than Scotland lose rugby matches to England.'

'That many?' Lou said. He looked down at the bedside table, scanning a small bottle of Lucozade, and a paperback novel of the escapist kind, SAS action stuff where men were men and women mattresses.

'I have a confession,' Colin said.

'Want a priest?'

'You'll do just fine. For the record, I'm a wee bit scared, that's all.'

'You? Scared? I never heard you say anything like that before.'

'I know, I know. Outdoor adventure type. Mountain-climbing. Kayaking. Freefalling from planes. Fearless bastard, that Colin Perlman. That's me.'

Lou said, 'There's nothing wrong in feeling afraid.'

'You say. I'm the one going down the long black chute, Lou. I'm the one whose fucking central pump is about to be explored and surgically altered — ' He was out of breath suddenly, sucking air quickly through his open mouth and looking irritated.

'You okay?' Lou asked.

'Just a bloody pain in my chest. I get them now and again.' Colin settled again, smiled weakly. He pressed the remote and the TV went off. 'Lou, I'm sorry, did I snap at you just then? I didn't mean to. It's just I've been lying here taking stock of my life and at some point in the horrible black armpit of a sleepless night I found myself wondering what the fuck I'd actually done with my six decades on this planet. Made pots of loot, fine. Took some downright amazing holidays. But isn't there supposed to be something else? I get the feeling there's a contribution I haven't made, only I don't know what it is. Am I talking about something spiritual that's missing? Is that it?'

'Maybe,' Lou said. A new Colin, he thought. *Spiritual?* Superman in the Versace business suit, wealthy overachiever, seeks true meaning of life in his hour of darkness. *Yea, though I walk through the valley of the shadow of death.* Lou supposed it came to us all, that narrow-angled introspection: what has my life added up to? Your face in the mirror becomes unfamiliar. Even the backs of your hands, your fingernails. You don't know who you are any more. *Pots of loot and amazing holidays*: why hadn't Colin mentioned his prime achievement, the love of Miriam?

'I regret I never had kids,' Colin said. 'Maybe what's bothering me deep down. No kids, therefore no stake in immortality. No continuance. I wanted children. Just couldn't have them. Did I ever tell you that?'

Lou shook his head. 'Never.'

'Something wrong with my fucking seed, would you believe? Miserly sperm-count. A horny old bastard like me and I don't have enough in the sperm division to make babies. God's not fair, Lou.'

'Sometimes I think God's a merchant in the souk, Colin. You want something, you pay a price. You got a good marriage and a life of

199

enviable prosperity. In the debit column, no kids.'

'Plus a dicky ticker.'

'That too.'

'You don't believe this shite, do you? That there's some celestial set of scales, and everything's measured?'

Lou shrugged. 'The older I get, the less I know what I believe.'

'Law and order, though. You believe in that?'

'It's my business.'

'And bad people deserve to get punished?'

'I go along with that.'

'Such uncomplicated convictions.'

'They work for me,' Lou said. He picked up the bottle of Lucozade and looked absently at the label, and wondered if Miriam carried around regrets about the failure to have kids. He wanted to ask why they hadn't adopted, but he knew he had no right to pry. Maybe Colin was too proud, too macho to admit, by the public act of adoption, that he couldn't impregnate his wife. A man's vanity.

'They gave me some Valium half an hour ago,' Colin said. 'My brain feels like that home-made jam our mother used to make. Remember that — gooseberry stuff, gooey and sweet? Maybe that's why I'm boring you with the story of my disappointment. Besides, you didn't come here to listen to me *kvetch*. You're here because of Lindsay.'

'You saw it on TV.'

'Yes. Apparent suicide.'

'He was murdered, Colin.'

'Murdered? I don't believe it.'

'Don't tell me. He was the least likely candidate for homicide you can imagine. Right?'

'Totally.'

'How well did you know him?'

'Not very.' Colin Perlman looked at the window where grey light lay on the panes and the wind stroked the branches of trees. 'He lived a boring little life, Lou. Why anyone would kill — '

Lou Perlman sighed. 'All I hear about Lindsay is how fucking dull he was.'

'But nice. Don't forget nice.'

Perlman swatted the air as if at a pestering fly 'Nice, nice, so where the hell does *nice* get me?'

'You've got a look on your face you must use when you're interrogating a suspect, Lou. You're frowning like a fog coming down. Suddenly I'm terrified of you.'

'Right. Tell me this. Why did you invite this nice boring little guy to dinner at your house?'

'You've been talking to Miriam.'

'She volunteered the information.'

'As I remember it, we had a client in common. Somebody Lindsay represented — the name slips my mind — had invested in one of those offshore funds I used to manage. We talked a couple of times. I was doing the polite thing by asking Lindsay to dinner. Also I was schmoozing him to send more business my way. It's really not very interesting, Lou. It's the kind of fiscal bullshit that always bores you.'

'Can you remember the client's name?'

'It's going back a few years, Lou. What

201

difference would it make if I remembered?'

'Who knows. Tell me about Nexus.'

'Nexus?'

'It doesn't mean anything to you?'

'Is it supposed to?'

'It's an organization Joseph Lindsay once belonged to.'

'Oh, *that*. I have an extremely vague memory of it, but I can't for the life of me think why . . . Maybe they bombed me with requests for a donation. What makes you think *I'd* know anything about Joe Lindsay's affiliations anyway?'

'Assumption. You knew Lindsay. Plus your old pal Artie Wexler named the organization for me. *Plus* the fact that Nexus was busy in our community for a time. Connections, Colin. I'm in the business of making daisy-chains.'

'Be wary of assumption, old son,' Colin said. 'Wexler was close to Lindsay. They go back to undergraduate days together. He's the one you should be asking these questions.'

'I already did. He wasn't much help.'

'He's ageing badly. He's puckered and jumps at the sight of his own shadow. Plus he farts a lot, and leaves an old man's whiff in the air. Like mouldy bran. I always expect to see him coming down the road with a cane. So where do you go from here, Lou?'

Lou Perlman shrugged. He'd half-hoped Colin might have illuminated a dark corner, a small candle flame at least. But no. And so the questions piled up like boxcars in a freight-train wreck, and nobody had sent in the heavy equipment to clear the line.

He laid a hand on his brother's shoulder. 'I hope it all goes well for you today, Colin.'

'I appreciate that. I wish you'd smuggled me in something to eat. A Bounty bar, yummy. They starve you before they operate.' Rifkind appeared in the doorway. White coat, stethoscope. His big domed head reminded Lou Perlman of an eccentric scientist in a sci-fi film he couldn't name. *The Invasion of . . .* whatever.

'Are you upsetting my patient, Lou?'

'Just wishing him good luck.'

Rifkind smiled, patted Lou's arm. 'What's luck got to do with it? I'm the best in the business.'

Colin said, 'Any man who blows his own fucking trumpet is a goddamn liar.'

Rifkind laughed quietly. 'I have testimonials.'

'Only from the survivors,' Colin said. 'The dead can't speak.'

Lou Perlman moved towards the door. He stopped, turned, looked back at his brother. Rifkind was listening to Colin's chest; the stethoscope joined the two men like an umbilical cord.

'Did you remember the name of that client?' Lou asked.

Colin Perlman said, 'Totally gone. Maybe another time, eh? If I make it through the hands of this white-coated assassin.'

Lou raised one hand in a slow gesture of goodbye. He went out into the hallway and back to the reception area. He was surprised to see Sandy Scullion in the centre of the room, his beige raincoat stained by rain.

'Lou,' Scullion said. He looked bleak.

203

'If it's bad news, don't tell me, Sandy.'

'It's not great.'

Perlman said, 'Fucking winter and bad news. They go hand-in-hand, don't they?'

'It would seem,' Scullion said, and frowned.

Perlman realized how rarely he'd seen DI Scullion, a family man of sunny disposition, make his face into a frown.

30

Rain fell across the swimming pool. Patterns on the surface of water, circles disappearing and reforming, transfixed Perlman. Some crimes shocked him even now; after all his years on the force, he still found certain acts of the human species outside his own compass. Acts, no, the word was too neutral. Outrages, yes, abnormal, misbegotten outrages at the extreme end of the behavioural spectrum where all the black and grey shades congregated. Where light was absent.

Confounded, he watched bamboo sticks float on the pool. He was aware of activity all around him, and yet removed from it. Medics, cops, forensics people, police photographers, all the buzzing and humming that came in the slipstream of a killing — but this one was different from most murder-scenes these people had catered, the buzz was muted, shouts shaded into whispers, whispers into silence. In this place dismay had accumulated a great weight, and with it came a hush.

Sidney Linklater approached and stood at Perlman's side. 'Beats me,' he said. 'It really does.'

Perlman didn't speak. He watched water slip through the holes in the bamboo cylinders.

Linklater cleaned his glasses with a rag. 'A sword,' he said. 'I think a curved blade, maybe ten to twelve inches long. I'll know more later. I have to . . . ' His sentence was a track that faded out.

Perlman turned and looked towards the back of the house. He saw Scullion, and a woman in a maroon raincoat and matching hat, Detective-Superintendent Mary Gibson, round-cheeked. forty-something, usually dressed in Laura Ashley. She looked out of place, like somebody who'd been interrupted in her greenhouse, or during a game of canasta. But that was superficial. She was tough, and she saw through anything bogus. Perlman liked her.

'A sword, Sid,' he said. 'What makes somebody choose a fucking sword?'

Linklater shrugged. 'Because he had one handy?'

'Not nearly enough. The word monster comes to mind.'

Perlman walked towards the house. He nodded at Mary Gibson. Sometimes she reminded him of a schoolteacher in a rough district, doing hard battle all day long with tough kids. Her makeup was immaculate, her short brown hair brushed neatly back at all times. She had a doctorate in psychology, Perlman remembered. Her husband was a functionary in the Inland Revenue.

'Some things just knock the feet out from under you, Lou,' she said.

'Aye, don't they,' Perlman said. He caught a whiff of her cologne, a bit on the peachy side, just enough to remind you of better seasons and happier places. 'Sid says a sword.'

Mary Gibson said, 'I think he's right. You

knew Artie Wexler, Sandy's been telling me.'

'A little,' Lou said. 'From the old days.'

'Anyone or anything come to mind?'

'Nothing out of the ordinary.' Perlman lit a cigarette. Rain dampened the paper. 'Where's Ruth Wexler?'

'Indoors. Sedated. Can I have one of your cigarettes, Lou?'

'Sure. Help yourself.' He offered Mary Gibson the packet. She took a cigarette and he lit it for her. Sedated, the only way for Ruth to be. But she had to wake some time and the horror was going to detonate in her face.

'First one in months,' Mary Gibson said, and dragged deeply.

'Good time for bad habits,' Perlman said.

'Ruth was the one who discovered the body. She came down looking for her husband at around eight, as far as I can gather, she became hysterical, alerted her neighbours . . . '

Discovering Artie. Discovering your husband like that. Perlman thought of the rich suburb all around him, the walls and electronic gates designed to keep out the scruff and the mad and the disenfranchised, the elaborate security systems configured to help you sleep at night. Nobody's safe. Not in this world. Not in this swank little Southside corner of Glasgow with its green enclaves and high-tech alarm systems. A swordsman in the dark. He could hear the rumblings of fear behind the wired gates and steel-shuttered windows as one hears the first deep stirrings of an earthquake.

Okay, he hadn't exactly liked Wexler, but who

207

would wish such a termination on him, so vile an ending? He felt drained, angry with the kind of anger that has nowhere to go but twist back in on itself like a reptile. He heard it hiss in his head, this serpent *thing* that inhabited a place beyond language.

Sandy Scullion said, 'The body's inside, Lou. We moved it out of the rain. You want to see it?'

'Not especially.'

'Neither did I, Lou.'

Perlman stared through broken glass patio doors into the interior of the house. Figures moved in the gloom. A flashbulb popped a couple of times. I don't want to go in there. Perlman's mind drifted to Lindsay, the cocaine-filled rubber shoved into his mouth, *here, swallow that*. Now Artie Wexler, sword-split, cleaved, sinking in the water of his pool.

'Let's go indoors,' Mary Gibson said. 'At least it's dry.'

Perlman followed her through the broken doors. He saw rain on slivers of glass, and a single bamboo wind chime that hung from a bent wire. Two photographers moved around with unusual restraint. Fingerprint guys did their thing softly. Murder was a way of life for some people. It kept them busy, gave them income. Their salary was blood money.

Sandy Scullion suggested they go inside the kitchen. Perlman was dazzled by the steel surfaces of the room. The granite countertops were smooth. Very modish, this pseudo-industrial decor. He remembered Wexler's face in the white beams of the Mondeo outside

208

Lindsay's house, that expression of — what? Surprise? Surprised by what? Perlman had a giddy moment, as if he were about to lose his balance. He clutched the edge of a counter and held on and the feeling went away. Murder on an empty stomach. It created mutiny among the intestinal acids.

Scullion said, 'As far as we can reconstruct this, Artie Wexler got up in the night and came downstairs — maybe he heard a noise, we'll never know — and somebody attacked him with a weapon, *probably* a sword, and he fell through the glass doors of the patio and he just kept backtracking to the edge of the pool. Judging from the blood patterns — admittedly disturbed by rainfall — he was struck once before he fell through the doors, and a second time when he was a few feet from the pool. The first blow was into the chest. The second was, well, the neck.'

Blow. This word softened the reality. Blow was what you did when you funnelled your lips and expelled air. 'How did this fucker get indoors?' Perlman asked. He glanced at Mary Gibson and he wanted to apologize for his language, but all the little etiquettes of acceptable behaviour had been cancelled in the circumstances. 'There's a security system, I saw the electronic keypad as we came inside, so how did this guy get in?'

Scullion said, 'We're not sure how he got round the system. We do know he killed the dog.'

'How?' Perlman said.

'The same way as Wexler,' Scullion said. He looked pallid.

'He took a sword to the *dog*?'

209

'The dog was decapitated, Lou,' Mary Gibson said. 'We can safely assume the assailant killed the dog first, to silence it, and then entered the house. As Sandy says, we don't know how the killer circumvented the security system. There's no evidence of a break-in.'

'Then maybe somebody had a key,' Lou Perlman said.

'Maybe,' Scullion said.

'Or Wexler himself let the killer in.'

'Another possibility,' Scullion said.

Perlman closed his eyes a second: welcome darkness. Except he had weird flashing impressions under his eyelids. 'Let's say he entered the house with a key. Start with that. If he had a key, then either he'd obtained it illegally, or Wexler had given him one. Right?'

'The only person who could possibly tell us about anyone having a spare key is Ruth,' Scullion said.

'So that leaves us tapping our fingers until she wakes,' Perlman said. 'Unless anybody feels like rousing her before the sedative wears off.'

'Let her sleep,' Mary Gibson said. 'There's no guarantee she'll be in any state to tell us anything when she wakes, Lou. Who knows what she'll be like? And I don't want to bring her back into the world right at this moment, because she's going to have a rotten enough time when she comes out of that sleep normally . . . '

Perlman agreed. It was the wise thing, the charitable thing. He walked to the doorway and looked into the living room. He thought: keys, fucking keys, it was more than a matter of

210

security systems and locked doors that discon-
certed him, more than the brutality of Wexler's
murder that perturbed him. Far more. He knew
he'd have to go places he didn't want to go, and
think thoughts he had no desire to entertain.
And he ran a hand down his face in a tired
massaging motion, and tried to conjure up
something warm and good, Sadie's face in his
bed, say, or Miriam's touch, but cheering images
were as thin on the ground as lilacs in frost.

He had a feeling of quiet desolation.

He stepped into the living room. He was aware
of Linklater on the edge of his vision, and the
fingerprint guys, and two medics in green coats
making shadows in the frame of the patio doors,
and a photographer saying *I've got what I need
now*. Perlman knew this snapper, a white-
bearded man called Robbie McPhail, AKA
Rumbleguts, because of his generally miserable
demeanour and his obsession with the movement of his bowels. *I'm passing what looks like
Guinness*, he'd say. Or *I'm hours on the lavvy
and it's all thunder, no lightning, catch my drift*?

Perlman stopped, stood very still, held his
breath.

The body lay on a massage-table, the kind you
can fold up and carry away. A sheet covered it.
The photographers would have taken pictures of
Wexler in the pool before uniforms drew the
corpse out of water and carried it inside.
Perlman observed Linklater pull back the sheet
and study the body, as if some new possibility
had just occurred to the young forensics expert.

He found himself staring at Wexler's bare

211

white shoulders and the red raw stump of neck, as devastating to the eye as something hung on an abattoir hook. Linklater said *nnnnn*, covering the corpse with the sheet and stepping back, lost in his own little world of death and echoes.

Perlman turned from the body, wondered where the head was, and then saw it on the coffee table wrapped in clear plastic of the kind you use to preserve leftover food, laid in a foam cooler and surrounded by ice, and weirdly fetal in appearance, a being half-formed and emerging. He was spooked by the sight of Artie's blind red eyes staring through creased plastic into absolute infinity, and the discoloured lips parted as if a word had been frozen in his mouth at the point of the sword's entrance to the neck.

What were you trying to say, Artie? What the fuck were you trying to say? Tell me now. He walked outside into the rain and lit a cigarette and his hand shook. Get it together, Lou. Stiff resolve, all that. Scotland the Brave.

Mary Gibson came up to him, tapped his shoulder. Sandy Scullion stood just behind her, holding a black umbrella over her head.

She said, 'I read your report on Joseph Lindsay. And Sandy's too. I also read McLaren's post-mortem report. Lindsay and Wexler, two old friends, Jewish — who'd want them dead? What had they done to anyone? I hope to God we're not at the start of something here, Lou . . . I hope we're not going to see swastikas and the desecration of synagogues or anything like that.'

Perlman saw in Mary Gibson's eyes a genuine

212

concern. The old highway of anti-Semitism was one he didn't want to travel. It ran through a landscape strewn with barbed-wire and Xyklon-B canisters and old newsreels of bones. He remembered his mother and how, whenever she served boiled eggs, she always said 'Hitler's head' as she cracked the shells with a spoon. A family ritual, this battering of shells and imagining it was Uncle Ade's skull you were breaking open.

'I don't want to sound complacent, but we don't get much in the way of *active* anti-Semitism in Glasgow,' Scullion said. 'I don't lie awake worrying that some fascist group is coming here to torch Jewish houses or places of business.'

'And visit our own little Kristallnacht on us, eh?' Perlman said. 'No, I don't believe Wexler and Lindsay had a lethal encounter with neo-fascism. A solicitor and a retired money-lender? They weren't prominent enough to be *Jewish* targets for some deviant National Fronters looking for headlines. What I *do* think — and this is gut — is that it's the same killer in both cases. Wexler and Lindsay had done something very wrong, at least in the murderer's eyes. Maybe they cheated him. Maybe they ruined him in some business deal. Whatever it was, the victim goes right off the wall looking for blood. More than that. He wants these men to die very badly.'

'He,' Scullion said. 'Or they.'

They'd walked round the pool twice. The rain was still coming down, but slowly now. The sky

213

over Glasgow was a grey membrane. Perlman paused at the deep end and gazed at the diving board, and he imagined Artie, flabby in swimming trunks, looking down at his own white body mirrored in blue water.

Mary Gibson took her gloved hands from the pockets of her raincoat. 'God, I need to smoke again. One bad situation and I'm reaching for the cigs without thinking about consequences.'

'Here.' Lou offered her his packet. He flicked his lighter and lit the cigarette she took.

'These things killed my mother,' she said. 'I swore never again.'

'You can quit after the one you're smoking now,' Lou Perlman said.

She smiled faintly. He imagined her pouring tea from a silver teapot into delicate china cups, and passing around a tiered cake-stand where delicate confections, some pink and others icy white, sat in virginal paper containers. *Do help yourself, ladies.* The other side of Mary Gibson, when she wasn't being a cop.

She said, 'Our first priority is to dig deeper into the relationship between Wexler and Lindsay. See what we can really establish there. We'll want access to all Lindsay's files. We'll want to know everything we can learn about Wexler's business. Maybe Ruth can help. Do you agree with that approach, Sandy? Lou?'

Perlman agreed. Sandy Scullion, who seemed a little preoccupied and remote all at once, simply nodded his head. They moved across the patio. Perlman stood aside, allowing Mary Gibson and Scullion, folding the umbrella, to

214

enter ahead of him. As he was about to follow them, he became aware of a uniformed figure approaching: Dennis Murdoch, the black and white chequered band on his cap discoloured from rain. His face was dark.

'I don't like your expression,' Perlman said. 'You're too solemn for a young man. You haven't earned the right to that look, Murdoch.'

'Sir?' Murdoch was puzzled. Perlman thought: Get used to bafflement. You'll meet it again and again. It's a constant in a policeman's lot.

'I wager you're here to add a little more weight to my general burden, son, right?'

Murdoch said, 'You asked last night about Terry Dogue, sir.'

'And you've come to tell me you found him.'

'Right.'

'Why is my spine icy all of a sudden?' Perlman said.

31

Shimon Marak purchased a Glasgow *A — Z Street Atlas* in Ottakar's bookshop in the Buchanan Galleries at the top of Buchanan Street. He bought a black coffee and flicked the pages while he drank. When he came to the index he found Lassiter Place. He turned back to the appropriate map page and saw yellow and white veins indicating roads and motorways. Lassiter Place was located close to a golf course called Whitecraigs on the far south side of the city. This meant a long taxi ride. He considered buses, but he was unfamiliar with the complexity of routes and numbers.

For that matter, he was unfamiliar with *everything* here. And this made him uneasy. He'd imagined it all so differently. He'd envisaged himself coming and going quickly, doing what he was here to do, then leaving without trace. But there had been deviations he hadn't anticipated, and bad attitudes. Ramsay. Ramsay's big friend, whose name hadn't been revealed. The little man in the baseball cap. The blonde woman in the lift.

This weird solitude he felt, this lack of grounding, he hadn't expected that either. He'd imagined he'd be too busy, the intensity of his focus so sharp he'd have no time for loneliness or uncertainty. Instead, it was the opposite. He had a sense of chasing spectres through a wintry city whose secrets were inviolate, even to those who lived in the heart of them. A mysterious river city made of stone, and yet somehow *insubstantial* to him, a holograph.

He walked down Buchanan Street where the Christmas lights glowed in the dim morning. The rain had quit. The shops were busy. A skinny man with a saxophone played a jazz tune on a corner. Shoppers, bundled up against the chill, went about their business in a dedicated manner. Starlings screamed in the wires above the street. A couple of dreadlocked teenage boys in green and white hooped jerseys rushed past, and one of them collided with Marak, who tried in vain to sidestep.

'Watch where you're going, you blind bastart,' the boy said.

Marak kept moving. He wouldn't let this rude little encounter rattle him. It was of no significance. And yet he wanted to turn round and go back after the boy and . . . and what? Strike him in the face. The mouth.

What was wrong with him? He didn't need such impulses.

He reached Argyle Street and walked to the knife shop he'd seen under the railway bridge the day before. *Victor Morris*. He was drawn by the brilliant display of knives in the window, hunting knives, skinning knives, stilettos, a gorgeous shining steel array. There were also airguns, air rifles, saxophones and guitars: a shop with a split personality. Violence and music. Harsh notes and gentle ones.

If he had a knife he'd feel less vulnerable.

He went inside, studied the displays. I want something small, he thought. Light in the hand.

'Yon's a beauty,' a skinhead boy said. He tapped a display case and pointed out a hunting knife.

'Are you talking to me?' Marak asked.

The boy, fifteen, sixteen, had a tattoo inked into his scalp. It was a face with an open distended mouth, a diminutive copy of 'The Scream', by Edvard Munch, done badly. It was a weird thing for a teenager to have tattooed into his scalp; such despair.

'Five-inch blade. Sheffield carbon steel. Samba stag handle. Great knife. You a hunter then?'

Marak didn't want to converse.

'I'd recommend that knife. Zall I'm saying.'

'I'll take your word.' Marak moved away. He sought out a salesman, an enthusiastic young man with a gold tooth. He bought the knife, and a leather sheath. He counted out the cash. Thirty-five pounds.

'Can't do a better deal than that anywhere,' the salesman said.

The tattooed kid said, 'I told him how good the knife is, so do I get a commission?'

'Commission? What you'll get is a kick up the arse if you keep bothering me.' The salesman looked at Marak. 'Boy's a real knife lover. You want this in a bag?'

'Please.' Impatient, Marak grabbed his purchase and hurried out of the shop. He turned left, passed a shop called Silks & Secrets that sold tawdry underwear, faux-fur bikinis, tiger-skin print

218

panties and matching bras: the blatant nature of the display caught his attention a moment, and he thought how little he knew of women, how small a role they'd played in his life. He'd never loved. He'd admired faces from afar, or the sight of somebody passing close to him in a hotel lobby or a street, or how a woman's perfume might spice the night, but he'd steered a course away from intimacy. Sometimes, in self-questioning moments, he'd wondered if he'd ever love, or if the life he'd chosen had killed the chance of such a possibility: how could anyone know what fate held?

He walked past the Royal Thai restaurant, smelled a sharp spice on the air — cumin, chilli. At the end of the block, he crossed the street. Outside a pawnshop on the corner of Robertson Street, he hailed a taxi. As he climbed into the back seat he wondered if he was still being followed, if the little man in the baseball cap had been replaced. He looked from the window of the taxi. So many faces, how could you tell?

'Lassiter Place,' he told the driver.

★　★　★

Lou Perlman was relieved to step out of Artie Wexler's house. The air was brisk and clean, didn't smell of death. He walked to the end of the drive and then turned to look back. White house, pale-blue window frames, red-tiled roof: all vaguely Mediterranean, the home of a rich man in a prosperous cul-de-sac.

It wasn't a house that shrieked bloody murder.

219

He faced the street. Four patrol cars, his Mondeo, Mary Gibson's Honda Civic, an ambulance, cars belonging to residents, a couple of uniforms hanging crime-scene tape in place, a few neighbours warily watching the house with the troubled expressions of people puzzled by this puncture in their airtight world. Word would be whispered back and forth between the houses: *somebody has murdered Artie Wexler.* Soon phone calls would be made, and the media players arrive in dozens, TV vans throttling the street. Ruth Wexler would be wakened by the commotion, and just for a moment she'd wonder why, and then she'd remember, and she'd see young WPC Meg Gayle, who'd been given the task of sitting at the side of the bed, and all the breath would be sucked out of her lungs. No dream, Mrs W, no nightmare. You saw what you saw, floating on the surface of the pool.

Sandy Scullion appeared beside him. 'This isn't professional of me, Lou. I feel sick. I mean throw-up sick.'

'You must have missed the news, Sandy. It's a sick world and it's getting sicker all the time. There are some neuroses out there that defy understanding. If you'd asked me a few years ago whether I'd ever see somebody beheaded in Glasgow, I would probably have laughed. When it actually fucking happens, funny it ain't.'

'No, it's bleak,' Scullion said. 'Ugly. Depressing. But not funny.'

Perlman shook his head. 'And now Terry Dogue.'

'I heard. Throat slit and dumped in the river.

It's a jolly sort of day altogether . . . '

Perlman experienced an internal slump. He longed to get away from this house, this cul-de-sac. 'We need Dogue's death on top of everything else. Sometimes the crap just keeps on coming. Now wee Terry's in that place where you can ask questions until you're blue in the bloody face about what he was doing in that parking garage at the same time as our Arab friend, and it's all fucking silence . . . '

He was quiet a moment. His head ticked like a clock. Organize, Lou. What to do first. That terrible word the Americans love: prioritize. He needed fresh input, a helping hand. He asked to borrow Scullion's mobile and then moved a few paces away from the DI and tapped in a number.

Perseus McKinnon answered in his deep voice. 'Cremoni's.'

'Perse, I need to fish.'

'Lou Perlman? My favourite Jew. I'll fish with you, Lou. Come and see me.'

'Soon as I can.' Perlman cut the connection, handed the cellphone back to Scullion.

'I eavesdropped,' Scullion said.

'I go back a long way with Perseus. He's supposed to be my secret weapon.'

'I know more than you think, Lou, about your secrets.'

'What a spooky notion,' Perlman said. 'Listen. When the media assault begins, you want me to talk to them?'

'You don't have the touch.'

'I'm smooth as velvet.'

'You're sandpaper, Lou.'

221

'You saying I rub people the wrong way? Fuck me, I always thought I was an old enchanter.' He moved the conversational tone to banter; keep it airy for a few minutes. He sucked on his cigarette. The smoke felt good in his chest. It belonged there. 'What line are you taking?'

'Mary Gibson wants me to go easy on the lurid details. Until we have the coroner's report.'

Perlman wondered how a coroner's report was going to make Wexler's death palatable for public consumption. There was no damn way round it: what happened to Wexler couldn't be soft-shoed. Then the public clamour would begin. The newspaper boys and girls would whip up a blood and fear frenzy. They were good at horror. They knew to jangle the nerves of their readers. *Ghoul Loose in Glasgow.*

He stared at the street, the knot of vehicles. He said, 'I've asked young Murdoch to see what he can get on this Nexus thing. It's a loose end I need to tie up because it's needling me. Murdoch can hunt through files, which saves me the slog. And this relationship between Wexler and Lindsay that Mary Gibson wants us to examine, Sandy — would you mind if I ran with that one for a while, unless you have other plans for me?'

Scullion shook his head. 'Do what you can. I'm heading over to Lindsay's office to secure his files and documents. Billie Houston has already prepared a list of his clients.'

Perlman tossed his cigarette away and thought of Terry Dogue with his throat pumping blood. Floating down the Clyde — at what point had he been dumped into the river? Almost anywhere. It didn't even have to be the Clyde. It might have been the Kelvin, fast-running and bloated by rains.

He was about to take a fresh cigarette from his packet when a black taxi turned into the cul-de-sac from the main road. It wasn't going anywhere. Too many vehicles restricted its advance. It could only back up. Perlman watched the driver turn to ask a question of the passenger, whose face was concealed by shadow. The driver shrugged, swung the vehicle in a tight circle and for a second Perlman found himself staring at the passenger's face in the window. *Christ.* He acted without pause, total reflex, running towards his Mondeo, which was blocked by the ambulance and an old Jaguar, red and glossy, lipsticked by recent rain.

He got behind the wheel and tried to squeeze his car through a narrow space between Jag and ambulance, but he wasn't going to get anywhere unless —

Unless he creased both vehicles.

Whoever owned the Jag was going to love him.

He leaned on the accelerator and the Mondeo started forward. Poor judgement of space: *get your eyesight checked, Lou.* The Mondeo became wedged between the other two vehicles. Perlman couldn't go forward, couldn't go back, couldn't get out through either front door. He clambered over the seats and struggled through a back door, then he ran in the direction of the taxi, which had already turned on to the main road.

Coat flapping, tie rising from his neck in the updraught, he chased the cab. Soon he was puffing, lungs in extremis. He ran and ran, hoping for a red light where the cab would stop. Two hundred yards, two-fifty, who's counting? A gathering of polka dots tapdanced in his vision as the cab went sailing further and further away. Enough, Lou. You're not a sprinter these days. Once upon a time maybe. Three hundred yards, three-fifty. Blood rocketed to his brain.

Five hundred. Six and rising.

He gave up.

Is this where it ends? Dying at the side of the Ayr Road while traffic whizzed north to the city centre, and south to Newton Mearns and points beyond? He sat on the kerb and stuck his head between his knees as the sky came falling down. He imagined cardiac arrest and the unacceptable irony of having to share a hospital room with his brother. Hello Colin, fancy seeing you here.

'Lou? You okay?'

He peered up into Scullion's face.

'What's the matter? You took off like a stallion in heat.'

Perlman held up a hand, meaning: wait. His chest was empty of air. When he recovered the power of speech his voice was dry as kindling.

'Did you circulate that print?' he asked.

'It went out late last night,' Scullion said. 'Why?'

'The guy's in a taxi heading towards the city.'

'Did you get the registration number?'

Perlman shook his head. He hadn't managed to get that close. 'It was a black cab,' he said.

Sandy Scullion immediately took his cellphone from his coat, and tapped in a number. Perlman, too proud and stubborn to collapse entirely, raised himself on one knee and stared at the sky and tried to level the capsized ship of himself, even as he wondered how long the chorus of effervescent polka dots would jitterbug in his eyesight.

'You all right, Lou?' Scullion asked.

'I *look* the picture of health to you?'

'Here. Let me help you up.'

'It's a matter of some principle, Sandy, that I get to my feet unaided. You know why? I see into the future . . . and I'm this frail old dosser in a nursing home . . . and I have no control over my bladder and I wear nappies and I can't move without the help of nurses.'

'And that's your nightmare.'

'One of a batch,' Perlman said. 'I don't want to live in my future before I actually have to, okay?'

'I think you've got a long way to go,' Scullion said.

'Must remember. *Never* sprint after fast-moving taxis.'

Perlman grunted, got to his feet, jiggled his arms as if to promote the circulation of blood, and peered at the stream of passing traffic. 'We need to snare that bastard, Sandy. He's got a lot to tell us.'

32

Marak sat in the cab, eyes shut and hands clasped tightly on his thighs. The cabbie talked endlessly.

'Did you see all the polis there? Has to be something really bad for that many patrol cars. Mibbe a murder. Mibbe a drugs raid. What do you think, eh?'

Marak made a cursory reply, a meaningless sound. He kept seeing the face of the man who'd given fruitless chase for a couple of hundred metres. And he remembered that same man in Bath Street in the company of the blonde woman who worked in Lindsay's office.

A policeman, clearly. The last thing he needed.

The cabbie hadn't mentioned the man diminishing in brief pursuit. Obviously he'd been too intent on making pointless talk to look in his side mirror.

'Were you intending to visit somebody in that cul-de-sac, eh? You got friends there? Do you think anything happened in the house you were intending to visit, eh? Something awful. Christ, I hope not. What do you think, eh?'

A cul-de-sac. Marak thought, I didn't know it was a deadend street. I wanted to look at the house. I wanted to see where Wexler lived. A glance, no more, at how the place was fenced and gated, how it lay in relation to neighbouring houses, what kind of alarm might be visible from outside. Reconnaissance, quick. But the street had been invaded by law officers erecting crime-scene tape around Wexler's house, and people who stood in fixated curiosity.

What had happened to bring so many policemen to the scene?

And the man who'd pursued the taxi. He'd seen Marak's face and reacted instantaneously, which indicated that he recognized him — but how? The blonde woman would have given the police a description — dark eyes, complexion, black beard, early twenties, foreign accent; what else could she offer? That scant verbal portrait wasn't enough for any policeman to identify him.

Had Ramsay betrayed him? was that possible? When it came to a man like Ramsay anything was possible if there was profit involved. But that raised another question: to whom would Ramsay betray him? The police? No. What was there to gain from that? Perhaps there were complexities of which Marak was unaware, loyalties divided by greed: greed was at the source of all this, after all.

The treason of greed.

Marak told the driver to stop. He stuffed some money into the cabbie's hands and got out, entering a big supermarket in Shawlands, an oasis of bright light in the gloom of the day. He cruised the aisles and wondered about his next move. Perplexity dogged him. He stood in the dairy section and stared absently at the yoghurts and skimmed milks and butter, half-expecting somebody to lay a heavy hand on his shoulder and say, *We need to have a chat, sir.* How long would it take the police to trace the taxi anyway? They'd call the cab companies, talk to despatchers, who'd talk in turn to drivers: everything was computerized, everything logged. The driver would be found, and he'd tell his story. He'd say he dropped his passenger outside a supermarket, and he'd specify the exact place, and the police would come.

And they might come very soon.

He hurried from the supermarket, walked a couple of blocks from the main road, found himself in side streets. Tenements rose above him like cliffs into which windows had been cut. Too many windows. Too many points of view. He found himself lost in a grid of streets. Tassie Street. Hector Road. Rossendale. He was moving deeper into a maze without a centre. He saw a face in a third-storey window looking down impassively. One set of eyes: his imagination multiplied eyes. In every window somebody observing . . . absurd. He had to stay calm and think clearly.

The rational man is the one who survives.

He came to a phone booth. Remains of pizza sauce had dried on the glass in streaky swirls. He opened the door, went inside. It was time, he thought, to make this call. He had to reassure himself, recharge his confidence. He gathered all the change he had in his pockets. He picked up the plastic handset, which was gummy to the touch. He knew the number, he'd memorized it. Why commit something to paper when you can store it in your head? He punched in the digits, and when he heard a voice answer he began to

228

feed coins into the slot. *Ding ding ding.*

In Hebrew, a woman was saying: '*Ha mispar she chiyagtem lo be sheroot. Ha mispar she chiyagtem lo be sheroot. Ha mispar she chiyagtem lo be sheroot* — '

Marak replaced the handset. *The number you have called is no longer in service.* Okay, he'd misdialled. Or something had gone wrong with the connection. He pushed the digits again, and waited, and after a moment he heard: '*Ha mispar she chiyagtem lo be sheroot* — '

He hung up, ran a hand nervously across his mouth. He'd remembered the sequence of numbers wrongly. Or. Or what. He felt panic.

He tried the number a third time.

'*Ha mispar she chiyagtem lo be sheroot* — '

Marak stepped out of the booth. He'd forgotten the number, that was it. He was too tense. He needed calm before his memory, usually a well-calibrated instrument, could function again. He walked and walked through unfamiliar neighbourhoods, and felt the temperature around him fall. By dark, ice would form on the pavements, the streets become treacherous.

Remember the number. Relax, let it flow back to you. A set of simple digits. It had to be easy. But he was blocked. He heard Zerouali's voice again: *you are doing a wonderful thing, young man, and may God be with you, and if you need a word of moral support at any time, telephone me here . . .*

Marak listened to a nearby train rattle past in the midday gloaming, and wished he were riding it, travelling out of this city without once looking back. The longer he remained, the more dangerous Glasgow was going to become for him; already it was beginning to feel like an icy prison in which he was being held without trial.

He walked until he came to a rubbish bin and there he ripped into slivers the photograph of Artie Wexler, and the manila envelope, and he dumped them, fisting them deep into the rubbish already inside the container.

33

Mould in the lungs? Spores and spots? Get an X-ray. *Cough me up a sample of lung, if you will, my good man.* Aye, doc, right, doc, anything you say, hack and spit. Lou Perlman pondered dire medical matters as he climbed the stairs of the renovated warehouse in Merchant City where a breed of people, the Loft Dwellers, had come into existence during the last fifteen years or so. Sharp boys in even sharper suits had refurbished the old tobacco warehouses of the nineteenth century, and turned them into comfortable spaces. The city centre, in particular those streets that had formerly been drab no-go areas between George Square and Argyle Street, had become modish. People lived here again. There were bars, shops, restaurants.

Perlman paused halfway up the stairs. Fucking lofts, he thought. Why did anyone want a loft? And why, when you truly needed it to work, was the lift jiggered? The world is in the process of breaking down.

The face in the cab came back to him. You see it once on videotape, and it's flat, half-real; you see it again behind the window of a taxi and suddenly it's flesh, it exists in other dimensions. The hot blast of recognition.

Sandy Scullion had reassured him that copies of That Face had gone out to all the

231

sub-divisions of the Force, and that he'd issue a priority follow-up.

The bearded man had serious questions to answer.

Perlman reached the top. He rang the doorbell that faced him. The door, he noticed, was a heavyweight item. Steel, with a peephole, and three keyholes. Keep bogeymen at bay. News flash for the world: bogeymen would always find a way in if they wanted access badly enough.

The door opened.

Miriam, in jeans and an old Levi's shirt, smiled at him. 'Come in, Lou,' she said, and she kissed him on the cheek. Her lips were chill. It was cold in this place, he thought. He stepped past her into a big space that initially seemed endless. The room went to infinity, and so did the window, which was a great band of grey light. He could see the dome of the City Chambers in George Square over the surrounding rooftops.

'You've never been in my studio before,' Miriam said. 'Red-letter day.'

'It's a hell of a place.' He rubbed his hands together and approached a canvas in the middle of the loft. Thickly applied oil glistened. The painting, half-done, was a collection of tiny squares in gradations of purple. The first word that came to Lou Perlman's mind was *painstaking*. Each little square stood on top of another. 'This isn't your usual colour explosion, is it?'

'It's my version of the patchwork quilt, Lou. Work for idle hands. Keeping my mind occupied.'

232

'I thought you'd be at the hospital,' he said.

'Twiddling the thumbs? Flicking magazine pages? Rifkind said he'd phone when the op was done. Up here I can work on my wee squares at least. I hate waiting rooms.' Her hands were purple from paint. Her hair was pinned up. Her neck was graceful and long. She looked slim in jeans. He was touched by the mauve streak of paint on her cheek. She was apparently unaware of it.

'I was pleased when you phoned,' she said. 'Serious bone to pick, though. You didn't tell me about Lindsay.'

'So can I help it if all my life I've hated being the bearer of bad news?'

'I imagine that's a drawback in your profession. You could've told me he was dead. You had the opportunity.'

'I know, I know — '

'Sometimes you go at things in a sideways manner, Lou. Like a crab.'

'I deny any affinity with crustaceans,' he said. 'I don't even eat them.'

'I read it was a suicide. Perhaps quote. The big maybe.'

'Want the truth? It was no suicide.'

'Somebody killed him? Do you know who?'

'Not yet.'

Miriam uttered a tiny sound of surprise. 'I think I need a drink. You want anything?'

'Water's fine.'

She opened the door to the kitchen. Perlman saw her take a bottle from the refrigerator. He was conscious of the height of the ceiling, where

233

a skylight the length of the loft permitted a view of the wintry sky. This space diminished him. He felt like a speck. He noticed stacked canvases, squeezed-out tubes of oils, brushes stuck in old coffee tins, rags.

Miriam came back with a shot of vodka and a glass of water. Perlman drank the water in an unbroken gulp.

'You have any idea of the motive?' Miriam asked.

'None,' he said. He wanted to back off, leave her be. Maybe what he had to talk to her about could be postponed for a while. He thought of Wexler again, pictures that kept coming at him, blood in chill blue water. 'This is a rotten time for me to come here, Miriam. Colin's on your mind, you're worried, you don't need . . . '

'Let me be the judge of what I don't need, Lou.'

'Okay. It's Wexler. Artie Wexler.'

'Something's happened to him? Tell me.'

Perlman walked to the big window. Pigeons on ledges, sparrows on chimneypots. He watched the birds and he told her. A stabbing; he quit there. He left out the decapitation.

She said, 'No,' and placed a hand flat against her chest, and then she sat on the floor with her back to the wall and her knees drawn up. 'Christ, Lou, who the *hell* would kill Artie Wexler? I saw him only yesterday. He came with me to the fucking *hospital*. You saw him. You were there. One minute he's driving me to see Colin, the next he's this puff of smoke?'

'And Lindsay was his bosom buddy. Two puffs of smoke.'

Miriam closed her eyes. Perlman longed to kiss the mounds of her eyelids. He heard a sound of bells and wondered if for a moment he was having an auditory hallucination associated with his flood of feelings.

Choral voices floated above the bells. 'O Come All Ye Faithful.'

'The floor below,' Miriam said. 'Choir practice. Some church group. Every day at this time. Bright little voices and handbells.' She drank her vodka.

'That would unravel me completely,' Perlman said.

'I'm so used to it I barely hear it.'

Joyful and triumphant. 'I wish I could bring you sunny news,' he said.

'Two puffs of smoke, you said. The killings are connected, Lou?'

'I think it's very likely.'

She looked directly into his eyes. There was a sadness in her face he yearned to eliminate. The deaths, had they made her sorrowful? Sure, but it seemed to him that there was another level of unhappiness inside her, one that wasn't related to the killings. He stroked her hand and then, a little surprised by his own boldness, he took a few steps back. 'How did it happen that Wexler went to the hospital with you?'

'He phoned to ask for news about Colin. He insisted he wanted to keep me company.'

'Did Wexler see Colin recently?'

'Not for years. Four, five, whatever. He never

called, never visited. Then Colin has a heart attack and Artie hears it on the grapevine and suddenly he can't stop phoning me. How's Colin? Is he going to be all right? On and on.'

'Why didn't he keep in touch?'

'Why do people ever lose touch? Why do they drift away? You'd know better than me.'

I probably would, he thought. He wished the infernal choir would quit. They were at it again. Bells. Angelic young voices. *Come ye, O come ye, to Bethlehem.* 'Were they avoiding one another?'

'I can't think why.'

'A falling-out? A fight?'

'Colin didn't say. Artie just . . . faded from the scene.'

'They were best friends from the old days, Miriam. They had a strong common history. Then for no apparent reason they stop seeing each other. They live in the same city, what — two or three miles apart, and they don't meet? Then Wexler just pops back into your life. How did he seem to you?'

'Gloomy one minute, a kind of forced cheer the next. Maybe a wee bit edgy. Mood-swings. He'd talk fast, then fall into a melancholic silence. I wonder how Ruth is taking this. Don't answer. It's a stupid question.'

'I don't know how people take grief,' he said. 'The loss of a spouse. The loss of a kid. I don't know where they find the resources to cope.'

'They always manage somehow, don't they?'

The Christmas bells again. He felt an affinity for Quasimodo going fucking mad in his belfry.

236

'Let's talk about Lindsay for a minute. What did he and Colin discuss when he came to your house?'

Miriam stood up, empty glass in hand. 'You expect me to remember that far back?'

'Try for me. Colin said they had a client in common. He'd forgotten who.'

'What has this got to do with Wexler, Lou?'

'Let me work that part out, Miriam. I'm only asking for a name.'

'Colin wouldn't want me to tell tales.'

'Two men are dead, Miriam. Your loyalty's priceless, and I admire you for it, but it isn't helpful.'

She was quiet for a while. Her face registered indecision. She walked up and down in a troubled manner, twisting her glass in her hand. Then she sighed long, as if she'd resolved some demanding problem. 'Okay. You're such a smooth talker, I can't resist . . . A man called Bannerjee.'

'As in the discredited MP?'

'Right. Lindsay handled some property transactions for him, I believe. Look, I didn't pay much attention to their business chat. That sort of stuff causes a crust to form over my brain. Colin had an investment fund, and Bannerjee was going to put a very large sum of money into it, and Lindsay was handling the details. That's all I know, Lou. I doze easily.'

'Lindsay, our nondescript little solicitor handling money matters for the jet-setter MP?'

'I'd guess Bannerjee trusted Lindsay. Maybe he knew his affairs would be dealt with honestly. The quiet family solicitor might be a better bet than some flash lawyer.'

'Could be,' Perlman said. Colin had avoided mentioning Bannerjee. Easy to understand. Who wants to be affiliated with disgraced figures? The fallen politician, the tarnished golden boy. Guilt by association. When an MP tumbled, he usually dragged others down, secretaries, hangers-on, advisers. Colin had been responsible for other people's *gelt*, a lot of it, and therefore had to be perceived as trustworthy. An association with Bannerjee might have ruined him. Okay. Fair enough. Business was played that way. Businessmen dined every day on the carcasses of former allies. Yesterday's pals were today's fricassee of beef.

Miriam asked, 'Does that help?'

'I don't know yet,' Perlman said. 'I'm looking for a road map. Colin and Lindsay and Bannerjee, fine. It's money, it's investments. Lindsay and Wexler, they met once a month like clockwork — why? what did they discuss? Why did Wexler persist in seeing Lindsay, when he didn't stay in contact with his boyhood pal Colin? I'm missing the glue, Miriam. I'm not getting these people to stick together the way I want.'

'You can't force some things,' she said. 'You can't make everything fit the way you'd like.'

'In my meshuganey wee world, dear, I'm always jamming square pegs into round holes. Sometimes what you get surprises you.'

'Maybe Wexler and Lindsay enjoyed one

238

another's company. Not everything in the world is sinister, Lou.'

Perlman watched a pigeon flap in panic across the skylight. Probably the bird had OD'd on Christmas carols. 'Do you think Wexler knew Bannerjee?'

'Lindsay had Bannerjee as a client, there's always a chance that Lindsay introduced his pal Wexler to his pal Bannerjee, isn't there?'

Perlman thought: Twenty or less days to Christmas, and he had violent death in a city whose inhabitants were expecting a fat fellow in a red suit and a gang of reindeers and a whiff of goodwill on earth. Oy. Another thought struck him: What if Colin was in danger from something other than Rifkind's surgery? Maybe that was a step too far, and Colin wasn't a target of whoever had killed Wexler and Lindsay — but Perlman had a sense of unease on his brother's behalf. Money, secret affiliations, business deals — perhaps something bound Colin to the dead men.

'Time to leave,' he said. 'I'll call the hospital this afternoon and see how Colin got on.'

'I'll be there around four o'clock.'

He touched the side of her face. 'You've got paint on you. Purple suits you.'

She placed a hand over his and said, 'I love Colin.'

'Why are you telling me something I already know, Miriam?'

'I felt like saying it. Maintaining a perspective, Lou.'

'I'm not sure what that means.'

'Don't you?'

She smiled, walked with him to the door. He raised a hand in farewell and left without looking back. He felt awkward, a bumbler. Was she reminding him of the inexorable fact he had no chance with her? Only if she knows what I feel, he thought. Only if she'd managed to see inside the bolted chamber of his heart. Had he given himself away unwittingly? He was embarrassed in the peculiar stinging, cringing way of adolescence. He thought he felt blood rush to his face, a blush. What was this — retarded development? You'll be writing wee love-notes next on scented paper, never to send them. You'll be strolling midnight parks in the misery of knowing your love was not only doomed, but that the object of your love had discovered your feelings and, effectively, had spurned you.

Spurned. I'm even thinking like a romance magazine. He went down the stairs. Halfway, he sneezed. Light fell through a stained-glass window and he saw the fine spray of his sneeze hang a moment in the air like powder. *I love Colin.*

Of course she does. And always will.

34

He moved along the lobby to the street door. He could still vaguely hear the choir at practice, but faint now. He reached for the handle, turned it. His exit was blocked by the figure of a man in the doorway.

'Did you shag her stupid, Sergeant? Did you make her come and scream, Mr Polisman?'

Perlman took a step back. He was aware of Eric 'Moon' Riley holding something in one hand, a stick, a length of metal, he wasn't sure at first. Riley was short, built like a concrete cube; he had a face that looked as if it was compressed by a nylon stocking mask. No beauty. No charm.

What did Sadie see in this gargoyle? Only dope and terror.

'Are you following me, Riley?'

'Did she suck your willie, Sergeant? Did you ram her up the arse with your hot rod?'

'What the fuck are you talking about?'

'She slept at your house, right?'

'She told you that?'

'Our relationship relies on trust, Perlman.'

'Trust my arse. You hit her, didn't you? You beat her, didn't you?'

'I didn't raise a hand.'

'I'm sure.' Perlman felt the day was caving in completely. It had become a landslide of slurry. He was up to his neck. He looked at the object Riley carried, a twelve-inch length of lead pipe.

He imagined it cracking his skull. 'If you hurt her, you fuckwit, I'll come after you.'

'On your white horse, Sergeant? I shake. Look.' Riley rolled his little eyes and shivered. His red leather jacket creaked. He had a brass buckle on the belt of his black jeans. 'Perlman's coming after me. I better get my arse outta town. Sheriff Perlman wants my ballocks in a sling. Oooo.'

'Is that the pipe you hit her with, Riley?'

'Naw, naw, I carry this for my general welfare, Sergeant. There are some rough punters in this town.'

'Where's Sadie?'

'Sound asleep.'

'Where?'

'The Sergeant and the Junkie. What a romantic story. You've got a thing for her, eh? I'm here to tell you only one thing. Hands off. You got that, Louie? Hands fucking off. She's my property. She's a no-go zone, bawheid.'

Riley flicked the air with the lead pipe. It passed within an inch or two of Perlman's face. Perlman reflected on the fact that in these times of broken-down authority you could no longer say *I'm a police officer, stop, do what I tell you or you'll be in trouble* with any hope of making it count. Say it, and you got whacked on the nut anyway. You might as well wave a lace doily.

'Tell me you get my message and I'm gone, Jewboy.'

'I get your message,' Perlman said. 'Here's one for you. You hurt her, you'll answer to me. I swear to God.'

'Hurting Sadie's like kicking your cat, for fuck's sake. Give her enough junk and she doesn't feel a fucking thing. She's a mindless hoor. What do you think? You're on some mission to save her? I pee laughing. She'll fuck anything for dope money. If I let her.'

Perlman had an urge to go for the throat, throw himself at this jerk, this moronic dod of humanity. The pipe was a major deterrent. 'You harm her — '

'Instead of handing out warnings, why don't you pay some attention to that poor arsehole with his head cut off out there in the suburbs?'

'How did you hear about that?'

'The radio. Always keep a wee tranny handy.'

So it had slipped out. It was public knowledge. You couldn't keep Artie Wexler's death in a padlocked box. Perlman imagined he heard the city draw a collective breath of astonishment. Everyday murder was one thing — the knifing, death by broken bottle, even the occasional gun — but this was the kind of slaying you expected in secretive Middle Eastern kingdoms where people had fingers hacked off for farting in public.

Not here, not in dear old heathery Scotland.

Riley turned towards the door. 'I hope you've listened, Perlman. I'm a vicious cunt when I'm upset.'

He was gone in a flicker of light. The door swung shut behind him. Perlman stood in the dim lobby, hands thrust into his pockets. The collar of his shirt stuck to his neck. He composed himself, controlled his breathing, stepped outside. He walked to Virginia Street, where he'd parked his Mondeo.

Sadie, he thought. What can I do for you, and where can I find the time to do it, lassie? I'm devoured.

Under the dull pearl light of a fading Glasgow afternoon, he sat in his car and lit a cigarette, thinking how the city, which he loved as a man might an unreliable mistress of vast and varied experience, sometimes coated him in a film of scum.

35

BJ Quick said, 'Good grass.'

Furf said, 'Cool.'

'Let's have the joint back, big man.'

Grass made Furf talkative and loose. 'You do the hokey-cokey and you shake it all about,' he said, and passed the blackened joint to BJ Quick, who toked deeply.

They were wandering along Anderston Quay on the north bank of the Clyde. The early-afternoon air over the river was tinted a little by a grainy mist. The giant Finnieston Crane, built in the 1930s to heave locomotives on to ships, stood like a forgotten metal cathedral.

They strolled past the glassy tower of the Moat House Hotel and the shell-like structure of the Exhibition and Conference Centre, known locally as the Armadillo. They paused and surveyed the river for a while before Furf said, 'I lived over there years ago,' and pointed with a gloved hand. 'Lorne Street.'

BJ Quick sucked on the grass. Smoke escaped through his nostrils. Dope made him feel a strange clarity. He knew it muddled the senses of most people, turned their brains to semolina, but it acted on him differently.

Furf said, 'There used to be a brothel over there. The Pox Palace. Got myself a bad case of the crabs there. See here, do you think I've got rabies?' He showed Quick the little bruises left by Dogue's bite.

'Rabies, fuck off,' Quick said. He coughed, then spat in a long arc. A neon light went on and off in his head: *club farraday club farraday club farraday*. He'd already decided to give his first interview, when the club opened, to the *Sunday Express*, because it hadn't harassed him like some of the other papers, such as the *Daily Record* or the *Sunday Mail*.

'I think we're getting away from business,' he said.

'So we are. We were discussing . . . Abdullah, right?'

'Here's what I want to know. How is it the names I pass on to him come to unhappy endings? Lindsay, okay. They say he did away with himself. Who knows if that's true? But this other punter, Wexler, was definitely murdered. So what does it mean when I give the names of two people to our mate Abdullah and they both turn up dead, eh? Coincidence? Not on your life.'

Furf frowned. He was having a hard time staying on track. 'I saw Abdullah go inside Victor Morris this morning. Tattooheid Jack, a kid that hangs around there, said he bought a knife. Then I saw him jump in a cab — '

'Fucksake, that's the *third* time you've told me. Your memory's shot every time you smoke grass, Furf. Now where was I? Righto. Do you know what's been crossing my mind? I'm thinking, okay, somebody sent Abdullah here to *kill* these people in the photos.'

'*Kill* them?'

'Why else are they feeding him the bloody names and addresses and photos? To deliver Christmas presents? You heard how Abdullah sounded off about Lindsay. *Killed my father, deserved to die, blah blah blah.* But the Arab's always too fucking *late.* Something happens to these people before he can get to them. First Lindsay pops his clogs, then the second bastard gets his head chopped off. I'm beginning to think he's not *meant* to reach his bloody targets. He believes he is, but somebody else gets in there ahead of him. He's one step behind the action.'

Furfee studied his worrisome hand again. 'Who the hell sent him here anyway?'

'Good question. And who's beating him to the punch? And who the fuck asked *me* to be the go-between? I mean, basically this job is delivering envelopes, and they're willing to pay *twenty thou?* How come *my* name was picked out of the hat?'

Furf said, 'It pongs, BJ. What do we do?'

'Do? We keep delivering the photos, what else? We go about our business and we ask no questions.'

'If it's dodgy — '

'Dodgy or not, either I deliver or I'm out of work. No moolah flows in. No moolah, no club farraday. And no future. See my drift?'

'Clear's a.'

Quick looked in the direction of the Moat House, where a white stretch limousine was drawing up. He watched a uniformed lackey leap into position like a startled scullery-maid, bowing, opening the passenger door. A long-legged woman and a tall man, both fashionably dressed, both too beautiful for this world, emerged from the stretch and glided inside the hotel. Quick was shot through with flames of resentment. He used to get the toady treatment in the Moat House. In The Corinthian, waiters jumped when he clicked his fingers. Yes Mr Quick, no Mr Quick, anything you say Mr Quick. He'd been a celebrity, and he hated the way it had all turned to shite.

Furf lit a cigarette. 'Listen. What if everything blows up in our faces?'

'Blows up how?'

'What if these people who are one step ahead of Abdullah decide they need to remove all traces of him, and everybody and everything associated with him?'

'What am I hearing? Are you *panicking*, Furf?'

'I never panic. Never.'

BJ Quick laid a hand on Furf's broad shoulder. 'One step at a time, big man. If it goes badly wrong, we bail out. Simple. Have I ever led you into a bad situation?'

Furf shook his head.

'See,' Quick said. 'Just trust me. I'll never let you down. Remember that.'

His mobile vibrated in his coat pocket. He took it out, flipped it open, answered. A man's voice said, 'Bear. You got another message.'

36

Lou Perlman parked the Mondeo outside a fish and chip shop called Cremoni's in Dumbarton Road, a couple of blocks from Partick underground station. The restaurant, founded by an Italian immigrant family years before, was no longer the property of the Cremonis. The present owner, Perseus McKinnon, had kept the name for the sake of authenticity.

Perlman stepped into a room filled with the scent of deep-fried foods, a familiar greasy perfume of hot melted lard in which fish and meat pies and battered black puddings and haggis were cooking. He listened to the bubble and hiss of the fryer where the chips were done. Satisfying, sniff sniff, redolent of childhood: it was all very old-style Glasgow, stainless-steel fryers and formica-topped tables and bottles of malt vinegar and ketchup spillage stuck to the floor.

He approached a doorway where strands of long coloured plastic hung. He pushed these aside, entered a small back room that was part storage space, part office. A black man in his late forties sat at a metal desk. He wore shades. He had a big plump face and a pile of unruly curls such as you might see on a child before his first haircut. A barred window, located behind his head, provided slices of daylight.

'Lou,' he said. 'Pull up a chair.'

'Brrrr. It's a cold one out there, Perseus.' Perlman gazed at Perseus McKinnon's black glasses, and considered the fact that, in all the years he'd known the chip-shop proprietor, he'd never seen the man's eyes.

'There's a new Monk collection on the market,' McKinnon said.

'I didn't know.'

'You should keep up, Lou. Serious jazz buffs like you and me, we'll be dinosaurs one day. Who played bass on 'Straight No Chaser', recorded 23 July 1951?'

'Tip of my tongue,' Perlman said.

'Want a hint?'

'I never take hints.' Perlman ransacked his overworked mind. 'Al McKibbon.'

'Well done,' Perseus McKinnon said. 'Your turn.'

'Okay. Name the backup vocalist on Gram Parsons's 'Hickory Wind'.'

'Aw, man, you're cheating. You know I don't follow that shite. How can you stand that country crap?'

'I try to keep an open mind,' Perlman said. 'I wish I had time on my hands the way you have. I'd gladly play trivial musical pursuits all day long.'

'You saying you're busy?' Perseus McKinnon had a staccato laugh that came from the depths of his chest; a bronchial woodpecker, Perlman thought.

'Up-the-Khyber busy, Perse. No-sleep busy.'

'Some bad boys out there.' McKinnon nodded towards the doorway, the city beyond. 'More

250

firearms in circulation than ever. Grenades, sub-machine guns. These are violent times, Lou.'

'This I don't know?'

Perseus McKinnon smiled. He had a big winning smile that made the recipient of it feel as if a blessing had just been bestowed. Perse was the offspring of a one-nighter between a black French seaman and an alcoholic red-haired stripper from Leith. His consuming interest was crime. He collected and collated the vital statistics of Glasgow's criminal world with the avidity of a Victorian collector in pursuit of cataloguing all known species of tapeworm. As some men sought out stamps and others souvenirs of the Golden Age of Steam, Perseus McKinnon gathered facts — about killers and thieves and conmen, loan sharks and debt collectors, hard men and their hired muscle. He stored on computer disks the data pertaining to a great assortment of crimes, the more extravagant the better, and he kept updated files on the prison sentences dished out to those miscreants the police apprehended. He was obsessed by the often incestuous happenings in the vibrant Glasgow crime scene, which he followed as if it were an addictive soap opera. He employed a small army of gossips, paying them with free meals or nominal financial consider-ations. He spent hours every day sifting newspapers, phoning his sources, updating his records. He kept backup copies of his disks in a safe-deposit box at a branch of the Royal Bank of Scotland in Partick.

'You got some problems at the moment, Lou?'

251

'You know damn well I do.'

'What I hear is that a certain solicitor died from too much force-fed cocaine.'

'Your sources gobsmack me.'

'Would you come to me if I was just some common or garden wanker?'

Perlman had quit wondering long ago about McKinnon's sources. He suspected there had to be at least one inside the Force, maybe a young constable who knew McKinnon might be helpful down the road, or an ambitious detective who understood the biblical principle that as ye sow so shall ye reap, and when you gave Perseus some tasty item you got something just as good in return eventually. It was pointless to speculate about this informant's identity. All Perlman knew was this: when you wanted information you were too busy to dig out through the usual avenues — pavement-plodding, door-knocking, unreliable touts — you came to Perseus. He had mishits, of course, items of utter nonsense and hearsay, but he was often reliable. Perlman's own knowledge of the Glasgow underworld was huge, but not so wide-ranging as McKinnon's, who'd amassed an encyclopaedic amount of intelligence on Big Men and Small, on Bosses and Gofers and Hangers-On. It was reputed that Perse's fascination with crime was rooted in his childhood, when his alcoholic mother dragged him across Glasgow to one gangster movie after another, four or five *noir* films in the course of a day. He always said he'd practically been breast-fed by Jimmy Cagney, and that instead of Winnie the Pooh or Rupert the Bear, posters of

George Raft and Peter Lorre and Edward G were taped to the walls around his bed. His mother, who'd died years ago from cirrhosis, had been besotted with baddies.

'I also hear a rumour you have a snapshot of an Arab in circulation, Lou.'

'What else do you hear?'

'On the Arab, *rien*. *Je regrette*. Why is he important?'

'Is the French really necessary, Perse?'

'*Mon père* was French. It's a wee link with my heritage.'

'Fucksake. You were born and brought up in Scotland. You've spent most of your life in Glasgow. Your accent's crap.'

'And *you'd* know good French, right?'

Weary, Perlman wafted a hand in the air. He was still trying to recover his dignity after the encounter with Riley. A young thug sticks a lead pipe in your face, you should *do* something about it. Maybe he'd get the chance some other day. It was a small defeat. 'The Arab's connected. I don't know how. He desperately wanted to see Lindsay. Why? I don't know. He turned up in a taxi in Wexler's street. Again, don't ask me why.'

'A criminal revisiting the scene?' McKinnon said.

Lou Perlman shrugged. 'Maybe. You know any swordsmen?'

'Not many,' McKinnon said. 'Bad boys with knives, sure. Plenty of them. I heard once of a guy mugging people with an épée. That was downright eccentric. But you don't behead somebody with an épée. At least I don't believe you do.'

Perlman leaned forward, thinking of the long day that stretched behind him already, and the hours that remained ahead. Some days seemed to consist of thirty-six hours, or forty-eight, unnatural loops of time in which day became night and slid back into day again, and you were jet-lagged without ever having flown anywhere.

'You heard anything about Terry Dogue?' Perlman said.

'Wee Terry. Now there was a lost soul.'

'Who was he running with recently?'

'Bad company.'

'He always ran with bad company,' Perlman said.

'He'd been seen with that well-known boulevardier and royal shitebag, BJ Quick.'

'The self-styled monarch of Glasgow Rock? Lover of tiny girls? Bankrupt, I heard. Does the king still have Furfee in his court?'

'The King of Rock and the Pollokshaws Peeler are seemingly inseparable.'

Perlman sat back, spread his legs. His calf muscles ached. He'd once interviewed Quick about an incident in which a hysterical thirteen-year-old girl had accused him of raping her, but then the kid had recanted. Perlman never learned if there had been a pay-off, or what pressure had been applied to her. Quick got away clean. As for Furfee, he was a seriously disturbed piece of work who'd done hard time in Peterhead Prison for violence of an especially nasty nature. He'd *skinned* the entire arm of some poor bugger in Pollokshaws with an open razor.

'I haven't seen or heard of the Peeler for a while,' Perlman said.

'He's out and about, sad to say. He's a fucking menace. He should still be in maximum security.'

'I don't make the laws, Perse. Sometimes I wish I did. Where do this ungodly twosome congregate?'

'No fixed abode. Try the former Club Memphis, Gallowgate area. You might find them there. One other thing. A wee bird was telling me that Quick and the Peeler have been seen in the company of Leo Kilroy.'

'Fat Leo, eh?' Perlman considered Kilroy, whom he'd interviewed a number of times. The fat man, despite a kind of cheerful willingness to help the police in any way he might, gave nothing away. His business interests and income sources were cloaked in fog. There were rumours of a high-dollar protection racket involving several of the city's elegant restaurants and boutiques and hotels, ownership of a freight company, and involvement in contraband cigarettes and single malts; a slew of stories, none of them verifiable. Inquiries into his activities had always dead-ended. Kilroy had powerful suck somewhere. Bigtime clout. Almost certainly he belonged in one of Her Majesty's Hotels, but you didn't get that kind of accommodation unless the law could make the shit stick.

'Why would BJ Quick be hanging round with Kilroy?'

255

'He's trying to buy his club back, Lou.'

'Is this a loser or what? He fails, comes back for more. Where's the money coming from? Kilroy?'

Perseus McKinnon said, 'Fuck only knows.'

Perlman got up. BJ Quick and Furfee, King and Jester. A joker with a taste for sharp razors. And Terry Dogue floats down the Clyde with a gash in his throat. Well well.

'I appreciate the assistance, Perse.'

'Glad to help.' Perseus McKinnon opened his desk and took out a canister of lemon-scented air-freshener and blasted the little room with such ferocity that a fog developed.

'I can't stand the stench of fried food, Lou. Never could.'

'So you bought a fish and chip shop?'

'It's the characters I meet, Lou. That's why I'm in the chipper business.'

37

Perlman drove back to Force HQ in Pitt Street. Without taking off his coat he sat behind his desk and hurriedly created a *Shit to Do* list. Underneath this he wrote down a number of tasks:

> *find out any responses to Arab print —*
> *see if Murdoch has got anywhere with his Nexus research —*
> *ask Sandy if he'd learned anything about the cab and where the driver had picked up and/or dropped off his passenger —*
> *contact Bannerjee, discuss Wexler & Lindsay —*
> *Quick & Furfee, find & question —*
> *Colin, check on health & security*

Moon Riley, who was outside the scope of his present inquiries, came back to bug him. He placed his pencil on the desk, rolled it round with the tip of his finger for a minute, then ripped the sheet out of the pad and stuffed it into the pocket of his coat and thought: Years ago I could have stored these notes in my brain, no paper needed, no reminders. A crick in the memory. Too many lapses these days. Too many synapses withered or snapped.

He sat back, sought a moment of peace, but phones kept ringing and the sound of a somebody's high-strung laugh irked him as surely as a person playing scales endlessly on a tin whistle. He tried to will himself into a state of stillness. Thoughts of Miriam slid through the baleen that protected his brain. *Maintaining a perspective, Lou.* That's fine and dandy, but a man can't help who he loves, my little *mandel.* Do you truly know what I feel?

He was restless, needed to move, had to get back on to the streets before long: the city waited like an unfinished crossword. He wasn't going to find the answers in Pitt Street. He rose from his desk and went upstairs in search of Sandy Scullion. His office was empty. Perlman went inside anyway, attention drawn to a little pile of Xeroxes on the edge of Scullion's desk. Copies of the Arab print. He picked one up, looked at the face, the determination in the eyes: the lips were parted a little, because the camera had caught him in mid-sentence during his encounter with Billie Houston. Who are you? Where did you come from? What did you want with Joe Lindsay? And why did you choke Terry Dogue?

He folded one of the copies and put it in the inside pocket of his blazer, then continued along the corridor, passing the open door of Mary Gibson's office. She saw him, called his name. He went inside, noticed a vase of carnations on top of a filing cabinet and a photograph of a smiling boy of about fourteen on the desk. Her kid, he assumed. Sandy Scullion, Mary Gibson, family people: they went home at night and immersed themselves in lives of pleasing regularity. They ate meals at decent times, and

258

bathed before bed. They brushed their teeth and gargled and slept in clean pyjamas. Scullion probably had slippers under his bed and Mary Gibson wore some kind of expensive moisturizer before she called it a day. Such lives of structure.

'Just the man,' she said.

'Looking for me?' He glanced at her wall-clock. Three p.m. on the nose. His mind wandered to Colin. He was anxious, more than he expected to be. Brotherly love. Hard to express, and hard to show, but it bubbled up from a mysterious well-spring in moments of potential crisis.

'Some talkative young constable spilled the beans about the murder,' she said.

He wondered how long it was since he'd heard that quaint phrase. 'You mean he spoke to the press.'

'Without authorization. I don't blame the boy, Lou. Those journalists pile a lot of pressure on. The boy buckled. He didn't know any better. Anyway, the greyhound's out of the trap and running, and now all Glasgow knows there's some maniac wandering about with a sword, beheading people . . . Oh, Ruth Wexler woke just after noon. I've got a brief statement WPC Gayle took down. Here, have a look.' She passed him two sheets of paper. 'There's a little bit at the end of the report you might find interesting.'

Perlman read:

Statement of Ruth Wexler, taken by WPC Meg Gayle.

I woke because my husband wasn't in bed.

259

Or maybe because I heard glass break. I thought it was a dream. It was four-thirty a.m. on the bedside clock. I went downstairs. The patio doors were broken. I cut my foot on a piece of glass. The room was cold. I walked outside. I saw a man in the swimming pool. I didn't know who he was, not immediately. I thought he was taking a swim. But the night was freezing and the pool wasn't heated. I remember seeing him float towards me and then I understood something awful had happened to him, and I must have screamed. I don't remember too well what happened right after that. The police arrived. They found our dog dead.

Perlman tried to imagine Ruth's voice. If Meg Gayle had captured the tone accurately, if she'd taken it down verbatim, then the voice came across as a repressed drone, a monotone.

He read: *I saw my husband's head had been severed.*

One stark sentence, he thought. Where was the hysteria? Where the turmoil of mind, the fractured recall? Maybe when she'd wakened more drugs had been administered for calming reasons, a little top-up of tranquillizer.

'Read on,' Mary Gibson said.

He turned to the next page.

I remember now. I thought at first it wasn't Artie, but another man. I wonder if I had been dreaming and when I went downstairs I was still confused. The man I thought I saw floating in the pool was called Colin Perlman. But it wasn't him. It was Artie. Poor Artie. I recognized his face.

(End)

'Colin's your brother, isn't he?' Mary Gibson asked.

'Right.'

'Scullion mentioned something about him being in hospital.'

'Cardiac problems.' Perlman looked at Gayle's report again. He imagined the inside of Ruth Wexler's head as much as he could. Strange twists of the brain, the eye, the horror of what moonlight revealed in the water. *Poor Artie. I recognized his face.* He pictured her again on the rim of the pool, her attention drawn initially to the body, and maybe moments later to the head, and he wondered at the sudden warp of recognition, the shock when you looked at two separate objects which, in everyday life, were *always* joined together. You saw a head, you assumed a body. You saw a body, you assumed a head. Suddenly you're in another world, one of terrifying amputation.

Scattered perceptions, mental disarray, illusion.

Mary Gibson said, 'Ruth was probably having a dream in which your brother was involved.'

'I talked to her on the phone yesterday and she asked how Colin was doing, so the name could've stuck. Who knows what inspires dreams?' He was guessing, firing blanks. Dreams were zoos where all the caged nocturnal animals were set free to roam.

261

'Can I use your phone? I'll only take a moment.' He called the hospital. He found himself connected to Fiona, the receptionist. 'This is Lou Perlman. About my brother — '

'Why don't I put you through to Dr Rifkind? Hold.'

A series of clicks, then Rifkind came on the line. 'Done and dusted,' he said.

'And it went well?'

'Of course. What else did you imagine? My hands are exquisite instruments, Lou. You'd faint if you knew what I paid in insurance premiums.'

'I'm sure I would, Martin. When can I see Colin?'

'He needs rest. Tomorrow, say.'

'Before noon or after?'

'Make it after. Tell me the truth, what's this I'm hearing about Artie Wexler?'

'It's true.'

'Somebody actually cut his head — '

'Somebody actually did.'

'Sweet Jesus Christ,' Rifkind said.

'How's the security in your hospital, Martin?'

'What are you asking? Are the patients and staff safe? Are the narcotics kept under lock and key?'

'Tell me about the patients.'

'At any given time there are four personnel, from a highly respected private security firm, on the premises.'

'I didn't notice any.'

'It's an expensive hospital, Lou. I want it to feel more like a five-star hotel. Security's discreet. Why do you need to know this?'

262

'I'm curious.'

'So am I. Tell me more about Artie Wexler. What did the cut look like?'

'Sorry, doc, have to fly.' Perlman put the handset down. He didn't want to launch into a description of how Artie Wexler had looked: he wasn't going to satisfy Rifkind's morbid curiosity.

Mary Gibson said, 'I assume your brother's all right.'

'It sounds that way.'

'Good. Why don't you sit, Lou? Bring me up to speed on what you've been doing.'

'I'm just on my way out, Super — '

'A minute of your time, Lou. Condense your world for me.'

He was uneasy. With Scullion, he was given all kinds of liberties. When he and Sandy discussed a case, they'd developed a form of verbal shorthand; besides, Sandy never asked for intricate details. He preferred broad strokes. Mary Gibson suddenly reminded him of a loan officer unwilling to be persuaded she should give him a line of credit.

He took his sheet of paper from his pocket and peered at it. 'It's all over the place,' he said.

'These things often are, Lou. But sometimes they culminate in something so simple you feel damn stupid for overlooking it. Talk to me.'

Something simple, he thought. I wish, how I wish. He ran through the tasks and names on his paper quickly, connecting this one with that, speculating here, guessing there, blowing air when he could neither guess nor speculate. He

263

was aware of Mary Gibson's unbroken stare as he talked. She could tell when he wasn't walking on firm ground. It was all in the look, the tilt of head.

'Three murders,' she said. 'You think Dogue's might have some as yet unspecified bearing on the others?'

'It's a possibility. Anything is.'

'You're working through a wide social spectrum here, Lou. The high, the upper middle, the low, and — let's call it the scum sector. Bannerjee may have fallen from grace, but he's climbing back up the slopes of Olympus. Don't underestimate him. Lindsay and Wexler, a lawyer and a businessmen, they're sort of upper middle. Maybe Bannerjee knows something about them, maybe not. Terry Dogue is down there, or I should say *was* down there. And his two associates, from what you tell me, are even further down, living with the manure and the slugs and the larvae. Our city in microcosm, Lou.'

'That's Glasgow for you,' he said. 'Everything converges sooner or later. Stand on the corner of Sauchiehall Street and Hope Street and eventually you'll meet everyone you ever knew.'

'And what a generous city it is. It even embraces outsiders. Like this mysterious 'Arab'.'

'Him I'll find.'

'Oh, I don't doubt it at all. You're persistent. That leaves us finally with Nexus, which brings all manner of things together in a comprehensible fashion. Maybe.'

'I'm not making that kind of claim, Superintendent.'

264

'Of course you're not.' She smiled. She had a good honest face. 'A few things before you dash off. I've set up a crime-scene office with a confidential twenty-four-hour freephone. So we may hook some information. Second, Ruth Wexler told WPC Gayle she has no knowledge of anyone possessing a spare key to her house.'

'She could have forgotten.'

'Admittedly. She's a very confused woman. One other thing, nobody in that cul-de-sac heard any unusual noises. They saw no strangers, no unfamiliar cars, nothing out of the ordinary. How can that happen? A man dies a violent death, a very brutal death, glass shattering, perhaps he screamed — but nobody hears a damn thing. What kind of society have we become?'

'People who can afford it live in cork-lined rooms with reinforced walls. Hear nothing, see nothing. What does that tell you?'

'We're mutating into bloody brass monkeys,' Mary Gibson said.

'Who don't feel the cold,' Perlman said. He edged towards the door.

'Answer me this, Sergeant. Are you a happy man?'

'I'm more a melancholic fatalist. As that well-known philosopher Doris Day used to say: Que sera sera.'

'And the future's not ours to see,' Mary Gibson said.

38

Inside the Brewery Taps BJ Quick accepted the envelope from Bear, who slid it surreptitiously across the counter.

'Who delivered this time?' Quick asked. 'Same boy on a bike?'

Bear said, 'No, different fellow. Came on a motorcycle, wore a black helmet, black visor. I didn't see his face. Big guy. Black helmet and the usual leather gear.'

Quick snatched up the envelope and went outside, where Furf sat inside the Peugeot. It was raining again, and cold. The afternoon light was dying fast. Quick slid behind the wheel and laid the envelope on his lap. Furf stared at him, red-eyed from dope.

'They sent a different messenger, Furf. I wonder why. I like consistency. Why did they change the messenger? Why didn't they send the guy that delivered the first two?'

'Mibbe he had flu. Something.'

Quick said, 'Aye, mibbe,' and opened the envelope.

The picture inside was a black-and-white glossy. He stared at it.

Furfee said, 'Looks vaguely familiar.'

Dry-mouthed from grass, Quick was about to reply when he realized the envelope contained something else. He tipped it over and a smaller envelope slipped into the palm of his hand. He ripped this open. Hundred-pound notes, a wedge of them. Oh Christ oh Christ, fuck out my eye and call me Long John Silver. Nothing felt better than cash, not even a smooth tit or that soft stretch of inner thigh beneath a young girl's honey-cake. Money money money! Money overruled all other considerations, cancelled misgivings, soothed anxieties. Whatever doubts he had were instantly dispelled. Money was the elixir. It turned base feelings into the gold of exhilaration.

His fingers trembled. He counted five thousand pounds. A slip of paper was attached by a pink plastic clip to the bottom note. *Final instalment due on delivery and completion.* The handwriting was unfamiliar. It wasn't the same as before. Different handwriting, different messenger.

So fucking what. Big deal. Money took the edge off paranoia.

'Half,' he said.

'Great,' Furf said.

'With the last chunk to come. Written right here.' He pressed a cold kiss on the money. It tasted good. 'My darlings, my wee precious darlings. Come to daddy, babies.'

Furf said, 'Fucking A.'

Elevated, heartbeat fast, Quick sang, '*Open uppa honey it's yer lovah boy me that's knockin'.*'

Furf did a truly awful impression of the dwarf on 'Fantasy Island'. 'De club, boss, de club!'

Quick stuffed the cash into his jeans. De club. Right on. Club farraday was his Jerusalem, and it burned silver and gold on the horizon, blinding him to everything.

39

Rain streamed across Perlman's windscreen. In Wellington Street, where lamps were lit, traffic was dense and ill-tempered: horn-blowers all. Incarceration in a motionless car diminished the zone of your tolerance, especially in the period leading up to Christmas. He couldn't find a parking space in Wellington, so he turned the car into Waterloo Street and deftly beat a slick young man in a Beamer to the only available space.

Three-thirty and almost dark. The wind, whipping through old shipbuilding yards, blew the rain from the river. Perlman drew up the collar of his coat and walked until he found himself outside Solway House, an office building made of glass. It looked fragile, like a big bright lightbulb. He went inside, checked the directory in the foyer, an area of muted lights and fancy palms in giant ceramic pots with African motifs.

He found the name he wanted, and rode the lift to the fourth floor, where he stepped into the reception area of *SB Worldwide (Scotland), A Registered Charity*. Glossy flyers and folders, descriptive of SB's good works in Africa and the Far East, were stacked on a coffee table.

Perlman approached the receptionist's desk.

The woman who sat there was a pleasant young Asian. 'Are you Mr Bannerjee's three-thirty?' she asked.

'Right. Perlman. I called.'

'You can go straight in, Mr Perlman,' and she pointed an elegantly bangled hand at a door on the other side of the room. Perlman thanked her, opened the door, entered another room, big but barely furnished.

He thought: Those who come back from the dead via the avenue of good causes can't afford to be ostentatious. Resurrected, these sinners need a nimbus of humility. Like Shiv Bannerjee, who was rising from his plain wooden desk and reaching out for a handshake. Well-dressed, good black suit, grey shirt, grey silk tie: a stylish little fellow. But nothing over the top, everything understated. There was something different in his look, and it took Perlman only a moment to realize that the full head of hair was white; in his Westminster days, it had been black.

Perlman took the man's hand, shook it. 'Thanks for seeing me at short notice.'

'No problem. I like to help the police when I can. Sit down, Sergeant.' Bannerjee gestured to a chair.

He likes to help the police, Perlman thought. Why not? He'd had plenty of experience cooperating with them in the past, when he'd been arraigned for an assortment of misdemeanours stemming from the fiscal 'irregularities' that occurred during his time at Westminster. Perlman believed, perhaps with the unjustified optimism of a man born in less cynical times, that anyone voted into public office had a moral responsibility. You get votes, it was the same as taking out a loan; you were indebted to your constituency, and if you

269

betrayed it then that was default. What could be simpler?

Shiv Bannerjee had defaulted in a major way.

A bone creaked in Perlman's leg as he sat. It was plainly audible and he felt a need to explain it. 'I've been exercising,' he said. 'Running. Probably too much for my age and condition.'

'Hard on the skeleton,' Bannerjee said. 'Be careful.'

Perlman felt like having a cigarette, but there was a no smoking sign on Bannerjee's desk. 'I try.'

Bannerjee ran a hand over his neat blow-dryed hair. 'We all do. Most of the time. I've had my moments when I was less than careful. You're aware of them, I dare say.'

'I'd have to be blind and illiterate not to be. As a matter of interest, do you feel a need to open up your old wounds? I didn't ask about your past, you brought it up.'

'Force of habit. People tell me I apologize too much,' Bannerjee said and smiled, a beatific little placement of the lips. 'Repentance is hard work, Detective.'

'I don't doubt it. I've never been very good at it myself. Everybody has something in their life they regret. Most of us are less public than you, Mr Bannerjee.'

'It's okay as long as you keep your indiscretions private, right? It's not always possible for a public figure. Call me Shiv. Everyone else does.'

Indiscretions? Perlman considered this a charitable way to describe graft and the sale of political influence. 'Fine. Call me Lou.'

'You mentioned on the phone you wanted to talk about Joe Lindsay.'

'Right. Your solicitor.'

'Oh, in a limited way only. He handled some property transactions for me some time ago. I didn't use him for anything else.'

A lie, a lapse in memory? Perlman wondered. Or had Miriam been wrong with her investment-fund story? He was biased: he trusted Miriam's version. 'So he only handled property for you.'

'Yes, poor fellow,' Bannerjee said. 'I had no idea he was capable of taking his own life.'

'He was murdered.'

'Pardon?'

'Murdered,' Perlman said.

'My *God*. Are you serious?'

'The suicide was a rigged job.'

Bannerjee rose and walked to the window and clasped his hands behind his back. 'I'm sorry. This distresses me. I liked Lindsay. I liked him a lot.'

'Enemies come to mind?'

Bannerjee turned, shook his head. 'None. Absolutely.'

The predictable response. Perlman moved on: 'Did you ever meet a man called Wexler? Artie Wexler?'

'I meet a lot of people.'

'Artie Wexler was a close friend of Lindsay.'

Bannerjee said, 'The name's familiar . . . wait, isn't he the unfortunate man . . . '

'Aye. He's the one. Spread all across the TV. The early edition of our beloved evening

271

newspaper splashed it on the front page. People buy murder, Shiv, the more exotic the better.'

'I didn't know he was a friend of Lindsay's.'

'You're sure?'

'Unless I'm forgetting. In my high-flying days,' and here Bannerjee smiled in a coy, self-deprecating way, 'I met hundreds of people, Lou. I don't meet so many now.'

Show me your open veins, Perlman thought. Break out the bandages. He sashayed in another direction. 'Colin Perlman, Shiv. Does that name mean anything?'

'A relative of yours?'

'Brother. Associate of the late Lindsay, in some small way.'

'I can't say I ever met him, Lou. Where are you going with this?'

'I'm a seeker after truth, Shiv.'

'And how can *I* help you along this difficult path you've chosen?' Bannerjee smiled. A gentle smile. You couldn't imagine a man with that smile perpetrating bad deeds.

'Let's run another memory test. Lindsay invested a large sum of money for you in a fund managed by my brother. Right or wrong?'

Bannerjee sat down. 'No, Lindsay didn't handle investments for me.'

'Think again.'

'I'm thinking. I'm just not getting anything.'

'Listen carefully, Shiv. If Lindsay invested money for you, what is there to be ashamed of? My brother managed a lot of funds, and as far as I know he operated a legal shop. Somewhere in Lindsay's files, I'm sure there's some reference,

272

even a tiny one, to the transaction involving you. What I'm saying is this: be careful when you lie to a cop, because he can get a warrant to take him into all the paper crevices where your average *schmuck* can't go. There's no hiding place in the end.'

Perlman chewed on a thumbnail and wondered what the fuck made people so reluctant to talk about this connection: Colin had denied remembering the name of Lindsay's client, and now Bannerjee was going down the same Avenue of the Amnesiacs. It's shite, Perlman thought, an information brown-out. And suddenly the events of the day broke over him like the rush of a toxic tide and he was impatient and angry. Bannerjee — who'd once spouted from the pulpit of high moral rectitude even as he'd been dipping into the till and fleecing the public — was beginning to irritate him.

'I can do it, Shiv. Believe me. I can get a legal paper any time to go through Lindsay's files with a fucking microscope. Try me.'

Bannerjee clenched his hands together loosely. 'Even if I did get Joe to invest with your brother — and I'm not saying I did, please keep that at the front of your mind — how does it help you catch Lindsay's killer? Or Wexler's? I fail to see.'

'I'll put it to you this way. You expose one lie, Shiv, and it's like peeling back a scab. And beneath that scab, who knows, you might find the original wound, the cut, the scar, whatever it is. You might find the source of an infection.'

'By the same token, you might find nothing.'

273

'Then all I've wasted is my time,' Perlman said.

'I think you've just wasted some, Lou.'

Perlman was jangling. *Smoke, I must fucking smoke.* Circumspection annoyed the hell out of him. He deplored obfuscation, shilly-shallying, tiptoeing. 'I have a question, Shiv. In this new incarnation of yours, that of a man projecting a saintly image, *mea culpa* et cetera, can you afford a police and/or Inland Revenue investigation of any hidden monetary investments?'

'Saint? I'm no saint, I'm not trying to be one.'

'Answer the question, Shiv.'

'Why are you so *hostile*?'

'Because you piss me off.'

'You don't bring much in the way of tact to an interview, do you?'

'Tact's a tool that only takes you so far. When it comes to a scrum, you need to get dirty and hustle. If I'm not polite, Shiv, it's because I'm a very weary man. I live in this amazing citadel of lies and frankly I'm tired of it. And I don't believe much of what you say, old son. Try again. Tell me you don't know my brother. Tell me his name isn't familiar to you. Look me in the eye and tell me you just blindly gave Lindsay a big sum of money and said, Here, Joe, invest this where you like, I trust you.' Restless, agitated, Perlman got up. The leg clicked again. He walked to the window and saw the streetlamps and sparkling rain fall through them. 'What the fuck is it, Shiv? Are you worried about having invested the money? Or are you really *more* bothered that I might find out the truth about

274

where the money came from in the first place. What is it?'

'I think I should have my solicitor present, Sergeant, before we continue.'

Perlman felt a buzz in his blood, a hum in his skull. He was rolling, getting into his stride. 'Solicitor? Great. Call him. I'll go and get a warrant that gives me total licence to scour Lindsay's files and records. No sweat, Shiv. See you in court. I'll alert the press, of course. They're always cynical about born-again sinners.'

'Am I to be haunted the rest of my life by my past bloody mistakes?' Bannerjee asked.

'Are you? Who knows? Do you have a conscience, Shiv? Can you salvage your life by good works? Or is this charity of yours really all showbiz and photo opportunities?'

'I try, I try, God knows I try, I really do.' Bannerjee picked up the telephone and Perlman moved towards the door.

Bannerjee hung up and said, 'Wait, Lou.'

'I'm listening.'

'There's no guarantee that Lindsay kept a record of this alleged investment.'

'I'll take the chance, Shiv. It's no skin off my nose either way. What about *your* nose?'

Bannerjee smiled somewhat sadly, and for a second Perlman weakened: I feel sorry for the bastard, he thought. Maybe he *is* climbing the ladder of salvation, a man who deserves the chance to re-create himself. Who am I to judge, to bring him down?

Except he's lying. And saints don't fabricate.

Bannerjee said, 'I can't afford adverse publicity all over again, and you damn well know it. I'm not going through that bloody circus. No way. So I'll tell you this. All right, I *know* Colin. We met a couple of times when he was structuring an investment fund. I agreed to put in money, and I let Lindsay handle the fine print. It was that simple.'

Perlman said, 'So bloody simple you had to lie about it? Why?'

Bannerjee made a little wigwam of his fingers, tip pressed to tip. 'I failed to report the investment to the appropriate authorities.'

'Ah so. The box springs open.'

'I should have declared it. I should have told the tax people there was x amount of money in a fund in Aruba or wherever. I didn't. I suppose I was arrogant enough to think that three months in jail was adequate recompense for my sins, so why shouldn't I keep the money?'

'Colin hid it for you. How?'

'I don't know the mechanics of it. I suppose he buried it inside a money fund, and buried that inside another, a paper trail. He told me he was good at that. Believe me, I didn't ask.'

Dismayed suddenly, Perlman thought: *Colin, Colin, oh laddie, what have you done?* He was quiet a second: any exposure of Shiv Bannerjee would draw his brother into the same web. Colin with his suspect money deals and his dicky ticker, Bannerjee with his aspirations to global philanthropy — they'd both be smeared by a court case. He wondered how he'd feel if he was involved in the prosecution of his own brother.

Like shite, what else? But he had no evidence against Colin, only Bannerjee's hearsay. *I'm good at burying money.* Is that what Colin would have said? His exact words? Nobody could ever prove it. Colin would deny it. Money, Perlman thought. It was complex, paper trails were complex and difficult to pursue, computers were deliberately programmed with misinformation, companies that began life under one name cloned themselves under different ones, and then, like amoebae, went on dividing to infinity, and each division bore a different identity. He realized, with hindsight, that he'd sometimes wondered in a vague way about Colin's business affairs, the trips to places like Belize and the Bahamas and even to Havana in recent years. He'd imagined Colin meeting bankers and pseudobankers and assorted moneymen, travellers on the dollar and deutschmark highways, keepers of secret accounts, Boss-suited scoundrels who buried enormous amounts of loot in places where Revenue officers couldn't find them. He'd taken it for granted that where there were piles of *gelt* that had to be concealed in hidden honeycombs, so there were grey areas where laws might be broken, or at the very least 'rules' might be bent. Wasn't that in the nature of capitalism anyway? Earn a lot and watch it grow and grow and grow. But he was out of his depth with the intricacies of finance, and he'd never thought it through, and he'd never questioned Colin either. My brother. I gave him leeway. I bestowed my blessing by omission; I never asked how he accumulated his capital. Naïve, Sergeant.

'Where are the funds now?'

'I channelled some into this charity. Seed money.'

'Very noble,' Perlman said. 'And the rest?'

'Less noble, I'm afraid. I bought a fine house, and I stuck the rest in more offshore accounts. You're thinking what an admirable fellow I am, eh?'

'The halo needs Brasso. How much money is left?'

'A million, a little more.'

'Tidy,' Perlman said.

'I can't go through another investigation, Lou. You have no bloody idea what that's like. The indignity. The family shame. I'm being honest with you.'

'Be even *more* honest, Shiv. One last effort. Did you know Wexler?'

Bannerjee sighed like a man harpooned and breathing his last. 'Yes, yes. I knew him.'

'Vaguely? Intimately? How?'

'Hardly at all. Lindsay introduced him to me.'

'And you didn't socialize? You didn't get into any funny-money schemes with Artie?'

'No, on both counts. I didn't like him much. As for money, no, I didn't trust him.'

'Why are they both dead, Shiv?'

'Now how would I know such a thing?'

'Their names weren't picked out of a hat. It wasn't some lethal lottery type of thing. Did they swindle somebody, Shiv?'

'I don't know,' Bannerjee said.

'You're not lying to me again?'

'No, no I'm not.'

Perlman listened to rain on the glass. Wind roared at the frame of the building. He thought of the same wind blowing up through Gourock and Greenock and Port Glasgow, ruffling the Clyde.

Bannerjee said, 'We've talked in confidence, I trust.'

'Are you asking me if I'll keep this information to myself? I can't give promises, Shiv. Not even where my brother's involved.'

'The fine upstanding policeman, eh? You're looking for a little nobility of your own, are you?'

'Nobility? That's too grand for me. I'm only trying to make sense of what's happening in this messy little corner of the world I occupy.'

'Infinitely more difficult than being *noble*,' Bannerjee said. 'I'd be careful, Lou. I'd be mindful of your brother's welfare. I really would.'

'Your concern is noted.'

'I mean it. Keep picking that scab you were talking about, and you may find out more about Colin than you really want to know.'

Did he want to know more? Did he want to know whether there might be other layers of deceit and sleight-of-hand? He didn't like to think of Colin sinking in a bog of fiscal shenanigans.

He opened the door.

Bannerjee said, 'You understand, of course, I can always deny we talked about anything.'

'Goes without saying.'

'Your word against mine.'

'I wonder who they'd believe, Shiv.'

'I wonder too,' Bannerjee said. 'SB Worldwide is sponsoring a programme to open schools for the blind in Soweto. We open our first next month. In the Sahara, we're working on raising funds for deep wells. What can you say *you're* doing, Lou?'

'In global terms I'm not such a *mensch* as you,' Perlman said. 'I spend all my time on the local level, digging through the hard outer crust of this city. Some days I think I'll never discover what *really* lies beneath Glasgow. But I persevere, Shiv. I don't know any other way. Thanks for your time.'

Perlman stopped in the threshold and swung round. One last sneak attack. 'When did you last attend a Nexus gathering?'

Bannerjee opened his mouth reflexively to reply, then he smiled. 'A what, Lou?'

'It doesn't matter.'

Perlman rode down in the lift, listening to Muzak, a sanitized version of 'Take the 'A' Train': sacrilege.

His nerves screeched. Colin, he thought. Stupid fucker.

★   ★   ★

Outside, he called Sandy Scullion's direct line at Force HQ.

'I was about to send a search party out for you,' Scullion said. 'What news?'

'Let's meet. I'll pick you up in Pitt Street in five minutes.'

'You're doing the *driving*?'

'Does that send a chill through your balls, Sandy?'

'Are you sure you have a full licence?' Scullion asked.

'Funny man.'

40

Marak stood outside an electronics shop in Maryhill Road and stared at some fifty TV screens transmitting the same image in the big front window. Black rain soaked him, but he didn't feel it. He was engrossed by the newsreel footage unfolding mutely behind glass. The cul-de-sac, the police cars, the ambulance, he recognized it all. He wanted to hear what was being said by the blonde female with the microphone, so he entered the shop.

. . . lack of any motive behind the vicious slaying of Mr Wexler. Detective-Superintendent Mary Gibson said she was shocked by the brutality of the decapitation. Strathclyde Police have set up a confidential hotline . . . Marak tuned the rest of it out, he'd heard enough, but the images fascinated him a while longer and he felt paralysed by the dreamy motion of light and colour. He thought he might somehow make an escape into the secret world behind the screen, a cathode-ray reality where everything passed in a blur.

A sales assistant, a young man in white shirt and black tie, asked if he could be of any help.

'Help?' Marak asked.

'Was there something you wanted to see? There's a special offer on Sanyo portable tellies this week. Dirt-cheap, lovely colour. Very sharp.'

Marak shook his head. He didn't want

anything. He backed away. The young man seemed surprised by Marak's sudden movement.

'You won't get a better price anywhere in the city, I give you my personal guarantee, sir.'

Marak retreated to the street. He stood in the rain and shivered. His shoes leaked. His socks were wet and clung to his skin. He was aware of the sales assistant watching him from behind the glass. He walked away with his head down, not absolutely sure where he was going. The flat was nearby somewhere, he only had to find the right street. But dare he go inside the building? What if the cop who'd chased him had tracked him down? Or what if Ramsay had betrayed him for reasons too obscure to be understood? How did things work in this city? How were transactions between men conducted?

Wexler had been murdered. Lindsay was dead.

Rain slithered into his eyes and he blinked. He dabbed his beard with his scarf. He felt he was turning into water. Everything he'd come here to do was being taken away from him. Somebody was dispossessing him.

He slowed his walk. Kids stood in the shelter of closes and smoked. They observed him pass. A stranger, bearded, a foreigner, somebody to mock. He heard them laugh behind his back. When he reached Braeside Street he climbed the stairs of the tenement and he paused, listening to the drum of his pulses. These nerves. He took his knife from his pocket, slipped it out of the leather sheath. He concealed the weapon in his hand, and continued to go up. When he reached the top floor he saw nothing out of the ordinary.

He unlocked the door and went inside the flat.

In the living room Ramsay stood with his back to the bars of the electric fire. The big man, Ramsay's companion, leaned against the wall and looked sullen. Ramsay's tuft of yellow hair appeared waxy. He held out an envelope which Marak didn't take.

'He's got himself a knife,' Ramsay said.

'Aye, I see,' the big man said.

'Handsome thing,' Ramsay said. 'Victor Morris, eh?'

They watch me all the time, Marak thought. Wherever I go.

'Put the blade away now, Abdullah,' Ramsay said. 'Take the envelope.'

Marak shook his head. 'The police know what I look like.'

'How do you come to that conclusion?'

'One of them recognized me today,' Marak said.

'You sure?'

'Of course I'm sure.'

Ramsay glanced at his companion a second. 'Buncha wankers, Marak. They know sweet fuck all. Don't let them bother you. Put the knife away and take the envelope.'

'How do they know what I look like? How could they possibly know? I went to that street in a taxi, and I had to turn around and leave again immediately when I saw all the police cars. One of the policemen chased me on foot. Why? How did he know me?'

'Listen. A cop sees a stranger in a taxi coming into a street where there's a big crime, you can

284

bet your arse he's going to be suspicious, especially when that somebody in a taxi makes a quick exit. Stands to reason. It looks suspicious, Abdullah.'

'Maybe so. Maybe you're correct. I don't know. They might even know where I live. They could be here at any minute — '

'Abdullah, they don't know where you live or they'd be here now, a whole fucking posse of them.'

Marak didn't move. 'What is the point of another envelope? Another picture, another name, what is the point? Lindsay died before I made contact with him. And now somebody murdered Wexler. Who killed him? How do you explain these things, Ramsay? Two names from you, both dead.'

'I can't explain. You're foaming at the mouth, friend. Screw the bobbin. Get a grip, for fuck's sake.'

Marak wiped the back of his sleeve across his lips. He noticed the big man gaze at the knife with more than casual interest. He thought: All this way to fail. Everything was spinning away, moving beyond his outstretched hand.

'Did you tell the police about me?' he asked.

Ramsay said, 'Think about that for a minute. You're my meal-ticket, Abdullah. You're my luncheon-voucher, for Christ's sake. Why would I drop you in the shite? Take the envelope. Do whatever you have to do. This is the last one, Abdullah.'

Marak stared at the manila envelope. He remembered pressing a cold wet cloth to his mother's fevered forehead, and Dr Solomon saying: *the prognosis is gloomy*. The motion of the fan, the bottle on the bedside table that contained aloe vera oil the nurses rubbed into her skin to keep it from drying out, the solitary lily, replaced daily, in a thin-stemmed vase. The memories that had filled him with sorrow and fogged his vision before — he *needed* them now, he needed to be in touch with the details of the hatred that had brought him here in the first place. Remember the horror. Remember remember. A man dies in a dry street on a blue day under a hot blood-orange sun. His hand touches yours as he enters the last darkness. He slips away from you, his hand goes limp in your fingers, there are figures in doorways, they rush towards the fallen man. And you, Marak, you try to keep the crowd away even as you hold your father's body. But people converge in shock, and women scream and cry, and little children stare numbly, there is always death here, always the gun, always. The music of this land is the music of the automatic rifle. Tak-tak-tak-tak. This is what you need to bring back in all its repugnance.

Otherwise, you will not be strong.

Ho chalashim lo matslichim. The weak win nothing.

'Take the bloody thing, Abdullah,' Ramsay said, pushing the envelope forward.

Marak looked into Ramsay's eyes. 'This is the last one? You're sure?'

'Aye. Then you can bugger off all the way home, Abdullah.'

Marak took the envelope. He didn't open it. My last chance, he thought. What lies in here might be my redemption. And then home. He realized he hadn't thought about the return journey. He understood that the machinery set in place for his outward trip would play no role in his return. It had probably been dismantled instantly for security reasons. It was the nature of these allegiances that they came into existence for only a brief time.

He'd be on his own. But it didn't matter. He'd make his way back.

'Have you ever hated, Ramsay?' he asked.

'A few people have regretted crossing my path,' Ramsay said.

'No, you don't understand. I'm talking about the kind of hatred that consumes you. It never stops. You nurture it. You're addicted to the feeling. When you lose sight of it, you're empty.'

Ramsay shuffled his feet, said nothing.

Marak thought: he grasps only localized hatred, specific moments of loathing. He doesn't carry it day to day, minute to minute, like an incurable ill in the blood. You have to hate with the certainty of sunrise, or the waxing and waning of moons. He had an image of his mother slicing melons on the long plain wood table at the back of the house in a neighbourhood near HaNassis Avenue, and his young brothers sitting and joking, and his sister combing her long black hair. Such a pretty girl. And his father, yes, presiding in his benign way over this regular family occurrence, this simple business of slicing fruit, sharing and laughing.

The dinners of spinach and haricot beans, sometimes called *espinakas kon avas*. Or Chicken Polo, rich with apricots and cinnamon. He could even taste the apricots; a remembrance of summer here in this city locked by the deadbolt of winter. He remembered the cable car between Stelle Maris and Bat Galim, the strolls along the promenade.

Those were sweet, sweet times.

And always laughter. Laughter was what he remembered most.

Except for the gunfire.

He opened the envelope. He looked inside.

Ramsay said, 'Listen, eh, Marak . . . Good luck, chief. Good luck.'

41

Leo Kilroy said, 'I told the cardinal to his face. Red isn't your colour, sunshine.'

'This is how you talk to cardinals?' Bannerjee asked.

'All the time. They know who butters their bread in this burg, Shiv. I get away with bloody murder. Pass me the tomato sauce, would you?'

Shiv Bannerjee slid the plastic tomato-shaped container across the table and wondered what it was that attracted Leo Kilroy, in his long brown cashmere coat and tan silk cravat and two-tone brown and white brogues, to such a greasy spoon as the Bluebird Café in Yoker. Yoker, for God's sake, nobody ever went to Yoker, which was beyond the western boundary of the city and famous only for its underwear factory.

And the menu here, oh dear lord — it consisted of some dreadful proletarian dishes: sausages, mashed potatoes and baked beans, Scotch mutton pie and baked beans, or egg and chips and baked beans. Bloody baked beans. The walls were dull dun and oily, and the window was steamed with condensation. A curtain of tobacco-cured lace hung against the pane. The grease-spotted menu, typed on cheap A4 paper, lay on the table.

Bannerjee noticed the only dessert was spotted dick. Why did they spot it? he wondered. Why didn't they just overlook it?

Kilroy speared a chip with his fork and studied it. It dripped red sauce into his fried egg. 'Formica Hell, am I right? That's what you're thinking.'

'Along those lines,' Bannerjee said.

'It's pure nostalgia. I love this place,' Leo Kilroy said. 'I was born in the next street. I've been coming here since I was wee and thin. I wasn't *born* looking like a bloody dirigible. The ambience here, Shiv. The sheer disregard of taste, style, colour. The idea that no dinner is complete without the garnish of at least one fried human hair or a couple of rodent droppings, this takes me back to when life was a simple matter. The old Bluebird hasn't changed in years. How's your sausage?'

Bannerjee said, 'It's a bit long in the tooth, Leo.'

'Gamey. As it should be.' Kilroy stuffed the chip into his small mouth and chewed. His fat cheeks wobbled. 'Wait till you try the coffee. If you don't find it lukewarm with undissolved brown granules floating on top, ask for your money back.'

An old woman in a very dirty apron appeared near their booth. She wore a hearing aid and shouted when she spoke. 'Everything awright there, Mr Kilroy?'

'Just dandy, Mrs Bane. As always. You never fail to impress. My compliments to the chef.' Kilroy made a kissing gesture of appreciation, fingers bunched to lips.

The old woman said, 'Don't be dropping any

290

grease on that good coat, you hear? Musta costa fortune.'

'I'll be careful, Mrs Bane.'

'I see some poor bastard got his head chopped off.'

'Dreadful business, Mrs Bane.'

'Aye, aye. World's been going to hell since Churchill passed on.' The woman shuffled away into a back room.

'Chef, did you say?' Bannerjee asked.

'Dear old Mr Bane does the cooking in what he calls a kitchen, and what the health authorities would gladly condemn. I've, ah, intervened a few times on Mr Banes's behalf. A little *baksheesh* does wonders.'

Bannerjee noticed that the only other diner was a rake-skinny man with thick-lensed glasses who read a newspaper propped against an HP sauce bottle. Part of the front-page headline was readable: *orror in Suburbs*. Poor Wexler and his fragile mental condition; he'd waded most of the time in the molasses of guilt. And now he was dead. And Lindsay too.

Lou Perlman had asked: *Why are they both dead?*

Bannerjee's thoughts drifted to the Detective-Sergeant; he decided Perlman wasn't really a danger. It came down to who said what and when, and the beauty of two-party conversations was the fact that either party could deny the other's claim to veracity. And if Perlman or some *apparatchik* from Pitt Street rummaged through Lindsay's files, what was he going to find that might not incriminate Colin? Given that Lindsay had *left* anything to find, of course. Bannerjee was fifty-fifty about that. Some snippet, some handwritten record, some diary reference from those times, it was always *possible* Lindsay had written a sentence or two down, perhaps even coded in some way, because the little solicitor loved secrets, and hushed conversations in the corners of quiet restaurants, and the idea he was privy to clandestine information. He was a small man who longed to hang around in places where the big boys traded gossip; a fantasist who buried himself in books about secret agents.

Poor old Joe.

And Lou Perlman, crusading for truth and justice out there in the alleys and dull-lit streets of the city, would surely draw the line when it came to his sick brother. You couldn't be certain, of course. There was never certainty. It was another fifty-fifty call. But Shiv Bannerjee had gambled most of his life. The trick was to make sure your arse was covered. He'd been truthful to Perlman, up to a point, that crucial point beyond which you do not go.

All things considered, he felt secure.

'My man worked out for you, I take it,' Kilroy said.

'Very well indeed,' Bannerjee said.

'I always felt that particular arrangement had a gorgeous symmetry,' Kilroy said. 'You pay him and it comes straight to me. Recycling cash. Keeping the flow rolling. You should see the pure *ambition* in his eyes. He carries around an aura that is eye-popping. I love to have somebody jigging on a wire. And all because he wants a rat-infested room at the top of a building shortly to be condemned. He doesn't know, of course, that the place is scheduled for the wrecking ball. Why spoil his fun? People entertain such sorry dreams. I sometimes think Glasgow is precisely the city for small dreams. I see disappointment all about me, sad faces, tubercular expressions, people hurrying through the rain looking miserable. Spotted dick, Shiv?'

'I'll pass.'

Bannerjee's stomach made a gurgling sound. He studied Kilroy a moment. He was a man of contradictions, bizarrely attached to this e-coli eatery on the one hand, and fond of a fine meal and a rich Havana at Number One Devonshire on the other. The eccentricities of his clothing suggested a desire for attention, and yet the details of his private life were scarce. Bannerjee could list on the fingers of one hand what he'd learned about Kilroy's world. He was a collector of twentieth-century Glasgow oil-paintings, a devoted fan of Partick Thistle Football Club, the least fashionable team in the city — excluding Queen's Park; he was a slum landlord, a devout Catholic, a pal of bishops and cardinals, and he consorted with some of the most notorious gangsters around. He knew judges and was said to be a friend of the Procurator-Fiscal.

Kilroy examined his hands, breathed on his rings, then buffed them with the sleeve of his coat. 'Are you finished with him now?' he asked in his honking way.

Bannerjee said, 'Done.'

'Then that's that. Is he paid off?'

'He will be very soon.'

'And what did he do for his twenty grand?'

'He delivered two envelopes.'

'Two envelopes? Very nice work if you can get it . . . This is one of my talents, Shiv. I bring people together and I make them fit. You want something, I want something, my man wants something. I join the dots. I knew he'd work out. So. End of story. In the immortal words of Zimmerman, the bard of Hibbing, you go your way and I go mine.'

'Next time we meet, Leo, let me choose the place.'

'We never meet, Shiv. Oh, we run into one another now and again at this function or that, limos passing in the night, but we rarely have a one-on-one these days. *Mano a mano*. We used to meet more in the old days when you were going like a bat out of hell for public office. I'll never forgive you for blowing it, Shivvie. It would've been very nice to have a sympathetic ear in Westminster. Useful too. My pal the MP.'

'But I was weak.' Bannerjee started to rise.

Kilroy touched the back of Shiv Bannerjee's arm. 'You're leaving? No coffee?'

'I have a date, Leo.'

'Do tell. Is she gorgeous?'

'The eye of the beholder,' Bannerjee said. 'She's too young for me, really. She has enthusiasms I can't even remember having in my youth. I won't go into detail. We meet every Thursday.'

'A standing engagement, if you'll pardon the expression?'

'You're forgiven.'

'My my. You're infuriating. You won't tell me about the girl. So talk to me about these two envelopes. What do they contain? I'm aching to know.'

'There's nothing I can tell you, Leo.'

Kilroy laughed and prodded Bannerjee with his cane. 'You sly old Indian, you don't give anything away.'

'We're an inscrutable race.' Bannerjee moved towards the door.

'I thought that was the Chinese,' Kilroy said.

'They don't compare, Leo.' Raising a hand, Bannerjee stepped outside. Kilroy watched him go. The small bell above the door shook and rung. Goodbye Shiv, goodbye.

'Mrs Bane,' Kilroy shouted. '*Mrs Bane!*'

The deaf old dear appeared, her head tilted in Leo Kilroy's direction. 'Did you call for me?'

'I certainly did. Bring me a cup of your finest java, wench.'

'I'll bloody wench you, Leo Kilroy. You're not so big I couldn't smack you a sharp one round the lugs.'

Kilroy laughed. 'You're a bold old biddy, Mrs Bane. Nobody else would even *dream* of talking to me like that.'

Mrs Bane didn't hear him; she'd already turned and gone into the kitchen. Kilroy looked at the door swinging shut behind her and thought: two envelopes.

Bad arithmetic, my Asian friend. Three.

42

Lou Perlman parked outside the Loch Fynne Mussel Bar in the Gallowgate, a thoroughfare that connected the East End of Glasgow with the boundary of the city centre, where the Saltmarket met High Street. The Gallowgate had always had a wretched reputation, a street of old tenements and mean-faced pubs and violence. Now, most of the tenements had been replaced by staid little houses, but in the slow-falling rain the area still looked drab.

A man in green wellington boots stepped out of the Loch Fynne and sloshed the pavement with a bucket of brackish water. He eyed Perlman and Scullion with open suspicion. A smell of the ocean wafted out of the bar into the rain.

Perlman sidestepped the flood and said, 'You want to be careful with that slime.'

The man said, 'It's raining, mister. What difference does it make if I pour water on the pavement?'

'You're in violation of City Regulation 3978,' Perlman lied.

'Take your regulation and shove it.'

'A graduate of the East End School of Charm, eh? I hope you claimed a refund of the tuition fee,' Perlman asked.

Scullion said, 'Lou, forget it. Come on.'

'What is it with some people? Is it something

296

they imbibe? Is there poison leaking from a faulty sewage-pipe underground?'

The man with the bucket glared at Perlman and said, 'Ford Mondeo, eh? Peesa shite car.'

Perlman gave into childish impulse and flashed a V. He wondered at the nature of this short encounter. The flood of water around his feet, the bucket swung with intent to soak, the general nastiness. Blame the way Glasgow, in monochromatic drear December when all things die, creates disaffection. The people succumb to the drab weight of the season. They huddle by fires, and hibernate in their own resentments. They dream of their own perfumed Araby: the lager dens of the Costa Del Sol.

Scullion said, 'Why let that arsehole rile you?'

Perlman knew the answer, but didn't say so. The man's hostility was irrelevant. Perlman's irritation had its source in Bannerjee's farewell shot: *Keep picking and you may find out more about Colin than you want to know.* How much do I want to know about my brother and his wrongdoings, if that was what they were? And how much was bluff from Bannerjee anyway? The man had been a damn chancer all his career. He was a liar, a villain who'd sucked the milk of the holy cow of high office.

Perlman and Scullion crossed the street through traffic.

Perlman asked, 'Any luck tracing the taxi?'

'We found the driver, no bother. He remembered the passenger. He picked him up at the corner of Robertson Street and Argyle, drove him out to Lassiter Place, did a swift turn, then dropped him close to Shawlands Cross. He thinks he saw the passenger go inside a supermarket, he wasn't sure.'

'Anything else?'

'Nervous guy, that was all he said. Told the driver he had somebody to visit in the cul-de-sac. Nothing new from the circulated print yet. You haven't told me what you've been up to. Mary Gibson thought you were going to see Shiv Bannerjee.'

'That's what I did.'

'Don't rush to tell me, Lou.'

'Lindsay was Bannerjee's solicitor. There's a whiff of financial knavery.' What to say that wouldn't involve Colin? And if evidence existed that *would* hurt Colin, its emergence would pain Miriam too. She loved her husband, after all. She'd made a point of saying so. Still, you'd protect her, wouldn't you? You'd be gallant, Lou, right? The lover's heart is blindfold.

It was a bloody balancing act, a wonky gyroscope on a taut string.

'What else would you expect with Bannerjee?' Scullion asked.

'He's working to repent. He says.'

'I'm Mother Teresa.'

'Under a wee bit of pressure, he admitted he knew Wexler. But . . . '

'But what?'

'I don't know how honest he was being with me. You know those characters that are halfway honest and they sound like they're spooning you rich cream, but they're really skimming? That's the feeling I got.'

They entered a building that had been a warehouse of some kind at one time. The air smelled of cats, excrement, cigarettes, dirty bedding: the dregs of a subterranean world. A half-hearted attempt, completely doomed, had been made to convert the building into something else, apartments and lofts, more lofts, Glasgow was threatening to become a city of bloody lofts.

Perlman and Scullion had to push aside some strands of barbed-wire and pieces of plywood to get inside. Scullion said, 'This should really keep out the riff-raff. By the way, mind telling me what we're doing here, Lou?'

'Quick and Furfee and the Dogue Affair.'

'Furfee? I knew he was out of jail, but I didn't know he was back in Glasgow.'

'He's back all right.'

An orange-tinted sign for Club Memphis — ROCK ALL THE WAY TO THE TOP ROCK-LOVERS! — peeled from a wall where a thirty-watt light hung from the ceiling. The two men climbed the stairs slowly, passing unfinished conversions, bare rooms where graffiti artists with demonic graphic styles had been at work, and electric wires dangled from walls covered with menacing multi-coloured runes. Glass crackled underfoot, lightbulbs, bottles, syringes. Vandals and winos dossed here regularly. A pong of used condom, rubbery and seminiferous, was apparent. Abrupt couplings in the dark, the exchange of body fluids between drunk strangers. *Oh, Jessie, I love you, if that's yer name.* There were empty sleeping bags here and there, and a kerosene lamp, guttered-down candles, some kitchen utensils, piles of clothing, little puddles of piss, a few fat jobbies in a corner.

A squat.

On the top floor they paused outside the glossy red door of Club Memphis. Messages and names and assorted arcana had been carved into the door.

Wee Cumby No Deid

WATP

FERGAL WANKA ☺

Perlman tried the handle; locked.

'So do we kick the door down?' Perlman asked.

'You up for it?'

Perlman shook his head. 'Christ no, I'd bounce off it. Jimmy the lock.'

'With what?'

'A hairpin.'

'I left my hairpins at home in my makeup bag, Lou.'

Perlman banged the door with his fist. 'Hallo. Hallo in there.'

No answer.

'I'll kick it down,' Scullion said.

'You fit for that?'

'We'll see.' Scullion shrugged, took a few steps back, and was about to lunge a foot when a voice emerged from behind the closed door.

'Aye? Who's there?'

'Police,' Scullion said.

'Whatcha want?'

'A minute of your time,' Scullion said.

Perlman had a slightly uneasy moment: you

never knew what lay beyond a closed door. Unarmed, you felt vulnerable. What if the door opened suddenly and a gunman faced you and you were a point-blank target? It had never happened to him, but it was always an edgy consideration as guns filtered into the city in increasing numbers. He loathed firearms. He was pleased he didn't have to carry one — but sometimes you felt the cold hand on the back of your neck and the fearful rush of adrenaline and you wished you had something more comforting than your fists and your luck to fall back on.

A crack appeared, a face in the slit. Scullion shoved the door with his shoulder. The impact forced BJ Quick to stagger a couple of steps back. Perlman followed Sandy inside. A big bare space, fag-ends on the floor, a chair: depressing. Club Memphis, if it had ever flourished, must have had all the ambience of a World War II Anderson air-raid shelter.

Quick asked, 'What's the fucking game?'

Perlman said, 'Hello, BJ, you sorry old shitebag.'

'This is a private club, Perlman, fuck off.'

'Don't be like that, Bobby J. We're pals. Should Auld Acquaintance Be Forgot and so on.'

'Up yours,' Quick said.

'Come on, don't offend me. I'm sensitive. Show me you care.' Perlman seized Quick's hand and squeezed it as tightly as he could. His grip was in far better condition than his lungs. 'We've been around the block together, you and me. Bloody magic to see you again, chief. How's it going? Not too well by the look of things here.'

301

Quick grimaced. His eyes watered. 'Hey, Perlman, let go the haaaaand, eh?'

Furfee emerged out of the shadows at the other end of the room.

'Look what the cat dragged in,' Scullion said. 'What's the story, Willie?'

Perlman asked, 'Skinned anybody lately?'

'I was in jail,' Furfee said and looked surly.

'Let go my fucking *hand*,' Quick said again.

Perlman didn't relent. He loved the idea that he still had this power in his fingers. It made him feel young and gallus. Superman, steel hands. His hair was dark and his stomach flat and his cape had no creases.

Quick said, 'Bloody police brutality.'

'It's a friendly handshake, Bobby,' Perlman said.

'My arse it is. You're hurting me, Perlman. Awright, you've proved your point. You're strong. I'm dead impressed.'

'I should waste my time trying to impress you, Bobby? Are you still interfering with underage girls?'

'Nobody's ever proved that, Perlman.'

'I can sniff the whiff of perversity on you, Bobby. I have half a mind to throw you out that window head-first. It would be my most worthy contribution to mankind. I'd get some kind of award for it. Mibbe my face on a coin, or a postage stamp.' Perlman released him. He didn't approve of Quick. He didn't like that whole sorry lifestyle, international Web allegiances and graphic porno website galleries where wee girls posed lewd, and the sleaze of it all. The way he'd squeezed Quick's hand was unprofessional, but he didn't regret the lapse; he knew he'd crush the hand all over again without thinking. And worse. All he needed was an excuse.

Quick said, 'Bursting the door down. Fucking police, think they can do anything. We live in a fascist state, Perlman.'

'What would you know about fascism, Bobby?' Perlman gazed round the room. The only chair in the place was surrounded by dried bloodstains. He walked in a circle round them. They were brown, but didn't look aged; they hadn't had time to be absorbed by the wooden floorboards. 'What happened here?'

Quick said, 'Shaving cut.'

'Must've been one hell of a big jaw.'

'What do the pair of you want anyway?'

Sandy Scullion said, 'Tell us about Terry.'

'Terry who?'

'Dogue,' Scullion said.

'You know a Terry Dogue, Furf?' Quick asked. Furf said, 'No.'

'You're pissing against the wrong lamp-post,' Quick said to Scullion.

Scullion said, 'Dogue was found with his throat cut.'

'Oh aye?' Furfee said.

Scullion said, 'And you being handy with a razor, well, you're on the list, Willie.'

'He's a changed man. I can vouch for Furf,' Quick said.

'Hitler once vouched for Stalin,' Perlman said. 'Let's go the easy route. It's less scenic, but it's direct. Where were you last night?'

Furfee looked at Quick for guidance. Perlman stepped promptly into Furf's line of vision. 'No cheating, Willie. No eye contact. Straight question. Last night. Where were you?'

'Here. There.'

'Can you show me here and there on a map, Willie?' Perlman walked closer to Furfee.

Quick said, 'Tell him nothing, Furf. I'll call my lawyer. Right now. Just tell this sarcastic old wanker fuck all.'

Perlman said, 'I object to that description of me, BJ. It's been years since I wanked.'

Scullion said, 'Call your lawyer if you like, BJ. It doesn't bother us. Look. Here's a phone.' He reached down and picked up an old black handset from the floor and passed it to Quick, who took it in a somewhat deflated manner.

'It's been cut off,' Quick said. 'I had a disagreement with those Telecom bastards.'

'Maybe there's another phone somewhere in the building,' Scullion said.

'This building? You're joking,' Quick said.

'Then you'll find one in a pub somewhere.'

'Try the Saracen's Head,' Perlman suggested. 'It's along the street.'

Quick tugged at his outcrop of hair. 'I'll do it later.'

'Afraid to leave Willie on his tod?' Perlman asked.

'Willie can handle himself, Perlman.'

Perlman looked into Furfee's eyes. They were dull, bovine. He was reminded of the eyes of a waxwork figure. He'd always found the likenesses at Madame Tussaud's sinister. As was

304

Furfee. He wasn't one of the front-runners in the brainbox steeplechase, but somehow that made him even more creepy and dangerous.

'You remembered yet, Willie?'

'I was walking.'

'And?'

'Had a beer somewhere.'

'Where?'

'Pub. I don't remember the name.'

'Where's this pub?'

'Bellahouston.'

'Bellahouston, eh? Alone?'

'Aye — '

'Barman see you? Anybody that might remember you?'

'No — '

'Try. Remember the name of the pub. The street.' Perlman moved very close to Furfee. 'Tell me. You carrying a blade even as we have this little tête-à-tête?'

Furfee said, 'No.'

'I don't altogether believe you, Furf. I'd like to have a gander. Okay with you? Turn out your pockets for me.'

Quick said, 'Don't let him search you, Furf. He doesn't have the *right*.'

'You're annoying me, Quick,' Perlman said. 'I'm simply asking Furfee if he minds showing me what he has in his pockets. It's up to him.'

'I mind,' Furfee said.

'So you're hiding something,' Perlman said. Furfee shook his head. 'Nothing.'

'You're sure, Willie?' Perlman asked.

'I'm sure,' Furfee said.

'Okay.' Perlman turned away: let Furfee stew in denial a moment, he thought. Change the angle. He walked back towards BJ Quick, who looked as tense as an eager dog restrained by a leash. 'Bobby, are you categorically telling me you have no knowledge whatsoever of Terry Dogue? I want you to think before you answer.'

The trick here, Lou Perlman thought, was to suggest that you knew the answer before you even asked the question; it was a matter of manner, of tone. *Think before you answer* was a handy little admonition that, delivered with just the right touch of assurance and authority, could place a spark of doubt in the other person's mind. *The cop knows something. He's got a snapshot of me and Dogue walking along the Broomielaw.*

BJ Quick wasn't buying. 'I never heard of him. That's the last time I'm telling you. We finished now?'

'One last thing,' and Perlman suddenly reached inside his coat and whipped out a copy of the still made from the security video and he flashed it under Quick's face. 'Tell me about this guy, BJ. Who he? What name?'

'Never seen him in my life,' Quick said.

'You're sure.'

'Positive.'

Irritated and impatient, Perlman said, 'Terry Dogue was seen following him. This guy's the one attacked Terry. Why would this character do that to Dogue?'

'This is fascinating, Perlman. Yawn. Zzzzz. Snore.'

Perlman turned, quickly shoved the print in front of Furfee's face. 'You seen this man, Furfee?'

'Never.'

'Look closer.'

'Nope. Never seen him.'

'Here. Look really fucking *close*, Willie.' Perlman pushed the print right up against Furfee's mouth. His impatience was changing to anger. It was a hot feeling, like standing in front of an open fire and unable to retreat from the flame because you were impeded in some way.

Furfee stepped back. 'Hey, hold on, wait — '

Perlman shoved the paper forward again, as if he meant to stuff it between the big man's lips. Paper couldn't hurt; what he wanted was something hard and sharp to stick into Furfee's big dumb criminal face; but it was more than that, more than Furfee, he wanted to take apart the mean stupidity of waste and violence he saw every day of his life, it was Moon Riley bursting Sadie's face with his knuckles, and anaemic teenage girls on the game, screwing drunks at the back of closes and giving blow jobs in alleys, it was BJ Quick scanning porno websites for naked nine-year-olds, it was the epidemic of vandalism, and the mountains of trash, the broken streetlamps and the burnt-out phone booths and the boarded-up windows of abandoned houses, and it was Furfee skinning some bastard's arm as you might the haunch of a dead stag, it was all this foul *stuff* that came rushing at him like black hearses in an insane hurry to disgorge their dead — and it crystallized in the sight of Willie Furfee's big sullen mouth.

'Here, eat *this*,' and he forced the creased paper against Furfee's teeth. He sensed the mouth behind, the black hollow, the throat; that was where he wanted to cram this print. Right down the Peeler's gullet, and may he choke on it.

Sandy Scullion said, 'Hey Lou, calm it, for Christ's sake.'

'Don't react, Willie,' Quick said. 'Don't lift a finger. Take what he gives and do fuck all about it, understand me? It's fucking *provocation*.'

Perlman stepped away from Furfee, suddenly aware of Furfee's shoelace-thin tie and the three-quarter-length coat and the black velvet collar. Something stirred in the hinterland of memory. Black velvet. He was breathing a little too hard for his own peace of mind. Keep the temper. Never lose the rag. It's bad for the whole nervous system. He tried to relax and to clamber out of the crazy mood that had overcome him a moment before, and he looked at Furfee in a manner that might almost have been one of patience, but not quite.

'Nice coat, Willie.'

'It's original,' Furfee said. 'Made in 1957.'

'And you're proud of it.' Perlman fingered the velvet collar. 'Fine stitching. Let me take a shot in the dark here, Willie. Were you at the Royal Infirmary last night?'

'What're you on about?' Furfee said.

'You were at the Royal last night and you took Terry Dogue out of there. Am I right?'

'No bloody way.'

Perlman said, 'It's easy to prove or disprove.

308

I've got an eyewitness, Furfee. Let her take a good look at you and we can clear this up in a twinkling.'

BJ Quick said, 'He's bullshitting, Furf. It's a scam.'

Perlman looked at Scullion. 'Can we take Willie to the Royal, Inspector, and let our eyewitness look him over?'

'Great idea.'

Perlman asked, 'You don't object, Willie?'

Furfee said, 'Telling you. I was nowhere near the Royal — '

'Then you don't mind a quick ride over there, do you?'

'Aye, well, as it happens — '

'Willie. You can do it the nice civilized way. Or we can send for a van and some uniforms and they'll cuff you and we'll all go to hospital together. What do you say?'

Furfee looked stricken.

BJ Quick shouted, 'You're under no *obligation*, Furf. None at all. These cretins don't have a legal leg to *stand* on.'

Furfee, an animal backed into a corner, stood as if petrified. It was clear to Perlman that the big man didn't know what to do; he was so accustomed to obeying the commands of BJ Quick he might have been the rockmeister's wooden-headed lapdummy. His brain was probably scrambled by sheer indecision. He was listening for messages, and hearing only static.

'Sandy, have you got your phone?'

Scullion took his mobile phone from his pocket. 'I'll buzz Pitt Street. We can have an

309

army here in less than ten minutes.'

Furfee had the razor in his hand and the blade open before Perlman even *registered* movement. He held the blade thrust outward. He lowered his shoulders and spread his legs. He went into pre-launch mode, tensed, muscles rigid, a big demon about to attack.

Quick said, 'You fucking *tit*. Put the razor away.'

'Good idea,' Perlman said. 'Just close the blade and put it back in your pocket, Willie.'

'The razor stays,' Furfee said.

Perlman stared at the blade. I keep truly dodgy company, he thought. Some hours ago he'd been looking at a lead pipe wielded by Moon Riley. And now this fine old-style open razor in the Peeler's hand. Sometimes you get days when all you run into are life-forms from the deepest dregs of the deepest stagnant pond, a place where pop-eyed tadpoles live among quivering black fronds and other unclassified species.

'Downright stupid, Willie,' he said.

'I'm out of here,' Furfee said. 'Anybody tries to stop me,' and he made a gesture with the blade. Bright steel shimmered. 'You. Put the phone down.'

Scullion set the phone on the floor. Perlman said, 'Leave here, Willie, and it might as well be a signed confession.'

'I'm confessing nothing.'

'Fucking bampot,' Quick said. 'Put the blade away, you big thick bastard.'

Perlman took a couple of steps forward, placing himself between Willie Furfee and the door. 'You skedaddle, Willie, and you're sending us a message, and that message says you don't want to run the risk of being ID'd at the Royal, because you don't want me to know you took Dogue out of there last night. And why don't you want me to know that, Willie? The only answer I can come up with is that you killed Terry. I'm prepared to bet that blade in your hand matches Dogue's wound exactly. I bet the blade fits right into the slit in Terry's gullet.'

Quick made a moaning sound of disbelief and said, 'Aw, *Jesus, Willie.*'

Perlman realized that Quick had made the assumption that the blade used to kill Dogue had been dumped. Why not? It was an obvious conclusion to draw. You kill a man, you clean the weapon and toss it. Bury it. Destroy it. Whatever. But Furfee hadn't dumped it because presumably he had an attachment to his antique razor that went beyond *Practical Murder and How to Get Away with It, an Introduction.* Rid yourself of the weapon. Don't forget that, students. Basic stuff. Maybe there was a mystical bond between the skinner and his tool, an attachment no average person could understand. Maybe Furfee slept with the damn razor under his pillow at night. It was a security blanket, a special toy, an object without which he felt a searing insecurity. Who knows? A psycho's mind wasn't an easy read.

The big man kept moving. When he reached the door he'd flee, and an unseemly chase would follow, and he'd sneak into the grid of dark streets that branched off the Gallowgate.

311

Perlman wondered if he had the courage to intervene. No weapon, no protection: what chance did he have against the Pollokshaws Peeler?

'Get out my way, Perlman,' Furfee said.

'Think,' Perlman said again.

'Step to the side.' Furfee waved the razor. It was as silver and fleet as a salmon leaping, and it came perilously close to Perlman's face.

'Next time it's your nose,' Furfee said.

'I'm attached to this nose, Willie. Had it a while.'

'You don't want to lose it, do you?' Furfee crouched as he made his way in the direction of the door. His reflexes were tuned to an invisible range in the upper register of instinct. A demented light had begun to burn in those hitherto dull eyes. The razor turns him on, Perlman thought. It's the source of his power, his thrills. He rules the world through a six-inch strip of honed steel. And I am his unwilling subject.

Furfee was a couple of feet from the exit now. Any second he'd be out the door and gone, lost in one of Glasgow's less penetrable neighbourhoods, narrow streets and back-courts and dank dunnies under the tenements. Perlman thought: Move, *do* something. But the notion was suicidal. Move and you get spliced to ribbons, flesh hanging off bone, blood geysering out of veins. He made an empty gesture with his hands, a so-what *I can't stop you leaving, Furfee.*

Then suddenly Quick was roaring past him, Quick as quick as his name, head down and charging. Perlman's first thought was that the deposed Monarch of Glasgow Rock was rushing for the exit but, whether deliberately or by accident, he collided hard with Furfee and the force knocked the big man back against the wall. Furfee gasped, reflexively slashing air with razor in criss-crossing patterns, gouging the side of Quick's neck with the blade.

'Ahhhh, holy Mary mothera *God*.' Quick held a hand to his neck and staggered away from Furfee, who turned to open the door, but Scullion was already at him, wondrously fast, swinging the chair in the air and bringing it down with marvellous ferocity against the side of the big man's skull. Perlman heard wood splinter and saw pieces of the shattered chair fly in the air and he remembered that Sandy had played scrum-half in his school rugby team, that he'd been a reserve for a place in the Scottish Under-18 national squad.

Sandy, a *nice* man, was also a tough one, tough enough to power in a couple of swift hefty kicks to the big man's head, then follow up with a knee into Furfee's adam's apple. Furfee crumpled, the razor fell out of his fingers and Perlman put a foot on it, then bent down to pick it up. It was surprisingly light, the handle smooth to touch. On his knees, Furfee looked up at the blade and blinked in the puzzled manner of a horse led up into light after years of working down a mineshaft. *I always wondered if there was a surface, a world outside*.

Scullion took the razor from Perlman, and held it against the back of Furfee's head, almost daring the Peeler to move, then threw his mobile for Perlman to catch. 'Call for assistance, Lou.'

'Right away,' Perlman said. He looked at Quick, who was lying under the window and bleeding freely from the neck.

'Mothera *God*. The *pain*.'

Perlman kneeled beside him. The wound was deep but it wasn't going to kill Quick, if he got attention soon.

'Thought you'd make a run for it, eh?' Perlman asked.

Quick stared at him. 'Run? Is that what you think? Run, my arse. I was acting like a good citizen. Man's a killer, for God's sake. And what thanks do I get?'

'Let me get this straight, Bobby. You *intended* to disarm Furfee?'

'Aye, I did. Of course I did.'

'You any idea how long it would take me to believe this pathetic story? Imagine the sun as a big black cinder and all the oceans dry. That's how long. You were *bolting*. You were obviously for the offski, Bobby. My guess is you realized Furfee hadn't tossed the razor and you didn't want to be implicated in anything he'd done and so you had some kind of brainstorm. But you made a right ballocks of it and ran head-first into your headcase associate. And you've just come up with this yarn. I hold my sides in laughter. And they said Vaudeville was dead.' Perlman began to punch in the number for Pitt Street.

'I was only thinking — mothera *Christ*! this cut *hurts* — how I might help you fellows out. Lend a hand like.'

'I hear music and there's no one there,' Perlman said. 'Let's stroll together into the real world. Nobody is going to believe you unless it's some *teuchter* down from his sheep farm for a day in the big city.'

'Perlman. Lou. Listen. If Furfee killed anybody — oh shite shite *shite* the pain — I don't want to be associated with anything like that. I stopped him getting away. Gimme some credit.'

'Don't even think about trying to con me.'

'I didn't know fuck all about him going to the hospital. Or any of this Terry Dogue stuff. I swear.'

'On your mother's grave.'

'My mother's not dead yet,' Quick said. 'But *I* might be if you don't get me some attention.'

'You're a self-serving prick. I'd love you to bleed to death. You want to survive? Talk to me about the man in the picture.'

'I know nothing about him, Perlman. Swear.'

'In the event of your demise, who do I call? Is there anybody who'd actually give a toss?'

'Christ. I'm fucking *pain*. Get on the blower to Pitt Street, Perlman. For pity's sake. Tell them to send a paramedic. Is this what I get for helping you out, eh?'

'Who's the face, Bobby?'

'Ah, fuck,' Quick said. 'This was a lovely club once. Many's the time we just boogied the whole damn night away. I want it back, Perlman. I want my *life* back.'

'I'm feeling tearful.'

'Don't be a heartless bastard, Lou.'

Perlman lit a cigarette, which he sucked on hard as he finished tapping the numbers in for Pitt Street. He was connected, patched through to Detective-Sergeant Bailey — or was it Bernigan? They sounded alike, the same nasal voices. Rodgers and Hart. He asked for immediate backup, gave the address, then shut off the phone and looked at BJ Quick.

'The bandages are coming,' he said. 'Now. What were we talking about?'

'This picture you're obsessed with.'

'I'll ask Furfee,' Perlman said. 'Maybe he'll know something.'

'Ask away.'

Perlman shook his head, and sighed. Why were criminals such dumb bastards? It didn't seem to have crossed Quick's mind that Furfee might be prepared to answer the questions Quick refused to countenance. Instead, in his fantasyland, in his Palace of Dreams and Mirrors, Quick was clinging to the fiction that he'd acted to assist the law, because of some new found civic-minded bullshit. Born-again BJ.

'Warning. Furfee's a clam,' Quick said.

'Clams open,' Perlman said.

43

A silver grey four-door Mercedes had been sitting for a couple of days in Kelvinbridge outside the house of a man called Teddy Gregorsky, an antiques dealer. Parking spaces were rare in Belmont Crescent where Gregorsky lived, and he knew that this Merc — which practically blocked his drive and thus made it difficult for him to get his Porsche in and out — belonged to none of his neighbours. So he telephoned the police in Pitt Street, and a Constable called James Brady was despatched to look at the car.

Teddy Gregorsky said, 'It's just been sitting here.'

PC James Brady, known as 'Diamond Jim' because of his enormous appetite, flicked on a torch and looked at the vehicle. The streetlamps were dim.

'I expected you to come out in daylight,' Gregorsky said. He wore a velvet smoking jacket robe with a monogrammed lapel.

'These are busy times at HQ, sir,' Jim Brady said. He strolled round the car.

'It's freezing cold. I'll leave you to do what you have to do and I'll go back indoors.'

'No problemo,' Diamond Jim said. Fag, he thought. Warms his arse in front of his fire, while I freeze my buns out in the street. It was zero degrees. A night for Guinness stew with totties

317

done so they were crumbly enough to soak up the gravy, the beef tender as a virgin's clitoris, and some encyclopaedia-sized chunks of crusted brown bread to dook into the leftover gravy. Oh, and three pints of McEwan's heavy to wash the whole thing down. Then half a Vienneta with a big dollop of vanilla ice-cream for afters. Followed by a Godalmighteeeee rip-yer-belly-out-yer-throat belch.

He leaned down and turned his torch on the number plate. Oh aye, what's this? He called HQ and asked for the number of the Mercedes that belonged to the dead solicitor.

The young WPC who'd answered said, 'Hold while I check.'

Brady pictured her. He'd categorized her when she'd first joined the Force: nice wee thing, shame about the face. She looked like a frog. But you just knew no Prince Charming was coming her way with a kiss. Ever.

She read him the number.

'Aye,' he said. 'That's it. Can you arrange for a tow-truck, hen?'

44

Shiv Bannerjee liked his women to wear silk underwear. He liked a slight convexity of navel. He enjoyed that expanse of skin leading from nub of bellybutton to pubic shrub. He'd spent some of his happiest hours with his head pressed to this plain of flesh. He enjoyed being equidistant from breasts and cunt. He liked sex in cheap hotels. He liked his women to talk to him during the act. He preferred Caucasian blondes such as Charlotte Leckie, who was presently inclined, legs parted, against the end of the bed in the Waterloo Hotel, situated above a Chinese restaurant in Sauchiehall Street.

Bannerjee penetrated her from behind, controlling her movements with hands on her hips. Her bottle-green silk underwear had puckered around her ankles. She'd ripped them in the act of stretching her legs to receive him. She was twenty-two, read the *Herald*, played three-card Brag for pennies with her mother every Sunday, and liked to watch football on TV. She shopped a lot. She had a charge card for the House of Fraser in Buchanan Street, and a Bank of Scotland Gold Mastercard with a credit limit of £5,000. She owned a comfortable three-room flat in Havelock Street in an area between Partickhill and Hillhead, although she preferred to say she lived in the latter because it had a more genteel reputation. She didn't smoke and

319

she rarely drank, except for the occasional glass of Babycham. She'd never used drugs. She sang in a choir that rehearsed once a week at the University. Sometimes she did volunteer work at the Royal Hospital for Sick Children. She wept whenever she read of little children with serious illnesses. She prayed for these kids. She thought the world was a cruel place, and God had some serious questions to answer.

These regular Thursday nights with Shiv were enjoyable, even if this hotel he favoured was far less pleasing than the places where she met her other men. But it made Shiv happy, and that was what counted. He was a gentleman, always kind to her, always thoughtful. He had his peccadilloes, but what person didn't?

She felt him grow harder. She gave her pelvic rotation more urgency and raised her voice from a whisper. 'Oh Shiv, Shiv love, oh Shiv, do me, do me, your big brown cock is making me come, Shiv, harder, deeper, oh I love it, love it, love it, take me to the moon, sweetheart, ride me ride me ride me, *Shiiiiv*, yes yes yes.'

Bannerjee's eruption was volcanic and prolonged. He spoke in Hindi. At least Charlotte Leckie thought that's what it was. She gasped as he came. She was never quite sure where the line lay between genuine responses and acting. She'd been playing this role for a couple of years now, the pliant mistress, the surrogate wife. Men like Shiv were generous to her. They didn't treat her as some common whore. They held her in esteem. They confessed things to her they couldn't tell their wives. This was a huge responsibility, she thought. The stuff she learned. The secrets she kept. She considered herself a courtesan of the old school.

She felt Shiv soften, then he slid out of her, and she turned around to face him. She held him in her arms as if he were a helpless boy, and she smoothed a hand through his thick white hair and called him baby, because she knew he liked this. In the distance kids were singing Christmas songs. Charlotte was touched by the sound. The Christmas period always made her feel vulnerable and weepy; all that tinsel and those silvery ribbons reminded her of something she'd lost, although she wasn't sure what.

Bannerjee said, 'I need to lie down.'

'Poor Shiv. I wear you out, do I?'

'You use up my energy, my dear. A man of my age.'

'You're not old. Don't say that.'

They lay together. Shiv Bannerjee caressed her breasts, kissed her nipples. He buried his face deep. He loved the weight of her tits. She sang to him softly. *'If that mockingbird don't sing, momma's gonna buy you a diamond ring.'* She had rather a sweet voice and Bannerjee was enchanted by it. Of all the women he'd bedded in the past few years, he'd allowed only Charlotte Leckie to get close to him. He was very fond of her.

The light in the room came from a streetlamp or traffic passing in the street. He liked this sense of being in the heart of city and all its clamour, and yet tucked away in a secret place. He smelled Charlotte's skin as he hid between her soft breasts. Here, the world didn't intrude. No peevish policemen, sharp journalists, Revenue agents. No criminal alliances, no slush-funds and secret accounts, no envelopes and messengers. And no immediate trips to some rank Third World sewer masquerading as a city where corrupt local dignitaries regarded you as a panacea. You could cure drought, famine, housing problems. They thought you could fly without wings.

Lying here in a cheap room above Sauchiehall Street, ah, now this was the simple life.

Charlotte Leckie looked at his face. 'You have very sad eyes, Shiv. Dark brown and inconsolable.'

'It's genetic,' Bannerjee said.

'You sometimes look like you have the weight of the world on your shoulders.'

Bannerjee smiled. 'Like Atlas.'

'Do you want me to massage you?'

'I'd like to rest. Nap a wee while.'

'I'll stay. If you like.'

'Of course,' he said. 'I don't mean to snooze for ever. I'll wake up filled with lust. And if you're not here, then I'll be *truly* inconsolable.'

She kissed his forehead. He shut his eyes. He listened to the carol singing in the distance, kiddie voices buried at times by the rumble of delivery-vans and lorries bringing Christmas goodies to the shops.

'Close your eyes,' he said.

She did so. 'You like it when we just hold one another, don't you?'

'I like it enormously.'

322

'If I sleep, and you wake before me, nudge me.'

'I'll kiss you awake,' he said. Lovemaking produced a sweet drowsiness in him. He was inside a dark velvet space. Charlotte, face down on the pillow, draped an arm across his chest.

The drift was lovely and smooth, down the brae all the way.

★ ★ ★

Marak entered the narrow hallway adjacent to the Jade Song and saw before him a flight of stairs covered with a tartan carpet, black and green, shabby and badly stained. He detected a scent of hot cooking oil. He climbed slowly, reached a landing where a reception desk was situated. Newspapers lay in disarray on a coffee table, and a cracked brown leather couch leaked tufts of padding. There was nobody behind the desk. A life-sized cardboard figure of a man dressed in a kilt moved one hand up and down in greeting. Marak could hear the whirr of the little motor that drove the motion. A cardboard balloon attached to the figure's cheerfully florid face read: *Welcome to Bonnie Scotland.*

He skipped past this effigy to the next flight of stairs. He moved softly. He was barely breathing. Up and up. He was hot. The place was overheated. Outside, pavements were frozen and lorries spread grit on the streets, and yet the heat in this building was almost tropical. He paused on the next landing and gazed upwards. At the top was a black skylight, a dome of glass

323

smudged by recent rain. He wondered if this was the right place, this shabby hotel, if the address written on the back of the photograph had been wrong. And why had a date and time been added to the address?

Neither of the previous pictures had come with that information. Perhaps this time was the only time.

He climbed again. He had a strong impulse to turn and go back down into the street and climb aboard the first bus that came his way and ride it to its destination, wherever that might be. But he kept ascending. He was beyond retreat. On the next landing a corridor went off at a sloping angle. The ceiling was crooked. A door to his right opened and a middle-aged couple emerged, the woman swaddled in an enormous fur coat and the man dressed in a pearl-grey overcoat that reached to his ankles. Marak turned away as they passed, coughing, covering his mouth with his hand.

The man said to the woman, 'Bloody Christmas rush. You know I hate that Princes Square. I'm knackered.'

The woman said, 'You're knackered? What about me? I've been carrying heavy bags all day.'

'What have we got in common, eh?' the man asked.

'I often wonder, Erchie. I really do.'

'Let's have a bloody good argument,' the man said.

'I'd prefer a bloody good drink personally. Mibbe we can do both.'

Marak heard them go down the stairs,

324

squabbling. He stood with his back to the wall. A phone rang unanswered some floors below. He touched the knife in the inside pocket of his coat. He heard his nerve-ends zing. *Turn and leave,* he thought. Listen to that earlier impulse. But he kept going. He owed the dead. When you had debts to the dead you didn't walk away from them.

He owed the living too.

He rose another floor, and now he was at the top of the building, standing directly beneath the dome. The rain on the dome was starting to freeze. It resembled an extra skein of glass forming over the first.

He was looking for room 408.

He stepped into a corridor where a sign read, *Rooms 400–416.*

He paused, fingered the sheathed knife. He knew how to use a knife, he knew the angle at which to drive a blade into the human body for best effect, which artery to sever and the slickest way to puncture the heart. He'd learned the art of the knife during his two years of National Service. He'd learned guns and grenades. He'd bayoneted straw-filled dummy figures and he'd fired machine-guns on target ranges. He'd learned hand-to-hand combat skills. He knew how to strangle a man efficiently.

He knew too much about killing.

He slipped the knife from the sheath, keeping the blade concealed under his coat. *408.* He'd reach the door, try the handle, and if the door was locked — would he knock and wait for an answer? For somebody to appear in the doorway?

He heard a woman singing from one of the rooms down the corridor. Quietly, liltingly. He couldn't tell what she was singing, but the sound captivated him. It released him. He was reminded of water running over stones, or the clarity of a monastery bell ringing slowly on a hill of ripe olive trees.

And then the singing stopped abruptly.

45

'Smoke?' Lou Perlman asked. He pushed a packet of Silk Cut across the table.

BJ Quick took one and Perlman leaned forward with his lighter. The interview room was small, lit by a little too much fluorescence. It smelled of old smokes and nervous tension. BJ eyed Perlman sideways, his mind flying like clouds on a windy day: where had they taken Furfee, and what was the big man saying? And how much did Perlman believe of Quick's story? *I was only trying to help, man.* The trouble with Perlman was you couldn't gather much information from his expression. His face was like a crumpled newspaper left out too long in the rain.

Perlman switched on a small cassette-player, punched the RECORD button. Quick's bandaged neck throbbed. For a while Perlman withdrew into silence, head shrouded with smoke.

'What now?' Quick asked.

'Just giving you time to readjust your thoughts.'

'They don't need readjusting, Lou.'

Perlman stood up. 'I think they do. This story of yours. It's puerile, BJ. You expect me to believe it? BJ Quick, scoundrel and perve, suddenly gets all holy and turns law-abiding? Character transformation just like that? Did the skies part above your head and God gave you a cheeky wee grin? Take the straight and narrow,

327

my child. All will be well. Yours sincerely, God.'

'God doesn't come into it, Lou.'

'You just had a seismic change of heart, eh?'

'Sudden like, aye.'

Perlman folded his arms. The tape-player hummed. The overhead strip of light flickered a second as if a spike had jolted the city's electric grid.

Quick asked, 'Listen. Can you not grant me some kind of immunity?'

'I couldn't grant you a free bus-pass, BJ. Immunity against what anyway?'

'Anything. The fact I was in Furfee's company. Guilt by association. Whatever. I mean, I helped the law, that's got to count for something.'

Perlman thought how some criminals lived in a fabulous world where cops could make quick hassle-free deals. There were no petitions involved, no consultations, no bargaining: it was just *gimme immunity, gimme a break. You can do it.* They didn't take into account the people with real power, those who sat Upstairs where all the important rubber stamps were stored. These were the men who could cut deals.

'No can do,' Perlman said.

Quick inhaled smoke. 'The way I see it, you fucking owe me.'

'Perspective is a funny thing. From my angle, you're a liar, you're withholding information, and you might be implicated in a murder. And I should help you?'

'Murder my arse. I had nothing to do with Dogue.' Quick saw club farraday float out to sea like a big abandoned galleon. Wind in the sails.

328

Disappearing to the horizon. He was depressed. Dead dreams did a terrible thing to your head.

'I wonder what Furfee is telling Inspector Scullion,' Perlman said.

Quick didn't want to think what Furfee might say. Probably nothing. Probably. In all likelihood. Which came down to: well, maybe. What the hell, Quick could deny anything Furfee said. He remembered Furfee producing the big razor and flicking the blade open and how at that very moment he'd felt his heart plunge deep into his intestines. That razor, that fucking razor. Furfee, you fucking moron, you braindead tit, you gorilla, you hadn't ditched the weapon. Hadn't bloody well thrown it into the river or dropped it down a sewer.

Quick tried not to think. He stubbed out his cigarette in the blue tin ashtray on the table.

Perlman said, 'Our man could be from the Middle East.'

'Shite. Not him again.'

'Suppose you just play your cards face-up, and tell me what you know about him.'

'I think I'd like to phone my lawyer now. I'll phone Binks. I should've done it before all this got out of hand.'

'Frazer Binks is a joke,' Perlman said. 'He couldn't punch his way through a wafer-thin brief. Last time he failed to save you a twelve month stretch in the Bar-L on a forged phone-card scam. Didn't he get his degree from some correspondence school in the wilds of Wales or somewhere?'

The door opened, and Scullion looked in. 'A minute, Lou?'

Perlman switched off the tape-recorder and went out into the hallway.

Alone, Quick helped himself to another cigarette. He shut his eyes against the harsh light and wished he had a way of reversing the flow of time to that very point where he'd thrown himself at Furf. Impetuous, aye, foolish, aye, but it had seemed to him at that moment he was doing the right thing, lunging at Furf and thinking he'd disarm him and ingratiate himself with the police . . .

He opened his eyes.

Who the *fuck* am I kidding? I was going like a rocket for the door. I wanted nothing to do with Furf and the bloody razor in his hand. I wanted *away* and club farraday be damned, Glasgow be damned. I had no bloody interest in helping anybody but BJ Quick. I was heading far far away, the Island of Arran, say, maybe find a cave halfway up Goat Fell.

No, no, nope, that wasn't it at all. It only *seemed* like that. I was *really* trying to help Perlman, right. Stick to that one, BJ. It's the better story. You're the hero of your own fiction. The nice thing about fantasies, you can pick the one that shows you in the best possible light.

He dragged on his cigarette and wondered what Scullion and Perlman were gassing about in the corridor. After a couple of minutes, Perlman came back in. He looks stupid in that old blazer, Quick thought.

Perlman said, 'Your friend Furfee can be a

talkative bugger sometimes, according to the Inspector.'

Quick smoked, staring at the tip of his cigarette and trying not to seem interested. 'Talkative my arse. He makes Charlie Chaplin seem like a chatterbox.' The cigarette burned his fingers and he dropped it in the ashtray. His wounded neck was aflame. He wished he could rip off the bandage and apply ice-cold water to his skin.

'Denies killing anybody, of course,' Perlman said.

'Zatso.'

'Denies knowing Terry.'

Quick said nothing, but saw a light in Perlman's eyes, a kind of predatory brightening. He didn't like it. 'And?'

'But he was prepared to talk about Abdullah.'

'Abdullah? Who's Abdullah?'

Perlman slapped the table hard. 'I'm tired of your shite, Quick. I've had a long day, and it's been a bloody cold one, and I'd like to get home before dawn. Don't fuck around with me.'

'Furf's the one fucking around.'

'He tells a very interesting story of you delivering envelopes to this Abdullah in Maryhill. But you weren't working for the Post Office. More a private courier.'

'This is a load of — '

'According to Furfee, you picked up the envelopes in a pub called The Brewery Taps.'

'The man's away with the fairies.' *Fuck you to hell, Furfee.*

Perlman pushed his chair back from the table

331

and stretched his legs. Quick noticed that the cop was wearing mismatched socks.

'Three envelopes, three deliveries,' Perlman said.

'He's on medication, you know that? He dreams up shite. He's always imagining stuff.'

'Right, right.'

'Some trank drug, fancy name — '

'Furfee says he went with you a couple of times to an address in Maryhill.'

Clammy, Quick forced a look of incredulity. 'Oh, aye, sure he did. Did he also tell you what was in these imaginary envelopes?'

'No, he went very quiet then. Said you'd tell us that. Quite emphatic about it, in fact.'

'How can I tell you what I don't know, Perlman?'

'Understand this. He's not pleased with you, BJ. In fact he said he'd like to cut your heart out. Exact words, *I'll cut that fucker's black heart out and stuff it up his arsehole.* The way he sees it, you prevented him from getting the hell out of that loft. I have the feeling that with a wee bit more pressure, he'll tell us anything we want to know.'

Perlman stood up. His glasses reflected light and his hair was a mass of unruly tufts. You'd never think he was a cop. Not in a hundred years. What did he look like? The guy who came to read the gas meter and looked sad because he couldn't remember where he'd stashed his winning lottery ticket. The broken-down door-to-door salesman, a one-time software hotshot made redundant,

332

peddling magazine subscriptions and hauling a heavy sample-case.

'So are you talking, BJ?' Perlman asked. 'Either I hear it from you, or I hear it from him. I don't care.'

'I'm telling you — '

'No, sonny boy, pin back your ears, *I'm* doing the telling. You just shut your gub and keep it shut. Let's leave the envelopes for a minute, and take something else into account, something new I just learned . . . Ready for this, BJ? Hang on to your chair. Our forensics man Sid Linklater, very experienced young guy, very bright, says there's every possibility that Terry Dogue's throat was cut by Furfee's razor — '

'Ballocks.' Quick felt clammy. His armpits flooded. He imagined how he'd react if somebody asked him to take a lie-detector test. He'd go into *melt-down*.

Perlman said, 'It's going to take more tests to be conclusive, but he's eighty per cent sure.'

'Okay, fine, so what, say Furf killed Dogue, it had nothing to do with me. Absolutely totally completely one hunnerd per cent nothing.' Quick made some motions of his hands, chopping the air like a kung-fu fighter.

'We've still got to break this forensic discovery to Furf,' Perlman said. 'How do you think he'll react?'

'Hell would I know?'

'My feeling is he'd want to be very cooperative, BJ. Don't you? I think he'd answer anything we asked. He's looking at a very long time in a bad jail, if the tests are indisputable. I

333

think he'll want to bring you down with him.'

'I was nowhere near *Terry fucking Dogue.*'

'Have a smoke. Take a few minutes and think through your predicament.'

Quick looked into Perlman's unblinking eyes. 'You're bluffing, you bastard. I just know it.'

'I never bluff. So you won't admit to any involvement with Dogue, and you won't tell us why you played postman in Maryhill, and what was in the envelopes. Fine.' Perlman walked to the door, clutched the handle. 'We'll see what Furf has to add. I'll be back soon, BJ. Why don't you sit here and marinate, okay?'

Perlman went out. Scullion was standing a few yards down the hallway. 'Well, Lou?'

'He's feeling the pressure. Give it half an hour. I'd kill for a cup of tea.'

'I'll keep you company.'

They walked together down the hallway to the place where a drinks machine was located. Hot tea, coffee, broth. Scullion stuck coins into the slot. The machine hissed, then issued liquid and a blast of steam. Perlman sipped from a cardboard cup and gasped as the hot tea hit the back of his throat.

Scullion said, 'When did Linklater say he'd come in and look at the razor?'

'Some time in the morning,' Perlman said. 'There's no hurry.'

'You're a cunning old fart.'

'I'm not that old,' Perlman said.

Scullion looked at his watch. 'You want to take a quick glance at the Merc?'

'Why not.'

334

Scullion's mobile rang and he removed it from his pocket and answered it. 'For you, Lou.'

Perlman took the handset.

He heard Ruth Wexler on the line, and the sound of her voice — thin, spectral, like that of somebody communicating from the place where the dead gather — unnerved him.

She said, 'You'll find the killer.'

'I know I will, Ruth.'

'Tell me you're certain.'

'I promise you.'

'I'm counting on that, Lou.'

46

Charlotte Leckie had dozed for a while but she still felt sleepy. She sang aloud the song that had been playing in her dream. It was an old Scots song, and she had no idea why she even remembered it, nor what she'd been dreaming. *'Twas there that Annie Laurie . . .* Weird choice, she thought. She hadn't heard that song in years. She didn't even like it.

She turned on her side. Shiv must have drawn the curtains at some point because there was no light from the street.

She looked at the luminous dial of her watch. Nine o'clock exactly. She'd slept for nearly half an hour. She realized Shiv wasn't in bed beside her. She heard water run in the bathroom. She felt very tired. She could easily drift back into sleep. What would it matter if she slept another fifteen minutes, or even thirty? She had no appointments. Shiv would expect her to stay until he decided it was time to leave anyway.

She listened to traffic, but it began to seem very far away. The Christmas singers were quiet now. Down the slope. She dozed. When she opened her eyes again she could still hear water running in the bathroom. The bedroom was impenetrably black save where a strip of light glowed under the bathroom door. Then a shape moved. The bathroom door opened. The sound of running water was louder. A white rectangle of light formed in the space, and the shape passed in front of this brilliance. She thought, *Shiv*, and was about to say his name when she realized that the figure entering the bathroom wasn't her lover but somebody else, a stranger, and all the while the water ran and ran.

She heard a noise. She wasn't sure of its source. It was almost the sound of air escaping, as in a sigh, but harsher. Harder. Or some object lodged in the throat of a person unable to expel it. Yes. But she wasn't certain.

She forced herself to move. Up on one elbow. Her view of the bathroom was limited by her angle. White walls, white light, white tub and basin and curtain shower. The tiles on the floor were another colour. Salmon? That was her impression. White and salmon. She saw the interloper move towards the sink but then he was lost to her. She thought she should stay very still. She didn't want to be seen. Why had she moved in the first place? She wondered why she hadn't heard Shiv cry out in surprise. His privacy had been invaded, after all —

The stranger stood in the doorway again. He saw her.

She tried to make herself very small. She sought invisibility. She knew something bad had happened. The air in the room had changed. It was unbreathable. She watched the man. She saw only that half of his face exposed by light. Half of a beard, one eye, a corner of a mouth.

She started to say something but he moved quickly and pressed a finger firmly to her lips and held it.

337

'Do not scream.' He took his hand away.

'Where is Shiv?'

'No questions. Please.'

'Where is he?' she asked.

He stepped back from the bed and moved to the front door. There he paused, turned, held out his hands in a gesture of dismay, and then he was gone. He shut the door as he left.

She rose from the bed, went into the bathroom.

'Shiv?'

The room was dense with steam. Hot water spurted into the basin. The floor was damp under her bare feet.

'Shiv,' she whispered.

She saw him then. He was seated in a chair, his head inclined over the washbasin. His arms hung at his sides.

'Shiv?'

She couldn't quite get her perceptions to work. Shiv wasn't sitting right. She thought it was like looking at something very familiar from a place outside her experience. If you were as small as an ant, a blade of grass would be the size of a tree. But that didn't do it, that didn't describe quite the distortion that affected her understanding. She saw herself reflected vaguely through the layer of steam that adhered to the mirror above the basin. She remembered she was naked. Turn off the water: that was her immediate response to the situation. Practical.

Do something very very simple.

Turn off the tap. All this waste of hot water.

She reached towards the basin, then she drew

338

her hand away again quickly. Through steam rising from the tap, she saw Shiv's face and his thick white hair.

Nothing else about him was familiar. This wasn't Shiv. This wasn't Bannerjee, her lover.

Something else.

47

The underground garage was cold as an igloo. Perlman blew into his hands. Fucking hell: temperatures in the city had plunged. By morning Glasgow would be one great construct of ice. No buses, no traffic except for the foolhardy, no trains, no planes, no escape. He stared at the four-door Merc that had belonged to Lindsay.

Inside, a Sergeant called Cameron Tubb was probing around, hands encased in latex gloves that looked like big multi-teated condoms. He wore a protective plastic suit and plastic boots. He was a thin man with an adam's apple the size of a prize-winning pomegranate. 'Lindsay kept a clean car, Lou. Fastidious fellow. A lint-free life. Contents of glove compartment. Car registration, an AA members' handbook, a small folded rag he might have used to clean his glasses. That's it.' Tubb placed these items inside a plastic bag and labelled it, then wrote with a felt-tip pen on the label.

'Anything else in there?' Scullion asked. His breath made a cloud on the air.

'Looking,' Tubb said. 'Sometimes I find. Sometimes I don't. I like to sing when I work. That trouble you gents?'

'Is it country-western?' Scullion asked.

'It bloody well is not, Inspector.'

'Then sing all you like,' Scullion said.

340

Tubb sang, 'If you throw a silver dollar down upon the ground . . .'

Perlman said, 'Jesus, you're really raiding the archives there, Cameron.'

'Fifties was a great time for popular songs,' Tubb said, and clambered into the back seat of the car. 'It will roll roll roll, because it's round round round.'

Scullion said, 'This is affecting my brain, Cameron.'

'Sorry, sir. I know other songs.'

'I've heard enough,' Scullion remarked.

'Everybody to his own, I say.'

Perlman lit a cigarette. He puffed smoke without taking the cigarette from his mouth because he stuffed his icy hands back inside his pockets. He thought about Ruth Wexler's call and the promise he'd so casually given her. What else was he supposed to have told her? Ruthie, look, it takes time, there are pieces to fit together. Somebody's murdered: it's like an explosive device detonating — and all a cop could do was sift the shrapnel the way Cameron Tubb was poking around inside the Merc. I have some of the fragments. I have to reassemble them. I have to see where they join.

Scullion said, 'I wonder how the car found its way to Kelvinbridge.'

'Whoever killed Lindsay left it there,' Perlman said.

'But what for? If you murdered a man, why would you drive his car away?'

'Maybe he was killed right where the car was parked,' Perlman suggested. 'Maybe Lindsay met

341

somebody, and they drove around talking, and then the killer asked Lindsay to pull over.'

'Which implies he knew the killer.'

'Right. Lindsay parks. All of a sudden there's a gun at his head, and a bag of cocaine going into his mouth.'

'Then what? He was transported to Central Station Bridge in another car?'

'Why not? But there are other alternatives, Sandy — '

'Save them for later, Lou. My brain's running on empty. Cameron, come on, I'm turning to a block of ice here.'

'You can't hurry this job, Inspector,' Tubb said. 'Suppose in the haste of my preliminary examination, I disturb something microscopic but essential? What would the lab boys say? See how I move in slow-mo, Lou? Time is frozen for me.'

'Well for me it's my fucking balls that are frozen, Cameron.'

'You're a crude man at times, Perlman.'

'I had a crude education.'

'Wait a minute,' Tubb said. He went into Mexican-accent mode. 'What ees thees leetle theeng?' He probed the space behind the front passenger seat and surfaced with a small crunched-up brown paper bag in his hand.

Scullion stepped closer to the Mercedes. 'What is it, Cameron?'

'Let's see.' Tubb opened the bag carefully and peered inside. 'Here.'

Scullion peered inside. 'Looks a bit like sawdust.'

342

Perlman gazed at the contents. He had a rush of familiarity. 'It's not sawdust,' he said.

'You know what it is, Lou?' Tubb asked.

'Only too well. I had a wife who ate it all the time, said it helped her stop smoking. That dust, pupils, is the residue of sunflower seeds. She picked up the habit of munching on said seeds during a trip to Tel Aviv. Told me everybody chewed on seeds over there. It was a bone of contention in our marriage. I was always complaining about her crunching on these things and spitting out the pods. She did it in bed — which was about the *only* thing she did in bed, as I remember.'

'Sunflower seeds?' Scullion said.

'She called it gar gar . . . something.'

'So our neat and tidy solicitor chewed on these seeds and then dumped the bag on the floor of his otherwise meticulous Merc,' Scullion said. 'And what did he do with the bits you spit out? Did he just expectorate from the open window? Why am I not seeing that clearly?'

'Maybe the bag belonged to somebody else,' Tubb said.

'The killer,' Scullion said.

'Careless of him if he dropped it, though,' Perlman said, and looked at Scullion. 'What was that phrase you used to describe him, Sandy? Arrogant amateur?'

'I remember.'

'So it just fell out of his pocket, and he overlooked it?'

'Possibly.'

Perlman snapped thumb and forefinger

together. '*Garinim*. That's the word I was looking for. That's what they call this stuff.'

Tubb tucked the paper bag inside a plastic one. He sealed it, stuck a label on it, scribbled something. 'We'll get it fingerprinted, gents.'

Perlman let his cigarette fall and crushed it underfoot. He was anxious to get back to his unfinished business with BJ Quick and Furfee. He imagined their tiny minds in turmoil. What to say? What half-truths? What might they fudge? They couldn't collude in a fiction either: how frustrating that had to be for BJ Quick.

Scullion said, 'Send us your report asap, Cameron.'

'Will do, sir.'

Perlman and Scullion moved towards the stairs. As they did, Mary Gibson appeared. She looked drawn, vitality drained. Her makeup had faded in the course of the day. The bloom was off, and her eyes lacked light. Perlman didn't like her expression. Something of sorrow, of anger, it was hard to tell. She didn't look like the Mary Gibson he saw on a regular basis.

'There's been another one,' she said. 'This fucking city's having a mental breakdown.'

Perlman had never heard her curse before. She pronounced the g in 'fucking', which gave the word a decorum it normally lacked.

'Another murder?' he asked.

'Another one. Correct.'

'Who's the victim?' Perlman asked.

'This'll kick-start you, Lou. Shiv Bannerjee.'

'*Bannerjee*? I saw him only — what? Four or five hours ago?'

'Then here's your chance to see him again, Lou. Just go to the Waterloo Hotel in Sauchiehall Street.'

Perlman didn't wait to ask more questions. He hurried to the stairs. He heard Scullion rushing behind him.

'I'll drive,' Scullion said.

'Be my guest.'

'My car's just up the block.'

The night air was arctic and brittle, the sky clear in the brilliant way of extremely cold weather. The moon, crystalline and indifferent, was motionless against the stars. A mental breakdown, Mary Gibson had said. Or a bad spell, Perlman thought, cast over the city by the black deeds of bad men.

48

Marak slipped on ice and fell as he ran. He struck his elbow and a pain scorched his arm. He rose quickly. The stretch of pavement in front of him was slick. He rubbed his arm and kept moving, more carefully this time. He didn't know where he was, none of the buildings around him looked familiar, all that mattered was to get as far away from the hotel as he could. He travelled a network of side streets, avoiding the main thoroughfares with their Christmas baubles. Darkness and silence was what he needed: an end to the nightmare his task had become.

He entered a railway station. It wasn't the one he'd been in before, when he'd used a telephone to call Lindsay's office — how long ago that seemed now. This one was bigger, brighter. He looked at the Arrivals and Departures board. The names of destinations flickered and changed in front of his eyes. Kilmarnock. Barassie. Ardrossan. He wondered about these towns and whether he could hide in them while he made plans for his journey home. He imagined small rooms, narrow streets, long bitter nights.

He had to get out of Glasgow now. Tonight. It was folly to stay any longer. He'd been tricked, manipulated. He'd come from Israel to kill certain men, and he hadn't had to lift a finger in anger to any one of them. Two dead, one suicide.

346

And now he wondered if Lindsay had really killed himself.

Or if it had been made to look that way.

Why had an elaborate organization been set up to send him here — with fake passport, money, travel arrangements, personnel in Israel, Greece, Scotland — if it was all designed to fail? He thought of the hotel, the woman in the bed, the sight of the dead man at the sink, the nausea he'd felt flood his mouth with bitter saliva, how difficult it had been for him not to throw up —

He'd call Zerouali. He'd do that before he did anything else. The Moroccan might be helpful, perhaps able to suggest the safest route across Europe. He walked to the public phones. The number, what was the number? He'd misdialled it before. He reorganized the digits in his mind until he had them in what he believed was the correct order.

He dialled the number, and when a woman answered in Arabic he began to punch in coins.

The woman said, 'Café Tahini.'

Marak spoke in Arabic. 'Connect me to the owner, please.'

'I am the owner.'

'I mean Zerouali. The Moroccan.'

'Zerouali?'

'He owns the Tahini.'

'There is no Zerouali here. Excuse me. You have a wrong number.'

'I don't think so. This is the Café Tahini, correct?'

'Yes. I told you. This is Tahini. But there is nobody here called Zerouali.'

More coins. Marak's hand trembled. 'A fat man, grey beard, Moroccan. Surely you know him?'

'Please. Believe me. There is nobody by the name of Zerouali here. And there is no bearded Moroccan. I think this is a mistake. I must go.'

'Wait,' Marak said.

'I tell you one last time. No Zerouali. Okay? I am hanging up on you.'

'No, please — '

But the line was cut.

Zero sound. The bottom of a dry well.

Marak hung the handset back in place then stood motionless in the forecourt of the station and felt dizzy, as if his body was rising upward to meet the high glass roof of the place. His hands wouldn't stop shaking. He was a mass of pulses, of systems breaking down. No Zerouali. Think. It wasn't the man's real name. Why would he use his real name in a clandestine situation? Why had he lied when he'd said he was the owner of Tahini? For the same reason: to protect his identity. You move in secret places for secret purposes, you leave behind your name and your occupation, you shed the outer skins of your identity: you keep only the kernel. Zerouali had dissolved into the scenery. Probably the kibbutz kid with the UCLA T-shirt had vanished too. The man in the Athens hotel who'd given him the passport, and the captain of the ferryboat — other players in this charade.

Now what, now what. He went inside a bar, a big gloomy room. A jukebox played a boring pop tune. Marak asked for water. He was given a bottle of Strathmore and a wet glass that contained one tiny cube of ice. He placed coins on the counter. The barman picked them up without looking at him. Marak drank the water quickly. The ice-cube rattled in the glass. He realized he should have left Glasgow when he'd learned about the death of Wexler, and when he understood that the police knew his face. That had been the time to abort the enterprise. But he'd been driven along blindly because he no longer knew how to open his eyes and acknowledge reality.

He wondered how he could contact Ramsay. But what help could he expect there? None. He knew that.

Has there been a plot against me? he wondered. Even if he couldn't define the precise nature of it, he was suddenly frightened. He sensed that he didn't have much time left to him in this city. He had to get away. He patted the pockets of his coat. He had his wallet, some Scottish banknotes. His traveller's cheques and his passport were back at the flat with his other few belongings. He left the bar, walked out of the station. The dark engulfed him. His feet were marble. His elbow ached. He'd go and fetch his stuff, discard what he didn't need, and then he'd be gone without pausing to look back. This was a city he'd forget, this a season he'd relegate to that junk room in the head where all bad dreams were stored.

49

The corridor outside room 408 of the Waterloo Hotel was crowded with hotel staff and guests. Perlman shoved his way through, barking at these witless spectators. Scullion, a pace behind, used his shoulders freely. A man who claimed to be the manager, fat-necked with the red fissured face of a boozer, was complaining loudly about how he was being denied access to a room in his own hotel, and what was going on anyway?

'Out the way,' Perlman said. 'Move it. Move it. Keep this passage free. You, manager man, get these people out of here, okay? Make it fast. On the double.' He forced his way into the room. A couple of uniforms were lingering in the doorway, keeping onlookers at bay. A man in a raincoat and an old-fashioned felt hat was standing inside the bathroom. He glanced at Perlman and shrugged. Rodgers, Perlman thought. Or Hart. He'd have to get them straight one day.

He noticed the woman on the edge of the bed. She sat with her hands clasped in her lap and a bedsheet draped round her like a toga. A handsome young woman, strong features, good healthy complexion, he thought: she was no cheapo pick-up, no pavement fodder. She had a stunned expression, a concussion in her eyes.

'You all right, love?' Perlman asked.

She looked at him, nodded her head very slowly.

'You want me to get a doctor for you?'

She spoke in a dry-mouthed way. 'No, don't.'

'Somebody shut the bloody door,' Perlman said. 'Give this woman some peace. And send that manager for some ice-water. Tell him to make himself useful.'

'Thanks,' she said. 'I appreciate it.'

Uniforms conveyed Perlman's order. The door shut, and the clamour in the corridor became muted. Perlman excused himself and stepped into the bathroom. Scullion was already inside, talking to the cop in the hat and raincoat.

He looked at Perlman. 'Bailey's been telling me about the woman, Lou.'

George Bailey spoke like a man with serious adenoidal problems. 'Name's Charlotte Leckie. Girlfriend of the deceased. The hotel manager says they met here every week, same night, same time.'

'She's no pro, is she?' Perlman asked.

Bailey took off his hat and ran a hand across his forehead. 'I don't think so. If she took money from Bannerjee, she probably thought of it as a gift. Maybe he gave her a bracelet here, a ring there. That kind of thing. That's the impression I get. I mean, when did you last hear a hooker who'd had elocution lessons? Talks quite lah-di-da really.'

Perlman stepped closer to the sink. A flashbulb went off, startling him. The photographer, 'Rumbleguts' McPhail, emerged from the

351

shower-stall where he'd been half-hidden by the curtain.

'We meet again,' he said to Perlman. 'Twice in one twenty-four-hour span. How about that?'

'Do you usually scare the shite out of people, Robbie? Christ, I'm blind.'

'Sorry about that.' Robbie McPhail ran off a couple of quick shots from other angles.

'Crowded in here,' Perlman said. His vision was filled with after-images, spikes of light. 'Tell me you're done, Robbie.'

'I'm on my way. Adios.' The photographer left the room.

'Cheerio.' Perlman rubbed his eyes, slipping the tips of his fingers under his glasses. He moved as close to the sink as he could get.

Bannerjee's face was pressed against porcelain darkened by blood. His white hair was red. Blood leaked from the left ear; whoever had killed him had driven a wooden-handled screwdriver deep into the eardrum. Perlman looked at the handle of plain unvarnished wood, and thought how ordinary it was, an item you could buy cheaply in any hardware shop.

He turned away from the sight of the dead man. You reach a point, he thought, where you say okay, enough. You've seen the city's underside, that place where people do barbarous things to each other, and you say enough, enough, this is where you draw a line. And you don't think you can go on without becoming totally numb, zombie numb. But you find energy inside yourself from some uncharted reservoir, and you keep going. He imagined the hand that

352

held the implement, and the immense force with which it had thrust the screwdriver into Bannerjee's ear.

He stepped out of the bathroom. He told the uniformed policemen in the room that he wanted privacy, and all three of them left. There was still a mumbling of discontent from the corridor. Perlman sat on the edge of the bed alongside the woman, who was holding a glass of water.

'They brought you a drink. Good.'

'It was kind of you to ask.'

'I'm told you heard nothing.'

She shook her head. 'I was sleeping . . . '

'And Mr Bannerjee went to the bathroom?'

'He must have. I didn't hear him go. I remember I woke up and . . . ' She sipped the water. 'I want my name kept out of this. Is that possible. I don't want my mother — '

'We'll do what we can.' Perlman patted the back of her hand. This one was no cheap *zoineh*, that was certain.

She said, 'I'm not on the game. I want you to know that. I'm not a streetwalker.'

'I believe you. What else did you hear when you woke?'

'I heard water running. This is dreamlike, Inspector.'

'Sergeant. Lou Perlman. Call me Lou.'

Scullion came into the room, as if on tiptoe, and stood by the bed. He looked at the woman with his customary empathy. Perlman thought he detected stress behind the expression, as if Scullion wanted nothing more than to go home to his family and lock the doors and draw the curtains and sleep for a week.

'This is Inspector Scullion, Charlotte.'

The woman gazed at Sandy. 'I'm just telling Lou . . . ' She paused. 'I was dozy. I opened my eyes. I saw somebody go into the bathroom.'

'Somebody other than Bannerjee?' Perlman asked.

'Yes.'

'This other man,' Scullion said. 'Was he in the bathroom long?'

'No, seconds. It seemed. I can't judge it. Then he came back out and saw me.'

'Did he say anything?'

'He asked me not to scream. I don't remember clearly.'

'Then what? He left?'

'Yes. Then I got up. I went inside the bathroom. And . . . '

Scullion asked, 'You think this man killed Shiv Bannerjee?'

'I assume he did.'

'Did you hear any sounds?'

'I heard a — I don't know how to describe it,' Charlotte Leckie said. 'Like somebody trying to clear something from the back of his throat. I don't know.'

Perlman said, 'You got a good look at the intruder.'

'I got a look. I don't know how good.'

Scullion crouched in front of the woman. 'Can you describe him?'

'Young . . . what else, what else. Dark eyes. Darkish skin, but not black. Lightish to medium

354

brown. It's hard to say.'

'Bearded?' Perlman asked.

'Yes. Right. He was.'

Perlman reached inside his coat. He retrieved the crumpled shot of the man he'd come to know as Abdullah. He smoothed the picture out as much as he could, and handed it to Charlotte Leckie. 'Is this the man you saw?'

She looked at the image and closed her eyes and whispered *yes* so softly that Perlman could barely hear.

50

Mary Gibson stepped into the interview room where BJ Quick sat smoking the last of the Silk Cut cigarettes Perlman had left him. He turned his head as the Detective-Superintendent approached. Good-looking for a mature babe, even if she was a cop. He'd never had any kind of encounter with a policewoman before. He doubted they were any easier to deal with than their male counterparts. Maybe even tougher. A lot of career women were fucking ballbreakers these days.

He watched her sit down at the other end of the table and he realized he should behave, cull the swear words, clean up the act.

Women liked men who projected manners.

'Sergeant Perlman's out,' she said.

'So I was told,' Quick said. He curbed the urge to add Your Highness. Don't play sarcasm cards.

'What did you want to see him about so urgently?' She folded her hands on the table. Manicured nails, subdued pale varnish. Stern look about her. This is one woman you wouldn't want to cross.

'You're aware of this, er, situation?' he asked.

She nodded. 'You have some problems.'

'Aye, well, that's your point of view. And you're entitled to it, don't get me wrong. The way I see it, we can come to some arrangement.'

'How cosy that sounds,' she said. 'Isn't there a

saying about lying down with dogs and getting up with fleas?'

BJ Quick played with the empty cigarette packet. 'Dogs and fleas, aye, right, ha ha.'

'What are you angling for? A deal?'

'Let's call it I scratch your back you scratch mine.'

'Scratch your back? I hardly know you.'

'Ha ha.' Quick heard this nervous laugh he'd suddenly developed, and he didn't like the sound of it. 'What I mean is we can work something out, like.'

'Like?'

'I've been sitting here thinking,' Quick said. And so he had. He'd been scanning the folly of his life. It was a superficial sort of examination, though; nothing deep, no analytical probe. Here he was in an interview room, looking at the possibility — vague, mind you, but a possibility nonetheless — of complicity in the murder of Terry Dogue. It only took a single sentence from Furfee for that to happen. *He was with me when I slashed Terry's throat, I swear to God.* Quick recognized that unless he could strike some sort of exchange with the constabulary, this situation was going to be like sinking into a big bucket of soft creamy shite.

'And what have you been thinking, Mr Quick?'

'Perlman wants a piece of information from me.'

'Oh?'

'Now,' and here Quick scratched the surface of the table with his fingernails in small circular

357

patterns. 'I'm thinking along these lines. Say I give him this information. Just imagine . . . In exchange, what's the chance I won't be drawn into any charges brought against that half-wit Furfee? If he killed a man, I swear, I had nothing to do with it.'

Mary Gibson stood up. Her skirt was pleated, Quick noticed. Warm tweedy material. Her stomach was flat.

'That's all you have to say?' she asked.

'He wants an address,' Quick said. 'I can give it to him. Understand what I'm telling you? I can give him this fucking address. Sorry. Beg pardon for the language.'

'I've heard worse,' Mary Gibson said.

Why wasn't she interested? why wasn't she agog? She just walked past him to the door.

He got up from his chair and said, 'Braeside Street.'

'Number forty-five,' she said.

'Right — '

'Top floor, no name on the door.' In a bored monotone. 'Tell me something I don't know.'

'Aye but — '

'This is exactly what Mr Furfee told me less than ten minutes ago,' she said. 'He's as desperate to help as you are. Funny to get as much cooperation. I sniff guilt. But you were just that little bit slower, Mr Quick. He who snoozes, loses.'

'Fuck fuck *fuck*. What the hell did you promise Furfee?'

'The moon,' she said. 'What else?'

'And what will he get?'

358

'He'll get justice, Mr Quick. He'll get a fair trial.'

'And me, what about me?'

'The same.'

She went out and closed the door and Quick, cursing the way the world worked, cursing his taste for underage girls and fast drugs and rock clubs, cursing everything that had conspired to bring him to this place at this particular time, including the moon and the stars and the drift of tides, tried in his anger to lift the table and topple it over.

'*Fuck fuck fuck*,' he roared. He quit when the pain in his neck became unbearable.

The table, he observed, was bolted to the floor.

51

Scullion took Mary Gibson's call on his cellphone in room 408 of the Waterloo Hotel and immediately pulled Perlman to one side. 'We're needed elsewhere. Now.'

'What about Charlotte Leckie?'

'Bailey can take her statement down. He writes, you know. I've seen examples.'

'What's the hurry?'

'I'll tell you on the way.'

Perlman turned to the woman and said, 'I'm leaving you in the very capable hands of Detective-Sergeant Bailey.'

'But — '

'It's okay. Really it is. Besides, he's nicer than me. He really is.'

Bailey came out of the bathroom, shutting the door quickly as if to hide the sight of something Charlotte Leckie had already seen.

Perlman said, 'Look after her. Take her statement.'

'Where are you off to?'

'It's a mystery,' Perlman said.

Charlotte Leckie said, 'I'd like to get dressed.'

'Bailey will be a gentleman and look the other way,' Perlman said. 'Won't you, Bailey?'

Perlman and Scullion went out into the corridor, where the uniforms had cleared most of the spectators away. They hurried towards the stairs, descended quickly. Perlman bumped along behind the Inspector. He'd yanked a muscle in his upper leg, probably when he'd given chase to the taxi. Now it had begun to ache.

They reached the street and walked to where Scullion's Rover was parked. Slippery underfoot. Glasgow was a city of whoopsadaisy surfaces, slick sheets of ice where any passing pedestrian might perform a pratfall.

Scullion unlocked his car. Perlman clambered into the passenger seat. 'Where are we headed?'

'You want to find Abdullah, don't you?'

Perlman buckled his seatbelt. 'Damn right I want to find him. Tell me you've got the address.'

'Furfee broke, gave it to Mary Gibson.'

'Furfee did? Well well well. Face to face with the mystery man. How far?'

'Braeside Street.'

'Off Maryhill Road. I know it.'

'I hate driving in these conditions.' Scullion switched on his de-icer, and wiped condensation from the windscreen with a rag he kept on the dash. He drove down Elmbank Street to St Vincent Street, where he crossed the motorway that slashed the gut of the city; below, the lights of slow-moving cars cut through the mist of exhaust fumes. He turned into North Street and headed for St George's Cross, and then Maryhill Road. Perlman watched the city go past in a tableau of dark buildings rising beyond street-lamps, the occasional illumination of a restaurant or bar. He was thinking of Abdullah, of the enigmatic envelopes BJ had supposedly delivered.

361

'Did Furfee say anything about the envelopes?' he asked.

'Not so far as I know. Christ, it's an ordeal driving.' The car failed to grip, slid, tobogganed a few yards to the right before Scullion had it under control again.

'I don't want to die in a car accident,' Perlman said. 'It's so bloody banal.'

'What kind of death are you looking for anyway?'

'Oh. Something heroic.'

'Tell me how you'd ever find yourself in heroic circumstances.'

'Saving a beautiful girl from drowning.'

'You don't swim, Lou.'

'That's why it would be heroic.'

Perlman pushed his seat back and stared out as Scullion drove up Maryhill Road. He thought of Nina with her *garinim* and the sheets of pretentious yellow bond on which she wrote her prose; funny how marriage could distil itself in so few sorry memories. He wondered if intensely cold weather induced an occasional melancholy in him.

More likely it was the three murders that stoked this mood; that, and the recurring anxiety he felt about Colin. No, wait, you're kidding yourself, Lou: it was more than Colin's physical well-being that bothered you. It was his fucking *past*. When he was healthy and back on his feet, would his history stand up to scrutiny? Or would Bannerjee's accusation be forgotten, as if the Indian's words had never been said in the first place? Shiv was no longer around to make any claims about Colin, and the comments existed only in Lou Perlman's memory; and who could say he wouldn't forget them?

But that question made him uneasy because he suspected he knew the answer: yes, yes, dammit, he'd protect his brother. He knew he would. He'd known it ever since the conversation with Bannerjee. He'd turn the old blind eye because the demands of blood were seemingly more compelling than those of the law. This revelation dismayed him. It came out of a place in his heart he'd never known about before now, an unlit corner where bad impulses hatched. He'd spent his life upholding the law, observing it dutifully, and now he realized he was actually prepared to look the other fucking way, like any sleazy cop on the take.

He had a sudden longing to speak to Miriam. Or simply to see her. Would she be at the hospital now? Sitting at Colin's bed. Talking quietly to him. Holding his hand. The loving wife.

'On the left, I think,' Scullion said.

He swung the car very slowly. He drove down a street of tenements, and when he saw forty-five he pulled the Rover into the kerb, where he switched off the engine. 'Here we are.'

'Do we know if he's home or if we wait down here until he appears?'

'We don't know,' Scullion said.

'You want to go in?'

Scullion said, 'I want a backup unit first. I'll call.' He used his mobile, made the arrangements for a second vehicle. 'I like a little extra security.'

Perlman looked at lit windows burning in the dark. The city compressed space, and thus compressed people. So many lives in boxes. His mind shifted briefly to Bannerjee, blood in that thick white hair, blood on porcelain. The impulsion of the screwdriver, the strength behind it.

His leg muscle twinged again and he changed position. A car slipped in behind the Rover, and flashed its lamps twice. Scullion got out. Perlman followed. There were two plainclothes men in the other car. Perlman knew them vaguely. He'd seen them around. He couldn't recall their names. They looked suitably aggressive, wide of shoulder, hard-edged.

'Watch the close,' Scullion said.

'Right you are, Inspector,' the man behind the wheel said.

'If you hear a commotion, get your arses in the building. The flat's on the top floor.'

'Gotcha.' The pair nodded. The one in the passenger seat, a bullock of a man, chewed gum vigorously.

Perlman and Scullion entered the narrow close that led to the stairs. They went up slowly. The lights on the landings were dim. The building had a feel of abandonment. Or like a vacuum. Airless and still, a space where nothing could survive. A food smell hung in the silence, but he couldn't identify it. Old lard, maybe, last week's bacon grease. He imagined people sitting in rooms in front of the hypnotic lights of TVs. People eating frozen dinners, reconstituted chicken parts and artificial mashed potatoes in

MSG gravy. But no sounds punctured the quiet of the building.

Up they climbed, Perlman lagging behind Sandy Scullion. Chasing taxis at your age. Not bright. He thought of the face in the cab's window. Was it a killer's face? How were killers supposed to look anyway? They came in all kinds of masks.

Scullion stopped. 'You okay?'

Perlman nodded. 'Dandy.'

He noticed Scullion's voice was a whisper. 'One more flight, Lou.'

Scullion started to go up. Perlman laid his hand on the banister. On the top floor, Scullion stopped again. Three doors on the landing, three separate flats, but only one door had no nameplate. Both men stood very still a moment, then Scullion pressed the bell and it buzzed inside the flat. He buzzed it a second time.

★ ★ ★

Inside the bedroom Marak was hurriedly stuffing his clothes into his backpack when he heard the bell. His heart skittered. At first he thought Ramsay had come to see him; but Ramsay had a key. Maybe it was the downstairs neighbour, the man with the blue snakes tattooed on the backs of his hands. But why? A drunken argument, a rant? Marak thought about his toilet items. He'd get them next. He'd ignore the bell and eventually whoever was on the other side of the door would go away.

He entered the bathroom and gathered his

365

toiletries and placed them in one of the outside pockets of the backpack. He zipped it. In the living room he checked the items he intended to carry on his person. Passport. Traveller's cheques. Cash. He was ready now. Ready for departure. *Wait* —

He drew from the left-hand pocket of his coat Bannerjee's photograph. He'd meant to dispose of it, but in his haste he'd overlooked it. Burn it. Just burn the thing. The doorbell rang again. Three long persistent rings. They left an electric echo in the flat.

He went inside the kitchen and found an old book of matches in a drawer and struck one, holding it to the photograph. The match was damp, and died. He let it slip into the sink. The bell rang and rang. He struck another match. The glossy caught flame briefly, then fizzled out. He lit a third match and applied it to the picture and this time the flame took, but it burned too slowly for him, spreading in a leisurely way from the corner of the shot towards the centre. Faster, he thought. Burn burn. He coughed as the chemical fumes rose to his face.

When he'd reduced the photo to a shiny black cinder, he dropped it into the plastic litter-bin. But the smell, that stench of petroleum by-products, lingered in the air.

Rrrrrrrrr. Rrrrrrrrrrr. Rrrrrrrrrrrrr.

He touched the knife in the inside pocket of his coat. He'd go to the front door. Just to listen. If he felt confident, perhaps he'd ask the person outside to identify himself. It was a nuisance, bad timing; he didn't need any interruptions

366

now. He was leaving. He was going home.

He walked down the hallway very quietly and listened. He heard nothing. The door had no peephole, therefore he had no idea who was out there, if it was one man, or two, or that drugged-out woman 'selling' raffle tickets.

He stood very still. Waited. Tried not to breathe. He was jangled. The doorbell rang again. The sound went through him like a saw on hard wood. A loose floorboard creaked under his foot. Perhaps the noise didn't carry beyond the flat to the landing. He thought he heard somebody whisper from the other side of the door, but he couldn't make out words. He couldn't even be sure he'd heard anything.

He backed away, returned to the living room. He glanced down into the street. Streetlamps glimmered on ice. He walked into the bathroom. He opened the window, looked out. The possibility of a fire-escape had popped into his mind, but he couldn't remember seeing any building in this city equipped with such a thing. The view was restricted to the back-courts behind the tenements, expanses of dark penetrated here and there by light from rear windows. You could see into other people's flats, other lives. A woman at a sink peeling something.

He leaned from the window: no fire-escape, only an arrangement of drainpipes bolted to the wall. What did people do in a fire? Jump? It was a long way down. He drew his head back in, shut the window, returned to the hallway.

The doorbell rang again. Two short bursts.

Marak felt like a man drawn down into a spinning funnel of water. Panic.

★ ★ ★

'Here,' Lou Perlman said. He'd gone downstairs to the car and come back again with the tyre-iron, which he handed to Scullion.

'It was your idea,' Scullion said.

'Aye, but you're fitter and stronger. You think you can get it open?'

'Worth a try.'

Scullion inserted the iron into the narrow space between door and jamb. He pushed hard on the length of metal. Wood splintered, little chips flew into the air. He kept angling the implement back and forth until the wood around the mortice split. The lock was a rusted antique, and it popped out easily. He pushed the door, which opened into a small hallway.

He stepped in, Perlman at his side.

There were four doors, two on either side. All lay open. Perlman glanced inside the empty bathroom, while Scullion opened a door that yielded to a cupboard stuffed with rusted old tins of cleaning solvents, brushes, paints. Nothing of interest. They walked to the end of the hall and stepped cautiously through the door on the right, entering a bedroom with greasy yellow wallpaper and a girlie calendar dated 1992. A crucifix hung aslant above a chest of drawers.

Perlman slid the drawers open. Empty except for outdated newspapers used as lining. The room smelled of damp wallpaper. There was another scent on the air, fainter, suggestive of burnt plastic.

'One more room,' Scullion said quietly.

'Wait.' Perlman nodded across the bedroom to a door, presumably a cupboard. Scullion turned the handle, an old plastic globe that slid off in his fingers. The door swung open, revealing a heavy-as-lead upright vacuum cleaner of a kind rarely seen since the 1950s, when these gadgets were more labour-intensive than labour-saving. A generation of women had schlepped these monsters, thinking them state-of-the-art. A couple of tweed jackets hung from a rod, and a punctured football lay on the floor.

There was something else, and Perlman almost failed to notice it. He bent down, shoved the dented football aside and fingered a plastic bag containing stuffed toys, a broken-necked giraffe, a furry monkey without eyes, a battered rodent.

A small black leather wallet was jammed between rodent and monkey. He opened the wallet, examined the contents. With a swift intake of breath, he handed it to Scullion — just as a noise from the lobby made both men turn to see a bearded young man, with a backpack dangling from one shoulder, step quickly towards the front door.

Scullion called out, 'Hey. You.'

The young man didn't stop.

Scullion moved with an unusual elegance, and ghosted sweetly and quickly into the lobby where he threw himself, arms extended, at the young man. He must have done this a hundred times on the muddy rugby fields of his adolescence. A swift tackle round the waist, and both men went down. They rolled together for a few moments, hands locked, expressions fierce, two men fighting for possession of an invisible ball. The young man freed one hand and prodded Scullion in the eye, and Sandy said, 'Fucker.' Perlman seized a broom from the lobby cupboard and smacked the kid across the back of the head with the metal shaft.

The kid, scalp bleeding, rolled over on his back. Perlman sat heavily on his chest. Scullion got to his feet and dusted his coat down with his hands and said, 'My eye, my damned eye. Christ.' He rubbed it with the tips of his fingers. Then he bent and searched the kid's inside pocket and found a knife and a bunch of papers.

'A nice knife, if you like these things,' he said to Perlman.

Perlman stared at the blade, which was impressive in a malevolent way. Glasgow was Blade City these days. He looked down at the young man. 'So where were you sneaking off to in such a hurry?'

'Out of here. Can I get up now?'

'I'm too much of a burden for you?'

'Yes.'

Perlman rolled away from the young man and stood up, then helped him rise. This was the face from the taxi. This was the face from the lift in the parking garage. Up close, it was less sinister than it had seemed on the videotape; younger, leaner. He probably had to work at looking tough and menacing. How old was he? Twenty-two, -three? Without the beard, he'd seem more like sixteen. Babyface with whiskers.

Scullion examined the papers he'd seized from the young man's coat. 'Okay. What have we here? One passport . . . Israeli. About three hundred pounds in sterling. Couple of hundred drachma. And a thousand US dollars in American Express TCs.'

'Let me see the passport,' Perlman said. He took it from Scullion and flicked the pages. A photograph, a name: *Shimon Marak*. An occupation: *Student*. An address in Haifa. 'No stamps. No visas. Why is that, Shimon?'

'Perhaps an oversight of your immigration authorities?'

'Lazy sods. They're always missing things. Where did you enter the United Kingdom?'

'Dover.'

'And how did you get to Scotland?'

'I took a bus from London.'

'We can check all that.' Perlman looked at the passport again. Shimon Marak. It didn't sound like an Arab name. 'Abdullah' was no Arab: he was more likely a Sephardic Jew of North African origin, perhaps Iraq, possibly Iran.

'Why are you in Glasgow?' Perlman asked.

'I'm a tourist.'

'In the dead of winter?' Scullion asked.

'I like the cold.'

'Right. People from all over the world flock to Glasgow in December for the cold. It's one big bloody cheerful freezefest. You can't get a hotel

371

room anywhere in the city unless you bribe the manager.'

Scullion was leafing through the wallet. He frowned at Perlman, then flashed the wallet under Marak's face. 'How did you get this, Shimon?'

'What is it?'

'What does it look like?'

'A wallet obviously, but I've never seen it before.'

'It belongs to a man called Artie Wexler. It contains his credit cards and a photograph of his wife. Do you know him?'

Marak shook his head.

Scullion said, 'Then how come his wallet is in your bedroom?'

'I can only assume you put it there.'

'Why would we do that?'

'You must have your reasons.'

Perlman realized he felt a curiously misplaced sense of pity for this kid. He was a long damn way from home, and in serious trouble; and who did he have to turn to for support? He was relying on a certain aloof arrogance, and making a show of being cool, almost disdainful, but this was a façade constructed with thin putty, and Perlman knew it would crumble eventually.

'Let's all sit down,' Scullion said. 'Make ourselves comfy.'

Marak rubbed his head. He had blood on his fingertips. Perlman held his elbow, and guided him inside the living room.

'I think I prefer to stand,' Marak said.

'The Inspector tells you to sit, you sit,' Perlman said.

Marak shrugged. He sat, looking bored.

'Is all this too much trouble for you, Marak?' Perlman asked. 'I mean, we can easily turn you over to people who are far less pleasant than Inspector Scullion and me.'

'I'm sure you can.'

Scullion, whose eye was swelling, looked at Lou. 'Do you think our boy is suggesting we planted this wallet, Sergeant Perlman?'

'Somebody had to,' Marak said.

'Since it wasn't us, who was it?'

'How would I know?'

Perlman said, 'Maybe you took it yourself. Maybe you stole it from Wexler.'

'Who's Wexler?'

'What were you doing in the street where Wexler lived?'

'Ah, *now* I remember you,' Marak said. 'You chased me. I found it amusing. You were puffing and huffing.'

'Glad I brought a smile to your face,' Perlman said. 'Don't irritate me, son. Just answer the fucking question.'

'The cab driver took a wrong turning.'

'So you didn't know Wexler lived on that street?'

'No — '

'Explain the wallet then.'

'I told you. I can't.'

'Got here by magic, did it?'

Scullion leaned forward in his chair. 'What were you doing in that particular neighbourhood anyway?'

'Sightseeing.'

'Right, I keep forgetting. You're a winter tourist. A man called BJ Quick said he delivered envelopes to you at this address.'

'Who?'

'Quick.'

'I have never heard of this person.'

'He knows you, Shimon. What about Furfee?'

'I never heard of him either.'

'Strange. He also says he knows you.'

'How odd.'

Perlman lit a cigarette. 'You're not making this easy on yourself, sonny boy.'

'But I have nothing to fear.'

'Mr Cool,' Perlman said. 'Thinks he can walk on fucking water, Sandy.'

'I only ever heard of one Jew who could pull off that stunt,' Scullion said.

'Aye, right enough.' Perlman glared at the young man. There was defiance in the set of face and the straight-backed alignment of body. You needed an ice-pick to chip away at Marak. 'What was your business with Joseph Lindsay?'

'Who?'

'Fuck these games. The solicitor. You phoned his office. You tracked his secretary.'

Marak looked as if he didn't remember.

'The fucking *garage*, Marak,' Perlman said. 'Where we got some nice shots of you, courtesy of the magic of closed-circuit TV, assaulting the secretary.'

Marak frowned and said, 'Yes. I remember now.'

'You've got a very selective memory.'

374

'I wanted to see Lindsay on a business matter.'

'Why did you need to see a Scottish lawyer?'

'I was interested in acquiring property in this country — '

'Oh, aye, so you could be closer to the cold. It doesn't explain why you assaulted the secretary, does it?'

'She was being obstructive. I lost control. I regretted it.'

'Do you lose control often?'

'No, I don't.'

Perlman looked for an ashtray. He couldn't find one. He walked inside the kitchen. There was that smell, that aroma of burnt plastic he'd noticed before, but stronger now. He tossed his cigarette into the sink and the butt sizzled.

There were spent matches in the sink. What had young Shimon been burning? he wondered. He looked around the kitchen. He opened the rubbish bin and saw the charred remains of what clearly had been a photograph. He picked it out of the rubbish with a gentle hand. It was flaky and would disintegrate if he didn't handle it gently. One edge hadn't burned entirely; a sliver of white border was blackened but visible. There were no images. The surface was composed of tiny black bumps as impenetrable as a sky without stars. Very carefully he carried the relic inside the living room and set it down on the coffee table, as if it were precious moth-eaten lace about to disintegrate.

'What's that?' Scullion asked.

'Let's ask Shimon. Why were you burning this photograph?'

'Is that what that is — a photograph?'

'That's what it is. We've got people with fancy machines, Shimon, and they can tease all kinds of information out of unlikely places. Take this photograph. They have some kind of computer that would restore the image you burned. Maybe it wouldn't be perfection, but it would be enough to see what you destroyed.'

'I destroyed nothing,' Marak said.

'Explain that smell,' Perlman said.

'I don't smell anything.'

'Judging from the pong, somebody's burned this within the last few minutes or so, Marak. And I don't see any other candidate but you.'

'I'll tell you again, I burned nothing.'

The old denial game, Perlman thought. See nothing, remember nothing. He made his hands into soft fists and wished he could *skelp* young Marak into answering questions.

Scullion sighed. 'Did you go to Lindsay's house?'

'How could I? The secretary wouldn't give me his address.'

Perlman thought about Joe Lindsay's abandoned Mercedes. 'You ever ride in his car?'

'That would also be very difficult, considering I never met the man.'

'Do you ever eat *garinim*?'

'What a strange question.'

'Just answer it.'

'Sometimes I eat it, yes,' Marak said.

Perlman sat down, sinking into a big sponge of an armchair, the kind that only a contortionist could escape with any semblance of dignity. He

376

heard springs creak. Good to take the weight off the aching leg. He stared at Marak. 'Summary so far. You don't know Lindsay. You don't know Wexler. You don't know how you came into possession of the wallet. You didn't burn that photograph. You don't know Furfee, you don't know Quick. Basically speaking, you know fuck all.'

'I think you are barking up a wrong tree,' Marak said.

This flat might have been a butcher's storage freezer. Perlman shivered and flipped a switch on the electric heater and heard one of the bars come on, clicking as it warmed. He smelled dust burning. It was like the stench of a mouse on fire.

Perlman asked, 'How did you hear about Lindsay? Were you sitting in Haifa one day with the Glasgow phone book in front of you and looked under solicitors and jabbed the page with a pin?'

Marak said, 'I knew his name.'

'How come?'

'I heard it mentioned in Haifa. Lindsay did business there now and then.'

'Oh aye? What kind?'

'I don't know what kind. I heard his name, that's all.'

'You're truly getting on my wick, son. Come on, tell me something you really *know*. Give me concrete. Hit me with gospel.'

'My date of birth.'

'I'm not easy to insult, but you're pushing me to the edge. Tell me something juicy.'

'Juicy? You mean interesting.'

'Bolt me to my seat.'

'I believe in justice.'

'I suppose that's a start. Isn't that a start, Inspector? You and me and Marak have something in common.'

Scullion said, 'Tell us more. Marak.'

'And I believe in peace,' Marak said.

Perlman said, 'Oh-oh. Justice *and* peace. We've got an idealist here, Sandy.'

Marak looked at the carpet, a soiled threadbare thing whose design had long ago faded into a few indistinct floral blotches. 'You're mocking me.'

'No. I was admiring your idealism,' Perlman said.

'I suppose *you* have none,' Marak said.

'I had most of my ideals kicked out of me working the streets of this city, son. A few wee bits and pieces are intact. Only just. Generally, I think idealism is a young man's game.'

'How sad,' Marak said.

'We're here to talk about your *tsurris*, Marak. Not ours. Face it. You've got serious problems.' Scullion blinked his swollen eye rapidly. It was almost shut.

'You can prove nothing against me,' Marak said.

'You think so, eh?' Scullion said. 'Check the list. Assaulting a police officer. The possibility of illegal entry into the country. The unprovoked attack on Joseph Lindsay's secretary. Possession of a wallet belonging to a man who was murdered — '

'Murdered? I'm to be blamed for that?'

Scullion said, 'Let me continue. There's the small matter of your presence at the scene of Shiv Bannerjee's murder.'

'Whose murder?'

'The Waterloo Hotel, Sauchiehall Street, remember? You were there, Marak. We have an eyewitness. She identified you from the print. What were you doing in that room at that particular time?'

'She's mistaken,' Marak said.

'I don't think so,' Scullion said.

Marak tilted his head back, laid his palms upturned on his thighs like a man seeking a source of relaxation. Perlman watched him and thought: Lindsay, Wexler, Bannerjee. Is this kid the one? Is this the killer? The connections were there, certainly, and they were strong enough to be audible. Marak and Lindsay, that fiction about buying a house was total *shtuss*. Marak and Wexler: how had Shimon come into possession of the wallet if he hadn't met Wexler somewhere along the way? And the Waterloo Hotel: he'd been present in the bathroom with Bannerjee, according to Charlotte Leckie.

But it was all circumstantial. Incriminating, aye, but still circumstantial. Where was the sword that had killed Wexler, and how had Marak acquired the cocaine to murder Lindsay, how had he coerced Lindsay into swallowing the condom unless he'd used a gun, and where was that gun now? The questions foamed and fizzed in Perlman's head. He tried to imagine this young man in the act of decapitation, but the

379

pictures were grainy. Nor could he see him force a gun to Lindsay's head.

And the wallet, that fucking wallet. That bothered Perlman. You throw away a wallet if you've stolen it from a man you've killed. True or false? You take the cash, dump the wallet. If you're prepared to gamble, you might nick a credit-card or two. No matter what you take, you dump the bloody wallet if you have any smarts whatsoever. Unless you were a *behayma* like Furfee, who'd held on to a murder weapon.

But Shimon Marak hadn't tossed it. So why not?

Maybe he didn't know it was in the flat. Maybe it had been placed there by somebody else.

Quick? Furfee?

Perlman pondered the idea of taking Marak to Pitt Street and confronting him with Quick and Furfee. It might be interesting, even revelatory. On the other hand, anything Quick and Furfee had to say would invariably be self-serving and consequently unreliable. There would be enough layers of exaggeration, false claims and accusations to keep a polygraph technician busy for years.

Perlman lit a cigarette. His throat was dry and raspy: if he was to break into song he'd sound like an old-time blues singer. Blind Lemon Jefferson, maybe.

'I think I'll talk to Linklater about what he can restore of the photograph, Sandy.'

'Go ahead,' Scullion said.

380

'It'll give us some idea if Shimon was destroying incriminating evidence.' He reached for the telephone that lay on the floor under the coffee table and he dialled Linklater's number. He got Sid Linklater's answering machine. 'Call me back, Sid. I'll be on Inspector Scullion's mobile. ASAP. I've got a nice wee restoration job for you.'

Marak said, 'He would have to be a magician to retrieve an image from that black stuff.'

'He's an alchemist, Shimon. He can take lead and turn it into the sweetest gold. Right, Inspector?'

Scullion, beginning to look like a prizefighter in need of a good cuts man, nodded. 'He's the best. Far and away.'

'As I told you, I have nothing to fear,' Marak said.

'Bully for you.' Perlman dragged on his smoke. 'You live in Haifa?'

Marak didn't answer.

Perlman asked, 'With your family? Are you married?'

Marak said, 'I don't discuss my family.'

'I'm interested in your background. Sisters? Brothers? What does your father do?'

'My father . . . ' Marak glanced at the ruins of the photograph on the coffee table then switched subjects. 'When you check, you'll see that my fingerprints are nowhere on that wallet.'

'Fine. We'll go over the wallet with a toothcomb, Shimon. What were you saying about your father?'

Marak slumped a little. 'My father's dead.'

'I'm sorry to hear that.'

'You didn't know him. How can you be sorry?'

Perlman said, 'Prickly, Shimon. I was expressing a common human condolence. Your father's dead, and I'm sorry. How did he die?'

Marak said, 'He was shot.'

'Who shot him?'

'It doesn't matter now.'

'I'm interested,' Perlman said.

'It doesn't matter,' Marak replied, a little pitch of sorrow in the voice.

Perlman sensed the young man's anger and loss. A damaged psyche was always difficult terrain to travel, but that didn't deter Lou Perlman, intrepid explorer. 'Somebody shoots your father, it doesn't matter? I don't believe that, Shimon. Why was he shot?'

'His associates thought he'd cheated them.'

'Cheated them how?'

Marak gazed at the floor. His hands were damp. They left prints on the dark wooden arms of his chair. He's in pain, Perlman thought. The death of his father is an open wound and he's covered it over in a gauze so thick, so congealed with old blood, it will never heal. Therefore the arrogance, the cold front, this was his armour.

'Cheated them out of what, Shimon?'

Marak stood up suddenly. 'Money.'

'But he didn't do it?'

'He'd never steal or cheat. He was a very honest man. He was the finest man I have ever known.' Marak clenched his hands so tightly his knuckles stood out like tiny sharp stones. 'They gunned him down in the street. I was fifteen years old and I saw it and I will never forget it. I don't want to talk about my father any more.'

Marak was silent. Perlman observed him, thinking how tightly wound he was, how tense his emotional sinews were drawn. A kid sees his father shot down in the street: what effect would that have on a life? Anger and loss and what else? A slow-burning fuse of vengeance? Something you tended carefully every day, making sure the fire hadn't gone out, a flame you fanned? Every day and every night, the same thought scalded you. And anything else around the edges, joy and love and laughter and music, lay in a shadow you couldn't penetrate because you were focused on only one thing. And so you prepare, and when you're ready, when you think you're old enough and tough enough, you make your move.

Settle old scores. Close the ledgers.

Marak said, 'I need to use the toilet. Is that permissible?'

'I'll keep you company,' Perlman said.

'I'm allowed no privacy?'

'In the circumstances.'

'Ah, of course, the circumstances.'

Perlman followed the young man out of the room. Scullion came behind.

'I'll hang around the front door,' Scullion said.

'Afraid I'll try to run away?' Marak asked.

'I'm not taking chances.'

Perlman went inside the bathroom with Marak and felt awkward when he heard the young man undo his zip and the sound of his urine striking water. He turned his face away: a small illusion of privacy, he thought. Why not? He heard

383

Marak flush the toilet, then zip his trousers up. The young man sighed as if with relief. And then suddenly the room was blasted with cold air, and Perlman swung his head in time to see Marak open the window and climb up on to the cistern and step out into the dark.

Perlman rushed to the window and saw Marak clinging to a drainpipe. 'You fucking *idiot*! Give me your hand. Come back inside.'

'I don't think so.' Marak was about four, five feet away, his hands clenched on the icy surface of the pipe. He couldn't climb in these slippery conditions, he'd fall, he'd go down until he struck the ground eighty or ninety feet below.

'Stay where you are,' Perlman said. 'Just reach out, I'll help you back inside.'

But Marak was climbing somehow, pushing himself up the pipe towards the edge of the roof, straining and grunting as he moved. His hard breathing steamed the air. Perlman heard Scullion come into the bathroom.

'Jesus Christ,' Scullion said. He stuck his head out of the window. 'Marak, don't be an arsehole. You're safer in here with us than you are out there.'

'I am safer where I am,' Marak said. He was already out of reach, a dark-coated figure flattened against the side of the building and climbing slowly.

'Where the hell do you think you're going?' Perlman roared.

'Where you can't follow.'

Perlman clambered on to the lid of the cistern and twisted his head to the side and watched

Marak continue his climb, arms hugging the drainpipe, towards the roofline. *I'm going out there*, Perlman thought. *I was the one that lost him, I have to be the one that brings him back down.* The lunacy of this act wasn't even a consideration: it was his responsibility, plain and simple. He had a good head of adrenaline going and his leg no longer ached and he felt weirdly youthful, as if the decision to go out into the precarious structures of the night rejuvenated him.

'No,' Scullion said.

'Watch me, Sandy,' and Perlman stepped on to the window ledge and felt the chill air sneak under his trousers.

'No, Lou,' Scullion shouted. 'For God's sake.'

'Here I go, singing low.' Perlman reached out for the drainpipe, and swung his body into space, and for a moment he thought he'd lost contact with the pipe and was going to tumble out into nothingness, which he understood was no philosophical abstraction but something dreadfully and inevitably real. It was where your life ended, and your world stopped. But he had the pipe, cold as it was, under the palms of his hands. The slick ice that had formed on the surface wasn't going to help him climb. Ice and gravity, co-conspirators. He looked up and saw Marak scramble on to the roof.

'Shimon, come back down, do it now, do it nice and slow and we'll be fine.' Perlman thought his own voice was a thin flute and unconvincing. Face it, Lou: you're clinging to a fucking drainpipe and hanging on for that condition people call 'dear life' and you're trying to convince some daring young guy to turn himself over to *you?* Dear life indeed. He glanced down, saw the wall of the tenement sheer beneath him, saw light from windows here and there, saw the outlines of the iron fences that marked one back yard from another, sharp railings; if you slipped there was every chance you'd be impaled. Very nice.

Cop kebab.

Looking down: wrong thing to do, Sergeant.

He shinned a couple of inches up the pipe. What an effort. He looked at the roofline above. He heard Marak's feet on the slates.

Scullion shouted, 'For fuck's sake, Lou. Get your arse back in here.'

'I don't think I can,' Perlman said.

'Don't move, I'll get some help, a ladder, the fire brigade.'

But Perlman was rising again, inch by hard-gained inch. His hands felt frozen to the pipe. He made it to the roofline, where the pipe adjoined a section of guttering, which looked too frail to support him. He had only two choices: reach up and grasp the guttering and hoist himself on to the slates and hope the whole arrangement didn't collapse, or begin his descent and pray he could make it back down to the ledge of the bathroom window without slipping off the cliff of the tenement.

'*Yippee aye o,*' he said, and scrambled up the last piece of pipe and hauled himself over the guttering and on to the slates. *Done it.* The slates

386

were so sleek they might have hosted an ice-hockey game.

Crouching, Perlman felt himself slip back towards the edge, then he countered this trend by flattening his face and body against the roof and locking every muscle hard in place and gripping any slight crevice he could find between the slates. The sky was high and starry above him. The city lit the air in blooms of orange and yellow. My funeral colours, he thought. Somewhere nearby floodlights burned unblinkingly around the edge of a stadium.

'Perlman,' Marak said.

Lou Perlman looked up. Marak was perhaps ten feet away, his back pressed to the base of a chimney.

'I thought we might continue our chat, Marak.' Perlman slid a few inches. He felt he was part of some strange deep earthly motion; tectonic plates were shifting beneath him. The earth was about to split. High in the Glasgow night, he sensed the city stretching away all around him, the thinning of lights as the river slogged down to the coast, the steadiness of its current disrupted only by the occasional vortex, the odd fluke of undertow. My river, my city, my place of my birth and my dying.

'You're going to fall,' Marak said.

'Absolute shite. I climb roofs in all seasons.' He slithered forward and up, still clinging to little crannies in the contours of slate. He was breathless, heart moving in his chest like an octopus flapping. His lungs pained him. He raised his face and looked at Marak. 'See? I'm so fucking nimble you wouldn't believe it, Marak.'

'Now what? Do you try to convince me I should give myself up?'

'I don't think you're ready to be convinced,' Perlman said. A plane roared above on a flight path to Glasgow Airport. The sound thundered in his head. The roof seemed to tremble.

Marak slipped suddenly, and sat down with his back to the chimney. 'I'm not used to these surfaces,' he said. 'How can you stand this city, this weather?'

'Born to it,' Perlman said.

Marak said, 'A man is killed in a street in Haifa. Years later, as a direct consequence of his father's death, his son sits on a rooftop in Glasgow in winter. Strange connections.'

'Aye, the world's a funny place,' Perlman said. His hands shook, his muscles strained. How long could he hold off the inevitable slide over slate and ice? 'Who killed your father, Marak?'

'You're asking two different questions, Perlman. Do you want to know who pulled the trigger? Or do you want the names of the real assassins?'

'Whatever you're prepared to give.'

Marak said, 'The men who pulled the triggers are of no consequence. They were once my father's associates. They accused him of embezzling an enormous amount of money that was supposed to reach them. And so they killed him. But they're dead now. I shot them three months ago in Tel Aviv. They were sitting outside a café, I went up to them while they were drinking wine. One I shot directly in the heart, the other the head. I walked away. I had a taste of justice. I'd waited a long time for it. The strange thing, it had no flavour.'

How casually Marak referred to these killings. Was some part of him numb? Had the muscles of his conscience been severed?

'Where did this money go?'

'The men who'd stolen it claimed they'd given it to my father to be disbursed for a noble purpose. I assume they kept it for themselves. What else would they do? Distribute it among charities?'

Perlman saw a sudden shooting star in the western sky, beyond the Campsie Hills, bright and brief and shocking. 'And this noble purpose — did it have something to do with the idea of peace in the Middle East?'

'How do you know that, Perlman?'

'I was always good at guessing games.'

'It's more than guesswork, I'm sure.' Marak's face was shadowed, his expression hidden. 'A few people dreamed they could change the climate of the Middle East. My father and his associates, for example.'

'And big dreams require big cash,' Perlman said.

'Of course. But the dreamers overlooked one fact: there is not enough money in the world to solve the problem of eternal hatred. Nor eternal greed. The money was stolen. My father was wrongly blamed, with tragic consequences.'

Marak moved away. He's almost lost to me now, Perlman thought. 'You told me you were an idealist, Marak. You don't sound like one.'

'Idealists have a cross to carry,' Marak said. 'I believe even as I doubt.'

Perlman laid a cheek against slate. He was fused to it by a film of cold. His thoughts tumbled. He had an after-image of the shooting star, dying lights flashing at the end of a tunnel in his brain. 'Let me see if I can guess the names of the thieves. Lindsay, Wexler, Bannerjee.'

'These were the names I received from a man who called himself Ramsay. Tall man, strange hair, weak chin.'

'BJ Quick.'

'Ah, he uses two names.'

'At the very least,' Perlman said.

Marak rubbed his hands together. A wind came up and blew across the rooftops. 'He gave me photographs, addresses. The burned photograph that so intrigued you was of Bannerjee.'

Perlman felt his coat rise and fall around his legs, the wind riding roughshod across him. 'I wonder how Quick got this information.'

'I didn't ask. All I know is I didn't kill them. The men were dead before I could ever get close to them. I was brought here only to be blamed for murders I didn't commit.'

'Why and by whom?'

'One day perhaps I'll think about those questions. My only interest now is to make my way home.'

'How do you propose to do that?'

'We'll see. What about you? How will you get down from this roof?'

Perlman raised his head. 'That's my problem, intit?'

'Yes. It is.' Marak moved slowly. In a moment he'd disappear on the other side of the sandstone chimney block. And then he'd be gone, and maybe he'd make it, maybe he wouldn't. Perlman called out his name, as if to stall him further and ask more questions, but the wind lashed his voice away, and besides Marak had vanished, moving behind the chimneys and heading for the other side of the roof, the downslope, and from there — who could say?

Perlman pressed his face into the slates. He was cold and weary. He heard Scullion's voice float up from a place below. *'You all right, Lou?'*

Perlman hadn't the strength to answer.

'We're coming up with a rope. Hang on.'

Hang on. Oy. I spend much of my life hanging on. He shut his eyes: dear Jesus, had he really climbed on to this roof? Was he truly lying here on this slick of tiles? Had he forgotten entirely the fact he suffered from vertigo?

And now he remembered, and his stomach churned sluggishly over and over and all the stars in the sky imploded in his head.

52

He was giddy for some time after he'd been helped down from the roof by means of a rope and the two beefy cops from the backup car. His impulse was to go home and sleep, and forget he'd ever been daft enough to climb on to the roof of a tall Glasgow tenement. But he went back to Pitt Street and began to work on a report of the encounter with Marak. He knew he wouldn't sleep if he went home. Things on his mind. Too many.

He typed a sentence on the portable Olivetti he liked, then quit. He pushed his chair back from his desk and pondered a call to the hospital, but it was almost midnight and he wondered if that was too late. Instead, he dialled Colin and Miriam's home number. He got the answering machine. Miriam's voice: *Please leave a message and we'll return your call as soon as we can.* Did that mean she was asleep, or that she was at the hospital? He was tempted to dial again, just to hear her voice. It had a richness, a chanteuse's lilt. It was a voice that implied more than it ever said.

He gazed at the paper inside the olive-green typewriter, and what he'd written, and his mind changed gears, and all of a sudden he was back on that iced roof, that parlous place. He knew tonight he'd dream of rooftops and chimneys and scary visions of himself dangling from a rope

392

knotted round his waist while the two cops fed him down slowly to the bathroom window, where Scullion watched the descent with concern. If he slept.

All this began with a man hanging from a rope under a railway bridge, he thought.

He pushed the typewriter away. The report could wait. His mind wasn't on it. He paced around his desk. He wondered if Marak had made it back down to the street, and where he might be in the city now. Scullion had patrol cars out looking for him, because he wasn't convinced of Marak's innocence. He wasn't buying the proclamation the kid had made to Perlman on the rooftop of a tenement. Why should he, without interrogating Marak thoroughly for himself? The city had been violated, and Scullion felt a deep responsibility, and as long as he wasn't sure of Marak in his own head, then he'd make every effort to track him down.

Scullion appeared in the doorway. 'You okay?'

'For a man with a few murders on his mind, fine.'

'When you climbed that drainpipe . . . '

'That's all I need, to be reminded.'

'I thought you'd fall. I was *sure* you'd fall. I kept thinking I'd have to ask Madeleine to cancel her plans to ask you to dinner next week.'

'What an inconvenience,' Perlman said.

Scullion patted Perlman's shoulder. 'You're sure you're all right?'

'Slight headache. Maybe a cold coming on. My leg muscles are sore.'

'And I can't see anything in one eye.'

'Such a catalogue of misery,' Perlman said. 'Incidentally, Quick admitted delivering photographs of the three victims to Marak. He doesn't know who hired him as courier. All done by phone, he says. Never saw anyone's face . . . '

'Anything else?'

'He believes Marak couldn't have killed Lindsay or Wexler. As for Bannerjee, he isn't sure. He thinks not. According to the impresario, Marak's a major loser.'

Scullion sat on the edge of the desk. 'If Marak's off the hook — and I'm not saying he is, mind you, because Quick's not famous for his veracity — who's the swordsman? Who's the killer?'

'Who indeed.' Perlman tugged a Kleenex from a box on his desk and blew his nose. He tossed the Kleenex directly into his waste-paper basket. 'Quick was trying to buy back the lease to that slum of a club belonging to Leo Kilroy. Do you suppose Fat Leo has any involvement in all of this?'

'It wouldn't *floor* me with surprise, because nothing Fat Leo does astounds me. But he doesn't come into the Lindsay-Wexler-Bannerjee axis, does he?'

'Not that I know,' Perlman said.

'I'm going to get a cup of coffee from the machine. You need anything?'

Perlman looked at the half-eaten cheese and cucumber sandwich on his desk. Stale, lathered with a highly dubious mayonnaise-based sauce that was whipped up in a local takeaway by grubby-fingered boys, it was utterly inedible.

'Nothing for me. I'm fine, Sandy.'

Scullion vanished down the hall. Perlman slumped in his chair, shut his eyes. Think think. He forced his eyes open, picked up the phone and called Perseus McKinnon.

'Perse, one question.'

'The hour is late, but fire away,' McKinnon said.

'You heard the news about Bannerjee?'

'It's been on the telly. Very gruesome.'

'I want you to tell me if you know of any connection between Leo Kilroy and any of the three dead men. Anything at all, it doesn't matter what.'

'How about asking me something difficult,' Perseus McKinnon said. 'Kilroy supplied some muscle when Shiv was just another ambitious Asian running for public office.'

'What kind of muscle?'

'How shall I say? Persuaders? Guys that got the vote out. They wore nice suits and charmed old ladies. They drove elderly people to polling stations. Every now and then I heard a story about one of them getting a wee bit argumentative. But Kilroy managed to keep a very tight lid on his boys.'

'So Bannerjee was indebted to Kilroy?'

'Big time. Kilroy wanted influence in high places. But Bannerjee, as history has duly recorded, fucked up.'

'Do they keep in contact?'

'That I couldn't say. Where are you taking this, Lou?'

'I don't know yet. Thanks.' Perlman hung up

and stared at the sheet in the Olivetti, then tore it out and crumpled it into a ball. He threw it at the wall. Bannerjee and Kilroy. This connection made him uncomfortable. Was it possible that Fat Leo belonged on the same bus as the three dead men? Had he bought a ticket and shared a trip with them, then he'd decided to get off before the point of destination? You'd never find Leo's prints on anything, because he was too smart; but that didn't mean he failed to leave some spidery little traces of his activities at least.

Okay. Was it possible that Leo Kilroy, for reasons that eluded Perlman, had engineered the deaths of the three men?

Think. Motives?

The money factor? Had there been some rabid falling-out, a fierce disagreement concerning loot and its disbursement?

Or was it less obvious?

Such as what?

He picked up his sandwich and stared at it critically. He sniffed it. Tainted. He dropped it in his waste-paper basket. There were clouds gathering in his head, and he didn't like their formation. He longed for some spike of sunshine to pierce the glum congregation. He thought about Colin again, like a man constantly drawn back to a lingering mystery; *bruder*, you kept some dubious company.

If you knew Bannerjee, did you know Kilroy too, Colin?

And then Perlman remembered, and he slapped his forehead in dismay at the failure of his memory. Murdoch. You *yutz*, Lou, he thought. You'd forget your name if it wasn't for your driving licence or your library card. He picked up his telephone and asked the switchboard to connect him to PC Dennis Murdoch.

Murdoch came on the line almost at once. 'I only just finished collecting that material for you, Sergeant.'

'Great. Let's get together. You hungry?'

53

Perlman met the young Constable at Café Insomnia, an all-night eatery in Partick. The clientele was mainly the post-pub set, young and ready to gorge themselves on carbohydrates. Wonderful smells perfumed the air, bacon, toast, coffee. You could get breakfast here all day long. Perlman asked for coffee and dry toast, Murdoch ordered a bacon roll and tea.

'Thanks for the material,' Perlman said, and laid the manila folder Murdoch had given him on the table.

Murdoch sipped his tea. 'I did it quickly. If you think I should spend more time on it. I'd be happy to — '

'You sound as if you don't want me to read it, Murdoch.'

'No, it's not that, Sarge, I think maybe I could've found more material if I'd had more time, that's all.'

'Let me look through what you've got before I make any judgement.' Perlman glanced at the young cop, who shrugged and bit into his bacon roll.

He opened Murdoch's folder. Inside was a stack of Xeroxed papers and some print-outs the young cop must have run from a computer. Perlman read swiftly, turning one page after another like a man anxious to reach the denouement of a mystery — and then he stacked

398

the papers in a pile and stared at Murdoch's face, which was expressionless. Perlman felt trapped in a weirdly airless space. His head filled with a darkening sense of disappointment. He lit a cigarette and blew smoke and thought the small cloud that floated away from his lips was the colour of dismay. He wanted to pretend he'd never read these papers. Put the omelette back into the eggshell, Lou. Go home and take a sleeping pill and enter the blackout zone.

'Where did you get this stuff, Murdoch?'

'The Jewish Telegraph was one obvious place. A lady there was very helpful. Then the Internet. There's a lot of information about Nexus out there, Sergeant. If you're patient enough to look for it.'

Perlman's hand shook very slightly. He picked up the pile, shuffled the pages until he found a newspaper clipping, badly Xeroxed, smudged but legible. It hadn't been attributed to a writer; presumably it came from a wire service. Dated September 1995, it described the murder of a man called Yusef Barzelai in Haifa by unknown assassins. He was 'a pioneer member of the Nexus group', according to the story; he'd been shot down in front of his son in a busy street. The son's name was given as Eli Barzelai: there was a poorly focused photo, snapped by some insensitive jerk, of a teenage boy holding his dying father.

When you looked closely you saw it was Marak, Shimon Marak cradling his father. The kid's mouth was open, frozen in a scream. How many times did you see similar photographs of personal horror and outraged grief, victims of terrorist attacks, innocent bystanders blasted by nail-filled explosives? Too often in this sad old world. Perlman looked into the devastation of the kid's expression.

So Eli Barzelai had travelled to Glasgow on a false passport. Why not? Maybe he was wanted by Israeli authorities in connection with the slayings of two men in a Tel Aviv café.

'Add a beard,' Murdoch said.

Perlman nodded. 'You'd get a close resemblance all right.'

Murdoch finished his roll and looked at Perlman, who nibbled on his toast, brushed crumbs from his lips, drank some coffee, then returned his attention to the papers. He leafed through them: *I'm just going through the motions*, he thought. *I'm stalling the inevitable. I've seen what I didn't want to see. And now I'm going to look at it again.*

He stopped at an obituary of Yusef Barzelai. Born Baghdad, 1939. Emigrated with parents to Israel, 1951. In Israel, Yusef established a successful career as a political journalist, and worked for various pacifist causes. In 1988, he'd co-founded Nexus, whose original committee consisted of four Jews and four Palestinians.

Murdoch, a conscientious boy, had gathered all kinds of items about Nexus, some no more than press releases, others analytical think-pieces on the group's slim chances of success in the volatile atmosphere of the Middle East. There were stories that covered fund-raising activities in the United States, France, the United

Kingdom. Indefatigable, Yusef Barzelai and his fellow founders had launched themselves passionately on the dinner circuits of the capitalist world, reasoning that you could broker peace only if you had financial muscle. An article in *The Economist* reported that by the early 1990s, the group had raised more than ten million dollars; and that was 'a conservative estimate'. And so Nexus grew, opened offices in Tel Aviv, Jerusalem, Haifa, hired energetic people dedicated to the aims of the organization. They sent out pamphlets on coexistence, and published a quarterly journal entitled *Pax: The Future of the Middle East*, which was basically a low-circulation house magazine for the cause. They established a Centre for Peace Studies in Jerusalem. The Centre was bombed in 1994 by extremists; it wasn't clear whether they were Israelis or Palestinians. The attack, in which five Nexus staff members were killed, slowed the impetus of the organization. By the middle of the 1990s, Nexus had closed its offices and ceased publication of *Pax*. The Centre was never rebuilt.

By the spring of 1995, according to an article in the *New York Times*, Nexus was in the process of 'regrouping'. The report also said that 'funds are still available for restructuring' the organization.

'Irrepressible optimists,' Perlman said in a dry way. Men dream of the unattainable, and sometimes even achieve it. But the house odds were always stacked against visionaries.

Murdoch asked, 'Is there anything wrong with a little optimism? Where would we be if we always looked on the gloomy side of things?'

'You're a cheerful soul, Murdoch. Your glass is always half full, eh?'

'I try to be upbeat,' Murdoch said.

'Don't lose that attitude, son.' Perlman drank his coffee then fidgeted with the rim of the cup. He gazed at the papers on the table. He picked another sheet from the bunch.

I didn't like this one when I first saw it, and I like it even less now, he thought. He took off his glasses, wiped them with a paper napkin, replaced them. 'This old shot. Where did you find it?'

'A back issue of *Pax* on the Internet.'

The Internet. The World Wide Web. A whole world I know nothing about, Perlman thought. He looked at the photograph, the smiling well-nourished faces, men of beaming prosperity. They wore tuxedos. On the right of the photograph Artie Wexler smoked a cigar. This was a slightly thinner Artie, but not by much. At the front stood Lindsay, smiling in a lawyerly way, as if he'd just demonstrated the validity of some arcane legal precedent. Behind Lindsay was Shiv Bannerjee, his tux a wee bit more fashionable than any of the others, his shirt frilly, the cuffs extravagant.

Perlman felt the weight of a grave depression settle on him. He couldn't take his eyes from the picture. It fogged in front of him.

'He's your brother, isn't he?' Murdoch asked.

'He's my brother all right.'

'I heard somebody say he was sick. Heart problem.'

'He had a bypass today.'

'Did it go all right?'

'I think it did, Murdoch.'

'He looks healthy in that picture,' Murdoch said.

'This was taken in 1992.'

'So it says.'

Perlman clasped his hands on the table. 1992. Ancient history. Let it go, Lou. What does it matter? Colin operated in some shady areas. You knew that. You knew he moved in the cool grey canyons of cash, in the ever-shifting scree of stock certificates and shares. Funny business. You'd had it confirmed by Bannerjee. Why be shocked by anything else you discovered?

You were even prepared to overlook Colin's past.

His eye travelled to the side of the group.

Colin looked directly back at him, his expression one of good cheer and good health; he emitted the confident glow of a man who's never been bruised by life, never battered. A man whose expectations have always been met, and more usually surpassed.

Perlman read the caption for what seemed to him the hundredth time. He was no longer really seeing it. *Friends of Nexus Dinner, the Savoy, London, April 1992: Our guests from Glasgow.* And a list of the names of this Glasgow contingent was provided in bold font after the caption. Perlman, who felt he'd stumbled into the secret of some ancient freemasonry, remembered his brother saying: *Nexus? I have an*

403

extremely vague memory of the name.

He scrunched the page from *Pax* in his hand and stuffed it in his pocket. Oh, brother, you never thought anybody would come across this old article from an obscure magazine neglected for years and left to decay in some dark underpass of the information highway, did you?

He got up from the table, patted Murdoch's shoulder. 'Thanks for all your help, son.' Then he picked up the folder and went quickly out into the night.

54

He drove across the river to the south side on roads as hard as diamonds. Streetlamps created glossy reflections, traffic signals burned red and amber and green on the ice. There were few cars around. The city's wintry desolation was total. Christmas trees seen in the windows of houses looked cheerless, already dying. Decorations hanging inside living rooms resembled paper braids from Yules a century ago.

Christmas was created for manic depressives, he thought.

Spring was years away. *You must remember spring*.

When he reached the Cedars he parked the Mondeo and walked directly to the building, in darkness except for a few pale lights upstairs. The front door wasn't locked. It didn't need to be, because a heavyweight security guard sat in the reception area. He was a crewcut man with a thick neck and a nose battered flat into his frightening face, a misshapen glob of bone and flesh. Perlman wondered if he ever heard little bells ring in his head. *Seconds out*.

'What can I do for you?' he asked.

Perlman showed his Force ID, which the guard scanned with a lack of interest. 'My brother's a patient here. He had an op today. I want to see him.'

'See him? This time of night? You're joking.

Come back during visiting hours,' the guard said. 'Ten a.m. to noon. Or four to seven.'

'I mean now,' Perlman said.

'The only way you can get to see your brother at this hour is if Dr Rifkind gives his okay.' The guard flashed a wrist, scanning the fattest wristwatch Perlman had ever seen, a great chunky slab of a thing. 'If I was you, I'd wait for visiting hours.'

'Then I'll speak to Rifkind. Is he here?'

'He went home hours ago.'

'I'll call him,' Perlman said.

'What's the bloody urgency?'

'It would take too long to explain, even if I felt like it, and I don't. Just give me Rifkind's number — '

'It's ex-directory.'

'So if there's an emergency you don't know how to contact the chief physician? What happens? Patients just expire?'

The guard said, 'If your brother's had an op, he needs rest. Last thing he wants is visitors.'

'He'll want to see me,' Perlman said. 'I have an uplifting effect on him.'

'At this hour?' the guard said.

Perlman leaned across the desk. 'Get used to this. I don't intend to leave without seeing him. What are you going to do? Restrain me? Assault a police officer?'

'I have my instructions, Sergeant.'

'Let's see what happens, shall we?' Perlman stepped towards the door that led to the corridor.

The guard hopped over the desk briskly.

406

'Don't do this,' he said. He positioned himself squarely between Perlman and the door. 'Now I've told you the visiting hours and I expect you to have a wee bit of respect for the regulations we have here.'

Perlman said, 'I can have a fucking squad car here in minutes. I can have you removed from the premises on the grounds of almost anything I choose to invent. I've been a policeman too long, and power's completely corrupted the fuck out of me.'

'You're putting me on the spot,' the guard said.

'Look away. Turn your back. Bend down and tie your shoelace. You never saw me.'

The guard's expression was one of exasperation. He was thinking of the consequences of a patrol car screaming into the car park, policemen rushing into the building, DS Perlman drumming up some ridiculous accusation that might affect his job with Strathclyde Number One Security, who never hired anyone with a criminal record. There was a pension involved, and a good health-plan, and bonus money every Christmas. Strathclyde Number One Security had been good to him.

'Fuck it. Okay. I'm not looking. Satisfied?'

'You're a great man.'

Bluffed, the guard walked back to his desk and Perlman stepped through the door into the corridor. At the far end a dim lamp glowed. The place was silent. No stirring patients, no night-time coughers or hackers, no sound of machinery monitoring anyone's health. Which room was Colin's? Wasn't it room 9?

He moved slowly past closed doors, checking numbers. Wouldn't Colin be in intensive care after heart surgery? He wasn't sure about that. Why were hospitals so inherently spooky in the dead of night? He'd seen too many movies in which psychotic nurses performed mercy-killings on terminal patients. He'd seen evil angels prowl darkened wards with a lethal syringe concealed under a towel.

He found number 9, stopped outside the door. 'Lou?'

Perlman turned. Rifkind was coming down the corridor towards him. He wore pyjamas and a robe. 'What are you doing here?'

'Visiting Colin.'

'He's asleep, Lou. Come back in the morning.'

'I'm tired of being told that,' Perlman said.

'He's exhausted.'

Perlman touched the door handle. 'The alsatian at the desk said you'd gone home.'

Rifkind smiled. 'He's paid to say what I want him to say. Sometimes I sleep here when I need to keep an eye on specific patients. I have a small apartment upstairs. If you're worried about Colin, there's no need. The operation went like a dream. Is something troubling you? You look fraught.'

Fraught, yes. Totally riddled with *fraught*. 'I just want to see him, Martin. He's my brother, for God's sake.'

'You sound very petulant, Lou. Will you stamp your feet next? I think we keep a jar of lollipops somewhere for naughty little boys. Would you

408

like one? Red? Green?'

Perlman said, 'I'm going inside.'

'No. Wait. You'll only disturb — '

'I won't wake him. I'll just look at him. How does that sound?' Perlman turned the handle, pushed the door, saw thin white light burning above his brother's bed. Colin sat up in bed wearing an unbuttoned pyjama top. His chest was bandaged, and he had an arm attached to a saline drip that made a quiet *glugging* sound.

'Well, brother,' Colin said. 'An unexpected visit. I'm lying here in a post-op haze, and the hell of it is I can't sleep. They give me painkillers and big fat jellybeans loaded with downers, but nothing seems to kick in. Prowling the neighbourhood, were you?'

'Sort of,' Lou Perlman said. 'I just wanted to visit.'

Rifkind said, 'Ten minutes. No more.' Then he went out.

Lou sat on the edge of the bed and scanned Colin's face. The saline drip *plopped*. There was bruising around the place where the drip went into Colin's arm.

'The operation was successful,' Lou said.

'They tell me,' Colin said. He looked healthy; maybe a little drained, which you'd expect, but there was colour to his face and a light in his eyes.

Lou Perlman was quiet. He looked at the Lucozade and Kleenex on the bedside table, the pills, a get-well card in which he could see Miriam's signature followed by a bunch of Xs. The sense of betrayal wasn't weakening inside

409

him; the knowledge that Colin had lied stoked his anger. And yet he wasn't ready to speak, because too many half-formed sentences went racing through his mind and he couldn't corral them cohesively.

'Say something, brother,' Colin said.

'You've heard about the murders?'

Colin Perlman said, 'I've heard. Wexler is dead.'

'Cruelly,' Lou said.

'I saw the story on the box. Who killed him, Detective?'

'I'd be guessing if I said anything.'

'No suspect in custody?'

'No.'

Colin made a gesture with his hand; the tides of fate were unpredictable. 'Hard to believe Artie's . . . gone. Artie and Lindsay both. Strange, eh?'

'And Bannerjee's dead. You see that?'

Colin said, 'Aye, I saw it.'

'What do you think of his murder?'

'I'm supposed to have an opinion on the death of this Indian *parech*? His passing doesn't mean anything in my life, wee brother.' Colin grimaced. 'Give me that little brown bottle, will you.'

Lou Perlman picked up the prescription bottle from the bedside table and handed it to his brother, who slipped a capsule out and conveyed it to his mouth with a short stiff movement of his arm.

'I hurt like a fucking pincushion,' Colin said.

'I'm not surprised.' Lou leaned a little closer

to Colin. What was it you said before, *bruder*? You were lying in this hospital bed *taking stock of your life*? Was that the phrase you used? I wonder if you reached any conclusions. 'You never knew Bannerjee anyway, did you, Colin?'

'I'm glad to say.'

'Never ran into him.'

'Didn't I just say that? Are you here to interrogate me or something?'

Lou Perlman laughed. It didn't sound right in his ears. A fake laugh, a cocktail-party whoop. 'Just passing through, Colin. Besides, I was worried about you. Wexler dead. And Lindsay. I wondered if there might be a hit-list, and your name was on it for future disposal.'

'My name? What have I done?'

Lou Perlman saw the opening. 'You've lied to me. We can start there, if you like.'

'And how have I lied, wee Louie?'

Wee Louie, Perlman thought. He hadn't heard that one in years. *Wee Louie'll clean up the mess. Wee Louie'll clear the chess pieces away.* He understood Colin was trying to put him back in his place of youthful servitude. Yessir, Colin. No problem, Colin. Happy to be useful.

'You lied about Bannerjee, Colin.'

'Oh? Did I?'

'He's the name you couldn't remember. Lindsay's client? The investor?'

'*That*. Slipped my mind. Big deal.'

'Bannerjee — whose name was practically a fucking synonym for scandal in Scotland — just *slipped* your mind? He was in every tabloid and broadsheet for months. The morality of our

411

politicians. Do ethnic-minority members make good politicians. Don't bullshit me, Colin. Don't start.'

'Is Wee Louie angry?'

'Fuck that Wee Louie *dreck*.'

'You're all grown up. I forget.'

'Bannerjee said you invested money for him. Illegally. Says you told him you were good at it. You'd done it hundreds of times.'

'Sweet Jesus. You don't grasp the truth about money, do you, old son? There's one and only one objective when you have it, Lou. To keep it. Nothing else matters. You vanish it. You put it where nobody can find it. You place it beyond the law, beyond the tax authorities, you stick it inside a trick cabinet, and when you open it — abracadabra, what cash? Where the hell did it go? It was here a minute ago, right? Illusion. There was no money. You only thought you saw it. I'm a fucking magician, Lou. I'm the *kuntzenmaker*. Years later, when you reopen the cabinet, the money's appeared again. Only this time it's more than you remembered. You put x into the cabinet, you get x-plus back. What a trick.'

'You're a crook, Colin.'

'With manicured nails. You're the cop, and your nails are all bitten down. What does that tell us?'

'Villains have more money to spend on their vanities.'

Colin smiled. The fetching smile, the charmer. 'I'm no villain. I manipulate the system. That's what it's there for.'

'You lied about Bannerjee, Colin. It comes back to that.'

'Amnesia happens.'

'Aye, right. I suppose you don't remember your association with Nexus either?'

'Again with the questions. It's like the Chinese water torture listening to you go on and on.'

'Take a gander at this, Colin. Refresh your memory.' Perlman took the clipping from *Pax* out of his pocket, hesitated a moment before he tossed it on the bed.

Colin picked it up and looked at it without expression. 'You dig up an old picture. So?'

'You told me to my face you had no connection with Nexus. You could hardly even remember the name when I brought it up.'

Colin let the clipping drop from his hand. 'I was somewhat preoccupied with my surgery, Lou. Let's say my mind was elsewhere. Do you understand that? Or are you too damned obsessive to grasp the idea that people don't concentrate *all* the time?'

'So this just sort of slipped your mind as well, Colin. It must be like a ski-slope in that head of yours. Look. See picture. Big dinner in London. Monkey suits. Friends of Nexus. Part of the prosperous Glasgow contingent. You were a cog in the Nexus machine.'

'I raised some money for them.'

'How much?'

'Oh, come on. Who remembers now? Lou, huge sums go through my hands all the time. I don't remember every transaction.'

Perlman picked up the clipping where his

413

brother had dropped it on the bedcover. 'Tell me how well you know this man,' and he pointed to a figure in the picture.

Colin peered at the shot. 'He falls directly into the acquaintance department.'

'And no more?'

'Why? Do you expect more, Lou? You want me to say we're bosom buddies? You want me to say we're joined at the hip and participants in evil schemes? That would satisfy you, would it? That would please your wee police brain, eh?'

I don't know what would please my wee police brain, Lou Perlman thought; and he looked at the photograph again. Slightly shadowed on Colin's left stood a fifth figure in the shot of the Glasgow contingent: Leo Kilroy, dressed in whale-sized tux and enormous cummerbund and outsized bow-tie. Kilroy's face was big and bloated, and his eyes were like slits made by a knife in a lump of pizza dough.

Lou glanced back at his brother. 'You know this man's rep? It's as rank as a barrel of bad herring, Colin.'

'I've heard rumours.'

'Rumours? Do me a favour. You worked with him to help raise funds for Nexus.'

'Our paths crossed. We attended some fund-raising dinners in Glasgow a few times, then Edinburgh. I think we went down to Newcastle and Leeds once or twice. It's fuzzy. We were never friends, Lou. And even if we were, I wouldn't fucking apologize for it.'

Lou Perlman took off his glasses and squeezed the bridge of his nose. 'Let me get it straight.

414

The money you raised for Nexus went into accounts you set up in funny places. Instead of transferring this money directly to Nexus, you took it and you played with it. You and your little gang. The Famous Five.'

'Are you saying I stole it, brother?'

'I imagine that's what I'm saying.'

'You disappoint me.'

'It's reciprocal. And don't give me that soulful hurt look, Colin.'

Colin Perlman sighed. 'I think I need to rest. I'd prefer it if you took your arse out of here.'

'A minute more, that's all.'

'No, now — '

'You didn't transfer the funds where they were supposed to go, and a man called Yusef Barzelai was suspected of having embezzled them. As a result, he was shot dead by some of his more rabid Nexus associates, who seem to have been judge and jury and executioners — '

'Barzelai? I don't know if that name rings — '

'Shut the fuck up. I'm not riding that old tramcar of yours, Colin. I know its destination. Feigned ignorance. You remember nothing, your head is fuzzy, it's all such a long time ago, yack yackety yack — '

'Go shit in the ocean, Lou — '

'Barzelai died because you and your wee gang cheated him.'

'Have you been smoking whackybaccy you confiscated in a drugs raid?'

Lou ignored his brother. He ignored the cold smile that was meant to be derisory. He had that certain tremor he always got when he suspected he was rushing towards truth; it had to be the same kind of shock that went through the hands of a man with a divining rod when he discovered a deep source of water.

'I had an encounter with Barzelai's son,' Lou said.

'His *son*?' Did Colin show just then a flicker of interest? Some movement of eye, or eyebrow, corner of mouth? In the bad light, it was hard to tell.

'The boy was sent here from Israel to eliminate Lindsay, Wexler, and Bannerjee.'

'Then you've caught your killer?'

'I wish I could say so. But I can't.'

'You just said you'd encountered this kid — '

'Encountered, aye. But I didn't say he was the killer, Colin. He wanted revenge for the people directly responsible for his father's death. Somehow he learned they're in Glasgow. He came all this way ready to do deeds. Except all the deeds were done for him, but in such a way it looks like he's the villain. He was here to be the fucking *patsy*, Colin ... Then one of my diligent constables provides me with this picture, and here's my own brother photographed alongside a character who's rotten to the marrow, somebody who certainly wouldn't be beyond arranging a few killings, if he had to.'

'Kilroy? Haul him in for questioning then.'

'He's been hauled in half a dozen times in the past couple of years, Colin.'

'You couldn't nail him.'

'Not on anything. He's always got alibis up to here. Takes a shite, he's got an alibi.' Lou paused.

416

'Here's my next question, Colin. If three men are dead, what's keeping you alive?'

'Why would anyone want me dead?'

'Easy. Because of your associations with the victims.'

'I'm sleepy.'

'Stay awake, Col. I have other questions. Who told the kid to come to Glasgow? Who give him the names?'

Colin Perlman kept his eyes shut. 'You're asking me?'

'What if I eliminate Kilroy as a candidate, who does that leave?'

Colin Perlman turned his face to his brother and smiled. 'You're serious?'

'Everything's possible.'

'I can't laugh in this condition,' Colin said. 'It hurts.'

'You were all taking bites out of the Nexus apple, right? You were all sucking on the same juice. So why are you alive and the other three dead?'

'Kilroy's alive also.'

'Play along with me, Colin. Take a short stroll through possibilities.'

With some difficulty, Colin Perlman manoeuvred himself into a sitting position, but kept his shoulders hunched. 'Let's nail this down. I'm your brother, your *blood*, and you're suggesting I might somehow be responsible for the deaths of these men? No, Lou. No fucking way. This is all about something else and we both know what it is, don't we? You've been waiting for years to get a shot at me. Years and years. All your life.'

'What does that mean?'

'You know what it means. *Jealousy*, wee brother. Jealousy that's eating your heart out. I got the looks. I got the brains. I got the girls. What did you get? Our father's melancholy turn of mind? What a gift. Thanks a lot, *Tata*. Fuck, ever since you've been a kid, you've resented the hell out of me, and now you see a chance to get back at me by pulling me into this bloody investigation. I'm not going down that avenue with you, Lou. You want to punish me, I say fuck you. I say get some treatment. Go for counselling. You need help, and you need it fast.'

Perlman felt his face flush, and wondered if he looked red. Where was all this bile coming from? What quarry was Colin digging in to produce this explosive outburst? 'I don't believe I'm hearing this.'

Colin said, 'Better believe it. It's not just the fact I'm rich, is it? It's not just my success, is it? No no no no, oh no. It's more than that.'

'Colin, stop there, just stop right there.' Stop before what? Before you go too far? But the door of Colin's mind was wide open and Lou found himself looking into a room he'd never visited before, and it wasn't very well-lit in there, and odd shapes stirred in the murk.

'You think I'm blind and don't notice, Lou? You drool like an idiot every time you see her. When you're in her company you're like some fucking eunuch anxious to obey his empress. You wear that big sick sloppy heart of yours on your bloody sleeve, Lou. You think I don't see? It's written all over you, *bruder*.'

'I like her, fine, I admit — '

Colin Perlman wagged a finger so firmly that his whole arm shook. 'No, no, you *love* her, Lou. You can't wait to get me out of the way so you can move in on her. Here's a laugh. She wouldn't want you. She finds your doting attention amusing. You're quaint, she says. Isn't Lou quaint? Isn't it funny to see a grown man so smitten?'

'Oh, Christ, Colin, give me a break, I don't want you out of the way. And I don't want Miriam. I like her. Maybe I love her, okay, maybe I do, it's possible. But I'd never *dream* of stealing her.'

'Stealing her? You're dreaming. Even if I wasn't around, do you think she'd fall into your arms? She wouldn't look at you twice. Unless it was to have you light her cigarette or scurry to freshen up her drink. You're a joke, Lou. You're like the cuddly toy every kid grows out of and abandons in some dark corner where the spiders live. You are pathetic.'

Lou Perlman fell into silence. He gazed at his brother. They locked eyes, and suddenly Lou felt all their shared history was rubble, like a town bombed by crazed pilots, and howitzers randomly discharged. He wanted to reach out and touch his brother's hand, but he understood that something had changed for ever between them. In one short rant of crazed accusation, Colin had razed their relationship, fragile and uncertain as it was at times, to the ground. Nothing after this could be the same. Everything in the future would be clouded by Colin's harsh discharge.

419

The room had the tense atmosphere of an electric storm, or that menacing aftermath when you think the lightning has passed away, but you can still hear thunder and you know the heavy sky will crackle with light again.

'Your IV,' Lou said. His voice sounded flat and unfamiliar to him. His words meant nothing. They were just sounds. He got up and walked round the bed. 'It's popped out of your vein. I'll stick it back.'

Colin Perlman didn't speak.

Lou caught hold of the plastic tube and looked for the entrance in Colin's arm. He slid the needle into the vein and then found himself gazing at the space between the edge of the pyjama jacket and the bandage. A strip of bandage, perhaps disturbed by Colin's agitated movements, had come undone, and was peeling from his chest. Colin Perlman, his mind elsewhere, made no move to adjust it.

Lou stared until his eyes felt dry: some things dawn on you badly. Some perceptions come through warped glass, and you're not sure you're seeing them properly.

'I'll fix that,' Lou said, and he reached for the bandage.

Colin Perlman pushed his hand away. 'No, call Rifkind, that's his job.'

'I can do it,' Lou said. There was a small tremor in his voice.

He reached out again and the dry bandage looped down over the back of his hand, and he caught his brother's eyes, which were the colour of iron. The bandage unravelled another couple of inches and Lou held his breath and listened to the way his heart motored. Colin put his hand over Lou's and gripped it tightly. The bandage, as it unspooled a little more, draped the hands of both men.

Lou thought: *The world is inverted.* It had become a somnambulist's universe, a place of spectral images. Truth was crucified in this world. Everything was shadow play.

Everything was the work of the *kuntzenmaker.*

'How did you think — how in hell did you even *think* you could get away with this, Colin? Jesus *Christ.*'

'I lie here. It's perfect. I'm immobilized.'

'It's not perfect,' he said. 'It's flawed, Colin. Because now I know.'

'I'm your brother, Lou.'

'And that makes a difference?'

'It has to.'

'After what you said?'

'I spoke out of turn, I'm sorry, I really am sorry, believe me, I lost control.'

'What are you sorry for? Which particular act? Which particular *fucking* act?'

Lou Perlman lowered his head. He was burning up, seized by a sudden fever. *I am falling sick,* he thought. *This world is sicker still.* Sham, everywhere you looked. Dishonesty. You were surrounded by deception and its master practitioners. He looked at the exposed area of his brother's chest.

No cuts, no stitches. The bandage was dry and free of bloodstain. He felt a strange drift in his mind, druggy.

421

'Was there ever a better alibi?' Colin asked.

Lou wasn't sure he heard the question. He was burning, his brain dry timber. He looked into his brother's eyes and for some reason he remembered how Colin would occasionally deign to play lead soldiers with him on the black and yellow chequered lino in the kitchen. Little men at war. Bam bam. Highland regiments. Cannon. Riflemen. Cavalry. Battles were fought.

Colin's men always won. Colin still wanted to win. Always.

'You set that kid up,' Lou said. 'You brought him here.'

'Passport. Money. Created a phony clandestine organization to smuggle him into Europe. He was so pumped-up with hatred he was just waiting to be hooked and reeled in.'

'Why have three men killed, for Christ's sake?'

'What we think are complicated questions often have really simple answers, Lou.'

Lou repeated his question. '*Why have three men killed?*'

'They couldn't be trusted.'

'Why couldn't they?'

'You want a catalogue?'

'The whole thing.'

'That silly old fart Wexler was having dangerous attacks of conscience that I attributed to the premature onset of senility. Couldn't sleep at night. Jittery. Coming undone. As for Lindsay, he was under investigation by the Scottish Law Society for certain improprieties unrelated to Nexus, and he was ready to confess *all* his wrongdoings as a bargaining tool to keep his practice. Poor fool.'

'Bannerjee?' Lou asked.

'He was angling for sainthood, and we all know saints can't be trusted to stay silent. Not when heaven is within sight. He'd talked about making appeasing overtures to the tax authorities concerning some of his hitherto undiscovered misdemeanours. Wipe the slate clean, start afresh. Shiv had had a sniff of the sweet narcotic of good works, you see, and he was stoned on the buzz of charitable acts, and no man is ever quite the same after that. He'd stopped seeing the world clearly. He wanted to sup with the Gods, Lou. He thought he'd found a way to freedom from his past. But it isn't that easy.'

And they had to die, Lou Perlman thought. 'Who did you hire to do the killings? Tell me.'

'Who did I *hire*? I went to a shop called Rent-a-Killer, of course. Where else do you go in Glasgow?'

'Don't do this, Colin.'

'Lou, Lou, little brother, you're not getting it. It's not coming through to you loud and clear, is it? There must be some static in the air. Or else you just don't want to believe.'

'Believe . . . ?' Lou felt a slowing down inside, a languid rearrangement of his thoughts.

'I had a little help now and again,' Colin Perlman said.

It struck Lou with the force of a jackhammer. The heart of the conspiracy was cold and twisted. This hospital charade, this 'operation', allowed Colin Perlman liberty to move in the city after dark, to slip away from the Cedars and do what he felt he had to, then come back to his sick-bed. No nurse would enter his empty room, because Rifkind, certainly an accomplice, would have issued instructions: *Patient not to be disturbed.*

But the patient was elsewhere.

Colin said, 'Naturally, I was worried about exposure any one of those three morons might have caused. And Leo Kilroy, well, he's a private man. He doesn't like coming out in the light. Something had to be done, Lou. Something had to *give*.'

'Did you have to . . . ' He felt a catch at the back of his throat. His saliva was trapped there. What was he going to ask? Did you have to be so brutal, Colin? If you had to kill, couldn't you have murdered with stealth and compassion? A painless poison. Overdose of sleeping pills. But these matters were of no relevance. Cocaine forced into Lindsay, the sword used to slice Wexler, the screwdriver into Bannerjee's ear: it was as if these deaths had become abstractions, like sepia photographs of unidentified First World War soldiers dead in muddy trenches.

Colin Perlman seemed to have read the unfinished question. He said, 'Yes, I had to. Everything had to appear truly brutal. Everything had to come back to the twisted psychology of the kid. He was filled with hatred and capable of anything, after all.'

'God help you.'

'God's not involved, Lou. He never is. You worry too much, wee brother.'

'Christ. How did you ever *think* you could pull

this off? Even if I hadn't seen your body, no marks, no stitches, nothing, what about Miriam? What would she say when she saw you?'

'Do you want an answer to that question, Lou? Think of the implications first. If I tell you that she wouldn't be surprised, then it means she's implicated in the whole pantomime. Do you want to hear *that* kind of thing about the woman you love, little *bruder*?'

Lou said nothing. Sometimes truth was the last thing you wanted. Even if you'd given your life to discovering it, there were times you didn't want to hear it.

Colin said, 'Relax, Lou — '

Relax? Lou Perlman wondered. What did that mean? How did you relax —

' — we don't have a sexual relationship. The last time we fucked, it had to be eight or nine years ago. Some things lose their allure. We haven't slept together since then. I haven't seen her naked in all that time either. She hasn't seen me. But it's a comfortable marriage after a fashion. Separate bedrooms.' Colin adjusted his bandage. 'What now, mon petit gendarme? Where do you go with all your little discoveries? Back to Force HQ? Talk them over with your superiors? Process warrants for my arrest? And Rifkind's too. Oh, and let's not forget Kilroy. He's an accomplice before and after the fact.'

Lou Perlman rose and walked across the room. It seemed to take a very long time. He wasn't sure if he knew where he was headed. He had no destination in mind. He couldn't quite recall where he lived or how to get there. It was somewhere in the eastern reaches of the city, a black house, a lonely house, he just couldn't bring it into focus. He had to get out of this hospital. That was all he understood. Get away. He clamped a hand over his mouth. He thought he was going to shed tears or throw up; some weight or fluid had to be released from his body, something to make him feel light again.

He thought of how damned his brother had become.

Colin said, 'I'm betting you do nothing, wee brother.'

Was there a veiled threat in that remark? A hint of something yet to come? Lou wasn't sure.

Colin looked sad all at once. 'Before you leave. I have something to say to you, Lou. I should have said it a long time ago. But somehow our family always had difficulty with emotional expressions. We stifled the things we felt. And you may not believe me now. But I love you, brother. That's all. No matter what I said to you a moment ago, no matter how deeply you despise me for what I've done in my life, that one fact doesn't alter.'

I love you.

White-faced, Lou Perlman went into the corridor and then moved in the direction of reception. *I love you.* What was that supposed to be — Colin's lifeline to cheap redemption? Three easy words. The magician steps from the magic cabinet and says *I love you* and all the world is right again and sunshine melts the snow away? *I love you.*

426

Didn't he know? Didn't he see? Everything was damaged.

Lou's step was heavy. What to do now? What to do with his knowledge? Outside he walked to the middle of the car park and he stood very still. He took the icy city into his lungs, sucking deeply as if to cleanse himself. The air was tack-sharp in his throat and nostrils. And if it smelled of anything, it was of Glasgow, of cold sandstone and tiled closes, frozen ponds and brittle leaves in the city's black silent parks.

He was aware of a figure emerging from a parked car, some kind of antique vehicle. He glanced at the man, who was moving in quick short steps towards the entrance. A big man, fat, a coat down to his ankles, hands gloved, a long scarf slung round his neck and trailing both back and front. As he approached the entranceway the man began to glitter as light played on the silvery pendant that hung outside his coat.

A man of the night, Perlman thought, a man shining in the dark.

Perlman reached his car and sat inside and tried to imagine the conversation between his brother and Leo Kilroy. But he couldn't. His brain wouldn't kick in. He felt half-dead, heart like a bag full of broken toys. He drove out of the car park, travelling too fast on treacherous roads.

55

He climbed the stairs. The lift was still out of
order. He knew it was too late at night to come
here, but it was the only place he could think of
— and yet, if you pressed him for a reason, he
wouldn't have had a single easy answer. Because
I love her. Because I'm sorry for her marriage.
Because the man she's married to is a monster.
The reasons were interwoven like inseparable
strands of tapestry.

Make it simple. I just want to see her, he
thought. That's all.

She was standing in the doorway of her studio.
She'd buzzed the downstairs security door open
for him. She wore blue jeans and a plaid shirt
too big for her.

'You look fragile,' she said.

She took his elbow and led him inside the big
space of her loft and he felt like an incontinent
old man in wet jammies being ushered to a
lavatory by a nurse. The nursing homes of his
future. The card games. The leakage of piss.
Drool Street, halfway house to the boneyard.

He stared at the big canvas covered in tiny
purple squares. He was reminded of something,
couldn't think what. A meadow of cube-headed
flowers. Once, from the window of a train
travelling south from Glasgow, he'd seen a field
of blue sheep. They'd been dyed by their owner,
and the dye had run in the rain. Blue sheep and

flowers with purple cubed heads. Why not?

'Sit down, Lou. I'll get you a drink.'

'No, no drink. You mind if I smoke?'

'Go ahead.'

He lit a cigarette and looked at Miriam as she dropped some paintbrushes into a jam jar of white spirit. 'You've been to the hospital?' she asked.

'I dropped in,' he said. 'Late.'

'I went there as soon as he was awake. I think he looked pretty good. Considering.'

Considering what, he thought.

'Rifkind said the op was a dream,' she said.

'Rifkind's a self-proclaimed genius.'

'What am I detecting in your tone?'

'You tell me.'

'Not sure. Snide?'

'More tired to the bone,' he said.

She sat on the arm of his chair and placed a hand on his sleeve. 'I still think that coat suits you.'

'Does it make me look like a cuddly toy abandoned in a dark corner?'

'Does it make you look *what*? . . . I don't know what's bugging you, Lou.'

'The world.'

'Did anybody ever say the world was easy? That cuddly-toy bit. That sort of popped out of nowhere, didn't it?'

He flicked ash into an empty coffee tin. 'Colin said it.'

'In what context?'

'He says that's how you think of me.'

She took her hand away. He longed to kiss her

429

mouth. He wondered if he could lose himself for ever in such a kiss. Never coming up for air, dying gloriously, mouths locked.

'I don't remember saying anything like that, Lou. It's horrible of him to claim I said such a thing.'

Lou Perlman shrugged.

She asked, 'How did a remark like that ever come up anyway? It's not the kind of thing people say out of the blue.'

'I forget the context.'

'He's on medication. He probably isn't thinking straight.'

Medication. Placebos in a little brown bottle. How could he ever tell her what had transpired in Colin's room? He couldn't. 'I just came by to see if there's anything I can do for you, Miriam. If you need anything. You know.' He looked into her small serious face. He touched her chin softly. Then he hugged her a moment, and felt her body relax against his.

'I can't think of anything, Lou,' she said. She looked nervous, he thought. 'You're kind to ask. You're always good to me.'

She took a step away from him. He realized she was crying.

'What's wrong?'

'I don't know. I'm not sure. I get weepy sometimes. Maybe it's that time of my life. Or it's the stress surrounding the operation.'

The operation, of course. The phantom waiting to be exposed, but he wasn't the one to do it. 'You can tell me anything you like, Miriam. You know that. You don't have to keep anything

430

back from me. What are pals and confidants for?'

She continued to cry quietly. He wished he had a hankie. 'Stop crying, dear. It upsets me. You don't want to see *me* blubber, do you? Not a pretty sight, I promise you.'

She smiled through her tears. Perlman thought his heart would break. How he wanted to hold and caress her and allow nothing to harm her. To be both guardian and lover. To take her pain when she was hurt. What kind of future did she have with Colin? *Only you know the answer to that, Lou. What now, mon petit gendarme? Where do you go with all your little discoveries? Back to Force HQ?*

Is that what I do?

And if I do, is it for the right reason?

Is it to bring justice into the equation, or because you want the husband out of the way? There was no dignity in some questions; and even less in the answers. He stretched out his hand and took hold of Miriam's. Tears continued to roll down her cheeks, even as she tried to blink them back.

'Don't,' he said. 'Please don't.'

'I love him, Lou.'

'Why doesn't that make you happy?'

'Because because, oh, a hundred things, Lou. A hundred.'

I could give you more firewood for your bonfire of sorrows, *neshuma.* 'What things?'

'Things. Stuff that happens in a marriage.'

'So much stuff happens in a marriage, Miriam. It's a wide spectrum of joy and pain and cruelty and sweetness, you name it.'

431

'I looked at him lying in his bed today and I realized how much I loved him and then I had this awful thought, and it stuck me out of nowhere, *Fuck you, Colin, I wish you'd died on the operating table* — '

'You wished *that?*'

'And I thought how everything had changed.' She paused, turned her face away from him, gazed at her canvas. 'Lou, you don't want to hear this. You have enough on your plate.'

'No, tell me.'

'It's the drift, the way we float apart, I'm not sure I'm saying it right. It's fucked, Lou. The train's gone off the tracks. It went down the side of a mountain a long time ago.'

'Elucidate,' he said. 'I'm not terrific at reading between the lines.'

She said, 'His fucking *women*, Lou. His *girls*. I'm so damned ashamed to say it aloud.'

'His women?' Why should Colin's infidelity surprise me? he asked himself. Colin's world had no known moral boundaries. He did what he liked. He plundered, he killed. What was a little infidelity?

'I wanted to tell you before. So many times I was on the edge of saying it. It's more than infidelity. It's more than just another pretty face that catches his fancy. I could get over that if it had happened once or maybe twice down the years. At least I think I could. But it's an *obsession* with him, Lou. Young women, middle-aged, it doesn't matter.'

Perlman said, 'You should have told me before.' And what would I have done anyway? he

432

wondered. Talked to Colin? Now look here, bruder, you don't know how much sorrow you're causing? Indeed.

Miriam said, 'It's like I'm the one who's failed, you understand that? Not him. Me. I'm the one who's let him down somehow. In bed maybe. Or does everything just go stale in the long run, Lou? Is that it?'

'I don't know the answer, Miriam.'

'I looked at him in his hospital room today and I thought what kind of idiot am I that I still love this man who treats me like shit? What does that say about me, Lou?'

Sadie drifted into Perlman's moment, a flash of her. What was the difference between Sadie and Miriam when you got right down to it? Only one of social standing, of possessions and money. Moon Riley beat Sadie. And Colin beat Miriam, but in places where no bruises showed. He patted the back of Miriam's hand, fingertips touching her wedding ring.

'I know, I know, we present this front, don't we?' she said. 'Husband and wife. Rich. Trips to faraway places. We're a couple, we're made for each other. What a twosome, people say. How lucky you are.'

'It fooled me.'

'And all the time, as soon as he's out of my sight, he's off screwing. Girls he meets. Teenagers. How does a sixty-year-old man attract teenagers? Okay, he looks fit and healthy, and he's got that accursed charm he can turn on and off. But teenagers? I suppose he flashes money and credit-cards and buys them good

433

dinners in smart restaurants. Sometimes it's hookers he picks up. Sometimes it's women I know socially. Ruthie Wexler. He was having a thing with her for years, off and on.'

'Ruthie? I didn't know.' He remembered Ruthie's statement, her sleepy recollection of seeing Colin Perlman around the time of her husband's death. The swimming pool. She was probably closer to reality than to the dream she imagined she was having.

'He had a key to her house, for Christ's sake.'

A key. 'He came and went,' Perlman said.

'I think you have that backwards, Lou.' She smiled, wiped her face with the cuff of a sleeve. 'See? I can joke about it. Brave of me. I'm falling apart, Lou. Don't let me.'

'Do you want me to stay with you? I can sleep on the sofa.'

'I'm tired, Lou.'

'You and me both.'

'I want to be on my own,' she said. 'Do you mind?'

'Can you sleep?'

'I have some pills for an emergency.'

'Take a couple. Go to sleep.' How could Colin betray this precious woman? How could he humiliate and hurt her so? Maybe the explanation was that simple-minded old standby, that glossy magazine self-help analysis: he's trying to prove age hasn't hampered his virility. Or maybe the low sperm-count drove him to demonstrate that he was hot in the sack even if he couldn't reproduce a little version of himself.

What did it matter?

Miriam caught his arm, raised her face, kissed him on the side of his mouth. Her hair smelled of paint, or some thinning solvent. He worried that he carried some trace on his breath of the tainted sandwich he'd half-eaten earlier. He wanted to stay. He wanted that sofa. He wanted to be near her.

'I unloaded on you, Lou. I dumped all that stuff on you. It's been knotted inside me for so long . . . Was that unbearable for you?'

'I take it in my stride. I sit tall in the saddle, my dear.'

'Except right now you're slouching,' she said.

He straightened his back. 'There. Soldierly. Proud.'

She kissed him again, all very proper, staid, a transaction of affection between people related by the accident of marriage.

He walked to the door. 'I'll phone you,' he said.

She walked alongside him. 'Maybe the worst has passed. Maybe getting it off my chest will make everything . . . I don't know, lighter? More manageable?'

It could get heavier, he thought.

'Maybe we'll even make things well again,' she said.

This was the worst. He shut the door, seeing the small fluttery wave she left in the air like a bird with a delicate skeleton.

56

Three a.m., then, and Egypt, silent Egypt. He parked his car outside his house and for a moment had no urge to go indoors. The blackstone building had a haunted look. Icicles hung from the sills and the guttering. *My ice house*. Perlman felt the day roll through him as if it were a series of aftershocks. You think you know something about people, and up to a limited point you do, and then something unexpected happens — and whatever confidence you might have felt about your insight into the human animal is suddenly as hollow and useless as a burnt-out lightbulb.

His hands shook in his lap. When he raised one to take the key from the ignition, the keychain trembled between his fingers. He was all pulses and jerky movements. Colin, Colin, where did you lose the way? How did that happen?

He opened the door and almost slid on the pavement as he stepped out of the car. He was ungainly, like a man made legless by drink. He faced the house. The windows were black slashes interrupted here and there by moons the streetlamps created. It wasn't a house that winked and smiled and said, Come in, draw up a chair, heat yourself by the fire.

I must move from here, seek a new home in a brighter part of the city, he thought. But where would that be — some unremarkable semi in Langside? A flat in a leafy part of the West End, near the BBC, say? Or, heaven help him, a loft in Merchant City?

A small dog might be company too. He'd walk it every night, regular as a chapel bell. A Scottie. Or a wirehair terrier. Something small, low-maintenance. He'd meet other dog-owners in parks and they'd talk about vets, or brands of dog food, or canine ailments. He might meet some good-looking widow walking her Labrador. He'd get used to the routine of it all. Easy.

He fumbled in coat-pockets for his door key. Every time he wanted to let himself in, he had to go through this same klutzy process, this ransacking of his pockets. Why couldn't he keep the key in one place? For the same reason your life is untidy, Detective. You're a creature of sprawl and clutter. The pile of fag-ends in an ashtray that so annoys some, you don't even notice. The collection of old newspapers, in stacks that teeter, might be an unsightly fire-hazard to certain people, but to you it's just something that has grown organically.

The key, finally.

He stuck it in the lock, twisted it. He thought: I can call Scullion, ask him to take me off the case. I want to step aside. And he'd ask why, and I'd say personal reasons, Sandy.

No way Sandy would buy that particular pokey-hat.

He pushed the door and stepped inside, flipped on the lobby light, and as he raised a leg to kick the door shut behind him, he heard

437

somebody move. Somebody, something.

He turned his face: *shit*. 'She isn't here,' he said.

Moon Riley said, 'I'm not looking for Sadie, Perlman.'

'So what the fuck are you doing on my doorstep?'

'This isn't a personal matter,' Riley said.

'Well, fine, call me at the office,' and Perlman moved to shut the door in Riley's face, but an intrusive foot blocked the attempt.

'This is professional, Perlman.'

'Professional like how?'

'Business, Lou. Plain and simple.' Riley pushed the door hard and Perlman didn't have the strength needed to fend him off. Riley was a tough well-muscled wee shite. He had the brute eyes of an enraged stallion. His red leather jacket made noises similar to old door-hinges opening and closing. He wore his hair shaven close to his scalp, so that it looked like a thin film of charcoal.

'What business would that be, Moon?'

'I'm here on a mission, Jewboy.'

'Sounds very serious,' Perlman said, trying to make it light, but he was troubled by what he saw in Riley's eyes and the way his voice was flat and purposeful. Physically, he knew he was no match for this hard young Riley, if it came to that kind of encounter. And he sensed that was where this locomotive was headed, and there was no emergency handle he could pull to brake the forward motion of events.

'A sword, they said. Wrong.' From under his

438

jacket Riley produced an implement with a hooked blade more than a foot long. 'I haven't heard them mention a machete, Lou. Lovely piece of work.'

Perlman imagined it slashing recalcitrant fronds in a jungle or hacking away gnarled branches. It would go through ancient knotted fibre like a blunt knife through soft margarine. What was it Colin had said? *I had help now and again.* He thought about the criminal interstices of the city, the spaces and intersections where lawless men colluded and plotted, and unlikely associates entered into murderous agreements out of convenience and profit.

He wondered if Riley had been involved in helping Colin drag the body of Joe Lindsay along the railway line and hanging him from Central Station Bridge. If he'd been instrumental in killing Bannerjee, maybe restraining him in an armlock while Colin drove the screwdriver into the ear. Or had it been the other way round? Had he swung the machete through the cords of Wexler's plump neck, or had that been Colin?

Perlman backed off a couple of steps and Riley grinned at him. He had very sharp little teeth, those of a gnawing animal. A beaver, or some kind of rodent. He lived in damp tunnels and earthen lairs and he came out only at night to kill.

'This is not an ideal situation for me,' Perlman said.

'Suits me down to the ground, Lou.'

'Aye, well, you have the advantage over me.'

'Isn't life just fucking *terrific*?'

'For some,' Perlman said. He glanced at the mezuzah, which was hardly visible under the old paint. Usually he touched it for luck when he entered the house. Tonight, he'd been interrupted. Hence, no good fortune. He stared at the machete and found himself thinking of its curved blade severing his neck.

'Your brother's some guy,' Moon Riley said.

'Lotsa fun to work with, eh?'

'Strong for his age, have to say. Impressed the hell out of me.'

'He's impressive, granted — '

Moon Riley suddenly raised the machete in the air, then brought it down with such force that it seemed to cut through the chill hanging in the house, creating a strange funnel of warmth. Perlman wondered if space had texture, and the blade had just sliced it. He backed away a few more steps, watching Riley smile.

'Just warming up, Lou.'

'I wouldn't like to see you doing it seriously.'

'You're about to.' And Riley swung the blade at an angle this time, not a downward slicing motion like before, but crossways, and level with Lou Perlman's neck. Surprised by the change of angle, Perlman stepped back and the blade missed him by a couple of inches. He kept reversing, knowing that sooner or later he'd hit a wall and could retreat no further. And if he didn't think of some way to protect himself very soon, he'd be headless in Egypt: which, he realized, had a biblical ring to it.

'I'm still warming up,' Riley said.

'I wish you'd keep it that way.'

440

'This one ought to do it.' Riley grunted. The swing was mighty, and fast, faster than Perlman's eye could follow. The blade came at him, curved and dreadful, and the sound it made was that of a person sighing. He tripped over a chair and fell backwards. He lay on the floor looking up at Riley, who laughed briefly.

'I enjoy a spectacle. The Jew cop lies helpless.'

'Are you by any chance an anti-Semite?'

'Me? Some of my best friends.'

'Right. Like Colin, you mean?'

'Colin and me. We're as close as thumb and thumbnail.'

Lou Perlman wondered if he could pull off The Stall, a desperate tactic where you engaged the killer in banter while you thought up some means of escape. But that wasn't going to be possible, because Riley was concentrating hard now, and he was all motion, swinging the machete furiously this way and that, a dervish of a man, swiping, slashing cushions, a sofa, whacking through the edge of a table, cleaving the upholstery of Lou's favourite armchair. It was snowing feathers.

'You see what this fucker can do? Eh? You see what it can cut?'

'How could I miss it.'

Riley was sweating heavily. He stood directly over Perlman, his legs spread apart. 'Impressed?'

'Scared would be closer,' Perlman said.

'You're right to be.' Riley slid on to his knees, straddling Perlman. 'You are fucking right to be.'

The machete came directly this time, no fancy angular stuff. The number-one route. It came

441

down with the speed of a guillotine. Lou turned his face to one side and the blade whizzed within an inch of his ear and razored the rug below him. Too close, way too close. Death was whispering to him. He could even make out what it was saying.

Riley cursed, laughed, raised the machete again, and said, '*Geronimo*,' and this time when he brought it down he had his angle correct and Lou looked up into the blade and wondered if he had time to roll away. His brain was working in fragments of time too tiny to be measured. Twist, turn, or at least raise a hand and take the cut there, you can go through life without a hand, people do, they do it all the time, they can live with a stump, a prosthetic attachment, but no, Riley wouldn't quit at just the hand, because that was a mere appetizer to a man who wanted the whole head supper. Okay, do it anyway, and Perlman raised his hand, fingers thrust up, palm turned out, the universal signal for stop.

The crack was very loud and rang through the house.

And Riley was no longer there. He'd slipped to one side in a listless way. Only the whites of his eyes showed. His mouth was open. The machete was still in his hand, but slackly held. All the force had been blasted out of him.

Moon had waned.

Lou raised his face and looked through the open door of the living room and the length of the hallway and he saw Colin, outlined in the frame of the front door and backlit from the street. He was wearing a dark coat and a dark

442

hat. His shirt was open at the collar. Lou rose to his knees and stared at his brother. He half-expected Colin to walk towards him, but that didn't happen. The gun in Colin's hand hung loosely at his side.

'It was Kilroy's decision to send Riley,' he said. 'I want you to know that.'

Lou got to his feet. 'You draw the line at killing your own flesh and blood, do you?'

Colin shrugged. 'I couldn't let Riley harm you. That's all.'

'You want thanks,' Lou said.

'I want nothing.'

'Okay. I'm grateful.'

'I said I want nothing.' Colin Perlman turned and began to walk. Lou moved, went after him, caught him before he reached the end of the drive.

'Now what?' Lou said.

'I take a hike far away. I have emergency funds I can access anywhere in the world. Or better still, I go back to the Cedars and see how things turn out.'

'You're still betting on me.'

'My wee brother,' Colin said, and laid a hand on Lou's shoulder. 'That bet would've been null and void if I'd let Riley carry out Fat Leo's instructions. What does that tell you?'

'I'm not sure,' Lou said.

'You think about it.'

'I'm thinking.'

'Good. You'll come to some conclusion. You usually do.'

Colin dropped the gun from his hand. He

443

looked at Lou and smiled. There was the old charm in the smile, the quack-medicine salesman's come-on look. Trust me. This snake oil's one hundred per cent. Cures everything, heartache included.

'So, Lou. Am I a bad man, or just a very greedy one who wandered off the righteous path and into the jungle of lunacy?'

'Don't ask me to judge you.'

'Right. You only get paid to do the legwork and apprehend the suspects. I forgot. The legal judgments are made elsewhere. As for the moral ones, who the fuck makes those?'

'Everybody and his brother.' Lou Perlman looked across the street. Ice formations hung in the dead branches of a tree. They gleamed like fireflies frozen at the exact moment of creating light.

'Goodbye anyway,' Colin said. He hugged Lou.

Lou realized he was desperate for this contact, he wanted a moment of intimacy with his brother. He needed the world to go back to where it had been before truth obscured the lies. The fabricated world was more comforting, the illusions were more pleasant. Colin held him tightly, and Lou remembered their mother and the way she'd died and the broken plate and the spilled crab-apples. And their sad sad father staring into the mysteries of a coal fire and longing for his beloved wife. All Lou's history welled up inside him, even as he understood that it was lost to him.

Father, mother. Brother.

'You know something, Lou? I just remembered that suicide you mentioned. Kerr, the milkman. I couldn't remember it before. Suddenly it flashed back. Boyhood, eh?'

'Memory,' Lou said.

'Funny old thing memory. We had some good times as kids.'

Lou heard a car somewhere nearby. It had a hoarse sound.

Colin moved away, then stopped. 'You know something else? I can't justify anything I ever did in my entire life, Lou. That's quite a depressing thought on which to take my leave of you. You think I should find the nearest tree and apply the milkman's solution?'

Lou shook his head. 'No, don't do that.'

'I accept the advice.' Colin waved a hand lazily and turned left on to the pavement.

Lou heard the car still, the meaty growl of the motor. Colin heard it too now, and stopped, turning his head in the direction of the sound and looking as if he recognized it. The lamps in the street, those that had any functioning bulbs, seemed dimmer than ever before. The car came into view, an antique, a classic, the one Lou had seen parked at the hospital. The one from which Fat Leo had emerged. He knew nothing about the makes of cars, just that Kilroy's was old.

Colin made a sharp sucking sound. He stared at the car as it moved under a light, showing a glossy pale-blue streamlined body polished to infinity, less a vehicle and more a moving sequence of reflections. The car slowed. A hand appeared in the open window. Lou saw Colin

445

lower his head. The flare from the window was brief and the noise abrupt and cheaply theatrical, like the explosion of an air-filled paper bag. Colin moaned and went down on one knee and then toppled to his side on the pavement; and the car, picking up speed, roared down the street until there was nothing left of it but a strange vibration that hung in the air like a piano key struck and still echoing long after.

Lou Perlman kneeled on the icy pavement and raised his brother's head up between his hands. Colin's eyes were shut, and his body had no tension in it, none of that tenacity of life. His neck lolled to one side, and his lips were wet and lax. His thick silvering hair was cold to the touch. Lou Perlman looked at his brother's face and then, lifting his eyes, stared the length of the street, listening maybe for a sound of the car returning, or perhaps seeking some sight of it, but there was nothing except silence in Egypt.

He stood up and shivered and all he could think of was how winter and grief were locked in a seasonal conspiracy, and he took off his glasses and pushed his knuckles hard into his eyes, a man lost in a strange grievous city that was the most familiar place on earth to him.

We do hope that you have enjoyed reading this large print book.

Did you know that all of our titles are available for purchase?

We publish a wide range of high quality large print books including:
Romances, Mysteries, Classics
General Fiction
Non Fiction and Westerns

Special interest titles available in large print are:
The Little Oxford Dictionary
Music Book
Song Book
Hymn Book
Service Book

Also available from us courtesy of Oxford University Press:
Young Readers' Dictionary
(large print edition)
Young Readers' Thesaurus
(large print edition)

For further information or a free brochure, please contact us at:
Ulverscroft Large Print Books Ltd.,
The Green, Bradgate Road, Anstey,
Leicester, LE7 7FU, England.
Tel: (00 44) 0116 236 4325
Fax: (00 44) 0116 234 0205